THE THORN QUEEN

ALSO BY SASHA PEYTON SMITH

The Rose Bargain

THE THORN QUEEN

SASHA PEYTON SMITH

First published in Great Britain in 2026
by Electric Monkey, part of Farshore

An imprint of HarperCollins*Publishers*
1 London Bridge Street, London SE1 9GF

farshore.co.uk

HarperCollins*Publishers*
Macken House, 39/40 Mayor Street Upper,
Dublin 1, D01 C9W8

Text copyright © 2026 Sasha Peyton Smith
Jacket illustration © Tran Nguyen 2026

The moral rights of the author have been asserted

HB ISBN 978 0 00 865751 2
TPB ISBN 978 0 00 874284 3
PB ISBN 978 0 00 874274 4
Export HB Exclusive 978 0 00 880225 7

Printed and bound in the UK using 100% renewable electricity at
CPI Group (UK) Ltd
1

A CIP catalogue record of this title is available from the British Library

All rights reserved. No part of this publication may be reproduced, stored in a retrieval system, or transmitted, in any form or by any means, electronic, mechanical, photocopying, recording or otherwise, without the prior permission of the publisher and copyright owner.

Without limiting the exclusive rights of any author, contributor or the publisher of this publication, any unauthorised use of this publication to train generative artificial intelligence (AI) technologies is expressly prohibited. HarperCollins also exercise their rights under Article 4(3) of the Digital Single Market Directive 2019/790 and expressly reserve this publication from the text and data mining exception.

Stay safe online. Any website addresses listed in this book are correct at the time of going to print. However, Farshore is not responsible for content hosted by third parties. Please be aware that online content can be subject to change and websites can contain content that is unsuitable for children. We advise that all children are supervised when using the internet.

For Casey,
I have you. I'm good forever.

There are places like this everywhere, places you enter as a young girl, from which you never return.
—LOUISE GLÜCK, "Averno"

For I have sworn thee fair, and thought thee bright,
Who art as black as hell, as dark as night.
—WILLIAM SHAKESPEARE, Sonnet 147

PRINCE EMMETT DE VERE

They keep forgetting to feed me.

It's my aching stomach that wakes me, not the rhythmic *drip*, *drip*, *drip* of water from the walls falling on my face. After weeks, I've grown used to that, but the hunger I can't tune out.

The first few days, they brought me trays of crusty bread and bruised fruit I didn't recognize. At least, I think it was daily. There's no light down here so I can't be sure.

But then the stretches between meals grew longer. "You have to feed me more often," I said to one of the guards. My voice was hoarse with disuse. "I'm human. I'm going to die if you don't feed me."

Bram might want to punish me, but he doesn't want me to die. If nothing else, I have to believe that.

The guard grunted and went on his way, muttering something about humans being too fragile.

That was five sleeps ago.

I reach up and prod at the fresh scar on my scalp where the hilt of one of the guard's swords knocked me unconscious my first day here. It's fully healed now, which is my only measure of time. It's been at least two weeks, longer probably.

I take stock of the rest of me. My shirt is torn all over, bloodstained and filthy. Under it, my ribs stick out, concerningly sharp. In the corner, my coat is balled up. I've been using it as a pillow. The rest of the detritus from the wedding, my dead boutonniere, my shattered pocket watch, the royal sash made of blue silk, are all shoved in the corner. I've sorted through them, found only one useful tool.

It stings worse than any wound to think of that day, but it's where my mind goes every time I close my eyes. *Her face.* The way it crumpled when she realized we'd failed.

I failed her.

Every moment I'm in this cell I'm failing her.

I'm not going to survive much longer. If I have any hope of escape, I have to act now, while I still have the strength.

I'm delirious, but I'm not imagining the footfalls on the stone stairs. This time it's a smaller guard, one I've seen before. That's good. I think I could overpower him if it came down to it.

He shoves the tray of food through the gap at the bottom of the bars, not caring that the cup of water spills all over the bread, leaving it soggy and me with nothing to drink.

I swallow the food in small bites so that I don't throw it up, and wait an hour or so for it to settle in my stomach. I've been waiting for weeks, hoping Bram would free me, but I won't have the strength to attempt an escape much longer, and

I refuse to just lie down and die. I'm more afraid of that now than I am of anything that lies beyond these bars.

I take the silver pin that once held my boutonniere in place and slip it into the iron lock welded to my cell door.

I feel around for the mechanism, and after a few agonizing minutes, something clicks and the door creaks open.

I nearly cry I'm so relieved, but I can't lose focus yet.

Along the edge of the wall, I stay hidden in shadows. There are a few other prisoners down here, but they're all huddled up in the corners of their cells, too unconscious, weak, or apathetic to rat me out.

I turn one corner, then another, through the serpentine dungeon, and then finally I see it: the rough stone staircase. My way out.

I make it up one flight and glimpse sun for the first time since the wedding. Warm yellow light pours through a gate at the top of the stairs like a beacon. I'm nearly there, hands outstretched, when footsteps rush up behind me. The guard doesn't say anything, just grabs me from behind and tosses my too-light body down the stairs like it's nothing.

My temple bounces off the edge of a step, sending blood pouring down the side of my face and out of my ear in a sickening rush.

He kicks me hard in the stomach, then brings the hilt of his sword down in the spot between my brows.

They say when you're about to die, your life flashes before your eyes, but I don't see anything but her. Ivy in the back of a dark carriage, Ivy covered in mud, the May Queen crown on her head, Ivy biting her lip in a garden, Ivy sprawled out under me in a coaching inn. The freckle on her shoulder I longed to kiss. A loose blond curl. Soft brown eyes. A flush across her cheeks.

Ivy. Ivy. Ivy. Ivy.

I can't bring myself to regret any of it. Not if it meant I got to have her.

As darkness claims me, my final thought is of Ivy Benton in her wedding dress, haloed by golden sun. I feel warm for the first time in weeks.

CHAPTER ONE
England, October 1848

"Tell me again, the story of the faerie king."

It's a pearl-gray evening, so cold even the heat of the roaring fire doesn't quite reach the bed. Rivulets of rain race down the warped glass windows, pooling into mist that floats in drifts along the cobblestoned streets below.

Bram looks up at me from my lap, his eyes the same gray as the sky, glinting in the weak light. His head is nestled in a pile of quilts, resting on my legs. "Tell me, Ivy."

I slip my fingers gently through his hair and sigh. "You need to rest."

His eyes flutter closed as he shakes his head. "Talk me to sleep." He kicks his feet under my duvet and I know there will be no getting him out of my bed now.

"There once was a faerie king who was beloved by his people," I begin.

Bram hums in the back of his throat, satisfied. I delicately trace the pointed tip of his ear and he curls up further, like a cat in a spot of sun.

"He was beautiful and benevolent and everyone who came across him was enchanted by his presence."

"Fun, too," Bram corrects me, eyes still closed.

I pull a bit of confetti from where it's stuck in the strands of his soft waves. "The absolute most fun."

This is the first time I've seen him in days. He's been absent, reveling with his court and their playthings.

"And handsome," Bram adds.

"Heart-stoppingly handsome." I lie to him all the time, but this particular statement is the truth.

I look down at his face—the delicate blue veins of his eyelids, his sharp jawline, full pink lips, thick eyebrows a shade darker than his sun-bleached golden-brown hair, his perfect nose. I trail my pinkie along the bridge of it.

My fingers itch to curl up into a fist and smash it. I can picture the way blood would drip into the hollow of his Cupid's bow, run down his chin and into the collar of his open green doublet. But it's not time for that—not yet.

It's been nearly four months since my ill-fated wedding, the one that ended with Emmett and Lydia missing and Queen Mor in chains. The country is in shambles after all her bargains were broken.

For the first few months of our marriage, Bram ignored me almost completely. I was left alone, locked up inside Kensington Palace with nothing but my ladies-in-waiting and Emmett's old dog, Pig, for company. I would have wondered if Bram remembered I existed at all, if not for the way I would wake to him sleeping in my bed. It started as a rare occurrence, rare enough that I thought perhaps, in his drunkenness after the revels, he got lost and mistook my bed for his. But then it started happening more frequently, as did the way he whispered my name in his sleep. I would wake at dawn most days to a broken chorus of *Ivy, Ivy, Ivy.*

He never acknowledged my existence otherwise.

Then, a few weeks ago, at the end of September, he declared we were moving to Bath for the autumn and instructed my maids to pack my things. Days later, our carriage rolled up at our new residence, a second carriage following to carry my abundance of trunks (all powder blue, embossed in gold with my new royal seal, naturally).

The Royal Crescent is the centerpiece of Bath's architecture. A half-moon arrangement of thirty terrace houses built of sandy-colored Bath Stone, featuring grand columns and intricately carved facades, all perched above a sweeping green lawn. The first order of business was a magical renovation project that took down walls and added secret, and not-so-secret, passages between the buildings, transforming the Crescent, functionally, into Bram's winter palace. It's a rabbit warren of secret passages, ballrooms, and Others lounging in ornate sitting rooms.

We've been set up at One Royal Crescent, the end unit with the best view of the city. Perhaps it's the smaller quarters, or Bram growing more complacent, but his visits are becoming more frequent. He comes to me, glassy-eyed at dawn, or in the midafternoon, or in the evening when the sun sinks low—whenever his revels end, really—and lays his head in my lap for comfort.

His breathing has slowed now, and I know he's nearly asleep. It's moments like this that he's least guarded. "How are they?" I ask him in a soft whisper. His eyebrows twitch into an expression of displeasure and I'm afraid I've pushed too far.

But then his face relaxes and he sighs. "I don't know what you mean."

I'm sure Emmett and Lydia are in the Otherworld; where else could they be? There's been no trace of them in England, despite my best efforts to search.

But Bram refuses to acknowledge them.

He had Emmett's portraits removed from Kensington Palace soon after our wedding, and I'm not allowed to even mention Lydia.

It's like the boy I love and the sister I adore never existed at all.

In my head I'm screaming, but I keep running my hands gently through Bram's hair until his breathing settles into a shallow rhythm and I know he is asleep.

I rise from bed once he's fully unconscious, and pray he sleeps through tonight's revel.

Outside of my bedroom, the house is a flurry of activity. Maids stoke hearths in every room, keeping fires alive against the October chill. Footmen race from room to room, ensuring everything is in tip-top shape for the evening. A bitter taste of fear lingers in the air. I do my best to protect our staff from his wrath, but no one wants to be on the wrong side of King Bram.

I cross the third floor to the other end of my private quarters and have my maids dress me in my evening gown. Among them, Lottie's face is a perpetual comfort. Emmett's longtime friend, she is one of the few people I can speak to openly. She is waiting, a hot curling tong in her hand. "You're late."

"I'm the queen; isn't everyone else early?" The joke doesn't quite land, but Lottie still lets out a hollow laugh.

"How is the king?" she asks as she dresses my hair.

"Asleep," I answer tersely. She knows me well enough not to push further.

She laces me into a celery-green moire silk gown and places a tiara on my head. I'm dressed more elegantly than I ever was back when I lived in Belgrave Square, but I can't help but feel I'm wearing a costume. I look at myself grimly in the mirror and exhale.

The tunnel into the revel is draped in a rainbow of streamers that keep getting caught in my tiara.

Emmy reaches from behind me and plucks another from my head. "You're going to show up looking like a chandelier."

"They wouldn't know the difference. They'd probably think it was human fashion and all show up to next week's revel wearing hats of crepe paper."

My four ladies-in-waiting—Marion Thorne, Faith Fairchild, Olive Lisonbee, and Emmy Ito—were formerly my competition for Bram's hand in marriage, but they have since become my closest confidantes.

As a group, we step into the swirling revel. The ballroom belongs to Rhion, Bram's closest friend and adviser. He was gifted the house next door to ours: fitting, given his position at court.

I'm always on edge at court revels, but tonight my nerves are reaching a fever pitch. Aurelia Vallen will be in attendance and I have a plan to execute.

I clasp my hands behind my back to hide the way they're sweating and glance anxiously at Faith.

"Just breathe," she whispers.

Something wet seeps into my silk slipper and I look down, praying it's punch, but find the floor is smeared with blood. It's early in the night for it, but I glance to the center of the room and see a group of glassy-eyed humans spinning around and around, their feet raw from dancing. I hate the way Olive stills at my side and grabs my hand for comfort. She's scared and it's my fault. It's my mistakes that allowed Bram to snatch power like this.

There's a shadowy interior balcony, adorned with dying cherry tree branches and beeswax candles, upon which a band plays a reel on a mix of human and faerie instruments. The thrum of a deep bass drum reaches right down to my marrow.

There is no veil of propriety at these revels. No dance

cards, no chaperones, no mamas trying to play the marriage market. There's no need to sneak away to the darkest corners of gardens to kiss, not when it's perfectly acceptable to push someone right up against the wall in front of everyone.

"Don't drink anything," I warn the other girls.

"Don't worry about us." Faith rolls her eyes. "We know by now."

The Others love a party theme and tonight's is the Wild Hunt.

The guests are dressed in a mix of classic English hunting dress, red coats and tweeds, and what must be traditional Otherworld clothing, finely wrought armor of gold and rich green tunics. Some are in costume as the animals themselves, a grotesque array of fox masks, boar tusks, and hellhounds.

I wear a quiver of arrows on my back, strung across the front of my gown with a strap of emeralds on a thick gold chain.

Marion nudges me in the side. "There she is."

Across the chaos of the ballroom, Aurelia Vallen stands against the wall, a golden goblet clutched to her chest. She looks down at the floor, but no one, save the five of us, pays her any attention.

"We better go now, before Bram wakes up," I say.

Olive still blanches at the thought of espionage, but puts on a brave face.

Aurelia Vallen is a little thing, unusually short for a faerie, with golden hair to her waist and overlarge sea-moss-green eyes. She's dressed in the fashion of Bram's court, with bell sleeves that trail to the floor, and an odd mishmash of human fashion: a partially visible hoopskirt, mismatched slippers, a red hunting jacket tied around her waist. To fit tonight's theme, she's got a pair of antlers on her head.

"It's *so* lovely to see you, Aurelia," I greet her with a smile. This isn't my party, but as queen, I'm always expected to act as something of a hostess.

"Rhion's invitation honors me, Your Majesty." She bows her head but her voice is thin.

I take the empty goblet from her hand and pass it to Marion who replaces it with a full one.

"How is your husband, is he well?" I ask. Pax is one of Bram's most trusted advisers. With blond hair and a sneering expression, he's one of my least favorites.

"He is well, Your Majesty," she replies, keeping her eyes trained on the floor.

I offer a warm smile. "Please, no need for all that formality. I hope you can think of us"—I pause and gesture to the other girls—"all of us, as friends."

This gets a small smile out of her. "Thank you, Your Majesty."

Marion steps beside me and expertly shifts the conversation to a recent visit to the modiste. The other girls chime in with easy chatter about building out their winter wardrobes for the coming colder months. This far west of London, the mornings are already icy, with winds whipping in from the nearby sea, though it won't be properly bitter for another month or two.

Aurelia seems to relax with the girls' talk of new gloves and fur-lined cloaks, and I relish it. This is all part of the plan. Tonight's revel is only the latest step in a plot that we've been carrying out for months.

It wasn't easy to find the weakest link in Bram's court. His advisers are unfailingly loyal to him, and their wives seem equally loyal to their husbands. I didn't trust I could say anything without risking it getting back to Bram.

But Aurelia was different. The first revel I attended I saw the other wives snickering at her from behind their insect-wing fans. Then one purposefully tripped over the tip of her pointed shoe and smeared cake all over Aurelia's dress. It was meant to look like an accident, but I could tell it wasn't.

It was then that our plotting began. First, Faith and Marion called on her, offering tips on how to clean buttercream out of silk. Emmy took her riding. I sent over a new shawl, claiming it matched nothing in my wardrobe.

Tonight is the culmination of all our work to get skittish Aurelia to lower her guard around us. We're circling now. Ready to go in for the kill.

I lean in and adjust Aurelia's slightly askew diamond necklace casually. "I've been meaning to ask, how was your journey here?"

"Oh, very pleasant, Your Majesty." She takes a sip from her goblet. "They've magicked the houses along the Royal Crescent to be connected, so I didn't even have to go outside."

"I didn't mean your journey to the revel, dear." I smile. "I meant your journey to England from the Otherworld."

She pauses, like a rabbit caught in a snare, and I'm terrified I've pushed her too far too soon, but then she takes a larger sip and lights up. "The journey to England was lovely! King Bram—"

All of a sudden, two of Bram's guards appear, pulling Aurelia off her feet.

She screams in pure terror and kicks her mismatched shoes.

"Put her down at once!" I command. "That's an order from your queen."

But the guards don't even look at me.

Aurelia sobs as they drag her from the ballroom. "Don't tell the king, please. I don't want him to be angry with me. I'll be good. I'll be good. I'll be good."

"Put her down," I insist, but it's like I'm invisible to them.

Aurelia's screams turn incoherent, no longer begging, but giving way to pure terror.

The guards pay her no mind. They pull her away and the door to some other house or passageway slams shut. I rattle the handle, but it's locked.

I yank again and again until my eyes well with tears of frustration. Emmy lays a hand on my shoulder. "Ivy, stop. You're making a scene."

I step away and wipe my eyes.

I now know two things. One: I have failed in the only real plan I had to learn about the Otherworld, the first step to getting Emmett and Lydia back. Two: Bram and his guards are watching me more closely than I ever could have imagined.

At that moment the music stops. The party goes still.

And Bram strides in.

CHAPTER TWO

Bram catches my arm as he bisects the crowd and pulls me into his side tight enough to hurt.

"I thought you were going to rest," I say sweetly. In fact, I'd counted on it, specifically waited for a revel that Bram was too exhausted to attend, but it seems my planning has been in vain.

Bram looks down at me, emotion flickering in his gray eyes. "I decided I'd rather be with you. If I didn't know any better, I'd be wounded. It's almost like you don't want me here." He keeps his face neutral, his voice soft, but I know Bram well enough by now to detect the simmering rage underneath. It's in the bruising pressure against my ribs as he clutches me to his side. To anyone else in the crowd, it might look like we're in love. Just as quickly, he lets me go.

Bram ascends the dais in the front of the room and gestures for me to join him. There is no second throne; I am expected to sit on his lap or stand behind him.

I long for the days when I could glance across a crowded

ballroom, catch his eye, and he would smile at me reassuringly.

I know now it was only an act, but he was so good at it, it might as well have been real. It was real to me.

I step up to the dais and plant a kiss on his cheek, making sure his courtiers are watching. One of the strangest things about Bram is that his body is never warm like a human's. His skin is always the same temperature as the air around it. When my lips brush him, it feels like I'm kissing something dead.

He doesn't quite smile but his eyes soften as he looks at me. A lock of sun-kissed light brown hair falls across his forehead.

"King Bram!" Some preternaturally beautiful woman with elaborately braided silver hair bounds up to him. "Dance with me!"

"I'm with Ivy," he says quietly.

She laughs, so big I can see right down her throat. "We don't know her! She doesn't matter!"

Bram steps down from the dais and kicks the woman's feet out from under her, sending her falling to her knees on the marble floor. He grips a fistful of her hair and yanks her head back, until she's staring up at me, gasping in pain.

"She's your queen," he says coolly. "Apologize."

"I'm sorry," she sputters.

"Your Majesty," Bram corrects her. "You're sorry to Her *Majesty.*"

"I'm sorry, Your Majesty," she squeaks. Bram releases her hair almost dismissively.

The woman glances at me disdainfully as she rises to her feet, but doesn't risk saying anything else with Bram so near. She is quickly scooped up by the elbow and pulled into a chain of Others, dancing in circles.

I look up at Bram and he plucks a streamer from where it must have been stuck in my crown.

"You didn't have to do that," I say.

"Of course I did."

I open my mouth. Close it again. I'm at a loss for how to respond.

It would be easy to imagine he cares for me, in small moments like this. But then I catch a glimpse of the group of enchanted humans and their blood-soaked feet in the middle of the ballroom and know Bram is incapable of true care.

What exists between us is something stranger and darker: not care, certainly not love.

"You should really be more careful." His face is unreadable in a way that turns my blood to ice.

"I'm not sure what you mean." Deny, deny, deny. That's the only tool I have in my arsenal.

"I have a gift for you. It should arrive tomorrow," he says, still remote.

And then he's gone, off to merrymake with some other group of sneering advisers.

Across the ballroom, Faith and Marion are doing their jobs flawlessly. They're positioned next to the banquet table, locked in conversation with Rhion.

Things with Aurelia may have gone sideways, but that doesn't mean our work tonight is through.

"Your Majesty." Faith waves me over to join them. Rhion is difficult to pin down, but I'm hoping Bram seeing me in conversation with him will make him happy. If I'm lucky, perhaps Rhion will even tell Bram how devoted, how loyal I seem.

Rhion tips his head in a bow as I approach.

"No need for all that," I say with a gentle laugh. "Not when we're in your home."

The insides of my elbow-length gloves are sticky with sweat. Rhion always makes me nervous.

It's not just his beautiful face—closely cropped black hair, moonlight-pale skin, violently blue eyes—it's the way he says everything like it's a joke, like he finds the cruelty of Bram's court hilarious.

I place my hand on the banquet table for balance but stick my palm directly in the center of a cracked pomegranate. Its jewel-like seeds squish under my weight, leaving my gloves looking bloodied.

Fiona Devon and Althea Jones saunter up to us, and I can sense Marion's annoyance. They both came out in society last year with us. Althea, who bargained with Queen Mor to become more beautiful, is back to the slightly mousy, familiar face of our youth. I heard a rumor that her new husband, Baron Rousting, was very disappointed when Queen Mor's bargains were made null and void.

"Ivy!" Althea greets me warmly. Then she blushes and corrects herself. "Your Majesty, I mean."

I still don't know how to behave around people I've known my whole life. I want to scream at Althea and Fiona to take their shiny new husbands and run as far from this court as possible, but British aristocracy has followed Bram to Bath. It seemed the fashionable thing to do, I suppose, and the humans were unable to resist the siren song of more magic, more bargains, more inhumanly beautiful Others.

"How have you been getting on?" she asks with two kisses on my cheeks.

"Oh, you know. It's always so taxing, setting up a new house," I reply tightly. "My parents stayed in London, and of course Bram is busy, so I haven't had much help."

"Where is Emmett these days?" Fiona asks lightly. The blood drains from my face. I can't think of him, not here, not now.

"He's not at court," I answer flatly. It's the same answer Bram gives. He's spread a rumor that Emmett has begged off, shirked his responsibilities as a prince, and is drinking his life away in a far-off, cozy country estate, seducing all the willing milkmaids he can find.

Only I and my ladies-in-waiting know the truth, that he's locked up somewhere for the crime of loving me. Or dead. But I can't bear to consider that.

"You'd think Britain's most notorious rake wouldn't miss the opportunity to seduce a whole new court of beautiful girls." Fiona giggles.

Althea frowns. "You know, he never tried with me. I'm a bit offended."

Fiona preens. "He kissed me once at Lord Gregory's Yuletide choral performance. Fabulous kisser. What a mouth."

"What happened after?" Althea gasps.

Fiona shrugs. "He got bored of me and moved on to Miss Tremaine. Then he got bored of her, and I think it was you next, Faith?"

Faith raises her brows. "Something like that," she answers tightly. The room shifts a little and I fear I'm going to be sick.

Rhion grabs my hand, the one that's sticky with pomegranate juice, and tugs. "Come with me to the fires!"

"No, I'd rather stay." I need Bram to see me performing my role as his devoted, dutiful wife after the disaster with Aurelia, but Rhion's grip is strong and I don't want to make a scene by resisting. Truthfully, I'm a little grateful for the chance to walk away from Fiona and Althea and their talk of Emmett.

"Nonsense." Rhion loops my arm in his and we exit the ballroom into the biting night air. The oval lawn in front of the Royal Crescent is transformed at night. It's dotted with half a dozen roaring bonfires, with groups of fae and humans alike reveling among them.

Some courtiers dance in dizzy circles, while others lounge on an array of velvet cushions, attended to by their human companions. Perhaps *companions* is too generous a word. *Pets* may be more apt.

All Emmett and I ever wanted to do was end Queen Mor's cruel bargain system. We may have achieved our goal, but now, instead of one faerie making bargains to contend with, we have dozens. It's like a hydra from the books my father used to read me. I chopped off one head, and one hundred others sprang up in its place.

It's constant now, the faeries playing tricks on the humans, luring them into bad bargains or impossible-to-win games. What's worse is the humans were used to Mor's code of conduct; she made her bargains with some sense of honor. These new faeries have none of that. The cruelty is the point for them.

Rhion settles us down next to one bonfire where they're in the midst of a drinking game. A tall blond faerie man is flipping a golden coin. Heads, he drinks; tails, the human next to him drinks. It lands on tails every time, and the human, in agreeing to play this enchanted game, is forced to bring his cup to his lips again and again. He's in tears at the faerie's feet, begging him to stop. His glassy eyes droop, nearly unconscious. He heaves and vomits all over his shirtfront.

The gathered fae just laugh and laugh as the man pleads and sputters.

I snatch the coin out of the fae's hand and toss it into the bonfire.

"Excuse me!" the blond faerie shouts in anger.

"Excuse me, *Your Majesty*," I correct him.

He keeps yelling but I pay him no mind. I kneel down at the

drunk man's level and whisper, "Go home. Go as far from here as possible."

With the last dregs of his strength, he pushes himself to his feet and wobbles away into the darkness.

But he is just one man and this is just one horror. All around me, the torture continues. One bonfire over, a group of fae have begun a game that I think is supposed to be some kind of replica of the Wild Hunt, tonight's party theme. I only know because they keep yelling "Hunt!" at the tops of their lungs. In a circle, around the bonfire, they chase a girl, who scrambles on her hands and knees, a deer mask pulled over her face.

I march over, mustering all the authority I have, and shout, "Enough!" But it's as if they don't even see me; they just dodge me on their next lap around the fire.

I bend and help the girl to her feet. She's petite, her mud-stained dress in tatters. I suspect she's a few years younger than me.

"Go home," I tell her like I told the other man. "Please, I beg of you."

Her mud-caked hands pull at the mask on her face; the overlarge eyeholes make it look something like a skull. Her own clear blue eyes are visible through it and she's crying.

"I can't," she wails as she pulls. The mask is enchanted, I realize. Some awful fae tricked her into this game with a bargain. "He told me I could join the court." She hiccups. "I can't even go home. My parents will know I've been here.

Who will marry me now?"

I turn to the group around the fire. "Undo it."

They don't react.

"I command you. Undo it!" I say louder.

A large man, wearing a child's christening dress as a scarf, belches, then looks up at me. "That was Westcott's spell. He's gone now. Sleeping or something. I don't know." Then he takes another sip from his goblet and returns to his conversation.

I've wondered, in the months since our wedding, why Bram keeps me around. Why bother with the trouble of making me queen when he has no intention of being loyal to me, or letting me participate in any official royal business.

Now I suspect it's because he knew I'd never get any respect from his courtiers. Even with my title and my status, I am utterly powerless. A joke, even.

Perhaps I am nothing better than Bram's pet, and he's enjoying torturing me the same way the fae around these bonfires enjoy their games. He keeps me close because it's fun to see me suffer.

It's either that or he feels some kind of affection for me, but that is even harder to wrap my head around.

There's a tug at my shoulder and I turn to see Rhion, his handsome face knit into an expression of confusion.

My stomach sinks. Tonight, I was supposed to be perfect. Instead, I've made a scene, screamed at Bram's court, and only further demonstrated my loyalty to our human subjects.

"My lady, you seem unwell. Let me accompany you home."

"Oh," I say weakly. "Yes. Thank you, Rhion."

I bend down to the girl in the mask and lower my voice to a whisper. "Come see me in the morning. We'll find Westcott together and force him to break the bargain."

She sniffles and Rhion pulls me away.

I cast one last look at the bonfire. The girl is back on her hands and knees as they chase her, the antlers of her mask silhouetted in the firelight. I don't know how else to help her. I've never felt worse about myself than I do in this moment.

Rhion leaves me at the steps of my home with kisses on both cheeks. Like Bram, his skin is the same temperature as the cool air around us.

"I'm sorry about tonight." I put on my best act. "I was rather hoping we could become friends. After all, you and my husband are so close, and we are neighbors."

Rhion smiles, and it lights up his whole face. "I'd like that as well, Your Majesty. Come call on me in the morning. We can discuss our newfound friendship over breakfast."

Breakfast is early for a fae courtier; most don't wake until late afternoon. He is unusual, indeed.

"I'd be honored," I reply with a fake smile.

"There's so much I've been meaning to discuss with you, so many human customs I'm desperate to know more about. For instance, is it usual for a lady-in-waiting to run errands in disguise?"

"I'm sorry?" I ask, confused.

"One of your ladies-in-waiting, the ginger girl. Wears a lot of green?"

"Olive?" I confirm cautiously. I don't know where this is going, but the curdling feeling in my gut says I won't like it.

"Why does she leave every morning around eleven wrapped in a drab cloak with a scarf around her face like some kind of beggar? Is that the fashion? Should I get one?"

"You must be mistaken. At eleven Olive would be at home. We usually meet around luncheon at the Royal Crescent."

Rhion just shrugs. "Humans!" he says with delight. "I'll never understand your customs. How thrilling to have so much to learn."

I walk into the dark of my house in a daze, through the echoing marble foyer and up the stairs. The maids haven't left any of the lamps on for me, so I have nothing but moonlight and long shadows to guide my way. Rhion would have no reason to lie to me about Olive, but I'd be a fool to try to find any logic in the actions of Bram's court.

I climb another set of stairs to the third floor, but when I open the door to my bedroom, I find a dim library, complete with spiral staircase.

I sigh. The rooms are always changing. I don't know if it's on purpose or something went wrong with the spell used to connect the town houses in the Royal Crescent.

I try another door and find a sitting room.

Another and it's a nursery. A slash of moonlight falls over

an empty cradle, an old rocking horse.

The third is a plain bedroom. Pushed up against one wall is a twin bed with a neatly pressed blanket. Next to it is a washbowl and pitcher in bone-white porcelain, set atop a simple table. It's probably meant for a member of staff, but I'm too exhausted to keep looking, so I fall onto the rough blanket of the single bed.

I'm nearly asleep when the sound of breathing startles me.

"Who is there?" I call.

No answer comes.

Outside, a gust of wind ruffles the dry leaves clinging to autumn tree branches.

There's a thump under the bed.

I lean down, heart in my throat, to find Pig, cowering. He looks as sorry as I feel, his tiny little body quaking with fear. He doesn't like this new, strange house, doesn't like the fae either. He barks every time one of them walks past my door.

He must have gotten lost when the rooms shifted and couldn't find his way back to my chambers either.

"Come here," I say softly. He burrows under the blankets and curls up against my side. I stroke his furry little head and let the tears flow down my cheeks.

I can't shake the feeling that Emmett would know what to do if he were here.

I miss him like a physical wound.

If Emmett and Lydia are in the Otherworld, as I suspect, I fear I may be running out of time.

Are their lives racing ahead like sand through a sieve while I plot and plan too slowly here? What good will rescue be if my sister is an old woman once I finally achieve it? Has Emmett spent years without me? Am I only a distant memory of some ill-fated young love? I can't think too hard about it or I'll lose hope, and hope is all I have.

I clutch Pig to my chest, and together, we face another lonely night.

CHAPTER THREE

The door slams against the frame and a shriek pierces the air.

Pig bounds off my lap as I bolt up and scream myself. It seems the correct thing to do.

There's a maid at the threshold holding her hand over her mouth. "Oh, I'm sorry, Your Majesty. I didn't know who was in my bed."

I rise sheepishly, still in my rumpled ball gown, my tiara on the pillow beside me.

"I'll give you your room back," I apologize. "I just got lost."

The maid delivers me like a child to Lottie, who is already with my ladies-in-waiting. Together, they rearrange me into something resembling a presentable queen. I can't stop glancing at Olive as Lottie winds my blond hair into a coronet of braids.

Olive notices me staring and pulls a funny face.

I hate Rhion for making me doubt her for one moment. I don't want to live in a world where there's one less person I can trust when the number is already so few.

The morning sun streams like water through the central staircase as I descend. I have no desire to spend my morning with Rhion, but I am a little relieved at the second chance to make a good impression after last night's disaster.

I pull my white ermine cape tight around my shoulders and step out into the brisk October morning.

The Royal Crescent is in complete shambles after last night's revel. The frost-covered lawn is covered in a rainbow of confetti, the burned-out skeletons of bonfires, and even a few fae, still sleeping off their hangovers.

At the bottom of our steps, I trip over something, barely catching myself before I topple over completely.

It's someone covered up by a maroon cloak. I nudge them with the toe of my boot, hoping to wake the drunkard and send them on their way.

They don't stir, so I nudge again, a little harder this time.

The person rolls onto their back with a flop and I stumble, gasping with my hand over my mouth. It's not a person, at least not anymore.

The lifeless eyes of the girl in the deer mask from last night stare up at me, ghost pale and unseeing. The deer mask lies next to her head, dirty and askew.

The footman must hear me scream, because he comes running out the door after me. "Your Majesty?" he asks. It's unsettling to hear his voice. Bram's cadre of servants so rarely speak.

"She's—" The words get stuck in my throat like day-old bread.

I don't need to finish my sentence. He sees it as clearly as I do.

He pushes past me, takes off his coat, and drapes it over her body. Her begging from last night rings in my ears, sharp like noon church bells. She asked me to help her and I did nothing. She looks even younger without the mask, no older than seventeen. I'm going to be sick. I kneel at her side, my tears landing in fat splotches all over her ruined cloak.

"I'm sorry," I whisper, even knowing she can't hear me. "I'm so sorry."

I never even asked her name.

Another footman appears, and with one carrying her arms, and another carrying her legs, they haul her away.

I'm left standing alone in tears on the sidewalk.

"Greetings!" comes a cheery voice behind me.

I turn to see Rhion poking his head out of his front door. "I thought you'd forgotten about me."

I wipe my eyes, but it's still clear I was crying.

"Oh no." Rhion's face falls as he sees me. "You're crying. Wait—let me guess why."

"Um," I hesitate.

"Burnt toast, bad dream, money trouble, unrequited love, homesickness—" He lists them out on his fingers.

"None of those," I reply. "But I'll take some unburnt toast if you have it." I have no desire to speak of the girl in the deer mask to Rhion. Either he'd understand my sadness and report my dissatisfaction with their courtly games to Bram, or he wouldn't understand and I'd be left trying to explain to an immortal why human life is precious. I've had four months to become an expert in hiding my emotions.

I get a better look at Rhion. He's dressed even more unusually today. He's wearing riding breeches, a woman's corset, a pale blue silk evening coat, and about a dozen diamond necklaces.

I'm struck, as I often am in the presence of the fae, by how young he looks. Rhion doesn't seem any older than eighteen or nineteen with his wild mop of dark hair and the faint smattering of freckles across his perfect nose. In truth, he must be nearly a century, if he's Bram's oldest friend.

In his receiving room, an elaborate breakfast has been laid out across side tables, coffee tables, tufted stools, and even the grand piano.

"I didn't realize we'd have company," I say, more out of surprise than anything. There are at least ten humans in this room, Rhion's pets, all dressed as oddly as he is. They're young, a little hollow-eyed, clearly hungover after last night. One man is still fast asleep, snoring softly on a chaise by the fire.

"Oh, there's always a rotation," Rhion says dismissively. A pretty brunette approaches him and he plants a kiss on her cheek affectionately.

"Your wife?" I ask as I take one of the few available seats.

He laughs. "Oh no. We met last night, I think." He cups his hands around his mouth and shouts, "What's your name, beautiful?"

"Libby!" she hollers, and goes back to sipping a bottle of champagne she's just pulled from between the floral couch cushions.

Rhion turns back to me. "I'm unattached. I don't share Bram's respect for the institution of marriage."

"Does he respect it?" It's too bold a question but I can't help myself.

Rhion takes a bite of croissant and shrugs. "You should hear how he speaks about you when you're not around."

I don't know what to make of that. I don't like the idea that Bram speaks about me much at all.

"And what of my sister?"

A curious expression flickers over Rhion's face. If I had to put a name to it, I'd call it *pain*. "Oh, Lydia" is all he says.

"You know her?" I gasp. "Is she in the Otherworld now? Is she all right?"

Rhion frowns. "I'd rather talk about you, Your Majesty." He plops down on a worn armchair by the fire, and, like flowers toward the sun, all the humans in the room shift toward him. Two spectacularly pretty girls position themselves at his feet and curl up like elegant cats.

"I'm grateful for your time. You've spent so much time learning our customs"—I gesture to his outfit, halfway sarcastically—"yet I still know so little of the Otherworld. Please." I can't stop myself from begging. My heart is racing at the mention of Lydia's name.

I look to the doorway and spot one of my footmen standing

like a tin soldier. He must have finished disposing of the deer mask girl's body. I wonder what they did with it. Every time I blink, I see her eyes staring up at me from the sidewalk.

I turn back to Rhion. With the footman watching me, I'll have to be careful. I can't ask about how to get to the Otherworld directly like I did yesterday. But maybe if I'm lucky, if I make Rhion like me, he'll let his guard down eventually. I don't doubt his loyalty to Bram, but he does seem to be careless.

"Did you ask your friend about her errands?" He completely ignores my previous remark and my hope deflates.

"There's no need, I trust her."

Rhion glances at one of his pets knowingly. "Tell me, Benedict, did I imagine it?"

Benedict, who is in an undershirt and a tricorne hat, strokes Rhion's shoulder affectionately. "No, my lord."

Rhion turns to me, as if to say *Ha!*

The freckle-faced girl at his feet passes him the bottle of champagne and he takes a swig. "What has a neck but no head?"

"Excuse me?"

"A bottle!" He laughs and offers it to me.

"I don't make a habit of drinking before ten a.m." I don't make a habit of drinking *ever*, particularly around the Others, but that seems rude to say.

"How have you found England? Is it much different than home?" I make a second attempt at conversation.

"Damper here. I don't know how you stand it. But I recently

learned about *the umbrella.* A fascinating contraption. We'd never have the patience to devise such a thing back home. We'd simply magick the cloud to stop raining. It's why I love you." I'm not quite sure who he's speaking to when he says *you,* but he reaches down and pats the brunette's head.

"If you dislike the damp so much, why stay through the winter? It's only going to get worse. You could return to the Otherworld. Bram and I could go with you. I could see my sister."

He gestures to the people around the room. I swear, five more have entered since we began talking. I don't know where they're coming from. "How could I leave now?"

"Are any more lords soon to arrive?" From what I have gathered, the Otherworld court doesn't bother with the array of titles we have here. There are no viscounts or dukes or baronets. There is simply King Bram and the lords and ladies under him. The first night the portal was open—our wedding night—Bram brought over the twelve most important lords, the men who make up his council, and their wives. In the months since, he's transported more aristocracy and members of his guard. Every few weeks he goes missing for a day or two, and suddenly revels look a lot more crowded. But any time I've tried to engage anyone in conversation about how traveling to the Otherworld works, I've been met with a stone wall.

Thoughts of the Otherworld consume me. If I can just figure out how it all works, I could go there, get Emmett and Lydia back, and then, maybe, find a way to shove Bram and his awful companions back through the door and bolt it behind them.

The one person who has ever spoken with me about the door to the Otherworld was Bram's mother, Queen Mor. The last time I saw her was on my wedding night, when her son had her imprisoned in the Tower of London. I went back to visit her again a few weeks later.

It was an ordeal, sneaking out of Kensington Palace through the tunnel system Emmett once taught me, crossing town in disguise, bribing a yeoman guard to let me inside the ancient prison on the bank of the Thames.

But up in the tower that once held her, I found only an empty cell, its gate squeaking as it swung open in the darkness.

It's another thing I'm too afraid to ask anyone about. If Bram knew I knew his mother was no longer at the Tower, he would also know I snuck out to conspire against him.

Again, Rhion makes no effort to address my question. "We're taking the waters today. Will you join us?"

"Oh." I'm startled by his request. Bram's court has been particularly taken with the old Roman baths since our arrival. They sit in the natural hot springs and breathe in the mineralized air. The humans say the waters are good for your health, that they can cure all sorts of ailments. But what good does that do an immortal?

"Don't you . . ." I hesitate. "You live forever, so I'm afraid I don't understand the point."

Rhion cocks his head, confused at my reply. "But it's fun."

He sounds so much like Bram I recoil unconsciously.

My efforts at reconnaissance are going nowhere. I can no

longer stand to be in Rhion's strange house, surrounded by his awful, glassy-eyed human pets.

I need to go home and find a private space to cry about the deer mask girl. It was a mistake to come here so soon after finding her body. I can't hold it together much longer.

"I do apologize. I hate to take my leave early, but I've only just remembered I have another appointment." I gather my skirts around me and start for the door.

Rhion stands, and a surprisingly genuine look of concern crosses his eerily beautiful face. "Will you come again?"

I pull my mouth into a smile with effort. "Of course, we're friends now, are we not?"

Rhion looks unsure. "Take the waters with us," he says urgently.

"Another day."

"Bring your ladies-in-waiting."

I'm nearly to the door when I stop and turn around, I can't help it. The diamonds around his neck sparkle in the watery morning light.

"You know Lydia?" I ask once more. My veins buzz with the confirmation that she must be in the Otherworld, that I've been right all along.

Rhion turns his gaze to the floor. "Can one ever really know Lydia Benton?"

It's a good question. One that's haunted me.

Rhion glances around like he's nervous we're being listened to. It sets me on edge.

He takes two quick steps toward me and shocks me by wrapping me in a tight embrace. "What can you shatter with just one word?" he whispers, lips nearly brushing the shell of my ear.

I pull myself from his grip. And then, as if nothing odd has happened, he snaps back to his cheery self and waves me out the door.

I take one last look back at him and realize, strangely, he didn't seem drunk at all.

I wish I could spend the rest of the day in my room, wallowing with Pig, writing letters to Emmett and Lydia, then feeding them to the fire, but a queen's work is never done.

It's been only four months since I was elevated far above my station, and given Bram's distinct lack of interest in running this country, it's all fallen to me. I may be powerless among Bram's faerie court, but in human matters, I'm the only one keeping things afloat.

I love Emmett and Lydia too much to let them come home to a country in ruins. So, by the bloody tips of my fingers, I am doing my best to hold it together.

First on the agenda is a charity tea with the other wives and high society girls at the Pump Room.

I'm taken down the hill in a sedan chair, essentially a chaise held up by two long sticks, with four footmen, one on each corner, to carry me. The ride is unsteady, and I'd really rather walk by myself, but I have to create some illusion of propriety.

All along the route people wave handkerchiefs and take off their hats in respect. I even hear a few echoes of "God save the queen!" Months ago, the first few times it happened, I was offended, automatically thinking of Mor, before I realized they meant me. I still have to bite my bottom lip to keep from laughing out loud.

The Pump Room is the most fashionable parlor in all of Bath, the place to see and be seen for all the ladies of the ton. Strangely, it's stayed mostly human. While other court activities have become a mishmash of human and fae traditions, our unwelcome guests have shown very little interest in joining us for afternoon tea in town. They're almost always sleeping until early evening after partying until dawn.

A hush falls over the crowd as I enter, and everyone dips into a hurried curtsy. In the corner, I spot Faith, Marion, Olive, and Emmy, but it would be impolite to head straight for them like I want to.

I circle the room, greeting dozens of duchesses, baronesses, and marchionesses. Gleaming tiaras of diamonds sit in their sugar-spun white hair, glinting in the afternoon sunlight streaming in from the arched second-story windows.

A grand crystal chandelier hangs above the assortment of round tea tables, and in the corner a stone Romanesque fountain bubbles with water pumped directly from the hot springs below us.

Somewhere in the second-story balcony, someone gently plays a harp.

I listen to the duchesses' and the baronesses' and the marchionesses' tales of woe. For hours, I circle the room, lay a comforting hand on their shoulders, and watch as they cry.

Some long for trivial things, like the return of their old nose, the one they got from Queen Mor that disappeared when her bargains were broken. But some tell me much worse stories. Lady Bexley weeps for her husband, Lord Bexley—owner of the most elegant gambling club in London. A group of faeries killed him two months ago over a game of poker gone wrong. They'd been enchanting the cards, and he tried to throw them out. He paid for it with his life.

Duchess Alton's daughter has disappeared, vanished in the night a few weeks ago, only days after complaining she kept hearing strange music in the garden.

Baroness Trilby's tenant farmers have abandoned their land after a charismatic group of faeries promised them bargains that would leave them so wealthy, they'd never have to touch a plow again. The farmers' whereabouts are unknown, but the market town surrounding their estate will starve once winter comes if a secondary source of food isn't found.

I pull out the small notebook I keep in my reticule and make a note to ensure extra wheat and preserves are sent to Ripon this winter. I'll send some letters as soon as I get home. We can pay for it out of the royal vault. I don't even think Bram checks how much money we have.

It feels as if there's no way I can do enough to save these people. *My* people, now.

After the ladies' tea, I'm carried back up the hill and begin my late afternoon meetings with the husbands.

These men—lords, dukes, and the like—used to be Queen Mor's advisers who would carry out the day-to-day tasks like collecting taxes, tracking farming, reading through crime reports, and the rest of the minutiae required of running a country.

Bram stopped meeting with them almost immediately upon ascending to the throne. The second week of his reign, when the chaos of Mor's broken bargains was still at its peak, he stormed out of a meeting, calling it "boring." He knocked over a vase for good measure and hasn't entertained their requests for an audience since.

But I saw all their letters, piled up on Bram's desk, detailing the problems our citizens are facing without a responsible adult at the helm.

I'd never call myself a responsible adult, but I am queen, so it's my job to pretend the very best I'm able.

Which is why twice a week, I put on my tiara and I sit with perfect posture on a remarkably hard chair and I listen to the men who were supposed to be Bram's advisers but who are now mine.

"It's called a steam engine," one of the lords explains, gesturing to a complicated diagram I only half understand.

He pulls out a stack of illustrations next. "With one of these locomotives we could move people between cities in a quarter of the time it takes to get there by horse and carriage.

It would open up commerce between towns. Other countries are decades ahead."

"It requires tracks?" I say, examining one of the pencil drawings.

He nods. "Yes, ma'am. We'd have to increase mining or imports." Lord Langley's got a curly gray mustache and a bowler hat slightly too small for his bald head. He is the current speaker of Parliament, a distinction that didn't mean much under Queen Mor's autocratic rule but now carries a significant increase of duties in her absence.

"Mor would never have allowed for that, but there's a decent chance Bram won't notice at all. Farmers would have to be compensated. It won't do to destroy our crops and people's livelihoods over this," I say.

He scribbles some notes. "Yes, Your Majesty."

"And the coaching inns. If people no longer need to stay overnight to travel, we must make sure they can still make a living somehow. Send solicitors out to speak with the proprietors."

A memory flashes through my head, a night at a shabby thatched-roof inn called the Swan. It was the first time Emmett kissed me.

"Are you quite all right, ma'am?" Lord Langley asks.

I blink hard. "Yes, of course. Please carry on."

For the next few hours we talk through all manner of bureaucracy, and I leave the meeting feeling satisfied. I so often feel like a sparkly but unwanted accessory in Bram's court, it's nice to be useful. It gives me something to think about other than my maddening terror for Emmett and Lydia.

※

I don't see Bram that afternoon, but I do leave a message with our footman that I'm dining out with Faith and Marion should he be looking for me.

Faith and Marion have taken up residence at an unfashionable address on Queen Street, a narrow town house made of Bath Stone with gutters that clog when it rains. They live with Marion's maiden aunt, Gabrielle, a woman of about ninety who is nearly always confined to her room. Marion and Faith, having lost the competition for Bram's hand, can never marry. Queen Mor's magical bargain with us has been broken, but Bram is eager to uphold it anyway. It seems it's the only one of his mother's bargains he agreed to keep. The day after our wedding, Emmy, Marion, Faith, and Olive were each delivered notes in Bram's hand that said simply, *The terms remain.*

It suits Faith and Marion perfectly fine. It's Olive and Emmy I worry about.

Marion and Faith's butler answers the door, and I show myself into the drawing room. I know the way well enough by now. From there, I exit through the back door and cut through the damp garden to the cellar.

"You're late," Faith scolds as I swing the crumbling wooden door open.

I swat away a spiderweb. "I'm your queen," I shoot back,

then glance at the watch pinned to my waist. "I'm also exactly on time. It's not my fault you're chronically early."

Marion pats Faith's leg. "I happen to like your timeliness, darling."

The cellar is dim and dark, lit with beeswax candles set atop dusty milk crates we're using for tables.

The first few times we met, it was just me, Faith, Marion, Emmy, and Olive, so we gathered in the drawing room. Then our little group grew. Now we have Marion's sister, Este; Lottie; Ben, an assistant cook in my employ; and, shock of all shocks, Eduart, a 410-year-old former banner knight who fought in the War of the Roses and bargained with Mor to become immortal.

When her bargains were broken and the rest of her immortal footmen turned to ash, Eduart remained standing. He didn't even know what had happened until about a month ago. News was slow to reach his hamlet in Hampshire. He also didn't have any friends, as his bargain with Mor had made him absolutely repulsive to others.

He ended up on my doorstep at Kensington Palace asking to see Emmett's now-dead father, Edgar. I took him to Marion's for safekeeping and explained the whole sorry story on the way.

With these numbers, our ragtag group of rebels can hardly gather in Marion and Faith's drawing room, in full view of prying eyes, so we meet here, in the cellar tucked away in the back of their garden.

"I'm aging." Eduart sticks his hand dangerously close to the flickering flame of the candle.

"That's dirt." Olive peers down at his hand.

"A freckle," Eduart argues.

Olive reaches down and tries to smudge it with her thumb. "Fine, a freckle," she concedes. "What does it mean?"

"It means after four hundred years on this rainy rock, I'm finally on my way out!"

We've spoken at length as to why Eduart didn't crumble to dust when Mor's bargains were broken. The bargains with her doomed footmen must have had different wording, bound them to her in some way she didn't do with Eduart. We know her bargains got more specific as the years passed.

It seems for Eduart, the clock of his mortality has simply started ticking again.

"That's wonderful, Eduart!" I'm genuinely happy for him. "Though I am sorry you're stuck with us for at least thirty more years."

"A mere blink of an eye," he says with a cheerful smile.

I glance at Olive next to him. She's in the same gray cloak Rhion described. "Have you been meeting without me?" I ask the table.

Their faces are startled. "No," Olive answers for the group.

"I would understand. I know my schedule can be difficult." I try to sound kind, unsuspicious. Rhion is just playing with me like he plays with those girls draped at his feet. I'd be silly to believe anything he says. I long for the days when I believed the Others could not lie.

"I swear it, we have not met without you. Why do you ask?" Olive says.

"Rhion says he saw you in disguise, running all around town."

Olive's face blanches and it makes my stomach sink. "When was this? I often go to the kitchens with Ben to try new recipes."

"Every day at eleven a.m.," I answer. Perhaps it's unwise to lay all my cards on the table like this, but I trust Olive. It would feel like losing to let Rhion take that from me.

Olive's gaze falls to her lap. "Is he trying to sow discord? You know how they are."

An uncomfortable glance flits between Faith and Marion. I'm envious of the way they can communicate with nothing but a look.

Could Emmett and I do that? I don't even remember now.

I lay my hand atop Olive's. "Of course. I didn't mean to accuse. I'm just so on edge these days."

Olive gives me a sidelong glance and pouts. "Sometimes I think you never forgave me for that stunt with the bracelet."

"Of course we forgave you!" I reply.

Olive's eyes well up with fat tears and Ben springs into motion, tripping over himself to pass her a handkerchief.

"I'm sorry," I say genuinely. "I shouldn't have brought it up." Olive is a hothouse flower, and in upsetting her I feel like I've let Rhion win.

"Can we please move on from this?" Faith sighs.

We spend the rest of our meeting talking through Rhion's strange riddles (verdict: useless), Mor's possible whereabouts (verdict: she could be back in the Otherworld by now), and ways to find the door between worlds (verdict: no one knows, and now that the Aurelia Vallen lead is dead we must start anew).

I return home feeling restless and unsettled. I whittle away the rest of the day in the manner to which I have become accustomed: desperately lonely and sick with fear.

Pig curls up in my lap as I sit at my desk by the window and work on my correspondence. I start with the business notes needed after today's meetings: the railway, the market town's food supply, a pending issue with a London hospital. When they are done, I smooth out a fresh piece of parchment and begin a letter to Lydia, as I do nearly every night. I know it's silly, but it makes her feel less far away.

> *It was another gray day here. I swear I can smell the sea on the wind. I miss London desperately, but am told we will stay in Bath through February. There's a shop in town that bakes the most fantastic buns. I wish I could share one with you.*
>
> *Your devoted sister,*
> *Ivy*

I close my eyes and try to picture my sister in the Otherworld. When we were little girls, we imagined it having fields of golden flowers and horses with wings. We'd jump around our garden pretending we were flying through the air on their backs.

I miss my sister. I'm nauseous with worry for her. But in these moments, when it's just me and my thoughts, another emotion creeps in, sour in the back of my throat—jealousy.

Next, I write a letter back to Ethel, my father's cousin, a woman in her mid-eighties who lives up north. We've been corresponding since I was a faerie-obsessed child. She was an eccentric adult who took me seriously, which felt like a lifeline at thirteen.

While I'm distinctly less enamored with the Others these days, she is still a beloved friend. She's written to me about her pumpkin crop. She thinks she's likely to win the county fair this year with the biggest one her garden has ever produced.

I'm so proud! I write back next to a little drawing of an enormous pumpkin and a tiny Ethel beside it in her spectacles.

I save my letter to Emmett for last. Today has left me wrung out and exhausted, so I keep the message simple.

I miss you. I love you. I'm sorry.

I toss the letters to him and Lydia in the fire and watch silently as they curl into ash. Then I blow out the candle at my bedside and fall into a fitful sleep.

I am awoken at dawn to Bram's nose nudging the bare bit of my shoulder where my nightdress has slipped.

"Tell me again," he whispers in the dark, "the story of the faerie king."

CHAPTER FOUR

He's still in my bed when I awake in the morning, his crown of golden oak leaves discarded on the bedside table. His dark eyelashes brush the tops of his cheekbones.

I consider his beautiful face, his sharp jaw, his thick eyebrows, and wonder if faeries can be smothered to death. It would be so easy to reach over and grab a pillow.

He blinks up at me, bleary-eyed, as the morning sun leaks across the floor.

"Your present is downstairs." His voice is hoarse with sleep.

"My what?"

He wipes his eyes. "The present I promised you at Rhion's revel. It arrived last night. It's downstairs."

"Oh," I reply flatly. I don't want him to see that I am afraid. I rack my brain for what it could be. I pray he hasn't brought my parents here. If I'm lucky, it'll just be a new carriage.

"That's all the excitement I get?" He smiles, and he looks so much like the boy from the spring, the handsome prince who I thought was only nineteen, who I believed might actually love me.

I smile artificially, wrap myself in a dressing gown, and pad down the stairs, Bram at my heels.

I check the morning room first; it would be the most logical place to put a present. There's nothing in there but a startled maid stoking the fire.

Bram frowns. "She was in here the last time I saw her."

"Her?" I ask, blood thrumming. "My mother?"

"No." Bram's voice lilts as he teases me.

"Lydia?" I gasp.

Bram's handsome face contorts into anger in a flash. "No. Not Lydia. When will you move on from that, it's been months. Really, Ivy, sometimes you're such a child."

I recoil. "She's my sister," I say quietly. I shouldn't say anything at all, but I can't help it.

Bram pushes past me and stomps through the foyer, then wrenches open the front door. "Ethel?" he calls.

"Ethel?" I gasp. She's so old it can't be safe for her to come all the way to Bath. She should be in bed recovering from her journey. I'll need to ask the cook to make soup and the maids to bring extra blankets and a hot brick for her feet.

Bram looks up and down the street, then turns to me and frowns. "She was right here, I swear it."

The Royal Crescent is quiet this morning, but from around the corner comes peals of rabid laughter. Faerie laughter.

Dread sinks like an icy stone in my stomach and I chase the sound, running outside in my bare feet with Bram behind me.

Two faerie men, one with dark hair and a cleft chin, the other lanky with a sickly complexion, are on the ground, clutching their stomachs with glee.

"Have you seen an old woman?" I jut my hand out at the height of my heart. "About yea high?"

This makes them laugh harder. They're doubled over, their eyes bulging.

A fat raindrop lands on my head. Then another down my nose. I wipe it away, but my fingers come away red.

No. I look up and there she is. Her fragile, elderly body tangled up in the branches of a tree.

"She was so excited." The sickly one chokes out through his giggles. "She wanted to make a bargain."

No. *No, no, no, Ethel.*

My friend. One of the only true friends I've ever had.

I never told her not to come to Bath. I never considered the journey would even be a possibility for her.

But I should have known she'd be unable to resist the siren song of a faerie bargain. Or maybe she just wanted to see me. She didn't often complain of loneliness in her letters, she was too cheery for that, but I could tell how much she missed me. For every letter of mine, I received three back. I meant to write her more. I should have been writing her more.

My knees give out. "No, please." Her blood splatters like dew on the grass.

"Asked us to make her fly," the dark-haired faerie explains through his laughter. "Didn't look up for branches. They ran her right through before the old broad had any idea what was happening."

"Get her down," I wail.

Bram doesn't seem to hear me. He's just staring at her body, high up in the tree.

"Get her down now!" I scream.

Bram sighs, like I'm a child who has asked him to rescue a toy.

"Fine."

"And kill them," I add. "Kill them both! I'm your queen, you bastards!"

I'm blinded by rage, kicking and screaming against the footmen who hold me back, their arms locked around my chest. I don't even know when they arrived. My vision blurs.

I'm in bed. My head hurts. My throat is raw.

I blink a few times, and then it all comes rushing back to me. Ethel's body tangled up in the tree. Her hat on the ground. It was a lumpy purple thing. She put it on this morning to see me and now she'll never wear it again. The thought of it lying in the dirt starts my sobbing anew.

Pig climbs onto my lap and I burrow my face into his fur.

The hope I held in my chest was a small flame, but a flame nonetheless; it flickered in the darkness. Ethel's death is the blow that has snuffed it out.

After a few hours of sobbing in bed, no one checking on me, I position myself in the chair by the window. It's closer to the fire and it feels less pathetic to be upright.

On the street below, life goes on. Ladies promenade, parasols balanced in their gloved hands, shiny carriages clatter by, and the green is dotted by a few picnic blankets.

But it all looks so bleak from up here.

Afternoon mist, blown in from the sea, pools in the streets below, giving the Crescent a seafoam-gray, dreamlike quality. The image of me, up here in this chair, must look serene from the outside, but inside I am raging. There is nothing sedate about my sadness. It's vicious. A monster clawing at my rib cage from the inside. I'll be shredded through completely soon if nothing is done.

It's only been four months and Bram's court has brought nothing but destabilization and horror to England. What will this country look like in another four months? In four years?

I'll be queen of the ashes.

Or I'll be dead.

Right now, I wish I was dead.

That's new. I've never really wanted that before.

The sun sinks below the horizon. I've done nothing but sit in this chair by the window all day, letting the gray world pass me by.

But now my stomach is grumbling and I have no interest in sleeping.

Still in my dressing gown, I pad downstairs to the kitchens, and pass Bram and Rhion sitting in the dining room.

They're discussing something intently over dinner. I hear

the words *forest, hunt,* and *queen.*

They pause when they see me in the doorway.

"Your Majesty, how lovely to see you." Rhion greets me without a second glance at my limp hair and bare feet. Maybe he thinks this is a new human fashion trend. I'll probably see him in a dressing gown at the next revel, with makeup mimicking dark bruises under his eyes.

"Oh, it's you," I reply weakly.

"Have you puzzled the answer yet?"

"I'm sorry?"

"To my riddle. What can you shatter with just one word?"

"Um—" I sputter. "I'm not sure. I was just looking for dinner."

Rhion pats the seat next to him and I want to die. "Plenty of room here."

I pause, desperate for some excuse.

Bram's gaze levels me. "Don't be rude, Ivy."

I drag my feet across the carpet and sink down in the seat next to Rhion. "I don't mean to interrupt your meeting."

"Oh, you're not interrupting anything. After one thousand years of friendship, we're out of things to talk about." Rhion laughs but Bram doesn't.

"What did you do with her body?" I ask flatly.

Bram looks up from his plate.

"Her body," I say again. "Where is it?"

He clears his throat. "Sent home to her family. I saw to it."

"And the men who killed her?"

Bram shrugs. "I don't know."

"You let them go?" I ask, horrified.

"She bargained with them of her own free will. I'm not a governess. My citizens can do as they please."

"She was an old woman and they killed her for entertainment!"

I push back from the table and my chair topples behind me. I want to tell him I hate him, but I know too well what harm it would bring. First it was the girl in the deer mask, then it was Ethel. It could so easily be Marion or my mother next.

I'm nearly to the door when Rhion's voice calls out. "A promise."

I stop and turn. "What?"

"That's the answer to my riddle. What can you shatter with just one word." He glances to Bram. "A promise."

That's funny. I would have said *heart*.

I'm not supposed to be in the kitchens. The poor old cook startles as I walk through the door, and the rest of the staff jump up and begin washing pots and sweeping the floor in an attempt to look busy.

"No, please," I say, but they don't listen.

I don't intend to stay for long. I'm only looking for something to eat—and more importantly, a moment alone with Ben, the most unexpected member of our little rebel group.

Only eighteen, he's the cook's apprentice, mostly responsible for breakfasts and desserts. He joined us completely by accident. The first time I took notice of him was two months ago when he walked into the morning room with a plate of scones, tripped over his own feet, and sent them flying into our laps.

He looked up and fell in love with Olive at first sight.

From that point on, he found excuses to come to the sitting room when she visited me. He asked me about her favorite desserts and made them for her with painstaking care.

And then he followed us to Marion and Faith's town house, innocently enough.

Olive had left her shawl behind and he was attempting to return it, and, he confessed to me later, have the opportunity to talk to her about something more than bread flour.

The problem was he arrived a moment too late. We shouldn't have been speaking so openly in the drawing room and Ben's footsteps as he approached were silent, a symptom of his years in domestic service.

"What did they use to lock up his mother—iron, was it? Could we get more?" Marion was saying as Ben hovered in the doorway.

I swore and jumped out of my skin when I saw him standing there. "Are you spying on us?"

"Are you talking about Queen Mor?" he asked plainly. "What an awful woman. Killed my dad. The son doesn't seem much better. It's a pity."

He was so profoundly unselfconscious, I trusted him immediately.

"That's my husband you speak of," I replied, just to see what he would say.

He bowed his head. "My condolences."

Everyone in the room burst out laughing.

Then Lottie vouched for his character and he was initiated.

I suspect he shows up more as an excuse to see Olive than because of any ambitions as a true radical, but he's relentlessly pleasant and genuinely helpful when it comes to spying on Bram's whereabouts.

I don't think Olive has even noticed how he moons after her.

He's stirring something purple on the stove when I find him.

"Want to try?" He offers the spoon to me.

"What is it?"

He smiles. "Grape jam."

He spreads some on two thick slices of toast when I explain I haven't eaten all day. We sit at the rickety staff dining table and I tell him about Ethel. He cries for me, which makes my tender heart swell, and then I explain the strange things Rhion has said about Olive. I'm desperate to think of anything but Ethel's body in that tree, and Ben watches everything Olive does. Really, I just want him to assure me I have nothing to worry about.

But he frowns. "She comes through the kitchens most afternoons. That's usually when I bake and she'll come sample things for me."

"That seems harmless enough."

"I agree, but there is one curious thing: her hair is always soaking wet."

"Soaking wet?"

Ben nods. "Like she's been swimming."

"That's very odd."

"I thought so as well, so I asked her where she'd been, and do you know what she said? She said she'd been taking the waters."

"The waters?" Since the Romans, it's been believed that the hot springs of Bath contain the power to heal an array of ailments, but Olive's never mentioned anything to me.

Ben nods. "That's what she said."

I'm at Marion and Faith's door at first light. Their beleaguered housekeeper leads me to the morning room, where a bleary-eyed Faith and Marion enter a few minutes later.

"Why are you here?" Faith asks. She's plaiting her long dark hair, still wearing her lilac dressing gown.

"Send for Emmy." I spring up from the love seat. "We're taking the waters."

CHAPTER FIVE

The Roman baths are in the center of town, down the hill from Queen Street. We approach the public entrance and are waved through by a startled attendant who recognizes me. I'm treated with such little respect by Bram's court, I often forget I'm still a national figurehead. My fame hasn't gotten less strange.

Steam pours from the pool outside into the gray October skies. The bubbling waters are surrounded by white columns and mosaics that are meant to look vaguely Roman. Above the pool, a marble statue of the goddess Sulis Minerva watches us reproachfully.

Together, we search the entire facility: the changing rooms, the tepidarium with its lukewarm greenish pools, the treatment room dotted with marble tables, the blue-tiled indoor swimming pool, and then finally the caldarium, the hottest room, where the white steam pools so thick, we can hardly see.

Marion pats her dark curls, trying to smooth the frizz from

the humidity. "Olive's not here." She groans. "And she's going to be so put out we went on an errand without her if she finds out."

I want to keep searching, but I know in my bones Marion is right. I'm upset with myself for letting Rhion plant even the smallest seed of doubt in my mind.

If Olive is taking the waters, then maybe she does have a health issue. If she hasn't confided in me, then it's none of my business.

But one thing nags. If she takes the waters every day at eleven like Ben says, then why isn't she here?

We emerge back out onto the chilly streets of Bath.

And then I see it. The flash of a gray cloak disappearing around a corner.

"Come on," I whisper to the others.

Emmy looks at me like I'm half-crazed as I take off running, but then I hear Faith gasp and I know she's seen her too.

We track Olive for a few blocks, staying far enough back that she doesn't see us through the throngs of people on the high street.

She ducks around another corner, but by the time we follow, she's disappeared completely.

This street is quieter, dimmer. There's nothing but a dusty, unfashionable haberdashery and a boarded-up print shop. Olive is nowhere to be found.

I swear under my breath.

"She didn't just vanish into thin air," Marion offers unhelpfully.

With what I've witnessed of magic, I'm not so convinced.

I drag my hand along the stone wall, searching for a seam, when suddenly, I feel nothing. I stumble and look up. Where my hand is, I visibly see a wall, but I wave my hand back and forth through it like it's made of air.

A faerie trick. A secret door.

My heart pounds in my chest. Is it possible I've found the entrance to the Otherworld by sheer luck?

I feel around the edges and identify the bounds of a door just large enough for a human to step through.

"Come on." I gesture to the others, and to their eternal credit, they follow without hesitation.

We enter into a dark stone corridor. In the distance, a flickering wall-mounted torch lights the way like a beacon.

Faith stumbles and Marion catches her by the elbow. The floor is an overlapping mess of shattered tiles, half-rotted wood, and crumbled mosaics.

We follow the torch around the corner, then down a sloping walkway. The air turns thick and humid.

Faith sniffs. "Ew."

"I didn't even do anything!" Emmy replies.

Marion tilts her nose up. "It's sulfur."

"Well, it smells like rotten eggs," I say.

We turn another corner, and it goes dark. There are no more torches to light our way as we travel into the underground labyrinth.

The four of us link hands and step over the treacherous

floor as carefully as we're able. I trip and Faith catches me by the arm.

"Are you all right?"

"What could Olive possibly be doing down here?" I answer.

Maybe it wasn't Olive at all. Maybe this is just some faerie trick and we're all about to be hunted for sport or boiled alive in the hot springs.

Just as my fear reaches a fever pitch, I spot a single pinprick of light in the distance.

We follow it until we enter an antechamber. It's lit up with torches on every wall, illuminating the strange room in firelight. The stone walls are weathered with time, and the floor is dirt except for the symmetrically spaced stacks of bricks every few feet. On the far wall, above an arched doorway, is a massive carving of a gorgon, his eyes wide, his beard and hair fanning out in all directions like a sunburst.

But that's not the strangest thing in the room. The sulfuric fog parts and we see her. Sitting on the floor, directly in the middle of a cage, is Queen Mor.

Her long dark hair hangs in a single braid down her back. She wears a simple white gown, stark against the dark bars of her cell.

"You again," she sighs as we enter.

It's shocking to see her, especially looking so serene. I haven't seen her since Bram's coup. It's like my body can sense how dangerous she is; I have a sudden urge to turn on my heel and run.

"Have you been in Bath this whole time?" I ask.

"My son loves me. He prefers me close by," she answers coolly.

The four of us jump at a clatter in the shadowy corner of the room.

Olive emerges, her gray cloak still pulled over her head. She's got a tray of food in her hands: a bowl of milk, a saucer of thick honey, glazed buns, and thick slices of bread. She calmly lays it on the floor and pushes it through the gap between the bars of the cell.

"Olive?" I say. It's the oddest thing. She doesn't even glance my way.

"You enchanted her?" I ask Queen Mor.

"My *son* enchanted her," she answers. "He needed someone to care for me."

Emmy grasps Olive's blank face in her hands. "Olive?"

Olive just blinks.

Faith approaches Queen Mor's cell with her hands on her hips. "If he loves you so much, why does he have you in a cage?"

"This is one of the things I hate about humans. Your lives are so short you have no stomach for conflict. This is simply a"—she searches for the right word—"brief disagreement."

"He's wreaking havoc," I say. "People are dying."

She levels me with a glare. "That's what people do. They die."

I point to Olive. "Undo it."

Queen Mor gestures vaguely to the bars. "I can't. But don't fuss too terribly, she'll be back to her old self the moment you leave."

I search for a response, but tears spring to my eyes and I'm afraid if I keep speaking, I'll cry with frustration. I don't want to cry in front of her.

Her head tips back and she rests it against the bars. "How is it I'm bored of you already?"

"Does anyone have a deck of cards?" I ask. The girls look confused, but Emmy raises her beaded reticule.

"I have my tarot cards," she says.

I extend my hand and she places the creased deck in my palm.

I sit down on the floor, as close to Queen Mor as I can manage, so close my knees are pressed against the cold bars, and shuffle the deck. Mor's dark eyes narrow as she watches.

I sift through the stack, pulling out every major arcana card as I go. The World, the Fool, the Hanged Man, the Empress.

Then, with only the minor arcana left, I shuffle.

The cards are thick, with golden edges, and not easy to shuffle, but I do a serviceable enough job, and then I begin dealing.

With two hands dealt, mine in front of me, and hers pushed just slightly through the bars, I stare her down and wait.

"What is this?" she asks cautiously. It feels like a victory.

"A game."

"Why?"

"If you're bored, we'll play while we talk."

She approaches me. Even in this cell, stripped of her jewels, she still holds her head like a queen and I find she still has the ability to frighten me.

"Fine."

"Gin rummy?" I offer, sounding as confident as I can manage.

"Fine."

There are fifty-six minor arcana cards, instead of the fifty-two in a regular deck, but divided among four suits, it's easy enough to play with them.

"It's unsustainable," I begin. "Bram has only been king for four months, but he won't be able to carry on like this for much longer. Any semblance of governance is gone. He spends all night partying with his court and then sleeps through the day. The Others make cruel bargains at every turn, and every day more people die. Citizens are afraid right now, but eventually that fear will give way to anger. You know enough about humans to understand that."

She considers the card in her hand, then discards. The eight of wands.

"So far, the only fae who have come through the door have been Bram's court and their staff. They're outnumbered significantly. If Bram carries on like this, there are going to be riots. People will fight back and he will end up dead."

I'm bluffing with that last part. I still have no idea how you kill a faerie, but Bram once told me he killed his own father—so I do know it is possible. The question that looms is whether I want to be the one holding the knife.

Mor's dark eyes flash, but she still doesn't say anything. She draws a new card. I do too.

"Tell me how to open the door between worlds, if not to save England, then to save Bram from himself. I know you don't wish to see him harmed."

She doesn't look up at me. She's on a roll now with her cards, discarding rapidly into matching piles until nothing remains in her hand. "Gin," she announces.

I fold, laying my cards upright on the ancient floor. "Lucky hand."

"This used to be a temple," she says after a beat of silence.

I glance up at the vaulted ceiling. We're underground now, buried in a ruin under the streets of modern Bath, but it's clear this was once a grand place.

A serene smile spreads over her flawless face, as unchanged as ever. It's as if we could have once been classmates or debutantes together. "My son put me in a place of worship because he loves me."

"He buried you underground because you're a miserable bitch," Faith says from behind me.

I turn my head to shoot her a glare. "Not helpful," I hiss.

Queen Mor pays her no mind. She stands up, and I do the same until we're mere inches apart. She has several inches on me and looks down at me through the bars.

"You want to know what I think?" she snarls. "I think if

you truly believed Bram was going to get himself killed, you'd just let him do it. You'd sit there and watch him self-destruct. You'd still be queen when it was all over. If he's gotten you pregnant, then your children and their children would rule. Wouldn't that be nice for you?"

I hate the way my face flushes. Bram comes to my bed sometimes, but the idea of letting him touch me like *that* makes me sick.

Queen Mor's cruel gaze pierces me as sharp as any knife. "You need me."

"I need you to save him from himself," I say once more. "If not for the love of England, then for the love of your son."

"I will not turn against him!" Her voices cracks like a lightning bolt across the cavernous space.

"Even though he has you in a cage?" Marion asks, her voice softer than mine.

Mor turns from me and walks to the other end of the cell, and I know the conversation has ended.

I curse. I pushed too hard too fast; that's just like me. No patience for anything.

I gather Emmy's tarot cards from the floor and pass them back to her.

In miserable silence, we walk out of the Roman ruins.

"What about Olive?" Emmy whispers.

She had wandered off in silence while I was playing cards. "She'll meet us back at home. We can decide what to do with her later."

We turn the corner into the tunnels that will lead us back to the street, when I hear footsteps.

We look to each other, panicked. In this narrow passageway, there is nowhere to hide.

"Olive?" I call hopefully.

A figure approaches from the darkness, at first nothing but a silhouette.

But the closer he comes, the more features I can make out. A man, tall, broad-shouldered, wearing a top hat.

After an agonizing moment, he steps into the lantern light.

Rhion smiles. "Hello, little rebels."

CHAPTER SIX

"Oh, thank goodness. We've gotten hopelessly lost on a women's historical society outing. Can you help us find the way out?" The lie springs to my tongue easily. Before I met Emmett, I wasn't a very good liar at all.

Rhion claps his hands together in front of his heart. "No need for that! We can speak freely now! Come, come." He waves his hand and it feels as if we have no choice but to follow him.

We end up in another dark antechamber, this one with a bricked floor and more little piles of bricks, like tiny ovens scattered throughout.

"The old caldarium," Rhion explains. "The Romans used to come here and sweat and gossip and do business. That was before my time, but my father didn't like the Romans much at all. Said they were so serious they never agreed to any fun bargains. They were too busy marching and building walls."

"Whatever you think we did, we didn't do it," Faith says. She's less scared of the Others than the rest of us, I think.

"That's a rather blanket denial," Rhion replies.

"We're ladies-in-waiting to our benevolent queen," she says dryly. "What business could we have with rebellion?"

I nearly snort a laugh at Faith calling me benevolent. She usually opts for *annoying, tiresome, naive*. She cares for me in her own way, I do believe that. But only four months out from the competition for Bram's hand, we're both still nursing the wounds we suffered at Bram's and Emmett's hands. She'd never confess it, but I know she still blames me for the way Emmett cast her aside. Her love for Marion has softened her but she's stubborn in nature. We have that in common.

Rhion takes off his top hat and holds it humbly in front of his chest. "Can we stop with the posturing? Bram is a monster. You're all smart enough to see it."

I pause.

This feels like a trick.

"I love my husband," I say slowly.

"You don't need to lie, not anymore," Rhion replies.

"I am devoted to my husband, King Bram. I love him truly. Now if you would be so kind as to show us the way out, we'd be much obliged."

Rhion shakes his head sadly. "He was my friend, my closest friend. My father was his father's closest adviser. We grew up more like brothers than friends. But then he snatched the crown from his mother, and the parts of Bram I loved—his humor, his kindness, his good nature—were warped into something cold and unrecognizable. His father was a cruel man and Bram learned well at his knee. Better than I'd realized. It took me too many years to realize the Bram I once loved no longer existed. It wasn't until his wedding that I understood just how gone he was."

It's a strange thing to say. Rhion wasn't at my wedding; he didn't arrive until the next day.

"He was kind to me, when we first met," I offer. I don't even know why I say it. It's like some primal part of me wants to comfort Rhion. The pain on his face as he explains who Bram used to be is difficult to look at.

"Bram has always been a skilled actor," Rhion continues. "Even in our youth, he learned how to manipulate others. I don't think he ever did a lick of his own schoolwork, there was always some girl who mooned after him doing it for him. Or, on rare occasions when that didn't work, some younger student he'd threaten into doing it instead. If they refused, he had no trouble acting upon his threats of violence."

"Cheating on his homework seems a rather small thing compared to patricide," Emmy says.

As Rhion paces, he leaves little indents in the felt of his hat from gripping it too hard. "I know, I know. I mean only to paint a picture. Bram was born troubled, and time and circumstances have warped him into a monster. We were young men by faerie standards when he led the coup against his parents. Queen Moryen and her husband, King Urien, ruled as true co-monarchs. But on one key issue they disagreed: the humans."

"I already know this part of the story, I think," I reply. Queen Mor told me months ago that her protection of the humans was what ultimately led to her exile from the Otherworld.

"Yes," Rhion sighs sadly. "Mor was sympathetic to the plight of the humans. It's not that she is a particularly empathetic being, but she does love law and order. She thought the brutality with which the folk treated the humans was undignified. She told me once she was sick of throwing away bloodstained carpets. When she decreed that the door to England was to be closed, there was outrage. The folk had grown used to their human playthings and they had also grown fond of England."

"And Bram used this against her?" Marion asks.

Rhion nods. "He did. That's the problem with immortality. In order for there to be a new ruler, the old one must be disposed of. There is no natural order of succession, only blood and betrayal and the blessing of the land. But there were those of us who agreed with our queen's decision. I had grown fond of humans, and not just as sport. Before the door closed, I had friends in London, and I could see they were just as complex and feeling as I was, even if their lives were shorter than my own. Bram ranted and raved about his mother, but I never thought he'd actually take action against her. I was naive. I won't be again."

"What do you mean?" Marion asks.

"We need to rid England of him. He is poison. Neither of

our worlds will survive for long if he remains on the throne."

"I'm still unsure of how that involves me," I say.

"You're his wife."

"I am, and I love my husband." I parrot my denial from earlier.

"And so, you are now a part of his family. We folk have funny rules about things like that. You can go through the door unaccompanied. I cannot."

My heart thrums. "The door?" I ask in a whisper, increasingly wary that this is a trap.

There's a spark in Rhion's eyes. "The door between our worlds. It's nearly impossible for one of us to die on English soil. Only in the Otherworld will you be able to kill him."

My blood sluices in my veins. This time, Faith says something before I do.

"We won't mention this meeting to Bram as a courtesy. We'll be going." She turns on her heel as Rhion shouts, "Wait."

I search for an emotion in his fathomless eyes and find sorrow. I don't know what to make of it.

"I love my husband," I say flatly.

"Surely there must be some way to make you trust me," he pleads.

"I've seen too much of your kind to ever trust a faerie again. It's nothing personal," I reply.

"I can't give up that easily."

"I'm sorry to disappoint you." I attempt to leave again, but he captures the sleeve of my day dress loosely in his hand, then drops it just as quickly.

"If not for England, then what about for Lydia?"

"Lydia?" I gasp. "You do know her, then?"

"I—" His voice hitches and he casts his glance at the ground. "I loved her—do love her, I mean."

There's only one way Rhion could know Lydia.

I can picture myself so clearly on that night, last February. The air was biting cold and I was near mad with anguish over Lydia's disappearance. In a last-ditch attempt to reach her, I tried to open a portal to the Otherworld like we tried to when we were children. It was the night I met Emmett. It was the night she returned.

I think again of those two weeks she went missing last February, and I know in my bones my suspicions were correct. "So she did go to the Otherworld?" I asked Queen Mor as much, back when I believed she could not lie.

Rhion nods. "Yes, she was there for months, long enough for us to get to know each other a little, but it must have been much shorter here."

"Only two weeks," I confirm. "And that's where Bram is keeping her now?"

Again, Rhion nods. "It is."

"Is she all right? Is Emmett?" The words come tumbling out of me; there are so many things I need to ask him. But then I remember who I am talking to. "Wait," I gasp. "I still don't trust you. How do I know you're telling the truth? This could be another lie or game or farce meant to trick me into sedition against my husband, with whom, I'll once again remind you, I'm madly in love."

The other girls and I wait, still and silent as Rhion gathers himself. He glances down to where his hands are clasped in front of him and then back up to us.

"I saw her for the first time in the middle of the afternoon. She was on her hands and knees, helping a maid who'd dropped a tray. Her voice was soft as she reassured her. I hadn't seen anyone do anything that kind in four hundred years. It's embarrassing to admit, but Lydia wanted little to do with me and I was too much of a coward to show her my true nature. I was afraid of Bram noticing just how much I noticed her. But I did . . . I noticed everything. She learned every servant's name and thanked them constantly. She played with the cook's children, spinning them until they laughed so hard they could scarcely breathe. A window in my room overlooked the garden and I watched her there, most days. She spent hours on her knees coaxing the castle grounds back to life, and then leaving a trail of petals on the stairs back up to her room. She was—" He takes a breath as if the force of his own feelings has made him unsteady. "I've lived for a very long time, but I'd never seen anyone so full of life."

My eyes well with tears picturing Lydia as he describes her, happy in the Otherworld. "You could be lying about this, too," I say.

Rhion just shrugs. "But I'm not."

And I shouldn't believe him, but I do. In my time among

the Others, this is the most genuine show of emotion I've seen.

"What of Emmett?" I ask.

Rhion shakes his head sadly. "I do not know. Bram doesn't speak of him and I haven't returned to the Otherworld since the day of your wedding, when he brought me here. I asked about Lydia when he was drunk enough to tell me where she was, but he said nothing of Emmett."

"But he has to be there, right?" I prod. "Bram wouldn't have killed him, would he?"

The corners of Rhion's mouth pull down. "I no longer know what he's capable of."

Rhion follows us up the hill to Faith and Marion's home on Queen Street.

Their poor housekeeper jumps upon seeing us all pile through the door and hurries off to the kitchens to fetch us stacks of cucumber sandwiches, scones, and miniature mince pies.

We send their footmen off with urgent letters and soon the five of us are joined by Ben, Eduart, Este, and Olive.

She rushes into the candlelit cellar and pushes the hood of her gray cloak off her head. "It's spitting rain out there." She pauses. "Why are you all looking at me like that?" Her eyes land at the head of the table. "And why is *he* here?"

Rhion tips his hat to her. "You're under an enchantment."

"Excuse me?"

"Bram has you under an enchantment. Every morning at eleven you go to the ruins of the old Roman baths and you feed and care for Queen Moryen, who is locked up there."

Olive's chest flushes. "I do not!"

"We saw you today, darling," I say gently. Between the glassy look in her eyes then and the genuine shock on her face now, I believe that Olive is completely unaware of what she's been up to. I know she's not that good an actress.

Rhion extends his hand. "Kiss it and I'll undo it."

"What?" Olive gasps, scandalized.

Rhion rolls his eyes. "A kiss for a broken curse. There needs to be an exchange. There's a way about these things. Quickly, please."

Reluctantly, Olive brushes her lips, just barely, against the smooth skin of his knuckles, below a thick emerald ring.

She blinks hard a few times and then murmurs, "Oh . . . oh. I am sorry."

I touch her shoulder. "You didn't know."

"But I could have told you where she was. All this time we've been discussing it and it was locked somewhere in my head."

Emmy shakes her head. "Don't concern yourself. You showed us in the end, didn't you? We followed you today, that's how we found her."

"It's not your fault," Ben pipes up from the edge of the room.

Marion and Faith try not to laugh. Only Faith succeeds.

"And it's where we found Rhion." I explain the circumstances of his being there.

"Which brings us"—I slap my hands down on the

pockmarked old table, more excited than I've been in months—"to the matter of the door. Rhion, I'll let you take the lead."

Rhion pushes back from the table and stands. "Once upon a time, back when England was still ruled by men, there were doors all over Britain." I'm so used to seeing Rhion take everything as a joke, it's strange to see him so serious. I wonder if this is a glimpse of the real him.

"We know!" Eduart heckles, and throws a small piece of cheese at Rhion, which he deftly catches in his mouth. He chews, swallows, then continues.

"Queen Mor's last act as ruler was to seal these doors behind her."

"She told me she enchanted it to let only Bram through. She hoped one day he would come find her," I say.

Rhion shakes his head. "That was a half-truth. The kings and queens of the Otherworld wield such power that they *themselves* are the conduit between the Otherworld and Britain. Queen Mor enchanted all the thin places, the places where the borders had been traditionally crossable, so that only one door remained—the royal family."

"What does that mean?" I ask.

"Bram can't open the door," Rhion says. "Bram *is* the door."

CHAPTER SEVEN

"I don't understand." Ben rests his head in his hands. "Maybe you all understand, but I don't get it at all."

"Nope, utterly and completely lost," Este replies. She looks like Marion in miniature. Same light brown skin and dark curls. Their eyes are the same too, big and brown and framed with thick lashes like a baby doll. At only seventeen, Este is the youngest in our little group. She speaks less than her older sister, but when she does, she does not waste words.

Rhion paces the room. "How do I explain? Bram, and Bram alone, can reach into the space between worlds and open the door. It's as simple as it seems."

"That's the reason Others have only come through in London and Bath," I say. "Bram has to let them in himself."

Rhion nods and snaps his fingers. "Yes, exactly!"

On the bright side, there is no door somewhere, swinging open, allowing droves of fae to cross over into our world. But it also means I need Bram to let me into the Otherworld himself.

Disappointment crashes over me like a tidal wave. I try

to swallow it, but a sob escapes my lips. Olive pats my back weakly.

"I'm never going to get them back, am I?"

Rhion pauses. "No. Don't say that."

I wipe a tear that's escaped down my cheek. "Why not? It's true."

Rhion crosses the room and bends at my knee so we're eye to eye. "Why do you think the folk love humans? So much we'd overthrow a queen and wait centuries to be reunited with you?"

"Because you're all pea-brained little sadists," Faith says under her breath.

Rhion doesn't take offense. "Not entirely untrue. But it's more than that. My kind may live forever, but we have one fatal flaw: our short attention span. The average human child has more ability for focus and self-control than a thousand-year-old fae. We love humans because we love human society. Our towns in the Otherworld are pale imitations of your cities because we couldn't be bothered to build them. There are no fancy stores with candies wrapped in wax paper or pleasure yachts that carry us down rivers. Our society is functional, but hundreds of years behind yours."

"And Bram means to halt all our progress," I say.

"That he will," Rhion agrees. "But there is another reason the folk love humans. It goes beyond fascination. Some of the folk can feel particularly strong human emotions. It's a hit better than any faerie wine."

"They're getting *drunk* off of us?" Emmy asks in horror.

"Not everyone. But yes," Rhion answers gravely. "The stronger the emotion, the greater the feeling of euphoria."

The sinking feeling in my stomach has only gotten worse. "I appreciate your information, but I'm still not entirely sure how this helps us get to the Otherworld or overthrow Bram."

"They're one and the same," Rhion says. "You need to get to the Otherworld to rescue Lydia."

All at once the puzzle pieces slot together in my mind. "You want me to get Bram drunk. Drunk on *me*."

Rhion grins. "Clever girl."

Brief elation quickly gives way to nausea. "I know that I am his wife, but I can't fake loving him. I don't have it in me."

"I didn't say it had to be love. What I said is that it has to be a strong emotion," Rhion answers.

We work well into the night on a plan, as the housekeepers bring us more beeswax candles to keep the room alight and trays of cheese, bread, and pickled vegetables to snack on while we work.

By the time I climb the hill back to the Royal Crescent, the first pale blue streaks of dawn are slipping across the sky, and I feel something like hope for the first time since my wedding day.

That night, I appear in the doorway to Bram's room as he readies himself for the revel. His private quarters are as spotless as his room at Kensington Palace. Not a scrap of parchment is out of place, not a bed linen wrinkled.

His valet buttons him into an elaborately beaded black cloak.

Bram eyes me in the mirror. I'm leaning against the doorjamb in my revel finest, a dress made of layers of sea-green gossamer, embroidered with tiny beads. I think I look a bit like a mermaid.

"If you'd come to me earlier, we could have matched," he says sarcastically.

I need him to like me, especially tonight, so I just smile and say, "Oh, are we going to be one of *those* couples?"

He almost grins.

This revel is held in Lord Huron's house, two over from ours, in the middle of the Royal Crescent. He's enchanted dragonflies, or maybe just trapped them, but they're flying all over the place and keep getting stuck in my hair and tiara. I swat them away, but can't stop flinching as they buzz by me.

I stay on the dais by Bram's side, lording over the party silently.

Rhion appears below us and offers a brief bow. "Come to the bonfires, Your Majesty."

I place a hand on Bram's shoulder. "No, thank you, I wish to stay here with my husband."

Rhion regards us. "You make a handsome couple. It's clear how devoted you are, my queen."

I clutch my chest like Rhion's compliment has taken me off guard. Bram smiles too; it pulls at the edges of his mouth, not quite enough to show his dimple, but enough it's clear he's pleased I've earned Rhion's approval.

"You have a lovely wife, Your Majesty." Rhion bows, then disappears into the crowd. The drum of the faerie band thrums through my veins, buzzing at the same pitch as the dragonflies.

Bram's arms snake around my waist and pull me onto his lap.

His breath is hot on my neck. "You look beautiful tonight."

A shiver crawls down my spine. "Thank you," I breathe out.

He picks up a loose blond curl and twirls it between his fingers. "You look so much like her."

"Like who?"

He trails a finger along my jaw. "Your sister."

Nausea claws up my throat. It takes all the resolve I have not to stand and run from this room or find the sharpest fork with which to stab him.

I pour Bram another cup of faerie wine from the decanter on the table next to us, and tip the goblet to his lips.

"I'm bored," I sigh. "Let's go home?"

He pulls me by the hand from the party. The tunnels connecting the houses are still full of people dancing, singing, passed-out drunk, or kissing passionately up against the stone walls.

The heel of my shoe drags through the thick pink icing of a smashed cake.

I kick off my shoes as we tumble through the doors of

Bram's bedroom. I fling myself onto his bed, giggling like a schoolgirl.

I try to kick under the blankets but the bed is made all wrong. The pillows are facing the wrong end.

I pull one from behind my back and examine it. "Why are these at the foot?" I ask.

"What do you mean?"

"Why are the pillows at the foot of the bed?"

He furrows his brow in confusion. "Do humans always sleep facing the same direction?" He shrugs. "How odd you all are."

The reminder of his lack of humanity always makes my hackles rise. Like some basic animal instinct is screaming from inside of my bones for me to *run*.

Instead, I interlace his fingers through mine and pull him onto the bed toward me.

This is it. The part I've been practicing in my head.

I imagine Emmett: the curve of his neck, the crinkle by the sides of his eyes when he grins, the way his hands gripped my waist. But mostly I think about how it felt when I glanced at him from across a ballroom. He was always a head taller than anyone else, easy to spot, and in that moment when his eyes met mine, I knew I had an ally. I knew that there was someone in that room who was looking for me, too.

I miss that feeling.

I miss him so much.

I close my eyes and cup Bram's face in my hands. He sighs and I let the feeling of immense love wash over me like a golden light.

The memories I've kept at bay for months because they're too painful to touch come flooding back to me: Emmett and me waltzing in his room, arguing in the corner of a dusty boathouse, sharing a bed in a coaching inn, spending our last night together in Kensington Palace.

It crashes over me like a wave and I'm lost in it, tumbling through the force of feeling.

I open my eyes.

Bram is looking up at me glassy-eyed. His chest rises and falls slowly.

I lean down, nearly kissing him. My bottom lip brushes his just barely.

"Ivy." He slurs my name.

He wrenches his lips from mine and trails them up the column of my neck. I arch against him. His touch revolts me, but I let him think it's passion.

"Ivy," he sighs.

I scrunch my eyes closed and grit my teeth so hard my jaw aches. My hatred crests over a dam I can no longer stop from breaking.

It overtakes me, the pure revulsion I feel for him. Like spiderwebs of ice, it races through the marrow of my bones.

I pull myself out of his touch and try not to gag. I needed to be strong enough for Emmett and Lydia, but I just can't do it.

I'll have to tell Rhion we need to find another way.

But then I open my eyes and look at Bram. He's tipped back

on the pillows, the sun-kissed waves of his hair around his perfect face like a halo.

Weakly, he interlaces our fingers and pulls me back toward him.

He's loose-limbed and pliant. Drunk, I realize. Drunk like we'd planned for.

"It tastes different," he slurs into my ear.

"What does?" I whisper.

He gazes up at me, a dark angel nestled among the snow-white linens of his bed. Shadows dance across his perfectly sculpted face. He sucks his full bottom lip between his teeth. "Love is nice, but your hate tastes so much better."

A chill goes through me.

A shadow fills the door. Rhion, waiting in the darkness.

"Show me, Bram." I run my fingernails along his scalp and he purrs like a cat.

"Show you what?"

"You know what. The Otherworld. Just a peek."

"I shouldn't," he protests.

"It's been my dream ever since I was a little girl. Remember, I told you that day in the barn back in the spring, the day you gave me your ring."

His hands are sloppy as they reach toward me, but his touch is soft. Silently, he twists the gold band inlaid with the small pearl that I've worn ever since that day. I take it off at night and set it in a dish next to my wedding band and engagement ring, my stomach turning as I slip them back on every morning.

He doesn't answer.

"You never got me a wedding present." I pout.

His eyes flutter closed. "You hate me."

"So, so much." I whisper so quiet not even Rhion can hear. "But only sometimes."

Bram extends an arm lazily across the bed, then with a turn of his wrist like he's opening a door, something clicks.

I blink against the sudden light flooding the room. I pry open my stinging eyes and see it: a perfect rectangle of verdant green landscape.

With the sharp edges of the door around it, the image looks almost like a postage stamp. The gently rolling hills are dotted with trees in a riot of autumn colors. Crimson leaves float gently on the breeze, landing on the ground in a silent flutter. I squint against the sunlight and can barely make out the vague shape of a shining castle in the distance.

"Go on." Rhion appears right behind me.

I stand from the bed, my knees shaking. I never actually thought we'd achieve this. For all my dreaming as a child, for all my scheming as queen, I didn't really believe I'd ever get to see the Otherworld.

I glance at Bram on the bed. His eyes are closed and his mouth hangs open.

"I've got him," Rhion whispers over Bram's sleeping form. "*Go.*"

I step one foot through the doorway and can't help but look

down. One slippered foot sinks into sun-warmed green grass and the other remains planted in the shadowed cream carpet of Bram's bedchambers.

I cast one last look at the room and at Rhion. If all goes according to plan, the next time I cross this threshold, Emmett and Lydia will be at my side and Bram will be gone.

"We all believe in you, Your Majesty," Rhion says with more reverence than I deserve.

I nod in wordless gratitude. Then I muster every ounce of bravery I've ever possessed, and step fully into the Otherworld.

CHAPTER EIGHT

Rhion slams the door behind me, and with a *click*, it's vanished, like it never existed at all. I reach out for it, but find nothing but the sweetly perfumed air of the Otherworld.

I tilt my head back and breathe, attempting to slow my rapid heartbeat. I'm going to need to have my wits about me and it's much too early to panic.

Birds chirp serenely as crisp fall leaves rustle in the gentle breeze.

My slippers sink into grass a slightly different shade of green than I'm used to, but the sky is the same blue-gray as it is in England.

I'm in an open meadow, surrounded on three sides by a sparse forest. Ahead of me, far off among the rolling hills, a castle juts up from the landscape.

It's grander than even Buckingham Palace, constructed of a strange opalescent material that shimmers in the sunlight.

It reaches up into the sky, marked by spires and turrets as sharp as canine teeth.

I hike up my skirts and head for the castle on the hill.

The landscape is bucolic. I half expect to find a serene herd of English sheep grazing on the soft grass, but the only other life I see is a man riding in an open cart pulled by one horse.

Neither the man nor his overlarge horse pays me any mind.

My thoughts race as I walk toward the castle. I'll find my sister, she will know where Emmett is, and then, together, the three of us will solve how to banish Bram forever.

Soon, I promise myself, I won't feel so alone anymore.

I can't let myself think of the other possibilities: that I might not find Lydia, that I might be taken prisoner, that there might be nothing left of my sister and Emmett to save.

I look down at my slippered feet and put one foot in front of the other. It's the only thing I have power over.

But even with my head so full, I can't help but marvel at the landscape around me. I wish I could grab my eight-year-old self by her chubby cheeks and tell her we did it.

The castle sits atop a hill, and at its base, I reach a small market town.

One short man shoves an overripe, unfamiliar fruit into my hand as I pass. I drop it the next street over, and it splatters on the ground, spilling seeds that look like tiny jewels and leaving my hands sticky and smelling of rot. Other stalls display sparkling cases of crystal figurines, little jars of tonics, books that rattle as if something lives within their pages.

The streets themselves are narrow, lined with crooked buildings plastered in bone white, or dreamlike pastels of robin's egg blue or blush pink, all framed by dark wooden beams. The top floors are wider than the base of the buildings and hang over the street, which is constructed of loose cobblestones with soft clover growing between the gaps.

At first, the Others pay me little mind, but the closer I get to the castle gates, the more eyes I feel on me.

Conversations stop and transactions are paused, coins in hand, as I walk by. My revel dress doesn't look much different from the clothes they all wear, more ornately beaded perhaps, but similar enough. My hair is in a style similar to that of the women, loose around my shoulders with three small braids sweeping my curls off my face on each side, attached by a jeweled comb in the back. Faerie women wear their hair long, and so it's become the fashion in my court as well. My hair reaches nearly to my waist now. Viscountess Bolingbroke would faint if she could see me. But despite my faerie fashion, there is no mistaking me for what I truly am: too weak, too small, too soft to be anything other than a human.

I reach the castle gates, but no guards stand at attention like at Kensington.

The metal is cool under my palms. All it takes is a soft push and the gates swing open noiselessly, as if welcoming me with open arms.

When I was a little girl and I imagined entering the Otherworld, trumpeters heralded my arrival and confetti rained down on me from a rainbow canopy of strange new trees. Reality is a dim comparison.

I tread anxiously along one of the snaking paths, nearly overgrown with snaking vines, dotted with purple flowers with sharp, thorny petals like thistle.

Then I see it—a row of hedges encircling neat garden boxes. Half of the hedges are trimmed back and wrapped for winter. Lydia's work. I'm sure of it. I recall hours of sitting with her and Mama in our garden planting bulbs and cutting back growth until our fingers were frozen and caked in dirt.

I can't help myself; I hike up my skirts and run down the winding path, as quickly as my exhausted legs will carry me.

The wind is knocked from me. I don't even realize I'm on the ground until I blink up and realize the blurry gray taking up my entire field of vision is the sky.

I wheeze and place a hand on my aching ribs, then roll over to try to push myself up off the gravel.

Two pairs of strong arms scoop me off of my knees and drag me toward the castle.

"Lydia!" I rasp, but there's so little air in my lungs my voice doesn't travel. "Lydia!"

The faerie guards are silent as they haul me away, too strong to fight against, but it doesn't stop me from trying. I kick and scream and bite and scratch with all the might I can muster.

The doors to the castle swing open for them as if enchanted, and they drag me through the halls wailing like an angry cat.

If Bram is going to kill or imprison me, I'm not going down without a fight. I'm sure Emmett and Lydia fought, too.

There's comfort in that, a connection to them.

The guards stop in front of a pair of double doors, snow-white and reaching at least three stories high. In place of handles are two massive stag's antlers, but the guards don't bother using them. With the heels of their heavy boots, they kick the doors open, then toss me to the floor like a pile of rubbish.

My knees strike the stone hard as the doors slam behind me. The music that had been raging whines to a sudden halt.

The silence weighs heavy, like the air after a crackle of lightning, before thunder erupts.

Still on my hands and knees, I raise my head slowly. My tangled hair hangs limp in front of my face and my mouth is full of metallic blood from where I bit my tongue when I hit the floor.

I look up and find myself in the middle of a faerie revel. On all sides are hundreds of courtiers, but they've scattered to the edges of the enormous ballroom, leaving a perfect aisle from me to the two thrones at the front.

I hear a soft gasp, and even in the tiniest of noises, I recognize her.

My sister, looking more beautiful than I've ever seen her. Atop her luminous blond curls sits a crown of diamond-encrusted branches. Her black gown is so long it sweeps past the throne she sits on and down the stairs of the dais, trailing beads like raindrops. In one hand dangles a bejeweled goblet, and her full lips are the bitten-red of faerie wine.

It's more difficult to see the figure in the throne next to her, as there are half a dozen exquisitely beautiful faerie girls gathered around it.

One with a manicured hand laid on his shoulder. Another standing behind him, her fingers wound through his hair. There's a girl lounging at his feet, her arm resting along his calf, and one perched on the armrest of his throne, a slit in her gown showing a scandalously long swath of leg.

But the one I can't stop staring at is sitting in his lap. She's got masses of long dark hair, and her gown is low cut enough to see how deeply her pale skin is flushed.

She's got one hand on his chest and the other in his mouth.

Globs of golden honey drip from her fingers, across his lips and down his chin. She pumps them in and out and he sucks softly, his eyes fluttering closed, his head tipped back. He, too, wears a crown. It's askew atop his dark hair, and his doublet—beaded black to match Lydia's—hangs open at his throat.

I gasp, and it must awaken something in him.

His eyes open and his gaze snaps not to me, but to Lydia. In that single glance, there is aching intimacy, pulled as tight as a bowstring.

Gently, my sister reaches for him and lays a comforting hand on his arm. Something glints in the torchlight—a wedding band encircling her third finger.

The sight of it is sickening, shattering.

His eyes land on mine.

I mutter only one word. "Emmett?"

It's as if a spell is broken. The whole party comes back to life suddenly, in uproarious, hysterical laughter—and it's me they're laughing at.

CHAPTER NINE

I turn on my heel and sprint from the room.

The world spins. I have no idea where I'm going, only that I need to be somewhere that isn't here.

Moments later I hear the doors behind me swing open with a crack.

"Ivy!" Lydia calls. "Ivy, stop!"

I turn, panting, tears blurring my vision.

Her eyes are glassy, her mouth hanging open in surprise. "Ivy." She says my name softer this time.

I look toward the doors. Emmett hasn't followed her.

My sister crosses the hall to me and tentatively grasps my hand, as if to confirm I'm really in front of her.

I blink and see again the twin thrones, Emmett by her side.

"How long have you been here?" I choke out.

Lydia looks to the floor, devastation all over her face. "Two years," she answers gravely.

Bile rises in the back of my throat, but I have to get the next question out. "And how long have you been married to Emmett?"

She yanks her hand back and looks beseechingly into my eyes. "It's not Emmett."

"Who, then?"

For the first time, I'm able to really look at her. Her blond hair hangs past her waist, and in addition to the bejeweled crown on her head, her curls are scattered with diamonds woven into small braids. Her warm brown eyes are lined with wet-looking black kohl and her lashes are long and dark. The light freckles that usually run atop her cheekbones are obscured with something that shimmers blue and purple like moonstone as it catches the light.

It's not that she looks older, it's that she looks *changed*, which is worse.

She sputters, shame creeping across her face.

"*Who?*" I half laugh. "No one could be worse than Emmett." For the briefest moment, I'm happy that someone has managed to capture my sister's heart.

"Bram." Her voice is so quiet, I'm not sure I hear her at first.

"Who?" I can't have heard her correctly.

"Bram." She says it more forcefully this time. Her eyes finally meet mine and I realize we're both crying. The kohl lining her eyes smears down her cheeks, leaving storm-cloud-gray streaks.

"No, I'm married to Bram." I twirl my wedding ring around my finger anxiously. She's got it all wrong, or maybe she's gone mad.

Lydia mirrors my gesture and spins her ring. "He married me first."

"That's not possible." Realization hits. My limbs go numb. "Oh."

"Yes. *Oh*," she replies softly, like she pities me.

My throat swells, but I get the words out. "Please, just, tell me everything. I can't bear another secret."

"My bargain with Queen Mor—I asked to experience something completely new and she sent me here as some kind of cruel trick, I think. I didn't remember anything when I returned home to England or I would have told you, I swear it." Her eyes shine with tears. "I didn't remember any of it until Queen Mor's bargains were broken on your wedding day."

"So he married you, then returned to England and married me?" I ask. My thoughts are tripping over themselves and I can't make sense of anything. "Why? How . . . how did it happen?"

"I lived in the castle with Bram, with very little memory of my time back home. You'll find that things like time and memory are slippery here. And Bram . . . he made me love him; you know how he is." She flushes with embarrassment. "It was only once he married me that I realized it was all an act. He was trying to break Queen Mor's bargains. When it didn't work, he realized the marriage must take place in England. That's why he announced his intentions to find a bride and married you."

"How did you get home the first time?"

Lydia frowns. "I hardly remember. I was running from the castle, and then I was back in England. It all happened so suddenly."

The doors to the ballroom creak open and the music and voices from the revel spill out into the hall.

Emmett stands haloed in torchlight in the doorway. The doors close behind him and for a moment he just stands there at the end of the hall, his chest hitching like he's run a very far distance.

"Ivy?" His voice breaks around the sound of my name.

Despite everything, my heart swells at the sight of him and the force of the love I feel for him nearly knocks me off my axis.

It's Emmett. My Emmett. Finally.

On heavy feet, he crosses the length of the hall to Lydia and me.

I expect him to run to me; my heartbeat is a roar in my ears. My arms are outstretched, but no—

He looks to my sister, then to me, then back to her.

Something wordless passes between them.

My arms go limp.

Two years.

I knew Emmett for only six weeks. Four months if you count our first encounter in the carriage, which would be generous.

I feel sudden terror that what we had doesn't compare to

whatever he now shares with my sister.

He looks as changed as Lydia. His hair is long, too, in dark waves that fall nearly to his shoulders.

Like Lydia, he's got a smear of kohl around his hazel eyes, though his is not as dark as hers.

I remember thinking his hands were too big for his body, but he's grown into them now. Everything about him is bigger, sharper, harder to look at. But his face is the same. There are those high cheekbones, sharp jaw, full mouth, straight eyebrows, and clever eyes. He's always been breathtaking.

Emmett lays his hands on Lydia's shoulders, a casual intimacy in it, the kind of gesture that passes between two people very used to touching each other. "It's not her," he says, voice thin.

Lydia looks up at him, her brows knitted together. "What do you mean?"

Emmett's eyes well with tears, but the line of his jaw is hard. "It's not her, Lydia. It's a trick."

"A trick?" I raise my voice. I hate them talking about me like I'm not here.

Emmett doesn't so much as look at me. It's as if he can't bring himself to.

"I should have told you years ago, Lydia. Ivy died the night of her wedding."

I cross the space between us and hit him on the shoulder. "I'm very much alive."

"Selkies and other Unseelies can shape-shift. Tell her

nothing," Emmett begs.

I take Lydia's hand in mine and tug her toward me. The way she looks at me with fear and hesitation shatters what little is left of my heart.

"It's me!" I exclaim.

Emmett ignores me completely. "I couldn't bring myself to tell you she was gone. I couldn't bear it. I've tried to protect you."

He looks so broken, but it's not me he's looking at.

"Emmett," I say loudly enough that he's forced to turn to me. "It's me." My voice cracks.

He stares at me in silent, awful suspicion.

"We once got caught at a coaching inn in the rain together. You told the innkeeper our names were Fern and Edward Bennett from Nottingham."

He presses his mouth into a tight line and shakes his head. "I told Bram that story."

I search my memories for something that only he and I would know. "We were together the night before Bram and I became engaged. The nightdress I wore was white with a pale pink ribbon. I left the ribbon in your bed."

His eyes are cold as he regards me. "I told Bram that, too. I've confessed everything."

Confessed like I'm just something he's guilty of.

I turn to Lydia; we have a lifetime of memories Bram could know nothing about. "Remember when you were eight you had recurring nightmares about falling out our upstairs window?

Papa had to install a lock on it just to get you to sleep."

Lydia glances anxiously to Emmett.

"Stop looking at each other," I snap. "Look at me." *Please just look at me.*

"It's true," she says softly.

Emmett shakes his head. "You don't know what the real Ivy told Bram about you, or what you told Bram the first time you were here. Nothing is to be trusted."

With one last agonizing look at me, he tears himself away.

"Emmett!" I scream after him. "Emmett, please."

His steps slow. It's as if he can't help himself.

From the end of the hall, he halts. Then turns back to me, like it pains him.

A storm rages beneath the surface of his hazel eyes.

"What do you see when you look at me?" The question comes out so quiet I'm not even sure if he hears me.

The love I have for him is the North Star I've been following. He's been the reason for everything I've done; every moment of survival was for him. I'd never once considered he might not love me back anymore.

I think of the girl's fingers in his mouth, of his intimate glances at Lydia. *Ivy died.* That's what he said, and he's wrong, but maybe he's right, too. There is a version of me that died the night of my wedding. And it appears the version of Emmett, the one who loved me so desperately, is dead too.

Britain's most notorious rake. Maybe I am a fool for letting myself think I was ever anything more than another notch in his bedpost.

Emmett's eyes bore into mine for a beat, searching for something he clearly doesn't find. He shakes his head, his longer hair a riot around his crumpled face, and then he disappears through a heavy door.

CHAPTER TEN

I begin to sob. It starts as big heaving breaths, but then they get stuck in my throat and I can't breathe as the tears fall.

Lydia wraps me tightly in her arms. "You believe it's me, then?"

She pauses and takes one long look at me. "If you are a selkie, you're doing quite a good impression of my little sister. I'll keep you around."

I laugh weakly. "You vomited on the table at Lady Trummer's autumn equinox tea when you were thirteen. You didn't tell Mama you weren't feeling well because you didn't want to miss the party."

Lydia presses her lips together.

"It was your most embarrassing moment. You never would have told Bram about it."

"You don't need to go on. I already believed it was you."

"You did?" I ask hopefully.

She nods. "No one else could look that shattered gazing at Emmett. There's not a selkie alive who is that talented an actress."

"I don't know what to say to convince him." I look down at my hands. This is nothing like how I imagined this going.

"He'll get there in his own time. Emmett is stubborn. He's afraid of getting hurt again. What he's gone through here . . ." She trails off.

"What has he gone through?" I ask, dread coiling around me.

Lydia averts her gaze. "It's not my story to tell."

As if to change the subject, she takes my arm in hers. "Come along, we'll have a room prepared for you."

The tug I feel toward Emmett is ever present. "I need to speak to him, make him understand—"

"Give him time," Lydia says.

"Time isn't on our side. Won't Bram come looking for me here? He'll notice I'm gone soon enough." In the plans I made with our little rebellion group, I pictured finding Lydia in the castle, freeing Emmett from prison, and fleeing with them, hiding somewhere for a few days until Rhion tricked Bram into reopening the portal and returning to England. I have flint and steel tucked in a pouch down my corset to make a fire in the woods. Never did I imagine I'd be welcomed into the castle as a guest.

Lydia's beautiful face is calm. "Hours in London are equal to days here. We have a while before he comes."

"I left in the night. He'll sleep through the afternoon."

Lydia nods. "That's good. We have two or three days then, at least. Long enough to come up with a plan."

"We can go to the woods. Rhion will open the portal as soon as he's able—" The words race out of me; I need Lydia to understand how dire this is.

"Rhion?" she asks, confused.

"He's helping us."

Her brows narrow. "That doesn't sound like him."

My stomach twists.

She smiles serenely. "We can discuss this in the morning."

I feel like I'm sleepwalking as I follow her up the central staircase of the castle. Like in Kensington, there is a massive tree growing up through the center. The tops of its leaves brush the domed, stained glass ceiling. Moonlight filters through the great hall in a pastel mosaic of colors. The sun has gone down fast.

Lydia leads me to a room on the fourth floor, a quiet corridor that seems to house rooms for guests.

She stops at a periwinkle door and turns the cut crystal handle. We step inside and she trails a gentle hand along the silk bed linens.

"I hope you'll find the room to your liking," she says like the perfect hostess.

The room is nothing like Kensington Palace. There is no dark mahogany, polished brass, or thick carpeting with geometric patterns.

One wall is made up entirely of windows that look out on the countryside, with its changing autumn leaves. The bed is white marble, with four posts that reach up to the ceiling.

The vanity is mirrored glass, even the drawers, which reflect speckles of starlight around the room.

"Don't do that," I say to my sister, suddenly exhausted. It's been more than a day since I last slept.

"Do what?" she asks innocently.

"Act like you're some prim and proper wife welcoming me to a weekend at your country estate."

I expect Lydia to laugh but she hesitates. "This is my home. I am queen of the Otherworld."

"Yes," I laugh, "but, like, not really."

Her brows furrow and I know, in that way sisters do, that we're about to have a fight.

"I've ruled this kingdom for years while Bram plays with you in England," she says harshly.

"Plays with me? He's tortured me! Every thought I've had these past four months has been for you and Emmett and your safety."

"Yes, exactly. *Four months.* You have no idea what it is to rule a kingdom."

I stare my sister down, the heat of anger rising in my chest. "I've been holding England together with my bare, bloody hands! Every morning we wake to new bodies in the streets. The government is barely functioning. I've had to learn tax codes, agricultural practices, social services—" I list them off on my fingers. "All the while hosting infernal luncheons for titled ladies because that is what is expected of me."

Lydia reaches up and brushes her eye, leaving a smear of

glitter across her cheekbone. The sight of it should infuriate me more, but instead it punctures me completely.

"I've had to be his tariffs and tea party queen. You got to be his magic queen." My voice cracks.

She puts her hands on her hips just like she used to when she chastised me for acting like a baby. "This is just like when we were children. You think it's been easy for me ruling the Otherworld as a mortal? I've had to fight for every crumb of respect I have here."

"It's not fair!" I can't help but yell. "I was the one who believed in magic."

This place is foreign, but this feeling is not. I am well acquainted with the emotion of looking at Lydia and wanting to be her—and then hating her for it.

Envy settles in my stomach sourly.

"Did you come here to fight with me?" Lydia frowns.

"I came here to save you."

I expect her to say something petulant like *I don't need saving*, but she pauses. It's as if she really looks at me for the first time. Then she starts to laugh. "You're the queen of England," she says in disbelief.

"I—I am the queen of England," I sputter, but then I start to laugh too and soon we're both hunched over, wiping tears from our eyes. It's all so absurd.

I cross the room and pull her into a hug. It's awkward with our heavily beaded sleeves and Lydia's sharp crown, but it's a relief nonetheless. "I missed you," I mutter into her unbound hair. "I'm just glad you're all right."

I feel her sigh. "I missed you too."

I pull back and look into her eyes, so like mine. "Do you love him?"

"Which one?" she asks, horribly. It's the worst possible response.

"I meant Bram, but either . . . both?"

"I loved who I believed Bram to be."

I don't want to ask the next question, but I have to. "And Emmett?"

She pauses, searching for the right words, her face so full of tender fondness, it makes me ache. "He's my best friend."

"That's all?"

"For two years, we are all the other has had. He's the only person I could be honest with, and him with me. What we've had to do to survive here . . ." She trails off uncomfortably.

The sadness in her voice makes me want to cry.

"I love him so much, Lydia. I'm afraid he no longer loves me back."

She places both hands on my shoulders. "I'd been here three months before I saw Emmett. He'd spent all his time before that below my feet in the dungeons, though I was ignorant to his presence in the Otherworld. He strode into the dining room, rail thin, bruises under both eyes, and you know what the first words out of his mouth were?"

"What?" I ask quietly.

"He said your name. Whispered it like a prayer is a more accurate description."

"Why would he do that?"

Lydia smiles sadly. "He thought I was you. It's a very large room and I was rather far away. No one who says your name like that could have forgotten you. You're rather hard to forget, I think."

I look to the floor, unconvinced. "Thank you."

She takes a step back and looks me up and down. "I'll send Eloree, my lady's maid, in to ready you for bed. You can trust her, but no one else. In the morning, we will plan, but you need your rest."

I nod, too exhausted to protest.

Lydia walks out the door and moments later a lithe faerie girl with sunset-colored hair that falls to the backs of her knees strides into the room.

She sprays my hair with a fine mist of oil that smells like rose petals after rain and looks at me with her overlarge eyes through the mirror.

"You look so like your sister," she says in a soft, high voice.

"We get that a lot. She's prettier, though," I answer.

"She is," Eloree says without hesitation. I don't know if her bluntness is a characteristic of the Others or if it's just her, but I find it endearing.

I raise my arms and she slips a nightdress the same blue as the light on the ocean, constructed of a floaty silk, over my head. She then passes me a wax-stoppered bottle with a light blue liquid inside, shimmering like the Milky Way.

I look up at her questioningly.

"A sleeping draught," she explains, and before I can protest, she unstoppers the bottle and tips it between my lips.

The draught tastes like a cold winter wind and I cough, trying not to swallow it, but it slides down my throat like oil.

I swat her hand away. "Don't do that," I sputter between body-racking coughs.

She looks at me with her uncanny, overlarge eyes. "Oh, most of us at court take them. The revels go on for so long."

"Well, I don't want one again."

She shrugs, as if confused by my reaction, then exits the room.

She shuts the door behind her with a gentle *click* and I lay my head on the pillow and try to swallow away the strange flavor of the draught. I hope I haven't just been poisoned. It would be embarrassing to make it all this way and be taken out by a lady's maid.

I've only been in bed for a moment when I'm startled by a frantic pounding on the door.

I grab a heavy golden candlestick from my bedside table and raise it above my head like a weapon.

What if Lydia was wrong and Bram's already found me here? I thought he'd taken all his most loyal advisers to England with him, but what if some remain in the Otherworld, and they're here to exact revenge on his behalf?

The pounding continues. "Who is there?" I call.

"It's me," Lydia's voice calls from the other side of the door. "Open up, I have an idea."

"How do I know it's you?" I ask cautiously. Emmett was so convinced I was a selkie, perhaps shape-shifting is commonplace here.

"You hid Mr. Froburg's brussels sprouts under your bed when you were seven because you didn't want to hurt his feelings, but then your room smelled so terribly of rotting brussels sprouts Mama almost fired our maid."

I crack open the door. "I should have thrown them in the fire."

Lydia cracks a smile. "With age comes wisdom."

She's in a nightdress similar to mine, an intricate lace dressing gown pulled over it. With a dramatic flourish, she gestures to the object at her feet.

"A bucket of water?" I ask. "I can't stink that badly."

"No, stupid." She rolls her eyes. "I just had the most brilliant idea. *Selkies.* They return to their true form in water."

It's vaguely familiar to me; there was a story about a selkie in Mrs. Osbourne's old faerie book. Once upon a time, I had every page memorized.

"Of course!" I shout, and haul the water from the floor. It splashes all over my hem.

"Which room is his?" I ask excitedly.

"Door at the very end of the hall," she says. "Good luck!"

But I only half hear her. I'm already racing down the corridor.

I drop the bucket at my feet and pound both fists on his sunrise-orange door.

From inside, I hear him stir, but the doorknob doesn't turn.

"Please, one second, that's all I ask," I beg through the wall.

"Go away," he answers miserably.

I pound until the doorframe shakes. "There is nothing you can say to make me leave. Crack the door. It's all I need. If this doesn't convince you, I'll leave you alone forever." I absolutely won't leave him alone forever, but I'd say anything to get him to open this door.

For a moment there is only silence, and I fear he means to leave me out here all night, rapping until my knuckles are bloody.

"Please," I beg so quietly he probably cannot hear me. My arms burn with effort and my fists throb.

Footsteps sound from behind the door.

Reluctantly, it creaks open a sliver.

"I don't know who sent you, but please let them know I have been tortured thoroughly enough." Emmett looks and sounds exhausted down to his bones.

The kohl from the revel has been washed from his eyes, revealing the bruise-like circles beneath them.

He takes a sharp breath at the sight of me like he's in pain.

I want to say something cutting like, *At least try to look happy to see me*, but I can't risk him slamming the door in my face.

In one fluid movement, I pick the bucket up and dump it on my head.

Emmett gives an abbreviated little breath. His eyes rake down my body to all the places my silk nightdress now sticks to every curve of me.

Then he wraps me in his arms, and he's kissing me.

His lips collide with mine with bruising pressure. His tongue slides into the gap between my teeth and he holds me against his body so tightly, I don't think there is a single space where we are not touching.

The exquisite relief mixed with scorching desire is the single best sensation I've ever felt.

It's like I've been aching with thirst for months and I'm suddenly being swept out to sea.

He winds his arm around the back of my head and tucks me into the crook of his elbow, tipping me back until we're both stumbling.

He lifts me up and I wrap my legs around his waist as my head hits the plaster wall behind me, but I can't bring myself to care.

I'm pinned now between Emmett and the wall, and I savor the heat of him, the hard planes of his body moving against mine.

He moans into my open mouth and all I can do is take it, feel it, feel him everywhere.

Then, just as suddenly as it began, Emmett lowers me to the floor and wrenches himself away from me.

He's as soaked through as I am now. His white shirt sticks translucently to his chest and his hair is plastered to his forehead.

He's breathing hard, looking at me wretchedly.

"I'm sorry," he gasps. "I can't do this." Then he disappears into his room and slams the door behind him.

PRINCE EMMETT DE VERE

It's hours later when I appear at the threshold to Lydia's room. She's used to my late-night visits by now, as I am to her unusual waking hours.

She opens the door after only two knocks, clad, as she usually is, in a nightdress with her hair wound up in a knot on top of her head, a few curls escaping around her face.

She waves the paintbrush she has in one hand at me. "Come in, you."

I plop down into the worn armchair by her fire and wonder how many hours, days, months I've spent in this exact spot.

I've never been able to think of the Otherworld as my home, but this corner in Lydia's room comes very close.

Lydia returns to her canvas, sparing a glance at me behind her.

"You look awful," she says.

"Thanks, Lyd."

"You need sleep."

"So do you," I shoot back.

"Where is Ivy?" she asks, ignoring my jab. "She did come to see you, didn't she?"

"Was the water your idea?" I ask.

She fights a smile. "You're too stubborn for your own good. I knew you just needed a push."

I roll my eyes, but she's too focused on her landscape-in-progress to notice. She flicks her paintbrush, and a smear of yellow starts to become a field of flowers.

"Where is she now?" Lydia asks again, perpetually the older sister.

"In bed," I say flatly.

Ivy banged on my door for what felt like ages after I slammed it in her face. When the pounding slowed to nothing I peered into the hallway and found her asleep at my threshold, splayed out like a doll.

I cursed under my breath, sure the castle staff had given her a sleeping draught. I don't want her tangled up in all the substances so readily available here.

I scooped her up and carried her back to her room. She flinched awake as I opened her door and blinked up at me with her big brown eyes.

"Emmett?" She sighed my name.

"Shh," I soothed her. "I'm just putting you in bed."

"Stay with me," she croaked, voice small.

I looked down at her in my arms and wanted nothing more than to slide into bed with her, wrap my arms around her, and never move again.

I tucked her under the quilt and watched as her blond curls fell in a cascade over her pillow.

Every part of me ached, like a fire had been lit inside of my chest and was spreading through my bloodstream until even the tips of my fingers were in pain.

Ivy fought hard to keep her eyes open, but even her strong will was no match against a faerie sleeping draught.

"Sweetheart," I said so low I hoped she couldn't hear me. Here she was, *my girl*, not dead, but alive and *here*—and I still couldn't have her. The pain of the dungeons was nothing compared to this.

I tucked the blankets up under her chin and plaited her hair into a loose braid so it wouldn't tangle in her sleep. Lydia taught me how to braid a long time ago, on a rainy afternoon when we had nothing to do but be together.

I allowed myself a moment of weakness in Ivy's doorway, where I stood for much too long watching the gentle rise and fall of her chest.

Then I walked to Lydia's room.

"You have to tell her," Lydia says now. "You owe her that much."

"I don't see the point. It'll just hurt her further," I reply. I don't know how to make her understand that I've become *of* this place, transformed. I may look well on the outside, but the veneer hides a rotting, foul center, like a piece of faerie fruit.

"So what's your plan, then?" Lydia asks, voice drenched with sarcasm.

"We'll do what we need to do with Bram, Ivy will move back to England, and she'll move on with someone more suitable than me. She was never going to be mine. I've known that since the beginning."

"And you and I?" Lydia asks quietly.

"We'll do what we've always done," I answer. *Survive.*

"If you think she's going to move on, you don't know my sister as well as you think. She won't just let this go."

I shrug. It's not often we disagree, but Ivy was willing to leave me for Bram even before all of this. Lydia has it all wrong.

"You have to tell her," Lydia says once more.

"I can't."

Lydia whips around to face me, her hands covered in thick oil paint. "She's in agony!"

"She can join the club!" I hate myself immediately for shouting at Lydia. She's always been my tether to the better parts of me, and I need her now, even as I long to push her away.

She flinches and I cross the room to her and wrap her in a hug. "I'm sorry. I'm sorry," I mutter softly.

Lydia lays her head on my chest, but she's breathing against me like she might cry. I know every hitch of her breath by now.

"I'm getting paint all over your shirt," she says.

"I don't care."

"I'll help you tell her. We can do it together," Lydia says gently.

I pull away from her. "Give me time."

Lydia chews on the inside of her cheek, looking so much like Ivy as she considers me. "I'm just not sure how much we have."

There's a heavy stretch of silence and I know Lydia is waiting to say something else. I flop back into my well-worn chair and wait for it. She finishes the shading on a cloud and then asks, "You really thought she was dead?"

I don't like to think of my first few months here, but the memories rush back to me in a torrent I'm powerless against.

I spent two months in the dungeons of the castle, locked in a damp cell, slowly starving to death, going mad with worry for Ivy and with grief for my father.

I attempted escape three more times after my disastrous first effort, but each time was unsuccessful and left me beaten to a bloody pulp. My left hand still can't make a fist after all the bones in it were shattered by a particularly enthusiastic guard.

I was lying on the stone ground, staring at the ceiling, when I heard Bram coming. After years of living in each other's pockets, I recognized him by only his steps.

I rolled over and followed the line of his shiny boots, visible under the bars of the cell, up to his face. He wasn't sneering. He was looking at me like he might be sorry for me.

Even after everything, I still felt a pang of love for him, like the clang of a bell in a church that burned down long ago.

"Have you come to mock me?" I asked.

"I've come to talk," he replied.

I pushed myself up to a sitting position and leaned against the far wall of my cell. Between the shadows and my too-long hair, Bram was less likely to see any of my reactions. I didn't want to give him the satisfaction.

"Talk, then," I said.

"Ivy is dead."

I gasped like I'd been hit, unable to stop myself. "No," I muttered to myself. "She can't be." Wouldn't I be able to feel it somehow? That very first night we met in the carriage, when she was out hunting for Lydia, she told me she'd be able to feel it if her sister was gone. I understood exactly what she meant. Even worlds apart, I cannot imagine I could go on living unaffected if Ivy Benton's heart stopped beating. Wouldn't something be fundamentally damaged within me? I should have been able to feel it like a broken bone.

But then—so many of my bones were already broken. Maybe I couldn't distinguish it from the pain I was already in.

"The night of our wedding," Bram went on. "After my mother's bargains were broken, there was a riot at the palace."

"The guards couldn't stop it?" I'd been worried about something like that happening, but had enough faith in the palace guards to keep us safe. I was willfully naive about a lot of things. I know that now.

"No. The gates were breached, and Ivy was killed in the chaos. I found her trampled body near the orangery. I think she must have been looking for you. I'm sorry to deliver this news, it brings me no pleasure."

"I don't believe you." The words were strangled.

Bram reached into the pocket of his coat and fished out a small object. He tossed it and it landed at my feet. In the low light of the cell, it took me a moment to recognize it.

I scrambled back in horror.

Lying in the dirt was a human finger wearing Ivy's engagement ring.

"I was fond of her, too," Bram said.

"Were you?" I asked, aghast, the devastation making my eyes blurry.

"I was," he answered, his voice a shade quieter.

"Get it away from me."

He lowered himself to the floor so he was sitting in front of my cell. He looked so odd sitting there in his fine silk jacket, a crown on his head. With surprising tenderness, he reached for the finger and tucked it back in his cloak.

All I could picture was her body, the same body I'd held and worshipped, bruised and broken against the grass. Had she suffered? She must have. It would have been a horrible way to die.

I leaned over and retched into the corner of my cell.

Bram just watched as I sobbed and heaved until there was nothing left in my empty stomach to come up but burning bile.

"Is this fun for you? Are you having fun?" I looked up at him through the damp strands of my hair.

Bram watched me like a parent watches an unruly child

throwing a tantrum. "Are you quite finished?"

"Finished mourning Ivy? How dare you."

"I've got business to attend to. Would you rather me leave you down here?" he answered in a bored voice.

"Is there another option?"

"I have a bit of a problem I need your assistance with."

"My assistance?"

"Now that I'm king of both England and the Otherworld, I'm finding myself stretched rather thin. Previously, while I was away, my most trusted advisers acted as regent in my stead, but now they're all in England with me."

My blood turns to ice, thinking of more fae like Bram running wild over my beloved homeland. England isn't perfect, but they don't deserve this.

"I need someone here, a regent to do my bidding while I'm away."

"And you want me to act as their personal punching bag?" I half joked.

"I want you to be my regent."

I sat up straighter, wary of a trick. "Me?"

"Despite the incident with Ivy, you really did have my best interest at heart. It was your plot all along to see me on the throne, and now you've done it."

He was right. In an awful sort of way.

"We were brothers, once upon a time," he went on. "Are you ready to throw all of that away for some dead mortal girl?"

Yes. But I was of no use to Ivy down here. I couldn't avenge her if I was locked away in the dark. I wouldn't last much longer. If I wanted to get out, this was my chance.

"There are always other girls." I choked out the words, false and bitter. "But I've only ever had one brother."

"That's what I hoped you would say." Bram grinned, and for a moment he looked so much like the boy I once knew it was heart-wrenching. "I think you've been punished enough for the Ivy-of-it-all. You've been down here for, what, a week?"

I glanced to the tick marks I'd carved into the stone wall with one of my cuff links. "Two months."

"Whoops." Bram pushed himself up off the floor. "Dinner tonight?"

"I'd be honored," I lied. It didn't seem much of a choice.

He disappeared out of the shadowy dungeon, and a guard came to free me from my cell a few minutes later. I was taken to my new rooms, washed and scrubbed and bathed. The giggling faerie maid smeared all sorts of foul-smelling potions on me to remove any trace of my imprisonment. But there are some scars that even magic can't heal; the damage is set too deep.

I was shocked when I saw Lydia at Bram's side that night in the dining room. For one heartbeat, I thought I was looking at Ivy again, before the light shifted and I recognized her sister. It was the night that everything changed for me.

At first, I was confused by Bram's trust in me, but I've learned in the years since he has a sick kind of possessiveness over me. It's genuinely never occurred to him that I could love anyone more than I love him. He wasn't on the lookout for any betrayal larger than a fight over a girl because he's always thought I believed in him as a leader, as *my* leader. I should be grateful for Bram's ego; it's the only reason I left that prison cell alive.

I blink back to Lydia's room and glance at the shimmering fire in her grate.

"Why did you think Ivy was dead?" she asks me gently.

"Bram told me she was, the day he freed me from prison. He showed me a severed finger, but Ivy doesn't seem to be missing any, so I suppose it must have been a glamour."

"Oh," she says sadly. "Why didn't you tell me?"

I chew on the inside of my cheek, watching the flames dance against the charred wood. "I didn't see any use in shattering your heart too. I was trying to protect you, I guess."

She walks toward me and tips my chin up with the handle of her paintbrush. "You could have told me. I want you to tell me everything. That's what best friends do, Em."

I reach over and wrap my pinkie finger around hers. She said it was something she used to do with Ivy when they were children, but it's somehow become our thing. "Best friends, Lyd."

She looks placated.

I leave Lydia's warm fire and climb the dark stairs up to the next floor where my and Ivy's bedrooms are located. It still feels so unreal that she's in the castle. I hate it. I'm terrified for her and I was barely functioning as it was. I'm a wreck over her; I always have been.

In an awful way, it was easier when I thought she was dead, because at least I knew nothing further could harm her.

The hallway is shadowy and silent; no one stays up here but me, usually. But in a castle like this, there is no real security to be had.

I walk halfway down the hall, strip out of my paint-smeared shirt, and ball it up to use as a pillow. Then I lie down in front of Ivy's door and sleep.

CHAPTER ELEVEN

My sleep is uncomfortably dreamless, as if my brain was snuffed out like a candle and relit as the sun rose.

It takes me a moment to remember where I am. I kick my feet like a grasshopper under the silk blankets of this unfamiliar bed and blink against the morning light streaming in from the ceiling-high windows. The whole room smells of dew-covered roses, the kind that grew in our garden back home in Belgrave Square.

The same girl with the sunset hair from last night is in my room, building up a fire in the grate. When she hears me stirring, she turns around.

"Good morning, miss!" she says cheerfully, and adds another stick to the crackling fire. The smoke here smells different, sharper, almost medicinal.

"Morning," I mutter, my throat too dry to say much of anything. I push myself up on my pillows and run a finger through my unruly hair, finding a braid I don't remember doing.

Eloree pushes a cup of tea into my hand, and its warmth leaches through the porcelain into my cold fingers.

I'm wary of eating or drinking anything in the Otherworld. I've read enough stories of young maidens eating a single cherry at a revel and getting stuck or sick for ages, but I'm going to have to eat eventually and my stomach is gnawing at itself with hunger. I take a tentative sip and find it close enough to English tea, if a little floral.

"Up, I must dress you," she chirps.

"For what?" I ask.

She doesn't answer; instead, she gestures for me to raise my arms. I do so reluctantly, and she slips off my nightdress and puts me in a clean chemise.

Over that, she laces an old-fashioned tab-waisted corset. The dress is snow-white, the square neck and bell sleeves adorned with golden cord. She leaves my hair loose around my shoulders, save for two small braids that pull away from my face.

She opens the door and waves me through. "Come, come."

"Where?" I ask again, but again, I receive no answer.

"Where is Lydia?" I raise my voice as fear begins to prickle at my arms.

"Her Majesty, Queen Lydia, and His Highness, Prince Emmett, are waiting."

It's jarring to hear my sister referred to as *Her Majesty*, but I suppose she is the queen of the Otherworld as much as I am the queen of England.

I follow Eloree down the grand staircase to the first floor, past a library with ceiling-high shelves of forest-green marble, and a strategy room in dark burgundies with an enormous map in the center. There's another rickety wooden staircase that leads down to a cellar smelling strongly of *something*.

The prickles of fear have turned into full-on, stabbing panic. The castle is silent and still. We pass no others, hear no voices.

"Where is everyone?"

"Waiting."

"Where?" I prod, but Eloree gives nothing away.

The doors to the castle are at least three stories tall, carved of white wood. They creak against the stone floors as they swing open on their own, revealing a crisp, blue day.

We walk all the way to the gates of the castle. They, too, swing open freely as we approach.

"Please," I beg, but Eloree doesn't so much as turn around.

I think about running, sprinting into the woods or something, but that feels useless. I have an eerie feeling there's nowhere in this kingdom Bram couldn't find me.

We've only been walking for a few minutes when I hear the distant roar of voices.

It starts so low I convince myself I'm imagining it, but as we get closer there is no denying the cacophony.

It brings to mind the day of the regatta, when hundreds gathered on the banks of the Thames to watch the boats race.

"What are they cheering for?" I ask.

"You."

We turn a corner, and I see them. The winding streets of town are packed with faeries who stand shoulder to shoulder.

Some hang out of upper windows, waving ribbons or sloshing wine onto the onlookers below.

The crowd parts reverently as Eloree and I approach, and this close, I can tell they've been up all night or longer. They have the glassy, bedraggled look of faeries at the end of a long revel. Their mouths and clothes are stained with bloodred wine, and their cheering is reaching a near frenzy.

In the very center of town, where four roads converge to make a square, a hasty platform has been built.

In the center is Bram. He's sitting on a throne, one hand holding up his bored-looking head, the other spinning a knife against the armrest.

I gasp softly upon seeing him. Some animalistic part of me, the place in my brain that has kept humans alive for generations, begs me to *run or fight*, but all I can manage to do is freeze.

Lydia said we had more time. I thought we had more time.

Bram's full mouth pulls up into a half smile, and he gestures at me lazily with the tip of his dagger. "You've kept us waiting long enough."

The crowd goes wild as I step onto the platform. In the far back, I spot little Aurelia Vallen and her husband who look just as delighted as the rest of them.

On either side of Bram are Lydia and Emmett. Lydia wears

a cream-colored dress similar to mine, and Emmett is in black court regalia like Bram, a golden circlet on his dark hair.

Lydia's eyes meet mine with a weight I've never seen in them before. No longer the vacant stare I grew used to in our last months together, but something desperately urgent. I used to be able to read my sister's mind with nothing but a glance, but in this moment she feels as far from me as she did when I was in London.

Emmett, on the other hand, can't even look at me. His eyes are fixed on the eaves of some far-off building.

Bram lounges on his throne, as handsome and relaxed as ever.

Not seeing any other choice, I shuffle up beside Lydia, so I'm standing next to Bram.

Now that I'm up here I can see the banners. They hang from every window in the town square, painted with borders of stars and moons and wildflowers, all bearing the same message boldly in the center: WELCOME, IVY.

This spectacle isn't something you could plan overnight.

My heart goes to my throat and I fear I might be sick, right here in front of everyone.

"You knew I'd come?" I whisper down at Bram.

Bram examines the shiny tip of his dagger. "You're not nearly as clever as you think."

Which means Rhion told him, which means my friends aren't safe. My mind spins.

"I've only ever wanted what's best for everyone." Bram

addresses the crowd now. "But it seems even my best-laid plans have unintended consequences. Two kingdoms, two queens seemed a rather neat arrangement, but I get the impression the Benton sisters are unhappy with the tangled web we've found ourselves in.

"Despite these temporary negative feelings, it's a great pleasure to have my people here to witness a joyous announcement. It seems we've found ourselves in quite a conundrum, but never fear, as I have a solution."

The crowd cheers and Bram preens.

I stare across the dais at Emmett and silently beg him to look up at me, but he's as still and useless as a statue.

"No—" I open my mouth to protest, so used to lying to keep Bram's temper at bay that it's my instinct to soothe him. My corset bites into the flesh of my waist.

He slams the tip of his knife into the arm of his throne, splintering the wood beneath. "Let me finish!" He takes a breath and composes himself. "As I was saying, the situation is untenable. We can't go on with all this—" He pauses and waves his knife mindlessly, searching for the right word. "*Scheming.* It leaves a bad taste in one's mouth, does it not?"

I look to Bram, ignoring the crowd. "I only missed my sister," I lie, the desperation to placate him clawing at me. It would be easier if he were angry, but this eerie calm is so much worse. The boning of my corset seems to grow tighter, and I suck in an uneasy breath.

"Let's not do that, Ivy," Bram dismisses me. "I have a plan

to solve all of this, and it's going to be so much fun."

Dread curdles in my stomach. Lydia reaches over and clutches my sweaty hand.

"I got the idea from my mother, actually," Bram explains. "She held a series of games to help me identify the most suitable candidate for an English wife. Why not do the same to identify who will be the best queen of the Otherworld?"

I'm going to be sick. The edges of my vision blur in and out as his words settle. *More games.*

"No, please, darling, let's go back to London and things can continue on as they ever were." I fight to keep my voice sweet and steady. There's no mistaking it this time—my corset *squeezes*, leaving me gasping.

Bram shakes his head. "It's impractical to have two wives. A folly of ambition. The people should have one queen."

"Long live the queen!" a few in the crowd shout, and I know it's not me they mean.

Bram's nostrils flare. "I am your king!" he snarls. The audience cowers and Lydia looks away, embarrassed.

"No, it makes sense," I say gently. "Lydia is such a perfect queen here, and I am so useful to you back home in England. You need us both." My corset constricts again, the pressure on my lungs nearly unbearable.

"I need you both?" he replies, voice thick with sarcasm. "So I can spend the rest of your lives watching you scheme behind my back? You have more loyalty to each other than you do to me, your husband. It's disgusting."

"But—" I protest. I can't take a full breath, so the words die in my throat.

For the first time, Emmett glances to me, worried, but just as quickly looks away, and his stony expression returns.

Bram sighs and tips his head back. "Do you ever stop talking?"

I sputter, all at once ashamed and terrified and filled with rage.

"What will happen?" Lydia asks, so quietly it's nearly a whisper.

Bram looks up at her. "What?"

Lydia doesn't look up. "What will happen to the one who doesn't win?"

Bram shrugs. "What is it your English aristocracy does? The loser will get a house in some backwater corner of the country and you can carry out the rest of your days living like royalty in the middle of a sheep pasture."

I hear the unsaid: *No matter what happens, you will never see your sister again.* I stopped Mor's games once; surely I can do it again.

Bram points his knife lazily in my direction. "I know what you're thinking, Ivy. There is no getting out of this. I am not my softhearted mother."

"But—"

He interrupts me with an exaggerated sigh and looks between me and Lydia. "You know, I'm tempted to pick Lydia. She talks back so much less. But then—" He looks at me.

"Lydia left me. Ivy, you've been so loyal."

He fixes his gaze on Emmett next. "She's never once faltered. She lets me into her bed as easy as breathing."

My skin burns red and I want to explain that it's not like *that*, but it wouldn't do anyone any good.

"I—" There's not enough air in my lungs to form the words. I gasp.

Bram looks to Emmett. "Oh, how I love those little gasps she takes. Don't you?"

Emmett just keeps staring ahead, his chest rising and falling.

"These games will make it all easier. And it's so much more fun this way, don't you agree?" Bram says.

"What if we say no?" I pant, my lungs screaming.

He frowns. "I was afraid you might say that. You're no fun at all sometimes, you know that?"

The crowd parts, revealing two figures, huddled together and flanked by armed guards. Faith is sporting a purple black eye. Marion's knuckles are smeared with blood, and I hope that means she got a few good blows in before they dragged her here.

Behind them, Rhion stands, his face unreadable, his gaze only on Lydia. My heart sinks. We were so foolish to trust him.

"You cut your hair," Lydia mutters.

Rhion's eyes widen, betraying an emotion I don't think he meant to show.

"I'll keep your little friends safe for you," Bram continues. "You can rest well knowing they're being taken care of in the dungeons. But if you stop participating . . . then I can make no promises of their safety."

I want to say something noble and brave like *You're a monster* or *I can't believe I ever thought I could love you. No one could.* But I still can't breathe.

Bram turns to Lydia. "I know what you're thinking—who are these girls to you?"

"I wasn't thinking that," Lydia replies softly.

"Oh, don't start acting all saintly now," Bram snarls. "Should *you* act out, I'll punish Emmett. Is that motivation enough?"

Lydia blanches. "I won't act out."

"Good," Bram says. "Then there's nothing to be worried about, is there?"

Emmett's eyes haven't left the eaves of that far building. It looks like his mind vacated his body long ago and all that's left is a husk of him.

"You won't send him back to the dungeons, will you?" Lydia asks like it pains her.

Bram shrugs. "Not unless you give me a reason to. Emmett has been a loyal regent and I see no reason to punish him unnecessarily."

Bram looks to me with his brows raised, as if to say *Look how reasonable I am.* Then he stands from his throne and claps his hands. "I know you have missed me, these many months

I've been in England, but let me remind you, *this* is who we are. Only I can bring you this. Let the games begin!"

The crowd goes wild, cheering and screaming and sloshing their cups. Someone hanging from an upper window magicks a cannon of confetti that flutters from the sky, leaving us coated in a rainbow of colors.

"Now?" I ask, shocked.

"Would you rather wait around? Your mortal lives are dwindling away at quite the clip. I'll never understand humans' lack of urgency."

Lydia looks to me, something dejected in her posture. "Let's just get it over with, Ivy."

Guards herd us away before we can say another word.

"I'm sorry!" I call to Marion and Faith, but I don't know if they hear me. I'm knocked unconscious as soon as I step down from the platform.

CHAPTER TWELVE

I wake up some time later, groggy, with the distinct, bone-rattled feeling of having gone on a long journey.

"Hello?" My voice is raspy and dry. I swallow and it hurts. "Lydia?" I try again. I can scarcely breathe. The corset hasn't loosened and it's squeezing my ribs with bruising pressure. The walls around me spin, and the inability to take a full breath is only making my panic worse. My vision goes spotty around the edges and the floor seems to sway beneath me.

I try to slip the tips of my fingers under the boning at my waist, to give myself more breathing room, but it's simply too tight.

My vision darkens.

I'm going to be so angry if I'm killed via suffocation by corset. What a profoundly stupid way to die.

The doors swing open and I blink against the sudden light. It's only now that I realize I'm in a carriage of some sort. No, *carriage* isn't the right word. A prison cell on wheels is more apt. Paneled in dark wood, with only a single hard bench to sit on, the transport vehicle is completely windowless. It's like they wanted it to feel as much like a tomb as possible.

A shadowy figure jumps in with me, the light glinting off a blade in his hand.

"No—" I pop upright and raise my fists.

He thrusts the knife toward me.

"Please—"

"Stop moving," the figure commands, barely above a whisper, and I recognize that voice.

"Are you going to stab me?" I ask him the same question he once asked me in a carriage a long, long time ago, but he doesn't laugh.

"Bloody corset," Emmett mutters. "It's enchanted to squeeze tighter every time you lie, and you did quite a lot of lying back there."

In one fluid motion he pulls my gown off over my head, then uses his knife to split open the corset laces up my back. The metal tip is cool as it just barely grazes my spine.

A parallel moment flashes through my head. A rainy inn. Emmett's low voice saying *I know my way around a corset.*

I heave in a full breath, my limbs tingling as the oxygen reaches my bloodstream.

"Thank you," I gasp.

Emmett's eyes graze down my body, now in nothing but a translucent chemise. Just as quickly, he glances away and bites the inside of his cheek hard enough that it looks like it hurts.

Hastily, Emmett helps me back into my dress. Then he

scoops the ruined corset up off the floor and hides it in the storage compartment under the seat.

It's only then that Emmett finally looks me in the eyes.

I open my mouth to say something, but there are so many questions raging in my head that I don't know where to begin.

Emmett looks pained. His brows are knitted, his lips pressed together, his hazel eyes alight with flame. His eyes flit from my mouth to my eyes, then back to my mouth.

The clatter of carriage wheels outside startles us both.

"I wasn't here," Emmett says in a rush, and then disappears out of the carriage and shuts the door.

A few minutes later, the silhouette of a man darkens the open carriage door. "C'mon, up with you." The faerie guard's harsh voice is in direct contrast with his angelic features. I'm quickly learning that's what the Otherworld is—cruelty cloaked in heart-wrenching beauty.

I'm once again tempted to run, but I know I have no choice but to go out and face whatever awaits me. If not for my friends, then for my sister.

I pointedly ignore the guard's outstretched hand as I hop down from the carriage. The delicate silk slippers I put on this morning crunch into a thick layer of underbrush.

The sweet smell of old-growth forest surrounds me, and the dried leaves of autumn rustle in the breeze from where they're stuck to spindly tree branches.

In front of me is a dark entrance, portal-like, through a copse of trees. Behind me, a ways off from the carriage, is the chatter of a crowd.

Bram is surrounded by Rhion and a few other courtiers I vaguely recognize from England. Emmett stands among them, looking remote, no trace of what he just did on his face. Behind them are a few dozen more faeries, gathered around cocktail tables, laughing behind insect-wing fans. A few are already drunk.

And beyond them are the stands. They're packed with faeries who sit shoulder to shoulder, their voices blending together in a roar.

To my left is a carriage identical to the one I just stumbled out of, and next to it is my sister. "Lydia—" I whisper, but Bram walks toward us and interrupts us with a hearty laugh.

"My girls!" he declares with a smile. He snaps and a footman steps forward with two long swords. Bram takes them and passes them to us in turn.

It's so heavy, I nearly stumble to the ground upon grasping it. It's got a thick hilt, inlaid with rubies that shine like beetle carapaces. The body of the sword is strictly utilitarian. A long blade spanning almost the entire length of my legs, sharp enough that its delicate edge catches the morning sunlight.

He turns to face the crowd, who go wild. "In the woods there is a creature that has been marked on its haunches with my coat of arms. The first person to bring me its body will be declared the winner." His voice must be enchanted; it booms like thunder over the clearing.

Bram raises a hand as they cheer. "I'm sorry we had to wait

so long for such merrymaking. I know having two humans in charge was dull. But never fear, I'm back!"

Lydia and I glance anxiously at each other. Bram looks between us both like we're extraordinarily slow. "Go on," he commands under his breath.

"I'd like to make a request," I blurt.

Bram nods. "I suppose that's characteristic. What is it?"

"If I win this trial, I'd like you to let Marion and Faith out of the dungeons. Treat them like the guests they are. They won't run."

Bram considers for a moment. "You know I love a deal."

"You agree, then?"

He nods. "Bring me the creature's body and your friends may have better accommodations."

"Say it again, say it better," I command, wary of a faerie trick.

"If you bring me the creature's body, your friends may move into the castle guest rooms."

"On the same floor as me."

"Fine."

"Tonight."

Bram shrugs. "Fair enough."

I spare one last look at Emmett, who is chatting casually with Rhion and the rest of them.

Look at me, I will, staring daggers into the side of his head, but he remains decidedly casual.

"Let us begin!" Bram claps and the trees themselves shake

and groan, their leaves falling to the ground like gentle rain.

Emmett's eyes flit to Lydia, who stands a few yards to my left.

"Good luck," he mutters.

She smiles at him, like there's no one in the world she's more comfortable with, and in that moment I hate them both with a fury so hot, I'm eager to pick up my sword. I want to turn to the nearest tree and start hacking and screaming until the anger inside of me is burned up.

The crowd is so loud my ears have begun to ring.

Without any further fanfare, I step into the woods. If Emmett was also going to tell me good luck, I'm not around to hear it.

"Ivy?" I hear my sister call a few moments later, but I'm so annoyed with her, I stomp off in the opposite direction without answering.

I'll win this trial for my friends and lose the rest. Lydia can be queen for all I care. I'll rot in some backwater country estate with no one but sheep for company. Forgotten, as I was always meant to be.

But you love her. You'll miss her.

Hot tears burn my eyes. I keep walking.

I don't know much about tracking animals, let alone magic ones, so I wander, mostly aimlessly, through the thick forest.

I remember, vaguely, a scene from a book where a girl followed broken branches to a water source where animals gathered, though for all I know animals in the Otherworld may not even need water. Maybe their rivers flow with something else, like champagne or blood.

But it seems as good a plan as any, so I turn my eyes to the ground and begin scanning for anything that looks out of place. It's difficult to discern because everything in this forest is one shade off from normal. The acorns scattering the brush are as large as two-pound coins, their caps shining gold. The leaves have pointed tips like tiny daggers, and in the treetops above me, birdsong rings out in a sharp, minor key.

Eventually, I find a gentle slope and follow it downward. My arms are burning with the effort of carrying my sword and I feel sick as the image of Emmett plays in my head in an awful loop. His eyes were so soft as he looked at my sister. There was so much kindness in the way he said *Good luck.*

He kissed me, that must mean something; but he left me, too. The sides of my hands are bruised from where I pounded on his door until the sleeping draught took me under. My ribs still ache from where he cut me out of my corset. I'm too wrung out to go over it again and again.

It feels like I've been walking for ages when I finally hear the gentle babble of a stream.

I collapse to my knees in front of it and cup my hands to take a drink. It's not champagne, just plain, cool water. It's probably unwise of me, but I fear I won't be able to go on much farther if I don't have something in my stomach. I'm ravenously, bone-achingly hungry. I don't remember the last time I had a full meal. It was back in Bath, but England feels so far away now, and time is so slippery here.

The water tastes normal enough, perhaps a little sulfuric.

I take a deep breath but can't stop tears of frustration from spilling down my face. They land on the rippling surface of the clear water and slip under instantly, like they never existed at all.

Suddenly, there's an odd clicking sound. Smooth river stones moving against each other.

There's a splash and something hops out of the brook onto the grassy riverbank.

At first, I think it's a fish—it's about the same size, no larger than the silk slipper on my foot, and it glimmers an iridescent fish-scale silver when the sun hits it.

I shriek and move back, then pick up my sword on instinct.

"Thank you," a high-pitched voice chirps, and I scream again.

The fish, which is distinctly *not* a fish, has moved to stand on two feet. They're difficult to look at straight on, like my mind doesn't know how to process something so far from human. They've got the general shape of a person—two arms, two legs, a head—but they're wearing an outfit like armor constructed of fish scales, including a pointy hat made of a fin.

Their eyes are overlarge for their small face, silvery-blue all the way through, no whites at all, and wet like they've been crying. The rest of the face is greenish white, like the waterlogged belly of a dead fish.

I scan quickly for Bram's royal seal but see nothing. I don't think this is the creature I'm meant to slay.

"I'm just going." I turn on my heel to leave. If four months in Bram's court have taught me anything, it's to regard everything from the Otherworld with caution and suspicion.

There's a tug on the hem of my dress and I turn to see the creature looking up at me. They stick a long, webbed finger in their mouth and close their eyes.

"Umm," I hesitate.

"Thank you for the tears." The creature's voice is the same pitch as the babbling water.

I hesitate. "Oh . . . you're welcome."

"What can I do for you?" Their teeth are long and pointed, like a fish's.

"Nothing, thank you." I step to go, but they cling to my hem.

"No, please!" They sound distressed now. "You gave me something, now I give you something."

"Why?"

"It is the way of things!" the creature exclaims. With one of their long hands, they pull off their hat, revealing two sharp little horns.

"What are you?" I can't help but ask, even though I'm afraid the question may be impolite.

If it is, the creature doesn't seem to mind. Their small mouth curls up into a grin. "I am Duddon. Sprite of this spring."

"Nice to meet you," I say.

Duddon bows. "It's been a long time since I met a human. Your tears were delicious."

"Consider them a gift," I reply, though in my experience faeries don't have a great grasp of sarcasm. "I'm sorry, I really must be going."

"Not a gift! It won't do! Where are you going?"

I gesture to my sword. "There is a creature I must slay."

Duddon nods enthusiastically. "The Questing Beast?"

"Um—I'm not sure. Something with King Bram's seal on its haunches."

Duddon does a full-body shudder at Bram's name. "Oh, yes. The creature you're looking for lies in the meadow beyond. I will show you the way. I saw the guards catch it and brand it this morning. It wailed so loudly all the forest folk heard. There were tears then, too, but not as tasty as yours."

"I'm sure I can find it myself," but even as I say it, Duddon bounds back to the water's edge and pulls out a smooth river rock nearly as big as they are.

Duddon traces the surface with the pointed tip of a green finger, leaving chalk-white markings on the stone.

"Follow the stream down, but you must be sure to avoid the brambles at the center of the forest," Duddon mutters as they sketch over the stone. "It is where the merchants harvest their fruit for the night markets and they are very foul indeed." Duddon's mouth turns into a pout. "They play awful games and kick us around like balls. We sprites stay away from them if we can."

"Thank you for the advice," I say earnestly.

Duddon preens a little, then hands me the rock, upon which they have drawn a crude but legible map.

I consider it for a moment. "How do I know this is not a trick?"

"A trick?" Duddon responds, horrified. "You gave me your tears. I gave you a map. It is a fair bargain."

As far as faerie logic goes, it's solid enough. "Then I thank you."

Duddon nods, their fin hat back on and bobbing wildly. "Please come back and see me again, my lady. Whenever you need to cry, I am here." With that, Duddon curtsies and swan dives back into the river, disappearing beneath the surface of the water.

The stone is cool and heavy in my hand as I follow its crude marking down the riverbank, eventually entering a wide, lush meadow where a path snakes lazily through the tall grass.

I cut through a ring of trees and then through a clearing of standing stones. I see bone-white cliffs in the distance, a sign that I am getting close to the large X marked on Duddon's map.

A high-pitched scream pierces the meadow.

I take off running, kicking off my useless slippers as I go, grateful I'm no longer wearing a corset. "Lydia, I'm coming!"

Brambles and rocks and who knows what else slice my feet as I sprint across the clearing, cutting left into another circle of trees.

Standing in the middle, dappled light pouring over her, is my sister. She looks like a warrior from heaven with her blond curls tumbling over her shoulders, her sword held aloft above her head.

She lowers it as soon as she sees me and lets out a breath of relief. "You shouldn't be here," she says.

"Because you want to win?" I reply sarcastically.

She doesn't respond. I follow her gaze to the edge of the tree line, where something moves in the shadows.

I think of my friends locked away in the dungeons, and I lunge, sword in hand.

Lydia tries to sidestep me, but I'm faster and reach the creature before she does.

It's nothing but a pale blur as it moves through the thick ferns, but I raise my sword, ready to strike.

All of a sudden, there's that scream again. It's not coming from Lydia, I realize, but from the creature before me.

It sounds like a child weeping, high-pitched and unbearable.

I swing but my sword misses, striking the ground with a spray of dirt.

The creature stumbles out into the soft grass, fully visible now, and I fall to my knees, dizzy at the sight of it.

It's a snow-white unicorn, its coat perfect and unblemished save for Bram's royal seal, newly branded and sticky with blood, on one side of its back legs.

Its horn is pale gold, its eyes a large, luminous brown, jarringly similar to the eye color Lydia and I share. But that's not the reason I fell.

It's just a baby. No bigger than one of Bram's hunting dogs, it's still got the chubbiness of childhood in its face, and it's unsteady on its spindly legs.

Lydia pushes past me.

"It's just a baby!" I cry out. My sword clatters to the ground, and I reach out in an attempt to stop her even as she raises her sword. "Please!"

I stumble to my feet and get a grip around the hilt of her sword, my hands on top of hers.

"Ivy, stop!" she screams. "Let me do this."

"We cannot!" I scream back. How marred will our souls be if we kill something as beautiful and innocent as this?

The unicorn has fallen now and is braying in an awful tone that reaches straight to the core of me.

I throw my full body weight to the ground, slamming my back hard against the dirt and dislodging Lydia's grip on her sword, which tumbles to the ground with a *clang*. Its blade falls so close to my head, it shears off a few locks of my hair as it hits the ground.

I push myself up and toss her sword and mine into the stream. They both sink under the dark water, disappearing.

Lydia's face is cold. She doesn't even look at me.

"C'mon. Let's just tell him we didn't find it. He can't keep us out here forever," I whisper, but Lydia doesn't respond.

I pick up my feet to run at her again, but a tree root writhes like a snake and reaches out to trip me.

I fall hard enough to knock the wind from my lungs.

In four long strides, Lydia is in front of the unicorn. I'm too far to stop her now.

She throws herself onto its back, and without hesitation, she snaps the golden horn off its head and stabs it into its soft neck.

The unicorn screams a death knell that will haunt me until the day I die. It hollows out something within me, and I have never wanted to be dead more than I want to be dead in this moment. I don't know if it's the unicorn's magic affecting me or if the simple act of watching my sister do something so horrible has undone me.

The unicorn gasps and keens as it drowns in its own blood, its little pink mouth opening and closing again and again uselessly. Its tiny body shudders, and maybe I'm projecting, but it's as if I can sense in it an emotion that all species understand; it wants its mother.

The unicorn dies alone in a field, its own horn the cause of the killing blow. I keep hoping it will disappear in a shower of sparks or dust, like the swan I once killed in a hedge maze. I'm desperate for *some* evidence that this is another magical faerie trick, but the unicorn lies limp and solid. Just another dead animal.

I retch, but there is nothing in my stomach but river water.

Lydia stands, panting and covered in silvery blood. Then she bends, scoops up the unicorn's limp body, and slings it over her shoulder.

"Did you really want to win that badly?" I sob. "Nothing could have been worth that."

She pushes past me wordlessly and begins the long walk back to Bram and Emmett.

She's ten paces ahead of me the entire journey through the forest. As I watch her silhouette bob through trees and step over stones and felled logs, I can't help but wonder if my sister is a person I know anymore.

It once felt as if our very souls were intertwined, as if we were two halves of a whole. I couldn't conceive of a time when it would feel like I do not know her, but in this moment, she is a stranger to me.

The Lydia I knew in London, who rescued abandoned kittens from the carriage house and fed them by hand until they were strong enough to open their eyes, never could have done what this Lydia just did.

I'm still crying by the time we reach the edge of the trees. Bram, Emmett, Rhion, and a few other members of the faerie aristocracy are having a party. A band plays a cheery tune as they lounge on overstuffed pillows on the ground, a buffet laid out on a low table in front of them.

Lydia dumps the baby unicorn unceremoniously at Bram's feet. "Here," she says flatly.

Bram claps his hands with glee. "Well done, you!"

Emmett's handsome face goes pale as he looks between us—at Lydia's gown now stained and sticking to her body with silver blood and my eyes rimmed with red.

Without saying a word to anyone, I climb miserably back into the transport carriage, sit down on the hard wooden bench, close my eyes, and tip my head against the wall.

"Come, Ivy. We're having a party!" Bram exclaims.

"I'd like to go home now." I wish I knew what I meant by the word *home*. Our town house in Belgrave Square, my childhood country estate in Oakham, Kensington Palace, and One Royal Crescent all feel as if they belonged to a different person.

For the first time, it hits me that I might never see England again.

I sit for a few hours, my mind far away from my body while Bram and his courtiers finish their merriment. I don't look outside to see if Lydia is on his arm. I don't know if I could stand it. The worst part is, I do not judge her for doing what it takes to survive. I am just afraid of the person it has made her.

CHAPTER THIRTEEN

When we return to the castle I head straight for my room and slam the door. There's a soft knock sometime later, and I open the door a crack, longing to see Emmett, but it's just Eloree with a tray of food. I have no patience for her after the trick with the corset this morning.

I'm sure it was Bram's doing, but she was party to it.

"Will you go to the revel, miss?" Eloree asks. "I can dress your hair."

"No, thank you," I say emphatically.

I instruct her to leave the tray, and then I break every rule of every fairy tale I've ever read, and eat ravenously. The food is richer with flavor than any I've ever had and I shovel it into my mouth so quickly I fear I'm going to make myself sick, but it's been so long since I've eaten and this is the only thing that's come close to soothing the ache inside of me.

Once I'm finished, I dress in a black gown made of a gauzy material, one of the simplest in my wardrobe, and slip down the main staircase. I'm underdressed among the revelers who race across the hall, the dark wine in their goblets sloshing over their sleeves and onto the floor. They pay me no mind as I take the stairs to the lowest level, where the earth is damp and dark.

As I descend farther into the castle, I hear the rhythmic drip of water and the low snore of a guard, asleep in a tipped-back chair at the base of the stairs. I snatch his ring of keys from its hook on the wall, careful not to let the heavy metal clang together.

On tiptoes, I sneak past him and into the rabbit warren of the dungeons. The cells look as if they were dug out by hand. The walls are jagged, the ceilings too low for someone as tall as Emmett to stand completely upright.

I follow the serpentine halls with only a few mounted torches to light my way.

"Marion?" I hiss. "Faith?"

"Ivy?" It's a weak voice in the darkness, but unmistakably my name.

"Marion!" I exclaim.

I turn the corner and see the two of them piled into a single cell, their familiar faces coated with tear-streaked grime. Their dresses are torn and splotchy with dried blood. They're both leaning against the back wall, Marion with her chin propped up in her hands, Faith tending to her swollen eye.

"I'm so sorry." I sink to my knees in front of the bars and slide a key into the lock. It doesn't fit, so I try the next.

Faith clambers toward me and gestures. "There—try the

thinnest one." There's a little resistance as I slide the key in, but I press harder. The lock slides open with a *thunk* and I swing the door open.

"I'm sorry," I say again, pulling Marion into a tight hug. She looks like she needs it the most. Faith's eyes gleam with a murderous rage. Hugging her would be like trying to hug a porcupine. I touch her elbow instead. "I'm going to kill him," she says. I don't know if she means Bram or Rhion, but I nod in agreement.

"Let's go." I gesture down the dark hallway, but Marion hesitates.

"Before we do that, we have something to show you."

"Show me?"

"Did you think we were just down here twiddling our thumbs? Give us more credit than that, Your Majesty."

She says my title like a fond little nickname but it still makes me wince.

I follow them deeper into the darkness, down to the very end of the hall, where the prison ends in a jagged dirt wall. Cold groundwater seeps into the soles of my slippers and a fat drop of condensation lands on the top of my head.

There's a figure huddled in the last cell. A flicker of torchlight illuminates my face as I step forward, and then I hear her laugh.

"Always a pleasure," I greet Queen Mor.

"Oh, there's no need to lie. I find it so distasteful." Her voice is as cool and regal as it was when we were in her Kensington

Palace throne room.

"He brought you here?" I ask.

She stands, straightening to her full height. Even in a simple white shift dress, she's so inhumanly beautiful that the sight of her causes my heart to leap into my throat. "I told you, my son loves me."

I gesture to her cell, the rusted bars, the water dripping from the crumbling earth above her. "Is this what it means to be loved by him?" I ask the question as much for her as for myself and Lydia.

"He wants me here."

"But he doesn't trust you."

Her perfect face betrays no emotion. "He's a wise and careful leader."

"He's a monster. Help me, please. Both your kingdoms depend on it, surely you see that."

She cared enough for humans once upon a time that she staked her whole throne—her whole *life*—upon it. Has she changed that profoundly in the years living among us?

"You want this brutality to stop. I *know* you do."

She retreats into the cell and sits down against the wall. With an exaggerated yawn she says, "Come back and see me when you're less boring, Ivy Benton."

I'm already walking away, but I pause and whip around to face her. "It's Her Majesty, Queen Ivy, now."

I can't be sure, but I think I hear a low chuckle as we walk out of the dungeons.

I take Faith and Marion directly up to my room and dress them in the gowns from my closet. Faith's is a pale blue the color of her eyes. Marion is in a deep purple gown with ribbons for sleeves. Together, we do our best to scrub the dirt from their faces and dress their hair with the variety of creams and brushes and combs we find in the drawers of my vanity.

"Where are the others?" I ask once we are alone.

"Safe, I think . . . I hope," Marion answers. "Faith and I bought them time to run. We believe they all fled north. That was the plan, at least."

I stay in my simple black gown, but at the last moment, I snag a diamond tiara from my wardrobe and place it on my tangled curls.

I lead them down the stairs to the ballroom. We pause at the double doors and take a deep breath. The three of us have survived in Bram's English faerie court—all of it was training for this moment.

The doors crack open and the music of the faerie revel pours around us like a tide, sweeping us into the undercurrent.

The ballroom is packed with bodies, and I suspect Bram's return may have something to do with it. Vines with dark, ripe fruit have been hung in garlands across the rafters. Golden orbs of enchanted faerielight cast the room in long shadows.

We cut across the writhing dance floor to the dais where Bram sits on his throne. His handsome face is vacant, his head propped up on his elbow.

He perks up as soon as he sees us, righting himself and grinning.

"Hey, I know you," he slurs as we approach. "You're all very pretty. Very pretty and *very mean*." His full bottom lip juts out in a pout. "Not you, Marion. You're too sweet for your own good. One day someone is going to eat you up."

I shift slightly, pulling them behind me. "I thought I'd show the other girls what a true faerie revel is like."

Bram claps his hands together. "Capital idea!"

"They are your guests, are they not?"

"I suppose."

I climb the steps to the dais and plop down in his lap.

From across the ballroom, my eyes meet Emmett's. He's leaning against the far wall, a goblet in one hand, girls surrounding him like flowers tilting toward the sun. Emmett's hazel eyes are glazed over, his full mouth half-open, his chest rising and falling like he's out of breath. One of the girls, the same dark-haired one from last night, trails her finger down his neck, into the hollow of his throat, which is exposed by his half-open doublet.

I mirror the gesture on Bram, trailing my pinkie down the line of his neck, keeping my eyes locked on Emmett while the party spins in a blur around us.

The girl presses her lips against Emmett's collarbone, the one that healed all wrong when he broke it jumping horses as a child, and the force of my jealousy is dizzying.

I do the same to Bram, savoring the awful way he shudders

against me, then trail my mouth back up.

"Can't we be done with this dungeon business?" I whisper into the hollow space right behind his ear. Bram hesitates. The faerie music thrums down my spine and it's as if I can feel this place making me someone else. I close my teeth around his earlobe and pull down slightly. Bram arches slightly against me. His breath hitches. "Please?" I purr. "It's beneath you."

Across the ballroom, Emmett's eyes drop closed, and he's too far from me to hear but I know what he sounds like when he moans, how it starts low in the back of his throat.

Bram sighs against his throne. "But you did not win. That was not our deal."

I rake my nails over his thigh, right above his knee. "Don't you want to make me happy?"

The corners of his mouth turn down. "Not particularly."

I resist the urge to roll my eyes. "Don't you want me to be grateful to you? Only you can give this to me."

This time it works. His face relaxes. "Fine. Go, be merry!" Then he gestures lazily to a footman and mutters something about having extra guest rooms made up.

I bound down from the dais and shoulder my way past the other girls, ignoring Faith asking "What the hell was that?" and Marion's disgusted laughter.

By the time I look up again, Emmett is gone.

CHAPTER FOURTEEN

I push through the revel until I emerge on the moonlit terrace, gasping for air. The air is crisp and clear, but it doesn't stop my head from spinning.

It's too cold for anyone else to be out here, and I take a moment to savor the peace, even though I can still hear the muffled sounds of the party from inside. A bit of golden light spills from the windows of the castle, but out here, it's just me and the expansive, dark blue sky. The strange stars and double moons of the Otherworld sparkle above me.

A door creaks open behind me and I turn. Emmett walks out onto the terrace. His hair hangs down across his forehead and he's got an unreadable look on his face. His footfalls are silent as he strides across the mosaic tile and joins me along the stone railing.

His hands are near enough to mine that I can feel the heat of them, but he's not touching me, as if on principle. We're standing side by side, both gazing into the garden like we can see anything but inky darkness.

"Who was that?" I ask.

"Who?" He sounds genuinely confused.

"The girl you were kissing."

"We weren't kissing."

"We're going to argue semantics?" I can still feel the heat of Bram all over me.

A muscle in his jaw jumps. "She was no one."

"Is that what I was, too? No one?" My voice is thick with venom.

He sighs and it comes from a place deep within him. I steal a glance at his perfect profile. He's holding so much tension in the sharp line of his jaw, but his eyes are sad. "You could never be no one to me."

"Then what am I?"

I'm begging for him to say something gallant like *you're the love of my life* or *you're the only person I've ever truly wanted*, but he disappoints me.

"You're . . . Ivy."

"I don't know what that means anymore." Moonlight has leached the color from the gardens, leaving Emmett and me looking like ghosts of ourselves.

I turn to walk away, but he captures my wrist in his hand and spins me to face him. The space under his eyes is dark with bruise-like circles; there's something about him that looks as wounded as I feel.

I hear the unicorn's death knell like an echo in my ears.

"Don't go," he says softly.

I tear my arm from his grasp. "I hate this place."

Devastation makes his shoulders sink lower. "Don't say that."

"Why not?" I ask. "It's awful. I used to dream of coming here, did you know that? It was all I wished for as a child. Every night I'd close my eyes and lull myself to sleep, picturing streams running over with starlight, faerie cakes that tasted of sunshine, and a noble, handsome suitor who would love me as I am. But it's nothing like that, is it? It's rotten to the core and it's rotted all of you with it. I don't know who Lydia is anymore and you—" I stop.

Emmett's eyes meet mine with bruising force.

"You used to love me and now you can barely look at me." My voice cracks.

"That's not—" He struggles to find the words. "This place isn't all bad."

"How could you of all people possibly say that?"

"Me of all people?"

I gesture to him, to the bags under his eyes, to his too-long hair, to his pallid skin.

"It looks like you're being devoured from the inside out. Whatever is happening here . . . it's eating you alive."

He physically recoils, but I don't relent.

"The Emmett I knew would have fought. He *never* would have left me alone in that forest to kill a helpless creature while he got drunk with Bram." Now that I'm yelling at him, it feels as if I can't stop. Heat races across my collarbones, down my arms, and into the tips of my fingers.

"I trust you to fight your own battles!" he shoots back. "And did it ever occur to you that me staying behind with Bram, making him think I am complacent, *is* protecting you?"

I laugh sarcastically. "You used to be filled with fire and now you're just a husk. You used to be better than this. You used to be *good*."

His eyes narrow. "I used to be a lot of things. The day I thought you died, I died along with you."

"But I'm *not* dead." My voice is strained. "I'm *here* and I need you."

"Do you? Do you really, Ivy?" He doesn't raise his voice, but I still resist the urge to flinch. He's never been angry at me like this before. We've bickered, but never truly fought.

A gust of icy wind blows a lock of dark hair across his forehead. "You're the one who left me first, I'll remind you. I was willing to run away with you. I was ready to leave everything I ever knew, burn my life down, just as long as I could have you in the ashes. But you walked across the hall to my brother's room like it was easy."

Here it is, all out in the air.

I think back to the night that he's referencing. Queen Mor had just told me that I had lost the competition for Bram's hand and so I knew if I still wanted to break her bargains and save England, I had to convince Bram to run away with me. But first, I stopped by Emmett's room. Things spun out of control, a spark that turned into an inferno. He took me into his bed and I let him. I wanted him to be the first to touch me like that, because, in a way, it made me his. If I was going to be ruined, I wanted Emmett to be the one to do it. But it didn't feel like ruination. Not even a little bit.

I can't believe he's throwing that night back in my face. "I was only doing what we'd planned for all along. You *knew* that I loved you. How can you possibly think that was easy for me?"

"Because you bargained to forget me!" His voice bounces off the frost-cloaked trees.

My breath comes out in a puff of vapor. I deserve every ounce of his ire and I'm foolish for believing I could outrun it. I've spent every moment of the past four months hoping that if I loved him hard enough, if I worked hard enough to keep things together in his absence, I could rewrite how things ended. But staring at him, all wide open and wounded, I know that I am not absolved. I can't just keep moving. Emmett is going to make me face what I did.

His knuckles are white where he grips the stone railing of the terrace. "I could never have done that to you, *never*. Even in my darkest days, when I thought I was going to die in that dungeon, when all the bones in my hand were shattered and both eyes were swollen shut, when I was delirious with starvation, *never* would I have chosen to forget you. You were my single light in the darkness. The memory of you was the only thing that kept me warm at night. The pain reminded me you were real."

His voice softens. "Sometimes it's hard to remember a time before this place. I would have lost my old self completely if I wasn't tethered to you. When I think of my life before, it's like a dream, like something that happened to someone else. But not with you. The memories with you are vivid, awake. *You make me exist.*"

I want to close the distance between us. It's only a matter of inches, but it feels uncrossable. "And you wanted me gone," he finishes gravely.

"I wanted the pain gone," I say, no louder than a whisper.

"Then that is where we differ. I relished my broken heart because *you* were the one who broke it. I would have endured one thousand years bearing the loss of you if it meant I got to hold on to the memories of what we had."

I wipe away a freezing tear from my cheek, unsure of when I began to cry.

Maybe that's all love is. Just something you endure.

"I was only doing what I thought you wanted of me. I thought you'd move on."

Emmett shakes his head. "Then you don't know me very well at all." It's exactly the right thing to say to wound me.

"You know what hurt me the most?" he continues "That you didn't really believe in me. Our plan was that by marrying Bram, the bargains would be broken. I still can't figure out why you bargained to forget me if you actually believed the plan would work."

"It's because I knew I'd never be able to walk down the

aisle and vow to be his wife feeling how I felt—*feel*—for you. I figured when the bargains were broken and all of a sudden I remembered you again, it would be too late and I'd be Bram's wife and it was something I could learn to live with while you went off and fell in love with some other girl. And if we were wrong . . . well, then, I would have been numb forever. It's not that I didn't believe in you. I didn't believe in myself." I've been shrinking into myself, but I can't help these words from coming out in a frantic burst.

"You really think my love is that fickle?"

I look to the ground, my eyes stinging. "I suppose I did. I'm sorry." *For so many things.*

"I'm sorry, too," Emmett says. "Today, I promise, I was doing my best to protect you. It made me sick to see you walk into that forest. But there are things here you don't understand, plans already in motion. I can't make Bram think I'm his enemy, not now."

"Then let me in," I plead. "We were partners once, we could be again."

Emmett sighs but doesn't argue with me. "Meet me tomorrow morning and I'll show you more."

"Tomorrow morning?"

He nods, a hopeful light returning to his eyes. I've never been good at saying no to him. This reminds me of all the nights last spring, agreeing to meet him in the dark of his room or in the sunken garden.

"All right."

I watch his shadow dip back into the castle and there's something horrible in the slope of his shoulders. Right before ducking inside, he turns back.

His eyes meet mine and his gaze is as tender as a bruise.

It looks like *You're two years too late.*

I watch the stars until my face goes numb. I'm about to go inside when movement in the corner of the garden catches my eye. It's an animal, no larger than a dog, but with silver-white fur that glows the exact same shade as the moon. It's far away and cloaked in shadow, but I swear it's got a jagged little stump in the center of its forehead. It's only then that I crack open and start to sob.

LYDIA BENTON

The walls hum with the music from the revel raging deep in the castle, nearly loud enough to drown out the knocking at my door.

I open it to find a sorry-looking Bram. His hair hangs in loose waves around his face and his full bottom lip is stuck out in a pout.

I exhale.

I skipped tonight's revel because I didn't feel strong enough to face him, but here he is, at my door anyway.

Like a phantom limb, my heart gives a little beat, pleased that he's chosen to seek me out. I don't think I'll ever stop chasing his approval, no matter how I loathe myself for it.

Emmett often chastises me about the way I follow Bram around the castle like a lost dog, but I can't help myself. I've been here, in the Otherworld, for years, but I only see Bram once every few months. His attention still feels precious, his approval like oxygen. My lungs sting and I get the sense I'm drowning without it.

He leans against my doorframe. "Are you cross with me?"

"No," I answer honestly. It's so much more complicated than that. I wish I could be like Ivy, who is brave enough to simply be angry with people. All my emotions are tangled up into a ball so dense, I have no hope of making sense of it. Love and hate and longing and resentment are all starting to feel the same.

"Then why did you skip the revel? It makes you look like a bad queen, like you're not even trying. Maybe I should just pick Ivy." He's loose-limbed but not quite drunk.

I flinch as if he's slapped me.

His face crumples and he steps into the room, shutting the door behind him. He reaches up and cups my cheek with one of his hands. I press into it and close my eyes.

"I'm sorry, I didn't mean it," he says softly.

I blink up at him. "I know you didn't." He didn't. *He has to love me, at least a little, right?*

He flops down into the worn armchair by the fire—Emmett's chair—and looks so unnatural there that I pause, but then he pulls me onto his lap.

"If you're not cross, what are you?"

"I'm sad." My chest aches as I remember all too vividly what it felt like as the unicorn's horn sank into its flesh. I'm disgusted with myself too, but that doesn't feel worth explaining.

"Sad about what? Everything is fine."

Emmett and Bram are so different. Emmett comes to my

room when he's hurting and wants to feel his pain in private. Bram doesn't want to feel his at all, so he makes the rest of us do it for him.

"Just because it's immortal doesn't mean it didn't suffer!" I snap at him unintentionally, and his eyes darken. All unicorns are ageless creatures, but infants like the one we encountered in the woods today are rare. It was probably around one hundred years old. Its silver blood will clot, its wound will knit itself back together, but the horn will take centuries to grow back. I shouldn't have snapped it off like I did, but it was the only sure way to make its heart stop beating temporarily. I didn't want Ivy to have to do it and I knew Bram would never let us rest until the game was finished.

I've learned, in my time here, that the Otherworld is a living thing. The land and the creatures alike remember actions like the ones I took today, and I know they will not look kindly on them. I didn't want Ivy's first act in the Otherworld to be one of violence; the land would never have forgiven her. I have some goodwill here, but I've no doubt burned most of it today.

"Oh, so you're offended by a game? We can't have any fun around here?"

"That's not what I'm saying."

"You don't get to style yourself as queen and then act all high and mighty, like you're above us," Bram says, petulant. "This is what we *do*."

"I know, I know." I soothe him even as his words sting.

I don't understand how someone I love this much can be so cruel.

"Just because you hold your little visiting hours and sit on a throne doesn't mean you hold any real power here, Lydia," Bram says harshly.

Emmett and I reinstated the open hours in the throne room once a week a few months into his time as regent. They existed when Mor and Bram's father ruled the Otherworld, and it seemed practical for us to have a place to hear from the citizens we're supposed to be ruling over. We've solved petty disputes between Redcaps, taxation among river sprites, property spats for a family of selkies. Bram believes the small folk aren't worthy of his attention, but listening to them—helping them, if I'm able—is the best part of being queen.

I suspect Bram's games aren't just to pit Ivy and me against each other, but to publicly humiliate me in front of the subjects who have grown to respect me.

I don't even really understand why I care for him the way I do. Sometimes before I drift off to sleep, I lie in the dark and search through my memories, trying to find the one that could have inspired such illogical devotion. Again and again, I come up empty. I've settled on only one answer: that Bram has a glow about him, and when he turned that glow on me, I felt special too. I fear I'll spend forever chasing that feeling.

I grew up thinking boys were dull creatures, but Bram isn't dull at all. I know there are hidden depths to him. I see glimpses of charity, cleverness, warmth, and some part of me believes he'll let me see all of him if only I'm good enough. But what if I dig deeper and the only thing there is more cruelty? Emmett has said he fears there's nothing good left in Bram, but I don't know if he believes himself.

"How did you even find it so quickly? The party was supposed to last much longer. You ruined it." He's pouting again.

"The flowers showed me the way." They bent and bowed the moment I walked into the forest, as if on a phantom breeze. The soft green grass flattened itself into a winding path until I found the unicorn lying in a spot of sun in that meadow. Even the unicorn seemed to expect my arrival.

Bram huffs out a frustrated breath. "They like you so much better than me."

I reach up and brush a lock of hair from his forehead. His eyes gently close. "No, darling, that's impossible. You're the king."

I still don't completely understand the link between the Otherworld and the Crown, but the bond is inexorable. The plants have a sentience about them, animated by magic itself. It's true the gardens seem to bloom more brightly for me than anyone else, but as I'm constantly soothing Bram, it doesn't mean much. His power to rule is derived from the land; it's impossible it favors me over him.

His eyes flit to my half-finished painting in the corner and I sense he's eager to change the subject.

"Weren't you working on that the last time I was here?"

It was three months ago. I'd just begun the underpainting. "Yes." I look up at him, smiling, waiting for a compliment. It's the most detailed landscape I've ever attempted and I'm quite proud of how it's turning out. There are still muddy sections where I've painted, covered up, and repainted, but it's my best work so far.

Bram glances to me, then back to the painting. He raises his hand, the one that isn't around my shoulder, and with a lazy wave, the painting changes. Color crawls across the canvas until every unfinished spot is filled in.

"Oh." I deflate, my shoulders drop, my eyes sting. I can't cry in front of him. He hates it when I cry.

"Look, it's finished," he says with an air of pride.

"Yes," I croak out. The places where Bram's magic has completed the painting are flat and wrong.

Bram tips my face toward his and sees the devastation there. "I can't do anything right, can I?" he says softly.

"I love it," I lie.

"It's better than you could have managed on your own. I was only trying to help. You're so ungrateful sometimes."

"I love it," I say once more.

Bram sighs like he'll never understand me and rises from the chair. He sheds his beaded doublet and flops down onto my bed. He spends most nights here with me on the rare occasion he's in the Otherworld, and this is how I love him most. He looks so much younger in sleep and it's easier to picture he's the person I hope he is, deep down.

Now that I'm grown, I'm ashamed of the way I poked fun at Ivy when we were children for her obsession with faeries and magic, because the truth is, I harbored my own fantasies. But my obsession wasn't magic, it was romance. I spent hours in the garden, weaving daisy chain crowns and dreaming of the boy I'd one day love. In a way, I've spent my whole life looking for Bram.

But I fear Bram isn't a partner, he's a sharp object stupid girls cut themselves on. Me, Ivy, even courtiers like Lady Thalia have all been left in tatters by him.

I snuff out the lantern and climb into bed next to him, this boy I love.

It's been a long while but I'm still staring at the ceiling. I think Bram is asleep, but then he rolls over and kisses me long and slow.

He pulls back, and I look deep into his eyes as we breathe in sync. It's easy to imagine he loves me too.

Featherlight, he trails his fingers over my knuckles under the covers. His careless fingers twirl my wedding ring, then he shatters the silence. "Do you think Ivy's having fun?"

I pull my hand away.

"Yes," I answer quietly, and pull the quilt up under my chin.

Bram flops over on his back to stare at the ceiling. "Do you think she loves me?"

"Of course," I answer flatly.

But she doesn't.

And so, I'll save her from him. But in doing so, I'll also

get to keep him for myself. Does that make me selfish or a martyr?

Bram has been sleeping for nearly an hour when I'm finally brave enough to slip out of bed and down the stairs.

The garden is navy-blue dark, speckled with starlight, and cold enough to make me shiver under my dressing gown.

I pad through the dark of the gardens, until I feel a certain *tug* toward a rosebush. As I approach, its leaves and flowers unfurl, revealing the unicorn resting in a hollow against the roots.

It whinnies and recoils as I approach. I extend my hand and wait for it to press its velvety nose into my palm. Its eyes drop closed, forgiveness in the gesture that I don't deserve.

Its silver fur is cool to the touch, but its heartbeat is strong.

"I'm sorry," I whisper, and it bows its little head like it understands me.

On unsteady legs, it rises and trusts me enough to follow me through the dark to the gates of the castle.

I press them open and gesture for the little creature to leave the castle grounds, to run as far from this place as possible.

The trees ruffle their leaves: in approval or condemnation I do not know.

The unicorn presses its little head and the jagged nub of its horn against my leg, then disappears into the night.

CHAPTER FIFTEEN

The lawn is dusted with frost like icing sugar that crunches beneath my feet and sparkles under the stark morning sun. Faeries usually sleep well past midday, so it's only me in the gardens this morning.

My fur-lined ice-blue cloak hangs heavy on my shoulders. I pull it tighter, fighting the wind that whips between hedges.

Emmett emerges from the mist like a vision. Golden sun reflects off his dark hair and the chill has turned his cheeks rosy. He's wearing a thick brown overcoat, similar to something he would have worn in London, but this one has metallic vines embroidered up the sleeves.

"I didn't think you'd come," he says.

"I've always come when you've asked."

I feel the fresh wound of our fight yesterday. I don't know how to act natural around him. We both said we're sorry, but I'm not sure how to go about healing. I'm terrified we're both too wounded to ever overcome what we've gone through and go back to the people we used to be. I long for the simple pleasure of bickering, toe-to-toe in a boathouse.

"Where are we going?" I ask.

Emmett smiles softly, like he's afraid I might spook. "To meet some friends of mine."

The walk takes us from the castle grounds through the hillside village and down into the glen where a few homes and businesses are scattered. Emmett talks blandly about the landmarks we pass. "This is the night market, it runs nearly every day after dark, except when the vendors forget," he says as we pass the empty stalls on the winding streets surrounding the castle.

He explains that faerie magic can't make something from nothing, but it can expand and transform. So unlike in England, where so much of our land and time is dedicated simply to the task of feeding the populace, the Otherworld has no real need for organized agriculture or farmland. A single berry is as good as a million berries. If you have enough food for one, you can simply wave your hand and have a feast for one thousand. A lack of agriculture means an economy never had a need to develop.

Those who do work, like the castle staff, are paid in the only finite resource in the Otherworld—land of their own. They earn mere inches a month. It can take a faerie centuries to earn a plot big enough to live on. The lords and other landed families are the lucky ones.

"The population of the Otherworld isn't focused on survival, only entertainment. It's why they're so obsessed with humanity. It's not just the way we make them feel, though that's a big part of it, it's that we're the model they have for society," Emmett says. I nod along as Emmett explains all of this, interested, but also concerned about all I'm missing back in England. I was supposed to talk with my advisers this week about building a hospital in the East End. They won't have access to the Crown's funding without me there to approve it.

"They call it Little Londinium," Emmett explains as we pass through the town square. "Most things here are a copy of something they saw in England, but the door was closed back in the 1400s, so it's turned into a bit of an off-kilter time capsule."

That explains the buildings, with their white plaster and dark wood, the strange fashion, and the odd way the Others sometimes speak.

"Some haven't been back to England since the Romans ruled. You'll sometimes see faeries wearing togas or poorly copied bronze armor. Some are nostalgic for the Middle Ages and still stage jousting matches."

He points out more businesses as we go: a dress shop where the seamstress insists on being paid in sugar; a tailor that went out of business after the proprietor made a bad bargain and was forced to speak only in limericks; a tavern that serves exclusively fermented fruit pies.

After walking for thirty or so minutes, the buildings thin and we reach the outskirts of Little Londinium.

We come upon a storybook cottage. It's got a thatched roof

and a chimney gently puffing smoke into the clear morning sky.

Emmett opens the gate in the knee-high fence and gestures for me to go through. "Ladies first."

I'm hit with a blast of heat the moment I step inside the building, which I realize isn't a home but a tavern.

"Uncle Emmett!" In a blur, two figures dart from the kitchen and throw themselves at Emmett.

He scoops the smaller of the two up off the well-worn wooden floor and tosses him high in the air. The boy's giggle pierces the room. The little girl at his ankles screams, "Me next, me next!"

The smell of pastries baking is nearly overwhelming. At this time of the morning, the small pub is empty, filled only with dust-flecked beams of light spilling from the rafters above. There are a dozen or so long tables and a stage in the corner with a few instruments propped up.

Emmett sets the little boy down and picks up the girl, who squeals with glee. The boy puts his chubby hands on his hips and looks up at me suspiciously. "You look like Queen Lydia, but you're not Queen Lydia."

"I'm her sister."

He gestures to the girl being swung around by Emmett. "That's my sister. She steals all my sweets and never goes to sleep when Mama and Papa tell her to."

I bend down and lower my voice. "Lydia was very good at listening to our parents. I was the naughty one."

The boy nods sagely. "Uncle Emmett says Queen Lydia is very, very good."

I've never seen a faerie child before. The boy looks no older than five, with big brown eyes and a mop of curly hair. His sister looks to be about seven, with spindly legs, her hair in two braids, the same fawn color as her brother's.

Emmett sets the girl down, out of breath and laughing. "Uncle Emmett?" I ask in a whisper.

"No blood relation, obviously. I just spend a lot of time here."

From behind the bar, a woman waves a towel. "Sit, eat!" she commands; then she pauses and her big brown eyes go wide. "Who's your friend?"

Emmett glances to me, then back to the woman. "Nan, this is Ivy Benton."

I turn and the woman gasps. Her eyes fill with tears, and then she rushes from behind the bar and wraps me in a bone-crushing hug.

"But she's—" she sputters, then leans back and grabs my face with both of her hands. "You're supposed to be dead."

"I'm sorry to disappoint?"

"Disappoint?" she gasps. "This is the best news I've heard in nearly a century!"

She releases me, then wraps Emmett up in a similarly tight embrace. "My darling boy," she sniffles. "I'm so happy for you."

Emmett's eyes well with tears, too, but he blinks them away rapidly and runs a hand through his dark hair.

The woman gestures to one of the empty tables and brings over a pot of tea and four cups. "I want to hear the whole story. Fennick!" she bellows. "Come quick!"

A startled-looked ginger-haired man appears in the doorway to the kitchen. He wipes his hands on his apron. "What is it now, dear? Oh! Emmett's here! How lovely to see you."

"Ivy's here!" Nan shouts.

The man, Fennick, shakes his head. "No, dear, she's dead."

I raise my hand awkwardly. "Alive, actually. Hello."

"She's alive!" Nan pops up behind my shoulder and echoes with glee.

Soon the four of us have steaming teacups in front of us and the children (whose names I learn are Orin and Veda) are sent to play in the garden.

Like all faeries, Fennick and Nan don't look any older than their early twenties, but there's a parental air about them. Maybe it's the crinkles by Nan's warm brown eyes or the gentle way Fennick holds his hands in his lap.

"Tell us the whole story, dear," Nan says. I take a sip of tea and begin with the night of my wedding to Bram, though I suspect she knows that part already.

"After Bram had Emmett taken away, I went with the other girls to the Tower to confront Queen Mor."

"Bram told me you were trampled in the chaos," Emmett says, his voice thin with pain.

I want to reach out to him, but I don't know if he'd accept

my touch. How do I comfort him over my own death? How do I make him feel better about something that was never even true?

"I am well," I say, but of course I'm not.

I continue my story, telling them about how the court moved down to Bath, how we found Queen Mor in the Roman ruins, how I'm doing my best to keep the country functioning as Bram's chaos reigns.

"Our Emmett is the same way," Nan says affectionately.

"I was going to ask how you all got to know each other," I say.

"Emmett has been such a help to us townsfolk," Fennick replies. "We wouldn't have a tavern at all if it wasn't for him."

"They're being too generous," Emmett says. "I came at first only because I was recently released from prison and looking for a place to get completely obliterated."

"The kids started screaming the moment he walked in," says Nan.

"I looked like a skeleton after all those months in prison."

"No," Fennick corrects him. "They'd just never seen a human before."

"So he sits down at the bar"—Nan leans toward me—"and he orders pint after pint, and it was only after three that he answered any of my questions. I thought he was pulling my leg at first, but I've since learned that Emmett doesn't like to lie."

I turn toward him, curious. "That's new." The Emmett

I knew was quite a proficient liar.

He looks toward the ground and shrugs. "Lying has never gotten me anywhere I wanted to be."

"I asked him how he'd come to be in the Otherworld. I hadn't seen a human since Queen Mor locked the door between our worlds and King Bram took over. I wasn't prepared for a love story."

"A love story?" I ask.

Nan captures my hand in hers. "He told us all about you."

Emmett's eyes catch mine. There's that spark of fire in those hazel irises I'd been missing. "She's being dramatic."

Nan swats him. "I am not! The way he described you, oh, my dear girl, I wish you'd been there to hear it."

"What was it?" Fennick taps the side of his face. *"Much too brave and smart to also deserve a face that beautiful."*

If I didn't know Emmett better, I'd think he might be blushing. "Well, you said he didn't lie." I smile but it feels out of place on my face.

My stomach lets out an embarrassing grumble. Faeries aren't really ones for breakfast, but Nan jabs her husband. "What are we doing? Get the poor children some food!"

Fennick disappears through the swinging door to the kitchen and reappears with four steaming meat pies.

"No pastries today?" Emmett says.

Fennick drops the pie in front of him. "You'll like this more."

While we eat, I hear more of Nan and Fennick's life and

how Emmett came to be a part of their orbit. After long days of ruling Bram's faerie court, Emmett began a habit of coming here to have a moment of peace.

"I realized they were different," he explains. "That not all faeries in the Otherworld were like Bram's courtiers."

"He saved us from those very courtiers," Fennick says gravely.

"Saved is too generous a term," Emmett replies.

Nan pats his hand. "You're always too modest. You absolutely saved us."

"We're a small family establishment. We want to be a place for the community to gather, but the nobles up in that castle had taken to coming here after their revels, so drunk they couldn't see straight, and destroying the place. One night it got so bad, they lit the roof on fire, right above where Veda and Orin sleep," Fennick says.

"And you know what Emmett did?" Nan asks. "He used his power as regent to declare any members of Bram's court were no longer allowed to visit the village on revel nights, and then he climbed up on our roof and fixed the thatch himself."

Fennick laughs. "We kept telling him we could just fix it with magic, but there he was, with his shirtsleeves rolled up, repairing it himself."

"Magic isn't always good at repairs like that," Emmett replies in a low voice. "I didn't want the straw to dissolve into mist during the next rainstorm and leave Veda and Orin all wet. It was easy enough to fix it myself."

"It wasn't easy at all! Nan exclaims. "He was up there all day, sweating buckets."

"But the courtiers have stayed away, and we love Emmett like another son," Fennick adds.

"Most of the faeries I've met here are like them," Emmett says. "Not like Bram and the rest of them at the castle."

"The worst of us, I'm afraid," Nan tuts. "I always agreed with Queen Mor's decision to close the door between our worlds. She's a mother, like me, and she knows if a child can't be trusted with a toy, you must take the toy away."

Again, I think of Queen Mor in that dark basement cell. So determined to stand by Bram that she's willing to spend the rest of her immortal life behind bars. The love she has for her son will be her undoing.

"Speaking of motherhood," I say, "I've never seen faerie children before."

Fennick looks fondly at his wife. "A rare gift. We tried for centuries, and never dreamed we'd be blessed with two so close together."

As if summoned, the children burst back from the backyard and scramble for purchase up on Emmett's lap. He lets them eat the last of his pie.

Veda presses her sticky little hands to his face, and in the blink of an eye, she morphs into a perfect, miniature copy of Emmett. She's got his dark wavy hair, his hazel eyes lined with thick lashes.

I let out a yelp of surprise.

Veda looks to me with a mischievous grin and changes into me. It's like looking in a mirror, if that mirror shrank me down two feet.

"Be nice to our guest, Veda. It's not polite to glamour yourself at the dining table."

"Glamour?" I ask Nan.

She nods sagely. "Every faerie can do magic, but some are blessed with particular talents. Our Veda here is quite the mimic."

Veda turns into Emmett again, but this time with a shiny, bald head.

Emmett springs up, arms outstretched. "You little devil!" he screams as he chases her. She squeals and laughs, only morphing back into herself once he catches her and lifts her off her feet.

After, we join them in the garden, where Emmett and Fennick push them on wooden swings tied to a gnarled tree.

Nan appears beside me and hands me a steaming cup of something.

"He loves you so much," she says.

"He did, once," I reply, too honest with this near stranger.

"A love like that isn't something you get over." She sounds so sure. But what do immortals know about moving on?

"I didn't even know him for very long," I confess. "He's lived with the memory of me much longer than the reality of me." How could I possibly live up to the idea of me he mourned?

"There's something I've learned about time in this very

long life," Nan says. "Sometimes a single minute matters more than one hundred years."

It's a nice thought. I'm just not so sure I believe it.

After Emmett is thoroughly winded from chasing Veda and Orin through the orchard behind the tavern, we give our farewells, with plenty of promises to return soon. We don't speak of Bram's new competition. It's as if I can read Emmett's mind; there's no point in worrying them over something so far out of their control.

Emmett walks ahead of me on the path. "Where are we going?" I ask.

He turns to me and grins, his face so beautiful in the midday sun I could nearly cry. "You didn't used to ask this many questions."

"That's a lie."

Together we walk to a nearby glen, secluded beyond the outskirts of town, where a waterfall pours over moss-covered stones into a babbling brook below. Flowers bloom for us as we walk along the winding path, and Emmett takes a blanket and lays it down once we reach the softest part of the grass.

"A picnic?" I ask.

"You were too busy pushing Veda on the swing to see her mother accost me and force me into taking all this food."

"They really love you," I say.

Emmett closes his eyes and tips his face up to the sun. It's been up long enough that the crisp autumn morning is yielding to warmth. "I love them too. I'd never seen a family like that."

"Like what?"

"That loved each other."

I feel a pang of homesickness for the kind of family I had before all of this. I hadn't appreciated the rarity of it until it was gone.

Emmett spreads the feast out over the blanket. Food that looks close enough to the sandwiches back home, but the tea cakes smell of raspberries and rain and are covered with candied flowers. Emmett peels one off and pops it into his mouth.

"Will you tell me about the last two years?" I ask. *Will you tell me if it's too large a gap to close, if I'll ever find my way back to you?*

He leans back on his elbows and brushes his hair behind his ears. It would be so easy to pretend we were in Hyde Park now, under a familiar sun.

"I think I'm quite good at it, actually."

"At what?"

"Being regent."

I smile. "I have my own confession."

He raises his brows.

"I'm not a bad queen." It's the first time I've said it aloud, the first time I've admitted it to myself, actually.

He grins, showing off his perfect teeth. I'm particularly fond of his canines, which are just slightly too sharp.

"I never doubted you."

I take a sip of something fizzy from a bottle and Emmett takes the moment to just look at me.

"How is Pig?" he asks. "I should have asked that the first moment I saw you."

"You were too busy accusing me of being a selkie."

Emmett plucks a blade of grass and picks at the white root. "Sorry about that."

"Pig is well," I say. "Misses you, though."

"I miss him, too. No one here keeps pets. They think it's undignified."

"Nonsense," I say. "Pig is so much more dignified than you."

We exchange stories of dealing with disgruntled nobles and sleight-of-hand diplomacy. He listens, rapt, while I tell him of our plans for a national railway, and I'm equally fascinated by the way he describes the court politics of the Otherworld.

He explains that in the spring of last year he and Lydia threw a revel so grand, it sated an ambitious lord who sought to replace Emmett as regent.

Emmett hasn't just helped Fennick and Nan; he's ingratiated himself with all of the Little Londinium businesses, and done a lot of dealmaking to establish him and Lydia as respected rulers.

Emmett reaches into the pocket of his coat and pulls out a package, wrapped in waxy paper, about the size of an apple.

"I wanted to show you this place isn't all bad." His voice goes a shade softer.

I peel back the edges and find a globe of whisper-thin glass. Inside is a pink flower, with six stamens pointing up from the center.

The stamens glow orange and I gasp in surprise.

"A preserved lux flower," Emmett says. "The center glows according to your emotions."

"What does orange mean?" I ask.

"I don't know. It's different for each person. What is it you're feeling now?"

Love. Fear. Bone-deep sorrow. Ache. Longing. "Awe."

Emmett's eyes flit from my eyes to my lips, then back again. *No one is going to want to kiss you if you can't look at them.* That's what he said to me before the first time he kissed me in a rain-soaked coaching inn.

He's looking at me now. Those sharp hazel eyes are the same, no matter what else has changed, and there is fire behind them.

"Please keep looking at me like that," I breathe.

Emmett's eyes shine with want, and his broad hands flex over the blanket. I have a sudden awareness of my own heartbeat, and the flush creeping up my neck.

This isn't anything like the frantic kiss in the hallway. I feel each nerve under my skin firing, the way the muscles in my arms go warm and lax.

I know just how his lips will feel, how they'll move against mine and how he'll take a breath before deepening the kiss. I know just how he loves to trail his mouth against the column of my neck, how he'll arch against me when I take a fist of his hair. He'll tip me back against the blanket and in the mist of the waterfall, I'll have him and it'll feel like coming home.

Each day we spent apart stretches between us now, and all I want is to close the distance.

I lean in, my eyes fluttering shut.

The grass rustles and I open my eyes to see Emmett pushing himself up off the ground and brushing dirt from his pants. "It's getting late."

My heart stutters, then cracks. I gesture to the bright blue sky. "If you're going to reject me, you need to come up with a better excuse than that." I can barely get the words out; they hurt too badly.

Emmett won't even look at me.

"You don't understand."

"Then help me! Let me in!" This feels like an awful repeat of our fight last night. "Do the girls you kiss at revels mean more to you than me?"

His hands clench into fists and then unfurl. "I beg of you, do not judge me for the way I've survived."

Emmett gathers our supplies from the ground in a hurry. I've never seen anyone fold a picnic blanket with so much ire. There's tension in every line of his body, like he's holding something back. "I have work to do." Emmett turns back toward the castle.

"With Lydia?" I spit.

"Yes, with Lydia. I will not allow you to throw that

relationship in my face."

"She's my sister!"

Emmett whips his head back around to me. "And she's my best friend."

"Then go, go to her." Every crack in my heart that had begun to heal splits open once more.

Emmett waits and extends a hand to help me off the ground.

When I put my hand in his, he glances from side to side and then up to the cliffs of the waterfall, like he suddenly fears we're being watched.

Just as quickly, he turns back to me and his face softens into agony.

"I won't trouble you with my presence any longer. I can walk alone," I say, my voice brittle.

Emmett shakes his head. "I'm not going to dignify that with a response."

"Leave me alone." I'm on the edge of crying and I don't want him to see me break.

I start walking and he's silent for long enough that I don't think he's going to respond, but his answer comes in a voice so low, I don't think he means for me to hear. "I've never been capable of that."

I walk faster, but he stays just a few paces behind me, like a watchful shadow, all the way back to the castle.

CHAPTER SIXTEEN

I've just finished crying when someone knocks at my door.

I've already had dinner alone, brought on a tray by Eloree.

"Leave me be," I call, but deep in my rib cage, my heart soars, hoping Emmett has come back to tell me he's sorry.

But it's not Emmett who bursts through the door.

Faith takes one look at my tear-streaked face and widens her eyes. "Has something happened?"

"Emmett—" My voice cracks and I start crying all over again.

"What about Emmett?" Faith asks.

"I don't think he wants me anymore."

"Oh, Ivy, I'm so sorry." Marion sighs. She's got a gold diadem atop her loose dark curls, and her gown is the rich blue-purple of spring violets. Beside her, Faith is a vision in molten silver. Her hair is half pulled back from her face, revealing a pair of earrings that trail down the column of her pale neck.

Faith puts her hands on her hips. "Want me to kill him for you?"

"No." I let out a watery laugh.

"Some light maiming?" she offers.

"Only if it's very light." I smile weakly.

Faith flops down onto my pillows and looks up at me, mischief playing in her pale blue eyes. "Cast aside by Emmett De Vere? Hmm, that story sounds rather familiar."

My first instinct is to defend him, but it's so much more complicated than that. They sit on my bed while I pace back and forth in front of the fireplace, explaining the situation.

When I am finished, Marion looks at me with pity. I know by now she's a true romantic. But Faith springs to her feet. "We're going to the revel."

"Ugh, please no," I protest.

"Emmett will be there," Faith says emphatically.

"That's exactly why I don't want to go."

Faith shakes her head like I've got it all wrong. "I know Emmett rather well. Well enough to know he loves you and well enough to know how jealous he gets. Sitting up in your tower weeping over him will do you no good. Let's make him cry over you for a change."

"I can't bear to see Bram," I protest.

"Bram won't be there," Marion pipes up. "He's in England for the next few days. Rhion sent word this evening."

"Rhion? After kidnapping you, that's rather odd."

Faith shrugs. "He's an odd man."

They stare at me expectantly, awaiting an answer.

I can't help myself.

"Find me a gown." I gesture to the wardrobe and Faith squeals.

I regret saying yes immediately. She riffles through the racks until she finds the most ornately beaded dress there.

She grins in triumph as she laces me into it.

"I can't go out in this!" I gasp in horror, looking at myself in the full-length mirror. The dress is constructed mostly of a pale blush chiffon, transparent and close enough to my body that I look practically naked. The skirt and bodice of the dress are embroidered with beaded vines of jet-black, crawling over my breasts and hips, the only thing giving me even a semblance of modesty.

"You look almost good," Faith says.

"Was that a compliment?" I ask in mock horror. The dress is borderline obscene. The mere sight of it might have killed Viscountess Bolingbroke.

"He's going to faint when he sees you, how about that?"

She slides open a velvet-lined drawer, selects a matching tiara of black diamonds, and places it on my unbound curls. "There." She smiles, then pulls out an aquamarine beauty and puts it on her own head. I raise my eyebrows at her, and she shrugs. "I'm not entirely altruistic. Let's go."

The revel tonight isn't held in the ballroom, but under a massive tent in the gardens. The court magicians put it up today while I was napping, and I awoke to the sound of snapping sail flags outside my window.

Inside, the grass has been covered with a mosaic of carpets, and a rainbow chandelier illuminates the hedges and flower patches in long, crawling shadows.

I find my sister as soon as I walk in. She's standing near the edges of the party, but people still orbit around her.

She adjusts a tiara made of teal-blue dragonfly wings and blinks twice at my dress. "Are you trying to kill the poor boy?"

"Only lightly maim," I shout over the music.

For once, I let the faerie music take me away on its current. I'm floating in it, lost in the rhythmic drum, so unlike the stodgy quartets back home. All around me are writhing limbs and bodies, seeking nothing but friction and escape.

I used to judge humans who got swept away in this and danced their feet bloody, but I understand now how good it feels to remove your brain from your body.

Someone presses a drink in a delicate pink glass to me and I down it without thinking.

I might drink another. Time gets so fuzzy here.

The revel goes blurry, my head spinning, or maybe that's my body. I've been dancing for so long.

There are flashes of clarity. Faith with her arms slung around my neck, grinning. Marion, asking if I'm ready to go yet, and me laughing in her face.

Someone's hands are on my hips, I don't know whose.

I come to, slouched on a silk love seat. It's set against the edges of the tent, hidden from the chaos by a series of geometric hedges.

There's a hand on my thigh. The gauzy layers of my dress

are hiked up above my knee, so the palm covers an expanse of bare skin. I watch in fascination as the long fingers leave dimples on my skin. They press nearly hard enough to bruise, as if holding themselves back from trailing higher.

My mind is swimming, like I've been dunked in a glass of iridescent faerie wine. I am nothing, no one, just a bubble floating to the top of the glass.

I follow the line up from the fingers, to the wrist, to the tan forearm, flexing with veins and muscles, until I finally reach his face.

Emmett's eyes are heavy, his full lips half-open, wine red, with a fleck of gold at the corner. The look on his face is absolutely desolate. An earring in the shape of a crystal flower pokes through the waves of his hair, curling gently around his flushed ears.

He lowers his mouth to my neck and I sigh.

"You're touching me," I say in awe.

"I am," he replies, sounding just as surprised as I am.

"I thought you didn't want me anymore."

His lips brush over my sensitive pulse point and I moan shamelessly.

"I want nothing but you." His voice is low, nearly a growl. "Every moment I am awake, there you are, in my head. Even in sleep, there is no relief. Visions of you torment me in dreams. It's nothing but *you, you, you.*"

The blood in my veins has been replaced with honey. My head swims with it, all sticky sweet and pulsating. I look deep into Emmett's eyes and in them I find a desire identical to my own. My own dark mirror. I suppose in a way, that's what he always has been to me—my most base desires, all my sins, reflected back to me in the shape of this brutally imperfect, beautiful boy.

His chest rises and falls like he's been running; his face is so open, so wrecked. I can't believe I was ever angry with him. Why was I angry with him? I don't even remember.

"Ivy." He moans my name and his mouth dips lower, kissing my flushed chest over the thin fabric. I want to tell him to tear it, rip it with his teeth, that I don't care, but I can't seem to find my voice.

I'm swept away in a tide of wanting. I am reduced to nothing but Emmett and the warmth of his hands, his mouth.

That mouth. It's sucking a bruise into the hollow of my throat.

I press both hands on his shoulders, and tip him against the love seat. His head lolls back and I hike up my skirts and climb onto his lap.

"Emmett," I sigh as I capture his earlobe between my teeth, tugging on the crystal earring there. Was there a reason we shouldn't be doing this? The thought floats out of sight like a petal on a breeze and I no longer remember or care.

He captures my chin with his hand and turns my face to him. His lips catch mine with the force of an inferno.

Nothing has ever been sweeter than the taste of his tongue invading my mouth. My teeth clack against his as I try to bring him even closer. I despise any space where we are not touching.

He winds one hand through the hair at the nape of my neck and presses the other against the small of my back. His wandering hands have never been less polite.

I can't break the kiss, not even to breathe. I'm drowning in it, but nothing, not even air, feels more important than him.

Emmett. Emmett. Emmett.

I want to die like this, pitched about like a sailor in a storm, lost in the tide of him. I used to think I'd never wanted anything as badly as I wanted Emmett De Vere, but now it feels as if I've never wanted anything *but* him.

"What are you doing!" Lydia's voice pierces the candy-floss-pink fog of my mind.

Still, we keep kissing. His mouth is so soft, so warm. I bite at the juncture of his neck and shoulder, then lick to soothe the toothy bruise I just left there.

"Emmett," Lydia says louder, and Emmett breaks our kiss with a gasp. He stumbles over his own feet as he stands up.

A sob starts in the back of my throat. "No, please. I need him."

He turns to Lydia, his face shattered. "I can't do this, I'm sorry, I'm so sorry."

The worst part is feeling the loss of his body heat as he runs away. The second worst part is that I don't know which of us he was apologizing to.

I'm properly crying now, hiccupping, barely able to catch

my breath. It's as if I've lost a vital part of myself, like I really might die if he doesn't come back and keep ravishing me.

Lydia sits down next to me and captures my face in her cool hands. My skin is burning as if with fever. "Ivy, calm down."

I wheeze in a breath, but the tears just keep coming. "You took him from me."

"What did you drink?" Lydia asks urgently.

"I—" I hiccup. "I don't know."

Lydia leans down and picks up an empty vial. The glass is an ornately engraved, soft fuchsia ombre that ends in a narrow, rounded tip. "Did you drink this?"

"I don't think so? Maybe while I was dancing? I wasn't paying much attention."

Lydia curses.

Through the pink haze, the logical part of my brain prickles with fear. I look up and see a crowd of faeries peering over the hedges, laughing. Their open mouths look like jackals, their cackles sharp and animalistic.

"Get me out of here," I whisper urgently, and Lydia hauls me to my feet.

I'm unable to stop crying all the way back up to my room. I try to run down the hall to Emmett's door, the need for him still clawing at my insides.

Lydia snatches my arm and pulls me back.

"No." I struggle against her grip.

She kicks open the door to my room and tries to pull me inside. I plant my heels into the carpet and pull away from her. I'm usually the stronger of the two of us, but the potion has left me weak and wrung out. Lydia slings my arm around her shoulders and drags me over the threshold. I claw at the doorframe. "No, please!" I beg, but Lydia pries my fingers off and slams the door behind us.

We're both panting now, and Lydia brushes a sweaty lock of hair from her forehead. "You were given a love potion," Lydia explains while helping me out of my gown. There's a fresh violet bruise blooming up my neck.

"Why would someone do that?" I sob. All the while my mind sings *Emmett, Emmett, Emmett*. It's as if there's a fist squeezing my heart and I'll die if I don't get back to him soon.

"Why do faeries do anything?" she says grimly. "For a laugh. I'd bet half the people in that room were dosed the same way you were."

"My friends—" I gasp, suddenly remembering how worried I should be for them.

"Are much smarter than you," Lydia answers. "They went to bed ages ago."

I sigh in relief.

"I was hoping you and Emmett were talking. I should have come looking for you both sooner, but I assumed Emmett knew better."

"Why would he take it?" I ask.

"Because someone tricked him . . . or he thought it was something else."

"You don't understand. I need him." A fat tear rolls down

my flushed cheek.

Lydia brushes it away. "And you can tell him that in the morning, when the potion wears off."

"Why does he keep pushing me away?" I sob.

Lydia's brown eyes soften. We're only two years apart, but her time here has made her feel so much older than me. "It's his story to tell."

"Then why won't he *tell* me?"

She shakes her head sadly. "Because he loves you too much to hurt you. It's misguided but it's true."

I lie back on my pillows and watch the ceiling spin. Nothing feels real. "What about you? Don't you care about hurting me?"

I think of the unicorn, the way Lydia tried to win so viciously.

"You're my baby sister." She helps me into a nightdress and leaves me with the curtains drawn and a carafe of water by my bedside.

It's only as I snuff out the lantern that I realize she didn't really answer my question.

PRINCE EMMETT DE VERE

"Shit!" Lydia exclaims. It's clear she was trying to shut the door to Ivy's room as silently as possible but hadn't expected to find me outside. Her eyes drop to the pillow and blanket I hold in front of my chest. "I won't let you go in there."

"I wasn't planning on it."

Lydia raises her brows like she doesn't believe me.

"I've been sleeping on the floor in front of her room every night," I confess. "I don't trust anyone in this castle."

Lydia rolls her eyes. "You're pathetic."

"I'm practical."

"You're a lovesick fool."

"I'm protective."

"Do you really think I trust you to be this close to her after you've both been dosed with a love potion?" she shoots back. "I should have you locked up in the dungeons for the night for your own good."

At the mention of the dungeons, I reflexively grab my left hand, the one that the guards shattered during my time there, and Lydia grimaces.

"If I hadn't just forced myself to throw up the rest of the potion, I'd agree with you." I'm sober now, though my head is still swimming with thoughts of Ivy. Her mouth. Her hair. The way her chest rises and falls. But I'm basically always thinking about Ivy, so it's really not too far off my default state.

Yes, I want her. But I always want her.

I would have cut off my own hands rather than go any further with her while she was in that state. I had just barely come to awareness when Lydia interrupted us. I know the potion doesn't make anyone do anything they weren't already thinking of; it doesn't alter your desires, it just lowers your inhibition. It's little comfort against the rising tide of my guilt.

I'm sick with the thought we might have done something that Ivy regrets. It only reinforces my desire to have her far away from this place. I might not think the Otherworld is rotten to the core like Ivy does, but she's far too good for a place like this, and every moment she's here is a moment she's in danger.

"I can't believe you were stupid enough to drink tonight," Lydia scolds. She never takes the substances at revels, while I've developed a reputation at court for being willing to participate in any kind of debauchery. I don't know if there's anything in the Otherworld that can be drunk, smoked, or snorted that I haven't tried at least once.

"It was only supposed to be faerie wine tonight, I swear it.

One of the asshole lords must have drugged me, hoping for a show."

"Or *her*," Lydia says with disdain.

I shake my head. "It wasn't her."

"You have to pray this doesn't get back to Bram," Lydia says tightly.

"Trust me, I'm praying." Praying isn't all I'm doing.

I take Lydia gently by the arm and escort her down the stairs to her quarters before she even realizes what I'm doing.

I bend to give her a quick kiss on the cheek, hoping she'll have forgotten all about the lecture she planned to give me come morning. "Good night, Lyd."

"Good night, Idiot."

"Your favorite idiot, though." I smile.

"You and Ivy are currently neck and neck for first place," she deadpans as she closes the door behind her.

I loathe returning to the revel, but that is where Lady Thalia will be. I had planned to fall asleep in front of Ivy's door, but every moment since I vomited has given me more clarity. Lydia's warning about keeping what happened tonight from Bram is urgent and I need to act quickly.

I spot Thalia's raven hair first, loosely plaited down her back and dotted with night-blooming flowers. "Darling," she purrs as I cross the crowded dance floor to her. She drapes her body over mine. Every nerve ending still feels raw from earlier; I just barely resist the urge to push Thalia away.

"Hello, beautiful." I brush my lips against her ear the way she loves.

She rocks to the beat against me, so close I'm not even sure if what we're doing can be classified as dancing. "That was hilarious earlier," she purrs. "I think I might be jealous."

"Of who?" I ask, putting on my best show. "Bram's human pet?"

"I'll simply never understand his fascination with those sisters. They're so dull, and so . . . blond."

"I agree. Whoever dosed me with that potion played quite the trick."

Her body shudders against me as she laughs. "Oh, how I love a trick!"

"Was it you?" I ask casually.

She pushes out her lower lip in a pout, but it's an unnatural expression on her sharp face. Her eyes are almost feline, the rest of her features small and pointed. "I wanted to see if you'd do it. You know, I really am quite jealous. I should punish you."

"It didn't mean anything." I'm terrified. If Thalia knows how I feel about Ivy, then Ivy is in even more danger than before.

"The potion only reveals what's already there."

I take a step toward her and crouch so our faces are eye level. "But you're my favorite, so what does it matter? I kissed her, but you're the one who has me."

She thinks and I rise back to my full height. "The thing about it is, darling, it can't get back to Bram. We'd hate to wound his ego; things always get so miserable when he's out of sorts."

She pouts. "Ugh, you weren't here, but after Queen Lydia left the first time, we didn't have any revels for *a month*."

I put on a show, really lay it on thick. "So, you understand why we have to make sure no one speaks a word of what happened tonight to the king."

Her fox-like eyes narrow. "It won't be easy."

I run a finger down her cheek and she leans into my touch. "Yes, it will. You're so smart."

She preens a little at this, a slight smile showing off her sharp white teeth.

Thalia was one of the very first people I met at court. She approached me at a revel just like this and promised to help me learn the ways of court life. She's a large reason I've survived as long as I have.

A large reason I'm so dead inside, too.

"It'll cost you," she says icily.

"It's hardly a price to pay when I enjoy my time with you so much." My words are as smooth as honey but taste like poison behind my teeth.

I think of Ivy sleeping soundly above me. I want nothing more than to be in bed next to her, watching her chest rise and fall, knowing she is whole and well.

"If we're going to do a little espionage, we should do it up, don't you agree?" I continue. The band plays a driving beat, and all around us, dancers spin.

She takes a delicate sip from her crystal cup. "What did you have in mind?"

"Bram's next trial for the girls," I say conspiratorially.

"It's being kept tightly under wraps," she replies. "No one knew about the unicorn until yesterday morning. I asked to have a coat made out of its pelt, but was rudely refused."

"Surely someone knows."

She shrugs. "Rhion, probably."

"Should we start with him?" I ask.

She shakes her head and her crystal earrings jingle like bells. "No, too difficult."

"Who else saw?" I ask, thinking of the blur of faces peering over the bush, laughing at Ivy and me. If I had anything left in my stomach, I might be tempted to vomit again.

"Only a small crowd. Lord Yarrow and his wife, the Gunner sisters, Lord Garrett, and that mousy little maid."

"Lyra?"

She presses her wine-stained lips together. "Yes, her."

"You start with Yarrow and I'll take the Gunner sisters?" I ask.

She nods and takes another sip from her goblet. If it were any other courtier, I might be worried that they're too drunk to focus on the task at hand, but I know Thalia well enough to know that she requires stronger stuff.

I spot the Gunner sisters across the revel, dancing with their lithe limbs flailing in front of the bandstand.

"You're looking particularly lovely tonight," I say.

One of them—Chessa, I think—narrows her eyes at me. "Which one of us?" It's a ridiculous question. They look exactly alike. Their limp white hair, sallow skin, and thin lips are identical, as are the dresses they're wearing. White spider's silk, old enough that it has begun to yellow, with hems and trailing sleeves that have been torn to shreds by tonight's dancing.

"You're a rake." The other one, Nessa, slaps my chest with her insect-wing fan. Her teeth are stained berry red from whatever is sloshing around in her cup.

"I'm an honest man." I give them one of my best smiles.

"You can't fool us. We saw you earlier with that human girl." Her voice is high and reedy.

"That's what I wanted to speak with you about, actually," I say. "I was rather hoping we could keep that between us. We'd both been dosed with love potion and the kiss was a mistake, but you know how Bram gets when he's jealous. We wouldn't want to upset him now, would we?"

They turn and blink in sync. I have the uncanny feeling they can read each other's minds.

"What are you offering?" Maybe-Chessa asks.

My expression hardens. "I'm sorry if I gave the impression this was a negotiation. You tell *anyone* I kissed Ivy Benton and I'll tell your father about the bargains you made with the selkies for those pretty pearl earrings."

Lord Gunner's prejudices against the small folk are well known. Like mirror images, his daughters both gasp and reach up to grab the pearls hanging down their necks.

"Papa will lock us up!"

"So, he won't find out. Will he?"

They do that blinking thing at each other again, then turn back to me. "I suppose not," Maybe-Nessa says glumly.

I put out my hand for a handshake, something I've found faeries believe to be binding.

They both put their cool, damp hands in mine and the three of us shake.

"A pleasure doing business with you girls. Enjoy the revel!" I call over my shoulder.

Thalia has just finished with Lord Yarrow and looks pleased with herself. "How'd it go?" she asks. She was the one who told me about the sisters' selkie deal this past summer; she has eyes and ears in every pocket of the Otherworld.

"I learned from the best," I say. "And you?"

"Yarrow is so easy, I just threatened to tell his wife about his trysts with the winged sprites from up north and he folded like a wet piece of parchment."

I take a satisfied sip from my goblet, though it's just water at this point. "Do you want Lord Garrett or the maid?" she asks.

"Garrett," I say. He's so drunk, there's a good chance he doesn't even remember.

"Wrong answer." Thalia smiles. Nothing brings her greater pleasure than seeing me uncomfortable.

"The maid is in love with me," I say. "I don't want her." I

hate the way she blushes and drops her tray whenever I come across her. It's so unbearably awkward."

She rolls her eyes. "They're all in love with you. Poor, sad, beautiful Emmett."

"Not all . . ."

She quirks a single brow.

I shrug. "Only most."

"I hate fighting like this, darling." She plants both her hands on my back and shoves me in the direction of the kitchens.

Lyra is standing over a tray of candied flowers, delicately dipping them one by one into a pot of molten sugar. Sure, she could replicate the candies by magic, but the court prefers things be done by hand as some sort of status symbol. That, and magic sometimes leaves an odd, burnt aftertaste.

It was Lydia who suggested the humans she found in the dungeons her first time in the Otherworld come to work in the kitchens, where she could protect them. They work alongside faeries like Lyra who have been employed here for hundreds of years.

Lyra startles and the violet in her hand drops and shatters at my feet. "My lord!"

"I told you, you don't have to call me that," I say.

She blushes deeply under a curtain of her white-blond hair. "What can I do for you?" she asks, a quiver in her voice.

"It's a bit embarrassing, but I came here to talk about something you may have seen earlier."

She nods. "Queen Lydia crying in the courtyard?"

That's something I'll need to check up on later.

"No . . . something with me and Queen Lydia's sister."

Understanding dawns and somehow she blushes even deeper. "You kiss so many girls at revels, but never me," she says.

"I respect you too much."

The poor thing tried to kiss me well over a year ago at some solstice bonfire. It was the best excuse my addled brain could come up with at the time.

She takes a step toward me. "I don't want you to respect me."

I take a step back. "I was dosed with a love potion tonight."

"I knew it," she says victoriously under her breath.

"We can't have King Bram find out," I say seriously. "Will you keep it a secret?"

She looks up at me. The kitchen smells of burnt sugar and violets. Lyra is such a sweet girl, but like so many others at court, she's fallen in love with a carefully crafted illusion. I think the only people who have ever truly known me are Ivy, Lydia, and Bram.

I pity Lyra and the other droves of maids and courtiers and bored wives like her. But to say I pity them is not to say I don't use them to my advantage.

Lyra may be sweet, she may be a servant, but she is a faerie, just like the rest of them. "What will I get in return for my silence?" she asks.

"A kiss," I say.

Her eyes go wide. "Please, please!"

"I kiss you and you will never speak of what you saw tonight to anyone. Do we have a deal?"

"Yes," she says.

I lean down and kiss her cheek. There's that snap, that sting of magic every time I make a bargain.

She stomps her foot. "That's not fair."

"You should know well enough that bargains need to be specific, love."

I pop a candied flower into my mouth and saunter out the door.

Thalia is waiting for me at the base of the staircase, a whole bottle of something dark slung in one hand.

"Done?" I ask.

"Done," she confirms.

There's no need for more talking; I know what comes next.

I follow her across the courtyard to the wing of the castle where a few select lords live on the castle grounds, but far enough away to give Bram privacy in the main wing.

It's freezing tonight, but I don't really feel it. I'm too numb.

Thalia's room always smells of sour smoke and spilled faerie wine. Her bed is the centerpiece: a behemoth, canopied and draped in rich red velvets.

It would be noble to say the first time I was here I was resentful, but that's not true. I didn't feel anything at all.

I think of what Bram said about Ivy. *She lets me into her bed as easy as breathing.*

I should hate her for it, just as she should hate me. But I don't hate her at all. I understand better than anyone.

Thalia pats the bed. "Come on, darling."

I unbutton my doublet and lie back on the pillows, feeling leaching from my limbs, thoughts floating from my head, until I'm barely anyone at all.

CHAPTER SEVENTEEN

I awake to a thump outside my door. Someone yelps. Another thump.

Barely alert, I throw a dressing gown over my thin nightdress and fling the door open.

Emmett is standing there, shirtless, a blanket and pillow on the floor beside him.

Next to him is Rhion, clutching his cheek and swearing.

"What is going on?" I exclaim.

Emmett shakes out his hand. "I punched Rhion."

Rhion curses again. "I tripped over him! He was lying on the floor in the dark!"

Dawn is rising, casting the long corridor of the castle in soft pink light and long purple shadows.

"Why are you outside my door?" I ask, sleepy and confused.

"I needed to speak with you, Your Majesty," Rhion says urgently.

I turn to Emmett. "And you?"

He doesn't answer, just looks at the floor. His hair brushes against his bare shoulder, and my eyes drift down his torso.

Look at his face, I chide myself. Now is not the time to be getting distracted by the planes of his muscled chest. His body has grown sharper in our time apart.

"Emmett?"

"I've been sleeping here," he admits.

"Excuse me?" I ask, confused.

"I've been sleeping here," he repeats.

"No, I heard you the first time. I'm confused as to why."

He gestures to Rhion. "To keep you safe from creeps like him."

"I'm on your side," Rhion protests. He's in a black doublet embroidered with purple crocuses; it's strange to see him not in one of his ridiculous outfits. The only human bit of his ensemble is a cameo he's wearing on a chain.

"You think I'm going to believe that after you brought my friends here?" I accuse him.

Rhion sighs. "Allow me to explain myself."

Emmett glances anxiously down the hall, clearly aware that anyone could see us here.

"Fine," I huff. "Come in, the both of you."

Like scolded schoolboys, they obey. I slam the door behind us. They take the two silk armchairs set by my fireplace. It's a little funny to see such large, masculine men in my decidedly fussy and feminine room. They're like toy soldiers in a dollhouse.

I perch on the end of my bed. The silk linens are mussed

from my fitful sleep. I've got a raging headache and would like nothing more than to be unconscious right now. The ghost of Emmett's kiss still haunts me.

I point between them. "Explain."

Emmett left the blanket outside, so he sits, bare-chested, wide-eyed in a transparent attempt to look innocent.

I hope Rhion thinks I'm staring him down as an intimidation tactic and not because I cannot bear to look at Emmett right now.

"Bram was always going to let you into the Otherworld," Rhion says. "He'd sent the invitations for the first trial weeks before."

"You put her in danger intentionally? I'll kill you," Emmett lashes out.

I have no time for Rhion's games or Emmett's petulance.

Emmett opens his mouth, but I hold up my hands. "Don't start."

I point to Rhion. "You—keep talking."

Rhion turns to Emmett. "Bram had his own plans already in motion. I needed to use them to our advantage."

"By turning on my friends?"

"I'll admit I was also the one who told him his other suitors would be at Marion Thorne's town house and to bring them to the Otherworld as leverage against you."

"So you were lying the whole time?" I say angrily. My friends are in danger because of my decision to trust Rhion. I think of Este waiting at home without her sister, of Ben and

Olive making tea cakes in the kitchen, of Eduart, completely alone in the world, save for us.

"You underestimate them," Rhion says emphatically. "They're rebels, radicals, they've been scheming and training for months. I had confidence you all could withstand whatever was coming. I tried to give them time to flee, but Faith and Marion stayed and fought to buy time for the others. I regret I wasn't fast enough, but it's not the worst thing that they're here in the Otherworld with us. More allies is a good thing."

"Still," I snap in return.

"I did it and it's done," Rhion says. "The girls put on a brilliant show."

"They were beaten."

"Not on my orders," Rhion replies emphatically. "I did my best to mitigate the damage. The guards who did it have been punished."

"But your actions still led to it."

"*Bram's* actions," Rhion corrects me.

"You betrayed me," I reply. I'm so foolish to have expected straightforward allyship from a faerie.

"I didn't. I swear it. I might have lied by omission, but we have the same goals. I knew Bram was planning on the trials, and I knew you needed an ally. He was growing suspicious after your visit to my town house. He didn't like that we'd been alone together. By my betraying you, Bram trusts me more than ever. I wield influence over him. You're here, in the Otherworld. That was always going to happen. Now you have two friends, and I have Bram's ear. I'm sorry I couldn't be more forthcoming with you, but I promise, from now on, I will be."

"I don't know how to believe you."

Rhion casts his gaze to the floor, his clear blue eyes full of pain. "Then don't. But know that I will do *anything* to ensure Lydia gets out of this unscathed. I have no regrets."

Emmett turns to Rhion, shocked. "Lydia?"

I roll my eyes, still annoyed. "He claims he's in love with her."

Emmett's expression darkens. "You're not good enough for her."

"I don't disagree with you," Rhion says.

"I'll kill you myself if you're lying about this," Emmett snarls.

"I'll help," I say.

Rhion shakes his head. "We share the same goals, the same as we always have. We need to get you and your sister through these trials, and we can use Bram's distraction to unseat him in the process."

"But how do we unseat him?" I ask. "We need a plan." I feel so hopeless, so naive. There's so much about the Otherworld I don't understand.

Emmett leans forward on his elbows. "I'm making progress there. I just need a little more time."

I look to him in surprise. "You are?"

Emmett glances sideways at Rhion, suspicious. "I won't give details, not with him here."

I'm so sick of not knowing, especially when it feels I'm finally getting close to what I came here for. This was always my plan: find a way to defeat Bram, and bring Lydia and Emmett back to an England that is safe from him.

I stand and reach for the doorknob. Both men look at me with surprise.

"Where are you going?" Emmett asks.

"Your room," I answer without breaking my stride.

Emmett stands to follow, then levels me with a glance, his hazel eyes as clever as ever. "My, Ivy, this is hardly the time to be seducing me." His voice is weak, though, and my heart hurts to see him trying to thaw the ice between us after the last disastrous few days.

I roll my eyes and point to Rhion. "Send for Queen Lydia. She's needed in Prince Emmett's room," I instruct. Rhion nods wordlessly and takes off down the stairs.

"Why my room?" Emmett asks once we are alone.

"Because you need to not be naked while we're having this conversation and I assume that's where you keep your shirts."

Emmett sidesteps me to unlock his door and I follow him inside.

"That's not fair." A hint of humor sneaks into his voice. "I'm only half-naked."

I take a seat on the bench by the roaring fire, and it's only then that a ripple of discomfort goes through me. It takes me a moment to identify why. It's because it looks so lived in, so *Emmett*.

There's a pile of leather-bound journals on the floor next to me. In the center of the room is a large desk, constructed of white stone with veins of lilac quartz. Atop it sits a stack of books from the human world, bound in leather with thick, uneven parchment, all from before Queen Mor shut the door between our worlds. One is opened to a handwritten copy of the Vulgate Cycle. There are other papers and dried-up inkwells scattered around it.

The blanket on the armchair behind the desk is the same color green as his quilt back at Kensington Palace. I half expect Pig to emerge, bleary-eyed, from beneath it.

There are a few cabinets that reach to the ceiling, but not much else in the way of decor. The bench by the fireplace is the only place long enough for Emmett to lie down, which might explain the blanket and embroidered pillow on the floor by my feet.

It's not a bedroom, I realize. It's an office.

Emmett crosses the room to his wardrobe and pulls a loose white shirt from one of the cabinets, then settles down in the window seat, adjusting himself on the silk pillows to face me. "I'm sorry about last night."

Involuntarily, my fingers drift up and brush against my bruised lips. "Don't be."

"Let me be, please," he whispers. "I would never . . ." He trails off and tries again. "I'd rather die than do anything you didn't want me to."

"I did want it."

"Not like that. Never like that." He pulls a hand through his hair. "I fixed it though."

"Fixed it?"

"Bram won't hear about it."

It hadn't yet occurred to me to be terrified of that, but of course, I should have been. "How?"

He looks so sad as he answers. "I called in a few favors."

He notices the way my eyes are roving around the room. "It's not Kensington," he says, like he's eager to change the subject.

"You never liked it much there, either," I offer.

"Not until you arrived," he says softly.

"This is your office." I don't mean it as an accusation but it sounds like one anyway. "Where do you sleep?"

He gestures vaguely to the bench I'm sitting on. "There, mostly."

I don't believe him. I want to prod at the subject, but the door swings open, and our eye contact breaks.

Lydia strides in wearing an apron over a white cotton dress. "Awfully early to pull me from bed. Quite rude, you two. No respect for your elders."

Emmett glances at her paint-smeared hands. "You weren't asleep."

Lydia glances at me, sisterly concern on her face. "Not the point. What did I miss?" she asks as she sits down beside me.

Rhion lingers in the doorway.

"Not you," Emmett calls.

Rhion's shoulders drop as the door shuts in his face.

Once settled back in the room, Emmett turns to Lydia. "I'm getting Ivy up to date on our little project."

"The updated dinner menus or the faerie-killing knife project?" she asks.

I blink. In my experience, faeries are invincible. Every injury is stitched back together as quickly as it was obtained. They never age. Never grow weaker. If I didn't know Bram had killed his father, I wouldn't think they could be killed at all.

"Faerie-killing knife?" Maybe it's stupid, but while I want Bram gone, viciously, completely, the thought of actually killing him leaves me reeling. Could I do it if it came to it? Could Lydia?

In my worst moments, I've thought perhaps Lydia was on Bram's side. That she'd stay loyal to him, win the competition to keep whatever power she has here.

Emmett can read the horror on my face. "We hope to just use it as a threat—something to convince him to abdicate his thrones for the good of both kingdoms."

"And if he doesn't?" I say uncomfortably.

Lydia pales. "He'll abdicate. I know he will."

"That's where Ferrinus comes in," Emmett offers.

"Ferrinus?" I'm lost.

"Ferrinus is the name of a legendary knife, one used to kill a faerie king. Bram used it to kill his own father after he banished his mother to England."

I'd always known in some way that Bram was responsible for his father's death, but it chills me to hear it said so plainly. "What kind of knife would be capable of killing a faerie? Is it magic?" I ask.

"Faeries can use magic to kill each other, but it doesn't touch Bram," Emmett explains.

Lydia nods. "It makes sense. The only way to have a new ruler is through regicide, so why wouldn't there be protections put in place for the king? Otherwise, it would be chaos."

"So a faerie can kill another faerie, but Bram can't be harmed."

"Exactly." Lydia nods gravely. "We believe only this knife can kill a royal."

"What kind of knife would be capable of that?" I shudder. But through the mist of memory, a page from *Faeries of the British Isles* comes back to me.

"Cold iron," I say. "That's what can kill a faerie."

Emmett snaps his fingers. "Precisely. Remember how those chains took down Queen Mor at your wedding?"

I prefer not to think of that day at all.

"Then we have to find it," I say. I feel horrible the moment the words leave my mouth. For all that Bram has done, not all of me wants him dead. But if we could use the knife somehow, to threaten him into giving up power or permanently closing the door between our worlds, then perhaps there is a way out of all of this. England would be free of him, and I would have my sister and Emmett back. For the first time since I came here, I feel like

I'm finally achieving what I set out to do.

"We're ahead of you there." Emmett crosses the room and pulls one of the journals from the stack at his bedside table.

He leans over Lydia and me, so close I can feel the heat of him. His long fingers riffle through the pages before settling on one in the middle.

"Here." In meticulous pencil, he's sketched a weapon. It looks less like a knife than a very sharp rock with a gilt handle.

"Cold iron!" I exclaim. "Cold as in *unforged*! It all makes perfect sense!"

"I've gathered accounts from hundreds of faeries and small folk alike," Emmett says. "As the story goes, after Bram banished his mother and killed his father, he disappeared for a day and a night. All we have to do is figure out where he went."

The door to Emmett's room swings open, making the three of us jump.

"If only you had someone who was there and knew exactly where Bram went." Rhion leans against the doorjamb gallantly.

Emmett sighs loudly and rolls his eyes. "You again."

"You're lucky no one ever uses this hall; your voice really does carry," Rhion replies.

"Or were you listening at the door with a glass pressed to your ear?" I retort.

Rhion shakes his head. "Nothing so undignified as all that." He pauses. "I used magic. Like a gentleman." His eyes flit to Lydia. I didn't think it was possible for Rhion to look bashful, but a blush creeps across the tops of his cheeks. "Your Majesty, I only want to help."

Lydia doesn't seem to notice; she's too focused on Emmett's sketch.

"Great." I stand. "Let's go. We could leave tonight. Rhion can tell us where—"

Rhion stops me. "You're not going without me."

There's tension in every line of Emmett's body. "I don't trust you."

Rhion sighs. "I won't let any harm come to—" He stops and his eyes land on Lydia. "I won't let any harm come to either queen."

"I don't like this," Lydia says softly.

"What if I gave you the knife to hold on to once we get it?" Rhion offers.

Lydia sucks her bottom lip between her teeth. "I suppose that could work. But then I must go with you to ensure you don't swap it out with a fake. I need to know it's the real one."

"Then I'm coming, too," Emmett insists.

"Then we must also bring Marion and Faith," I counter.

Emmett looks horrified.

I toss my hands up in frustration. "I'm not leaving them alone in this castle without us."

Emmett's face falls and I know he has relented.

Lydia turns to Rhion, who still can't meet her gaze. "How much longer will Bram be in England?"

"Not long: two days, maybe less. He told me he only needed

a day at court in England to tend to business. He's already been gone for a day and a half here. We don't have much time to waste."

I cross to the window and look out over the ragged landscape of the Otherworld. Far off in the distance, golden beams of light cut through the clouds to illuminate a dark forest at the base of a shadowy range of jagged mountains.

"We can't all leave," Emmett says. "Even with Bram gone, if both queens, his adviser, his regent, and his hostages go missing for two days, people will talk. This court runs on gossip."

"There's a revel tonight," Rhion says. "We'll go make an appearance, be very respectable, and then sneak out in the chaos. We'll have until late afternoon the next day to return. People will assume we're sleeping off our hangovers and Bram will be none the wiser when we return."

Emmett narrows his eyes. "I still don't like it."

"Tonight," I affirm.

"Bring a lock of hair, the button from your favorite coat, and something shiny," Rhion says.

"I can't tell if you're joking," I reply.

Rhion joins me at the window and looks out onto the expanse of the Otherworld. His long fingers flex against the windowsill. "I never joke about a quest."

CHAPTER EIGHTEEN

Faith and Marion are already under the tree when I arrive. Their shadowy figures are huddled together in the dark, but I recognize the shape of the gossamer veil Faith wears over her long dark hair. It ruffles in the breeze gently behind her, making them both look like phantoms.

The theme of tonight's party was Arthurian legend, and Faith dressed as Isolde. Beside her, Marion is Tristan, in brown leather riding boots and chain mail.

The drawstring pouch clutched in Faith's hand catches the moonlight as she holds it up. "I've got everything Rhion asked for."

She borrowed her shiny object, a pair of diamond earrings, from my wardrobe when we dressed for the revel together earlier tonight.

Tucked in the pocket of my cloak is a gold button, a small lock of my hair tied with a ribbon, and a sapphire ring.

There's a rustle in the dark blue shadows of the garden as more footsteps approach.

Lydia emerges, followed closely by Rhion, looking like a lost dog in her wake.

My sister's medieval-style dress swishes behind her, and she looks so small against the acres of the garden my heart aches with the desire to protect her.

She joins us under the boughs of the tree and glances up at the double moons in the sky. "Emmett will be just a moment."

"What's he doing?" I ask.

Lydia casts her gaze to the toes of her silk slippers in the dirt. "Tying up some loose ends."

Rhion has got a roll-top canvas pack slung on his back. He's wearing a linen tunic with a lion on his chest, the Lancelot to Lydia's Guinevere.

We wait a few minutes in tense silence, jumping at every snapping twig and rustling branch, until Emmett's shadow emerges from the cool mist.

"Sorry for the wait," he says as he approaches.

"Tying up loose ends?" Beneath my teasing is a genuine wish he'd tell me what he was doing. His life here is still almost entirely a mystery, and I know there are things happening at court he isn't telling me.

"Something like that," he says airily. "Shall we?"

Rhion nods, and we follow him dutifully out of the back gates of the castle, and into the dark expanse of wilderness.

The air feels immediately thicker here, under the dense canopy of leaves. The trees in the old-growth forest are spaced a few paces apart from each other, leaving gaps for shadows to dance like ghosts. I jump in fear and Emmett grabs my arm to steady me, then lets it go just as quickly. I take the opportunity to look at his costume. He's wearing a hooded chain-mail shirt with a breast plate, inlaid with stars. "Who are you supposed to be?" I ask. He shrugs vaguely. "A knight, I think."

I roll my eyes. "You're the laziest fancy-dress party attendee I've ever met, did you know that?"

"What about you?" He waves his hand at my navy-blue gown, my silver diadem with little crystals that hang down over my forehead.

"I'm the Lady of the Lake," I say indignantly.

"How long a journey will it be?" Lydia asks from up ahead.

Rhion tilts his head to the sky and takes a breath. "It depends on how kind the forest is feeling tonight."

"And how do we get it to be kind to us?" Faith asks. She lays a pale hand on the trunk of the nearest tree. "Please be nice, I'm already having quite a bad week."

Rhion looks at her, aghast. "Stop that. The trees hate sarcasm."

We walk in silence, our shoes crunching through the underbrush for what feels like ages.

Up ahead, the trees glow like something from a dream. It's difficult to tell if they're lit from within or if it's a trick of the light, and it sets my teeth on edge. "What is that?" Marion asks for all of us.

Rhion shoots a glare at Faith. "The seasons are changing. The trees are annoyed."

"I didn't realize they could hear me!" she protests.

"Hush, the both of you," Lydia scolds. "The trees aren't annoyed, they're . . . concerned."

As we approach, it's like we're stepping through time. In a blink, the dark, crisp autumn gives way to damp spring, ablaze with midday light.

I shield my eyes from the sun, so disoriented it's like the world has tipped beneath me.

Rhion is silent for a moment, like he's listening to a message on the breeze. "It's just a trick. We should carry on."

Our moods are noticeably tenser as we continue. My slippers quickly grow damp with dew, rotting fruit, and crushed pink flower petals that litter the ground. The sun on the back of my neck is making me sweat. It plays over the leaves, casting patterns like light on water.

And then there's the weight of Emmett's gaze on me.

After an hour or so of walking, we come across a silver babbling brook, and above it, a quaint little bridge in the shape of a crescent moon.

"We'll go over one by one," Rhion explains. "Does everyone have their button?"

I brush the cool metal where it rests in the pocket of my cloak. We all nod.

"Good," Rhion says. "There's a spirit who lives under the bridge. Drop the button into the water while you think of a memory associated with it."

"With the button?" Faith clarifies.

"Yes, the button."

"How do we know it's not a trick and you're not just bargaining away our bones to the creature or something?" Emmett asks.

"Your *bones?*" Rhion asks, his blue eyes wide with disgust. "Emmett De Vere, you have a horrifying imagination."

"But, like, just the bones?" Faith asks.

"We'd be gooey but otherwise unharmed?" Marion adds.

"Ew." I swat Marion's arm. "Don't use the word *gooey.*"

"Floppy?" Marion asks.

"Nothing is going to happen to your bones!" Rhion shouts. Lydia laughs.

"I'll go first, how about that?" Rhion offers. "You'll see that my bones and I are completely unharmed."

Emmett bites the inside of his cheek. "We've come this far. I suppose that's fair."

The bridge looks as if it could have been constructed yesterday. The wood is shiny and free of rot. There are even two baskets of fresh pansies hanging cheerily off its posts.

"Follow quickly," Rhion instructs, and we all arrange ourselves into a single-file line behind him. "I don't want you in this part of the forest without me."

With one last, longing glance at Lydia, he steps onto the bridge. His footsteps echo as he crosses the wooden planks, but right as he reaches the crest, he disappears. Gone. Like he was never there at all.

"Rhion!" Lydia calls. She's so panicked her voice cracks

around his name. "Rhion!"

Emmett looks at her with shock, at this evidence she might actually care for Rhion in return.

"Follow, quickly!" Rhion's voice is a few shades quieter, as if it's coming from the rustling green leaves in the trees surrounding us.

"I'll go." Faith plants a quick kiss on Marion's lips and steps onto the bridge. Like Rhion, she vanishes a few paces in, but this time, I listen close enough to hear a splash as her button hits the water.

Marion follows closely after, then Lydia, leaving Emmett and I alone.

The sun shifts and bends like candlelight, and the air clings thick and hot to my skin like a velvet cloak. The dappled light of the trees dances over his dark hair as he looks at me.

"You go," he says, his voice low and gravelly. "I'm not leaving you here alone."

"You think I want to leave *you* here alone?" Despite everything, or perhaps because of it, it's awful, unnatural, to be separated.

He reaches down and squeezes my hand. "Go on," he urges, "I'll see you on the other side."

The quicker I go, the sooner it will be over with, so I gather my courage and step onto the bridge.

The hollow wood makes a dull *thunk* as my feet hit it, and then the whole world shifts.

An icy wind whips my cloak around me as the lights go

dim, like the sun was snuffed out by a rolling thundercloud. Drifts of snow flutter around my feet like phantoms, and the forest seems to spin around me like a top.

"What have you come to offer me?" The voice is young and old. Soft and screaming. It could belong to one person or one hundred, and it's coming from inside my own head.

I reach into my cloak and am relieved to find the comforting, smooth surface of the button. I tore it off a white coat I found in my wardrobe late this evening before the revel. Marion and Faith have the other two.

"This." My voice trembles.

I extend my hand, revealing the button resting in the center of my palm. Tiny shards of ice carried by the wind sting as they pierce the delicate skin of my wrist.

"Mmmm." The voice purrs, pleased. "And the memory?"

The memory, the memory . . . My brain scrambles, trying to find something. Rhion said a memory associated with the button, right? I cast my mind back to my room, how I giggled with Marion and Faith as we ripped off the buttons and snipped small locks of our hair.

The voice in my head snarls like a cornered animal. Its claws scrape against some fundamental part of me and I shiver. "Not that, that's *nothing.*"

Nothing, nothing, nothing. The word clangs like a bell. I want to clap my hands over my ears, but I know that won't make it stop.

"What about this?" I offer, fully panicking now. Through

the drum kick of my heartbeat, I picture Emmett walking through the forest beside me, the broad line of his shoulders, his perfect face lit up by beams of silver moonlight, how I ache for him, even when he's close enough to reach out and touch.

"This means nothing to you." The voice in my head is disgusted. "You have insulted me."

"No, no—" I protest, but the forest stops, then whirls counterclockwise around me. I blink and find myself suddenly somewhere else.

I land hard enough to knock the wind from my chest, splayed out on cold, hard dirt.

I wheeze in and out for a few shaky breaths, and though my lungs eventually fill, it does little to calm my racing pulse.

"Emmett?" I call, but I hear nothing save for the far-off snapping of twigs and soft whisper of leaves in the dark. The air is cool, layered with the sweet smell of autumn once more.

I push myself to my feet, and through the thick wall of brush in front of me, I see the glowing, faintly purple lights of the castle.

I realize I'm right on the edge of the garden, where we began our journey. It seems my punishment from the bridge spirit was being spat out of the forest entirely.

My heartbeat slows and I sigh in relief. There are far worse punishments than being sent back to my warm bed for the night. The knife's edge of anxiety still cuts me, but I have confidence Marion, Faith, Rhion, Lydia, and Emmett are more than capable of finishing the journey on their own. Surely it doesn't take more than five people to find one knife.

The gardens are quieter than they usually are on revel nights. Perhaps without Bram or Emmett here to encourage merrymaking, the court isn't in their finest form tonight.

The doors to the castle swing open silently, and I'm surprised to find the great hall has changed colors. The walls were sage green when I left this evening, but someone has magicked them to a pale purple. It's a strange choice. It doesn't particularly match tonight's Camelot theme and I can't imagine Bram will be pleased to find his castle altered when he returns from England.

It's not my problem. At least, it's not my problem tonight. Exhaustion hits me like a physical object, like I've been awake for days, and I look forward to flopping into my own bed and not moving until morning.

I've only climbed one stair when a gasp from behind startles me.

It's Bram.

His face is one of shock. His full lips hang open, his brows knit together; even his hair looks strange. It's shorter than it was when I saw him last, just two days ago. It's not like him to change it.

"Ivy?" He chokes out my name.

"Oh, darling!" I put on my cheeriest voice, but inside I'm terrified. I must distract him so he doesn't notice the others are gone. "You've returned so soon!"

He keeps standing there, frozen, his mouth agape like he's seen a ghost.

The doors to the throne room open and an old man steps into the hall. He's got a full head of snow-white hair and a closely cropped beard to match. His face is lined with age, but he's retained the height and straight posture of a much younger man.

I'm taken aback, realizing he's the first elderly human I've seen in the Otherworld. It's disorienting. He must have quite a story to have survived here for so long.

"Bram?" the old man asks, and I'm even more confused, wondering why he's so familiar with the king.

But then he steps into the light, right at Bram's side, and recognition hits me like an anvil to the heart. It's as if I can feel each one of my ribs snap in unison.

It's the eyes.

Those clever hazel eyes are exactly the same.

"Ivy?" Emmett's voice is hoarse with age, but I'd recognize it anywhere.

I'm sobbing now. Big heaving breaths I can't catch. My lungs won't expand fully. It's like I'm drowning. I can hardly get the words out.

"How long have I been gone?" I cry. The spirit under the bridge cast me out as a punishment, but I never imagined this.

I can't look at Emmett's wizened hands, the blue veins stark against the thin skin. Instead, I look at Bram. Ageless, perfect Bram, forever eighteen.

I've missed it all. Emmett's whole life, the life we could have shared together. I thought two years was agonizing, but this is *everything.*

It's over. It's done. I've missed it.

Bram looks to Emmett, then back to me. I collapse, no longer able to support myself, and they both catch one arm before my knees hit the stone stairs.

"Seventy years," Emmett says in a pained whisper. "You disappeared seventy years ago."

FAITH FAIRCHILD

Rhion takes my hand as I hop down off the bridge. I'm shaking a little, but at least it was over quickly.

That awful voice rang out in my head, and for a moment I was terrified it wasn't going to accept my button, but then I gave it a memory of kissing Marion under the tree before the others arrived and it was satisfied.

"That was horrible," I say to Rhion. In the branches above us, the birds sing a cheery song.

Rhion looks to the bridge anxiously, awaiting Lydia, I suspect. "The spirit is mostly harmless. Its bark is bigger than its bite."

"How do you know?"

"I've been coming here for many, many years. We're practically old friends by now."

Marion appears and I breathe a sigh of relief and extend a hand to help her down. She gives me a quick peck on the lips and I smile. "Well, that was terrifying," she says.

Lydia appears just a few moments after and Rhion rushes

to her, but she refuses his hand, leaving him crestfallen. "I'm fine," she says, voice a little thin.

It's funny; Emmett and Ivy may be skeptical of his devotion to Lydia, but I have little doubt it's genuine. It's hard to fake looking that forlorn. The way he yearns for her is nearly palpable.

We all face the bridge, waiting for Ivy, but minutes tick by and she doesn't appear. Marion and I share an uncomfortable glance but don't voice our fears.

Finally, we hear the dull echo of footsteps, but it's not Ivy who comes down from the bridge. It's Emmett's boots that step onto the soft spring grass.

He scans the four of us, and a look of panic crosses his face. "Where is Ivy? She went through before I did."

Rhion curses under his breath and, without hesitation, steps back onto the bridge, disappearing like vapor.

Lydia stands on her toes and strains to look after him, but he's vanished completely.

She lets out an audible sigh of relief when he reappears, just moments later.

"I have good news and bad news," Rhion announces. "Which would you like first?"

"The good news?" Lydia says cautiously.

"Ivy is fine."

"What?" Emmett roars.

"I just said she's fine."

"Little comfort when you just said there's also bad news."

Emmett's brows furrow in anger.

Rhion's dark hair is wild and tousled. "The bridge spirit didn't accept Ivy's button. He was very offended by the lack of memories attached to it. He's sent her back to the castle."

Emmett's shoulders drop and he exhales. "She's safe, though?"

"As ever." Rhion nods.

Lydia presses her lips together hard enough that the blood drains from them, then takes a sharp breath. I can tell she's uncomfortable with the whole purpose of this quest but is trying to be strong for Ivy. Perhaps for Emmett as well, but I can't quite parse the particulars of their relationship. Marion says I'm too nosy, but I prefer the term *curious*.

"Let's keep going, then," Lydia says quietly. "Where to now?"

Rhion points up ahead, to a path of pastel cobblestones that winds through the darkest part of the wood. "You must remember, for most of Bram's life, he was the crown prince and the castle was his parents' home. We constructed this cottage when we were little more than boys as a private retreat. The night Bram—" Rhion hesitates, searching for the right word. I also believe his love for Bram is real. He and Lydia seem similarly pained at the prospect of harming him. I don't share their reservations.

"The night Bram took the throne," Rhion continues, "we came here, to the cottage."

Lydia's eyes flash, and I know she's picturing it. Bram's

hand dripping with blood, Rhion beside him, panicked as fires burned and chaos reigned in the castle.

It was the night Mor came to England and made the bargain with King Edward IV, the night that started everything.

"What was Bram's dad like?" I ask.

Rhion takes a sharp breath through his nose. "A lot like Bram."

We walk for another half hour or so, and no one seems brave enough to talk. There is an omnipresent eerie feeling that there are many listening ears in this wood. I hold Marion's hand and hope it communicates all I am unable to say with words: *I'm here, I love you, don't be afraid.*

But I know Marion well enough by now to know she's not afraid. Much like me, she reaches anger much quicker than she gets to fear.

She's been particularly outraged these last few days. At first, she wanted to wring Ivy's and Rhion's necks for getting us kidnapped and stuck in the dungeons for a night. She tolerated the discomfort just fine, but she was incensed I was uncomfortable for even a moment.

Our quarters now are much more comfortable, but we still spend most of our time talking about what we'll do when we're home. Marion's bargain with Queen Mor to make her a talented writer might have been broken, but she never needed it in the first place. Her ability to sell her stories, to make income on her own, has opened the whole world to us.

It's Emmett I can't quite read. It's eerie to see this new,

slightly older, faerie-touched version of him. The humidity is causing his longer hair to curl around his ears and his mouth is set in a scowl. Somehow, I think he's gotten even taller than the last time I saw him in Kensington.

There was a time I thought I knew him better than anyone. I don't think I know him at all anymore.

I quicken my steps until we're walking next to each other. "She'll be fine," I whisper.

My words don't seem to give him much comfort. His smile is tight and doesn't touch his eyes. "Thank you."

Ahead of us, Rhion slows. We've reached the cottage.

It sits in a circular clearing in the woods, bathed in a perfect beam of yellow sunlight. It's constructed of the same pastel stone as the path, with an arched wooden front door and window boxes spilling over with flowers.

Marion points to the chimney, puffing smoke into the clear blue sky. "Someone is home."

"Shit," Rhion hisses. "I feared this might be the case."

He marches up to the door and pulls the handle, but it doesn't budge. "You're trespassing!" he calls as his fists pound the door.

The door opens a crack, revealing one large green eye at the height of Rhion's knee. "We weren't expecting visitors," a reedy voice answers.

Rhion puts his hands on his hips and looks down. "It's my cottage."

The door swings fully open and a hand with long, sharp

fingers waves us in. "Come in, come in, then!"

Marion looks calculating.

"Should we stay out here?" I ask.

"I might trust the woods less than I trust the cottage. Besides, he can't be more than four feet tall, right? We could overpower him."

The five of us shuffle into the cottage and the door slams behind us.

I blink rapidly as my eyes adjust to the sudden low light. The creature who waved us through the door isn't alone. I spot six others in my immediate eyeline bustling around the cottage. One has a feather duster and is climbing up the curtains; another stirs a boiling pot of soup on the hearth.

"Let us offer you something to drink," the one from the door says. He's got a mostly human face, but a mouth that seems slightly too full of teeth. His clothes are dark green, constructed of leaves sewn together, and on his head, he wears a top hat. In fact, they're all wearing strange headwear. The one at the hearth is balancing a pot on his head; another wears a massive, upside-down flower.

"No," Rhion replies with a gracious wave. "We won't be staying long."

"The cottage was vacant when we found it," the creature at the hearth pipes up.

"We haven't been here in many years," Rhion explains. "But I fear the king may not take kindly to your presence, if it is discovered."

"Will you tell him?" the one by the hearth asks.

"I will not," Rhion answers. I immediately like him a little better, because I can tell he means it.

It's strange to see such small beings in a cottage clearly meant to accommodate much larger men, like Bram and Rhion. The cottage itself is homey, if a little dark. Dust-flecked beams of light stream through star-shaped windows, and the furniture is mostly navy-blue and deep purple. In addition to the overstuffed armchairs and sofa, there is an array of carved wooden chairs. It's hard to determine what decor was Bram and Rhion's and what belongs to their squatters. In front of the hearth, a row of strange animal skulls are strung up, and I have to hope they're a more recent addition.

My nose stings with the smell of firewood, herbs, and something slightly metallic.

Marion, Emmett, and I sink uneasily onto the sofa in the middle of the room, and Rhion positions himself protectively in the chair nearest Lydia.

Despite our insistence that we didn't want anything to drink, another man appears at our feet and pushes a pewter cup into each of our hands. They're full of a dark liquid that smells of wet dirt. Rhion shakes his head slightly, a sign not to drink, but I didn't need his warning.

"We're here on an errand," Rhion explains. "I'm looking for a knife a friend of mine left here a few hundred years ago. It would probably be in the back of a wardrobe. If you'll allow me to look around—" At the suggestion, every one of the cottage's inhabitants freezes. The stirring halts. The dusting stops. A scrub brush drips water onto the floor from where it's held in midair.

"No!" the one from the door answers. "That won't be necessary. We'll bring you every knife we have and you can tell us if it is the correct one."

Before we can protest, they scurry off in a dozen different directions. Crashes and clangs come from the adjacent rooms, and soon they reappear, their arms full of items wrapped in a rainbow of fabric scraps and old rags.

"I'll go first!" one wearing a stocking cap pipes up.

He lays an object about the size of my forearm, wrapped in a dish towel, on Rhion's lap and then looks up at him expectantly. Rhion rolls his eyes, then reaches into his pocket and fishes out a ruby brooch.

The creature reaches out with one of his eerily long fingers and snatches the brooch, then holds it up to the light, apparently satisfied.

Rhion unrolls the object on his lap and sighs in disappointment as he reveals a kitchen knife.

One by one they come stand at our knees and one by one we give them the shiny objects we carried with us into the woods. In exchange for an earring, I receive a paring knife. Marion ends up with a whittling knife, Emmett with a butter knife, Lydia with a small hatchet.

But in the corner by the hearth rests a pile of more wrapped objects. We haven't gotten anywhere close to revealing every potential knife.

"We have nothing more to give," Rhion says. "Please let me search through the remaining knives and we'll leave you with our warmest wishes."

The creatures glance between themselves, their clever eyes not quite human. This whole place gives me the creeps. I long to take Marion by the hand and leave at once.

"No, no, you have more to give," the one stirring the soup says.

"I assure you—" Rhion begins to say, but he's interrupted.

"Your shadow, perhaps?" the one by the window says.

"A day of your life, but I pick which one!" the creature at the fire offers.

"Please—" Rhion holds up his hands, but he's interrupted by the creature sitting at his feet.

"Kiss her!" He points to Lydia with his sharp fingernail. "A kiss for a knife!"

"No," Rhion says forcefully, and at once, the easygoing, good-humored version of him disappears. It's in the deepening of his voice, or the squaring of his shoulders. I understand at once why Rhion is Bram's best friend, his closest adviser. His easy smile hides frightening strength beneath.

"But you love her!" the creature shouts, his voice sharp and dry.

Lydia blushes deeply and shifts in her seat. Rhion can't even look at her, but he doesn't deny it.

"*You love her! You love her! You love her!*" All of them are singing in chorus now. The creatures seem to be multiplying.

A leg swings down from the rafters, grazing my head, and Marion throws her weight protectively over me. Emmett stretches his long arms out over us both.

"That's enough," Rhion commands.

The one closest to Rhion stands on his tippy-toes and puts his hands on his hips. "Fine, I'll kiss her myself!" he declares, then scrambles up onto the chair and puckers his lips. Lydia recoils and both Emmett and I stand to pull him off of her, but before we've even had the chance to stand from the couch, Rhion's kitchen knife is through the creature's chest. "You will not touch her," he growls.

Blood drips off the hilt into the worn fabric of the sofa.

Rhion wrenches the knife out, the body thumps to the floor, and chaos erupts.

Immediately, sharp nails dig into my back as the creatures behind the couch attempt to climb onto me. Marion wrenches them off, then kicks to get them off her own leg, but hers won't budge.

"Damn Redcaps!" Rhion yells as he drives his knife again and again through the throng, but they just seem to keep coming. They spill from the side rooms, from the rafters, even wiggling down the chimney to bound over the fire toward Lydia. One's dirt-covered nails are primed to gouge her eyes out, but Rhion doesn't let him get close enough. The Redcap is dead before he hits the floor.

Lydia runs to the corner and crouches down at the pile of knives. She unwraps them as quickly as she can, kicking away the Redcaps who come at her.

As we fight, their strange hats fall off, revealing they each wear an identical stocking cap of bloodred.

Marion is still shaking her leg wildly, but the Redcap holds on, digging his fingers into her flesh. The minute I see he has drawn blood, my vision flashes red and I pick up Lydia's small axe, discarded on the sofa beside me.

There's nothing but instinct and thrumming fear as I hack and hack until the Redcap is in pieces and Marion is free.

"I'm going to kiss you about that later!" she calls as she grabs her own knife and goes to help Rhion, who has at least six Redcaps clinging to his back and screaming as they try to take him to the ground.

I smile and taste blood in my mouth.

Emmett is trying to make his way to Rhion, but is too busy fighting his own battle. A Redcap has dropped down onto Emmett's head and is using his sharp nail to leave a long bloody scratch across Emmett's cheekbone. He shouts and drives his dull butter knife into the creature's eye socket. Now without a weapon, he uses his fists to pummel the crowd trying to bring him to the ground until I can't tell if the blood on his knuckles is his own or the Redcaps'.

Lydia sprints for the door, hurtling over three who try to stop her. "I don't think it's here!" she calls.

"We won't harm you!" one shouts from Rhion's back. "You're so pretty and so kind to all forest folk. All hail Queen Lydia!"

Lydia hesitates; it's clear she has no desire to harm these creatures, which is almost funny considering how willing she was to dump that unicorn's body at Bram's feet. But I understand Lydia even less than I understand Ivy.

The boys are both wearing chain mail, which helps a little, but their necks and limbs are still exposed. The creature sinks his sharp teeth into the soft skin of Rhion's hand, and Rhion lets out a cry of pain.

Lydia's eyes darken, and with a swift kick to the Redcap nearing her feet, she wrenches the door open. The Redcaps recoil against the light and hiss, their bloodthirst seemingly reaching a fever pitch.

Rhion tries to force his way to the bedroom, but there are simply too many of them. They cling to his arms and legs, slowing him down like quicksand.

"We must go!" Lydia shouts over the din.

"We need the knife!" Rhion retorts in a strangled voice. There's one hanging around his neck, choking off his airway. I don't know if faeries need to breathe the same way humans do, but his face is turning purple and that doesn't seem good.

Marion and I keep hacking away against the endless stream of them as we make our way closer to the door. For each Redcap we fight off, another appears to take his place. The once-brown floorboards run red with blood, but the Redcaps seem delighted by it. They slip and slide and dip the tips of their caps in the mess with glee.

"You'll never find it!" The one at Rhion's back lets out a

sharp giggle. "Never, ever, ever!"

"It's not here?" Rhion chokes out in horror. Blood drips off his knife and onto the fabric of his breeches.

"We need to go!" Lydia shouts again. "Please, Rhion."

And because it's her who asked, he relents. I watch as the tension falls from his shoulders and the fire in his eyes dims to embers.

He raises his arms above his head and brings his knife down with brutal power. In three stabs, he is free.

But another yell pierces the air and the air grows thicker as I notice Emmett, still trapped deep inside the chaos. A Redcap jumps from the edge of the sofa, flying at Emmett, a blade poised to strike him right in the side of his neck. It's as if time slows. I can't get there fast enough. "Emmett!" I scream.

His eyes meet mine. I'm so panicked, so agonizingly sad that my friend's life is going to end like this after all he's endured.

But right before the knife sinks into his jugular, the Redcap is struck with a flying dagger. It lands with a *thwack* in the center of his chest and he goes falling to the floor.

Emmett tosses the other one he's fighting off his back and checks the small wound on his neck. "I had it!" he calls to Rhion, who rolls his eyes across the room.

Lydia stands with the door wrenched open. "Now!" she screams.

Blood-slicked and panting, we tumble onto the front porch. The bright, clear day is jarring after the chaos inside.

Lydia leaps off into the grass and Marion and I soon follow, leaving Emmett and Rhion staring up at the house together. For a moment, I'm terrified they're about to go back inside, but Emmett whispers something to Rhion, who nods, then presses his hands together. When he pulls them apart, there's a small ball of fire balanced between his palms. He takes a breath, then hurls it onto the thatched roof of the cottage.

The straw goes up like a match, immediately burning down to the rafters and filling the clearing with thick smoke.

The Redcaps shriek and wail, and it sets my teeth on edge.

"We need to go, *now*, before they come out and chase us," Marion says.

Rhion nods, but just as he turns to leave, a Redcap sticks his little head through what's left of the smoldering chimney and lets out a laugh that cuts straight to my bones.

"You'll never find it, you fools! We threw it in the Isern Caves!" He laughs and laughs until the smoke is so thick, it blocks him from view completely. I think I still hear his giggle as the cottage collapses.

Emmett stomps through the clearing and runs a hand through his hair, which is now crusted with dirt and blood. Our faces don't look much better. My heart pounding, I turn to Marion and place my hands on her face, tipping and prodding until I'm satisfied she's unharmed. She leans down and gives me a quick peck on the cheek. "I never thought I'd long for rainy England," she whispers in my ear, making me laugh.

I love her so much it makes my chest hurt.

We follow the path out of the clearing, back to the footbridge.

"The caves—" Rhion starts, but Emmett marches ahead of him.

"I'm not discussing any of this until we find Ivy," he says tightly.

Which leaves the rest of us trailing behind him, trying to keep up with his long legs. Emmett always walks too fast—it's one of the most annoying things about him, and there's plenty I still find annoying about Emmett.

Rhion takes a position at the back of the pack, seemingly unwilling to let Lydia out of his sight. "Thank you," she says quietly, after we've been walking awhile.

"For what?" Rhion asks.

"Saving Emmett."

I don't turn back to look, but Rhion lets out a disappointed sigh. "Of course. Anything—" He stops himself. I'm fairly certain he was just about to say *for you*.

"I didn't need saving!" Emmett calls without turning around.

"You were about to be stabbed in the neck!" Rhion replies.

"Just say thank you, Em," Lydia says.

"Thank you, Rhion," Emmett groans, and Marion and I both stifle a laugh.

The spirit of the footbridge doesn't demand payment for our return journey. I say thank you anyway, and that haunting voice pops into my head, all huffy this time, and says, "I have a sense of honor, you know."

Emmett lingers a little too long and I know he's asking about Ivy. When he exits, some of the anxiety has left his face, but his shoulders are still tense. "It says it sent her back to the castle gardens."

The woods turn from bright spring back to midnight autumn in a blink, leaving me shivering. I lost my cloak in the cottage, so Marion and I huddle together for the rest of the journey.

"I understand the button and the jewelry," I say as we walk through the trees, "but why the lock of hair?"

Rhion fishes into his pocket and pulls it out. At first, I think it's a trick of the moonlight, so I lean closer. The hair has gone white, completely leached of color.

I pull my own lock of hair from my pocket and it's exactly the same.

"The forest likes to play tricks," Rhion says. "My friend Lord Fernly's hair is still white after a trip to the cabin in our youth. It's best to provide a decoy."

I can't wait to never set foot in this forest again.

We don't hear the screams until the castle is back in view, a glowing opalescent beacon in the dark.

Emmett doesn't say a word, he just takes off running, suddenly in a full sprint. His boots crash through dried leaves, and he leaps over bushes and dodges trees until he's gone from sight.

The rest of us follow, the high-pitched, terror-filled shrieks as our guide.

It isn't difficult to find her. Emmett has beat us to it, but not by much.

Ivy is on the ground in the fetal position, rocking back and forth and whimpering. Emmett pulls her onto his lap and brushes her tangled hair away from her face.

"Shh," he whispers. "You're safe, you're safe," he says soothingly.

Ivy gasps, as if waking up, then begins sobbing anew. She reaches up and grabs his face with both her hands. "I thought I lost you," she chokes out. "I thought I missed it."

"Missed what, sweetheart?" Emmett asks, his eyes so full of longing and agony and love I feel almost guilty witnessing this moment.

"The life we're supposed to have together." Then she crushes her mouth to his. Emmett stiffens and then, as if giving up on some internal battle, he melts and kisses her back.

CHAPTER NINETEEN

I pull back from the kiss, dizzy and disoriented. I cling to Emmett's broad shoulders for purchase, and gasp when I see him fully.

"What happened?" I ask. Every part of him is covered in blood. It's crusted in his hair, running in streaks down his face and splattered over his chain-mail shirt.

My head spins. Just a moment ago, I was in the castle, sobbing on the stairs, and now I'm here.

"What happened to you?" Emmett asks, his hazel eyes full of concern and focused solely on me.

"The bridge spirit didn't accept my button and sent me back to the castle, and you were there but—" I swallow a sob as the image crashes back to me. "You said I'd been missing for seventy years, that I was too late."

Emmett plucks a dried leaf from where it's stuck in my hair and flicks it to the ground. "And then what?" he asks softly.

"And then I blinked and you were here, covered in blood." His hazel eyes are nearly green in contrast to the crimson rivulets that have dried down his face. It's a shocking sight, but I'm just so relieved to see him looking like himself again.

"It was a trick," Rhion says from behind Emmett. "A cruel trick, but nothing more than a nasty dream."

My heart slows but the tears don't stop coming. Emmett pulls me tightly to his chest. "Shh, it's all right."

"They're happy tears." How do I begin to explain the depth of my relief? The new clarity?

I glance at their empty hands. "I take it you didn't get the knife?"

Emmett helps me to my feet, and we walk through the icy gardens back to the castle. They tell me of their bloody encounter with the Redcaps.

The six of us cut through the revel up to Rhion's private quarters, which strongly resemble his house in Bath. I have to duck to avoid the fishing net adorned with forks strung up over his doorway.

"It looks just like your house in England," I remark, thinking of his strange group of fawning humans. "Sans all your . . . friends."

Rhion pauses and glances to Lydia, then back to me. "I hope they think of me as a friend. I was trying to save them from Bram and the rest of the court. I attempted to get that poor girl in the deer mask to come inside, too, but she refused me."

I regret my petty comment and am reminded of all we have to lose if we don't succeed. "That was kind of you, Rhion."

We move papers and books and silk shoes to find surfaces on which to sit. Emmett and I end up folded together on an armchair near the fire, with Marion, Faith, and Rhion all perched on the edge of his bed. Lydia chooses to stay standing and spends more of her time looking through the titles on his bookcase than at us.

"So they threw Ferrinus in these caves?" I clarify, still playing catch-up. My eyes keep lingering on Emmett, young and whole, beside me. My heartbeat has yet to return to its normal speed.

"That's what he said." Rhion sighs and lies back onto a beaded pillow, his dark hair a fan around him.

"So why not go get it? I'll bring a better button next time, I promise."

Emmett cuts me off. "The caves are forbidden for obvious reasons. Cursed a millennium ago. No one goes near them."

"Cursed?" I ask. "Cursed how?"

This time, it's Lydia who answers. "No one quite knows. The only thing the legends say is that what exists in the caves is pain, pure pain."

"But the Redcaps went?"

Emmett shakes his head. "No, they likely just stood at the mouth and tossed the knife into its depths to be rid of it. I'm sure it made them squeamish."

Marion snorts. "They seemed plenty comfortable with sharp objects to me."

"They say the blade is cursed. Its existence makes everyone uncomfortable. Regicide isn't exactly a dinner table conversation. Not even for Redcaps," Rhion replies. "No one wants to think about what it takes to kill the unkillable."

"But we're not going to kill him," Lydia adds sharply from over at the bookcase. She's thumbing through a volume bound in sky-blue leather, but I can tell she's not reading a single word.

"Someone will have to rule after him," Faith says. "Are we putting Mor back on the throne?"

Rhion chews on the inside of his cheek. "Perhaps, if we could guarantee she wouldn't use her power to come back to England. If not her, there are other candidates, a few lords I don't completely despise. Lady Thalia. Emmett."

Emmett stiffens. "Or you."

"I don't have a taste for it," Rhion replies. "What about you?"

Emmett sinks his teeth into his bottom lip. "I'm unsuited to rule."

"What if the land won't accept anyone but Mor?" Lydia says.

"The land?" I'm confused again.

"Do you remember when I explained to you how the door between worlds works?" Rhion asks. "How the magic between the regent and the Otherworld itself are deeply intertwined? It means the land must approve of the new ruler. Ferrinus may pierce Bram's heart, but unless the land feels we have a worthy replacement, we will be left without a ruler and chaos will reign."

"But that almost definitely won't happen," Emmett assures me.

"And we're not going to stab him in the heart, Rhion," Lydia scolds. "He'll abdicate once we present him with his options."

"A figure of speech!"

Lydia keeps scowling. I'm terrified to ask her what comes after. What if she plans to stay with him?

"None of this works if we don't have the blade," I say instead. "Send me to the caves."

"It's not possible," Rhion says. "The caves are a full day's journey, and Bram will be back any moment now—and not leave for several more weeks, months even. He'll notice you're gone."

The idea hits me like lightning. I bite back a smile. "Then we'll bring Bram with us."

I catch Lydia's eye from across the room and she nods almost imperceptibly, but we're sisters, which means I can read her mind.

"Convince Bram to make it the second trial. Send us both in."

It's not quite dawn when I find Emmett at my door. Daylight is only a vague promise, a pencil-thin outline of orange along the mountains in the distance.

I'm bleary-eyed in a white nightdress, and Emmett looks

like something from a dream. In the soft light, he looks so perfect I still find it difficult to believe he's real.

"What are you doing?" My voice is gravelly with disuse.

"Looking at you," Emmett says softly as he leans against my doorjamb. His hazel eyes are heavy-lidded with sleep, his mouth full, his tan neck exposed by the open collar of his shirt.

"Then come in and do it properly."

If this were six months ago, he would have made a joke, said something like *Oh, Lady Ivy, what about your reputation?* Or *Are you that eager to be ravished by me?*

But this new Emmett is as impossible to grasp on to as wisps of smoke. Something haunts him, and his easy jokes have evaporated on the wind.

Plus, he already had me, in the dark of his room in Kensington Palace, when we did something together we can't ever take back.

My room is dim with only the flickering in the fireplace for light. The fires never seem to need extra fuel here; they just keep on burning.

I suppose it's a little like how I feel for Emmett. He could give me nothing in return, but the desire I feel for him never lessens.

I crawl back into bed and motion for him to follow. The anxiety over what I might face today in the caves is like a physical weight around my neck, dragging me down.

It wasn't difficult to convince Bram to make the caves the

second trial. Rhion needed only to make Bram think it was his idea. It took a few days of mentioning the caves during dinners and revels before Bram announced his brilliant new idea to court. It took just two days to organize after that. We'll leave this afternoon, and I'd be lying if I said I wasn't terrified, but I'll be glad to have it over with.

Yesterday, Emmett pulled every book from the library, and still, the only information we could find was *What lies within the Isern Caves is pain. Pure, unadulterated pain.*

It's as if any additional details have been intentionally struck from the record.

I don't relish the idea of feeling pain, but I know it will be temporary. I will take this gladly over another creature suffering on my behalf.

Emmett stands now at the edge of my bed. "Get in." I pat the mattress.

He slides in without protest. The heat of him next to me is such a relief, my eyes prickle with tears. I've been trying to get him alone for days, but he insists spending too much time together at revels, or even walking around the grounds together, is too risky. He's always glancing behind, like he's terrified someone is watching him.

"I'm sick about today," he starts quietly. "I want to run to Nan and Fennick's and hide you in their attic, or wrench the door back to England open and take you as far from this place as possible."

But he knows I wouldn't let him. He knows, because

he's the same as me.

"That wouldn't solve anything," I reply gently. "You have to trust I'll be strong enough to take it."

Emmett reaches for my hand under the duvet. "You're the strongest person I know. I just wish you didn't have to be."

His knuckles are still split and bruised after the fight with the Redcaps. I bring them to my mouth and press my lips to each one.

Emmett captures my chin in his hand and tips my mouth to his. The kiss is long and slow, like we're not on borrowed time. He's methodical as he slips his tongue between the seam of my lips, then pulls back to trail down the column of my throat. I shiver as the cold metal of his earring brushes my bare shoulder.

I could confront him about the push and pull he's put me through, ask him why he won't just let me in, but instead I choose to take what he'll give me.

"I don't want to let you go," he whispers.

"Don't be afraid." I smile against his mouth. "I'm not."

He does us both a favor and lets me lie to him.

Emmett holds my hand until first light, then slips out of my room, ready to play his part for the day, as Bram's devoted regent and loyal brother. I know it will hurt him.

"Check on Lydia, please," I say as he walks away. I have the distinct feeling that he knows how to care for her better than I do.

He turns back and nods gravely.

By noon, I'm in a carriage, hurtling through the countryside into the unknown.

I'm awake this time. I assured Bram I wouldn't fight, and I won't.

The journey takes nearly a day, just as Rhion warned. We stop periodically for breaks to rest and eat and water the horses, and although we're in a caravan with dozens of other carriages, I never interact with anyone but castle guards, who refuse to speak to me. By the time we arrive at the caves, I've cycled through all the stages of fear and acceptance twice over.

The carriage finally comes to a halt and a guard swings open the back door. I hop down, ignoring his hand.

Next to me, Lydia steps down from her carriage gingerly, gracefully accepting help.

The space where our eyes meet is pained, and I know we're both thinking of the unicorn.

I want to hug her, to tell her it's all going to be all right, that we'll find a way out of this, but before I can, a pair of rough hands shoves me forward.

I whip my head around. "There's no need for that!" I snap. "I'll go willingly."

It's the smell that hits me first. The salty brine of the sea is picked up on a rough breeze, where it intermingles with the fresh, bitter scent of pine.

The caves are a yawning mouth on an expanse of cliffs that fall directly into a dark, writhing ocean. The sun reflects on its churning surface thousands of feet below. I shudder to think what kinds of creatures live within its depths.

The cave itself is unremarkable, which makes it all the more terrifying. I'm not sure what I was expecting, but it wasn't this.

The mouth reaches perhaps fifteen feet high, large enough to drive a carriage through.

Standing at the entrance, we can see a few feet inside, just a dirt floor and jagged walls. Then it disappears into darkness.

Lydia walks over to me, no sense of fear in her. Her shoulders are square, her head held high. Her cloak is snow-white, and she wears the hood over her blond curls. I peek around it to take a look at her face, which is stony.

Behind her, more carriages pull up and nobles stream out of them. There are colorful poufs set on the ground, and a long table where castle staff are setting up a noontime feast. Someone has pulled out a fiddle, and a cheery tune fills the stark cliffside.

"How do we win?" Lydia asks Bram. He's distracted, getting his cup filled by a servant, while the rest of court settles in for the party.

Bram grins. "Whoever lasts the longest."

CHAPTER TWENTY

From over Bram's shoulder, I spot Emmett and Rhion standing together. Emmett is doing a good job of playing loyal regent, but his face is gray with worry. Rhion, on the other hand, has never looked happier, his handsome face lit up with a radiant grin. When his eyes snag mine, though, they turn serious. He mouths *Good luck.*

"All right then." I turn to my sister. "I love you. I'll see you later."

Bram frowns. "No trying to lose on purpose. I'll know and it'll hurt my feelings and then we'll have to do the second trial all over again."

I reach up and press my palm to his cheek. His skin is rough with stubble and cool from the wind whipping up from the sea. "I wouldn't dream of it."

Lydia leans in and gives him a kiss on his other cheek. "I'll see you soon, my love." And then, without fear or hesitation, she steps into the cave.

And so, I do what I've done my whole life and follow my sister.

The noises from outside go silent. The only sound is my ragged breathing and a rhythmic *drip, drip, drip* from the water running down the walls.

I clench my jaw and brace myself for a pain that doesn't come. I feel entirely normal. Maybe the legends were just that—stories parents tell children to keep them from wandering off into dangerous places. I nearly laugh at Bram's stupidity. He got it all wrong.

"Lydia?" I call into the darkness. I'll find her, and once we've located Ferrinus we can sit for an hour or two, enough time to satisfy Bram, and then emerge together, looking wan, with some fabricated story of torture.

My voice echoes from the back of the cave. *Lydia, Lydia, Lydia.*

"Do you feel fine? I feel fine," I call. Still no answer. *Fine, fine, fine.*

With my hands out in front of me, I step a few feet farther into the cave.

There's a glint on the ground a few paces back.

"Lydia?"

I walk deeper into the cave, still feeling nothing except the strange, hollow silence.

The toe of my silk slipper connects with something solid on the soft earth floor.

I bend and push my hands around in the dirt blindly. The heavy fur cuffs of my cloak get in the way, so I pull them up in frustration and try again.

Sharp pain cuts into my palm and I yelp and yank my arm back.

I bend once more and feel around gingerly. My fingers close on a rough hilt. I rise and bring it as close to my eyes as I am able.

I lick the blood away from my palm and laugh with relief. In my hand, I hold a rough-hewn dagger with an ornately jeweled handle. I tripped directly over Ferrinus. The Redcaps must have stood at the mouth of the cave and tossed it in, just as Rhion suspected.

"Lydia, where are you? I found it!"

My heart rate picks up. This cave isn't large. She should be able to hear me. "Lydia?" I call, properly worried now. "I'll let you win if you want, just tell me you're all right."

I take a few more steps, then smack directly into a wall. Not one of jagged stone but something smooth, like glass.

I whip my head around and see nothing but darkness. I can't have walked more than twenty feet into the cave, but the ray of light from the entrance has disappeared completely. Like I've been sealed inside.

"Lydia?" I call, so panicked it's making me dizzy. My heart pounds in my ears; my limbs go ice cold.

Something deep within me *lurches*.

My head spins. My vision goes white.

I might be screaming, but everything has gone deadly silent, as if a thread has been snipped and I'm excised from my body completely.

Am I dead? It was a painless but stupid way to die.

My heart longs for Emmett, then breaks that he'll have to mourn me twice.

And where is Lydia? Did she die just before I did? Is that why she wasn't answering me?

But then—I see it. The first flecks of warm light, prickling at the edges of my vision.

The blackness retreats like a fog and there they are. *Lydia and Emmett.* We're back in the garden of the castle.

The opalescent towers of the castle glow in the bright sunshine and all around us the gardens are a riot of color. Pink roses bloom as large as dinner plates, and sparkling violets trail along the tan gravel path. A fat green dragonfly buzzes by lazily.

"Lydia! Emmett!" I shout, but they don't turn.

They're sitting side by side on a stone bench. Lydia is crying into her hands, her shoulders heaving while Emmett lays a comforting hand on her back, his face pained.

"Hello," I shout again, now directly in front of them.

My stomach turns as the realization dawns. They can't see me.

I take another look at the trees in full bloom.

It's summer.

Lydia and Emmett look different, too. Their hair is only slightly longer than it was when they left England. Emmett has no piercing in his ear.

I'm in a memory.

Emmett's eyes are hollow and his doublet hangs off of him, exposing sharp bones. Lydia looks less gaunt, but similarly haunted.

She reaches into her bodice and pulls out a delicate gold chain. The charm on the end of it glints in the light. I take a step closer, then gasp.

"What is it?" Emmett extends a bruised hand and takes it. But I already know.

"It's Ivy's baby necklace. We left them at the base of a tree when we were little, trying to summon a faerie. It was a silly childhood game. Mine was there the next morning—I'd planned to hide them both and keep up the fantasy for my sister—but Ivy's was gone. I figured maybe a magpie had snatched it, but then when I came back here after the wedding, I found it in my room."

Emmett visibly shudders. "What do you think it means?"

Lydia frowns. "It means Bram has been watching us, and going back and forth to England, for longer than any of us have realized."

She gestures to the garden surrounding us, and it's only on a second look that I realize something about this place is wrong.

The tips of tender summer leaves curl into brown. In the tangle of roots below, fruit is split with rot, festering in the noonday sun. Patches of grass have turned a sickly yellow, and the purple flowers lining the winding garden path are wilting.

"I think the land is sad when he's not here," Lydia says.

"Sad?" He rubs his hand, which is mottled with a yellow bruise.

Lydia blinks hard, and I know this look well. She's about to start crying. Sure enough, her face goes red and Emmett gently brushes away a tear. "That sounds stupid. I don't know. I just feel it," she says.

"I don't think it's stupid."

A summer breeze floats by, brushing gently through her golden curls.

To anyone spying from afar, they'd look like lovers.

"I don't know what to do," Lydia cries.

"About what?"

She tosses up her hands. "Everything. Bram has just left me here. He hasn't returned in a month and I'm trying my best to keep his court together, but no one respects me. Lady Thalia petitioned to allow taking changelings again, Emmett. *Changelings.* When I tried to put an end to it, she muttered something about me having no real authority here. The worst part is, she's right. I'm trying my best to be queen, but I can't seem to manage it."

"You're a wonderful queen," Emmett says softly.

My ribs ache as I watch. I'm glad they had each other, truly, but it's clear they have this unreachable *thing* together and I'm right back where I've always been—on the outside, in Lydia's shadow.

And what's worse is I hate myself for the jealousy when there are so many things that matter more.

I'm supposed to be saving England, and I can't manage to be anything more than a heartbroken girl, forever jealous of her older sister. Maybe I'll never be anything but this.

I feel the tug of magic, of the cave asking to take me somewhere else.

"Show me more," I say aloud.

The garden shifts and the memory blurs. Suddenly, I'm in the dark corner of a revel. Emmett is lounging, glassy-eyed, on a silk love seat. He's got streamers in his hair and a goblet slung lazily in one hand. The party swirls around him, a blur of bright colors and drunken merriment.

A dark-haired woman, so beautiful it hurts to look at her, appears beside him. She's got that carved-from-ice quality Faith Fairchild has, but even more perfect, in the eerie way all faeries are. Her eyes are golden, unnatural in their beauty, and they're boring into Emmett.

"Prince Emmett," she purrs.

His eyes lock onto hers. "Lady Thalia." He's doing a poor job disguising his loathing.

"Don't look at me like that," she sneers, and I recognize her as the girl who was sitting on his lap at the revel the first night I arrived here. She was also the girl he was kissing against the wall the night we got into our big argument on the terrace.

"Like what?" Emmett's voice is a low drawl.

"Like I can't help you."

"What could you possibly help me with?"

"You need allies," she answers curtly.

Emmett takes a sip of something dark from the goblet, ignoring her.

"You can act all aloof, but a regent with no allies is no regent at all."

"What makes you think I want power?" Emmett tips his head back against the brocade wallpaper.

"I don't think that at all. But I know one thing with certainty." Lady Thalia extends her elegant hand and points to the front of the room, where Lydia sits on a throne, surrounded by fawning courtiers. "You want to protect *her*. With Bram gone, the wolves have come out to play and her position is precarious. It's easy to undermine her politically. Even easier to arrange an accident for such a fragile, *mortal*, young queen. You'd do anything."

"Is that a threat?" he snaps.

"It's a warning. Without allies, neither of you will last long."

Emmett takes another sip.

"Together, we'd be formidable," Lady Thalia drawls.

"You proposed allowing the taking of changelings again in a council meeting this week. It upset the queen quite a bit. Why would I want an ally like you?"

She sticks her nose up in the air, every inch the haughty aristocrat. "I have sway with the council of lords. I could easily withdraw the proposal and push through your agenda instead. What is it you want? Increased protections for humans and the folk who live in the valley below? Fewer bargains?"

Emmett pulls himself upright, looking wary. His long fingers drum on the arm of the silk love seat. The fabric is ripped, revealing the batting beneath. "What do I have to offer you?"

Lady Thalia extends a manicured finger and runs it along the edge of Emmett's jaw. He shudders, perhaps with disgust, but also like he hasn't been touched in a very long time.

"You are gorgeous," she answers. "And so, *so* sad. It's delicious."

Emmett's eyes drop closed.

"I used to be Bram's, but I could be yours," she whispers against his skin. "I bet that would make him very mad."

My vision tunnels, the darkness closing in like curtains at a play.

Show me more.

The image shifts and we're in a dim bedroom. The bedclothes are a tangle of dark silks, and Emmett's pale form lies stark among them.

Lady Thalia crawls across the bed to him on her hands and knees. With agonizing, methodical slowness, she undoes the buttons on his shirt one by one.

His eyes are dark and desolate. The bruises beneath them have never looked bluer.

I don't want to watch, but everywhere I turn, there they are. I try to close my eyes, but I can't stop seeing. I'm without a body, without eyelids to close. The only thing I can do is witness. The force of it carries me away like I'm being swept out to sea.

She lays her head on his chest and smiles like a cat that has caught a fat mouse. "We're going to have so much fun together."

Show me more. I have to see; I have to know the truth.

The room shifts again and again until I'm dizzy with it. I'd be vomiting if I had a body, but I am nothing, no one but these memories.

Lady Thalia dancing with Emmett at a revel, her pupils blown out and glassy while he stares blankly at the ceiling.

"You've never made a bargain?" Lady Thalia asks, one perfect eyebrow quirked. Emmett shakes his head and she smiles venomously. "Then I'm honored to be your first. Let's make it a good one."

Then they're in a dark room, standing opposite each other, a third person in navy robes between them. The room is lit with thousands of candles flickering against the dark.

Emmett takes Lady Thalia by the hands. A garnet ring on her finger glints in the firelight.

Emmett tilts his head up to the ceiling, then looks back at her. "*I do.*"

Something inside of me shatters.

But before I can even understand what I'm seeing—what he's *doing*—the room shifts again.

More. I need to know more.

He's with Lydia, sitting on the chair in her room in front of the fireplace. His legs are slung over the armrests, his head in his hands. His hair is getting longer and the bruises under his eyes are worse.

Lydia's face is red and pinched with fury. "You married her!" she screams, and Emmett flinches. "You promised me you'd never make a bargain, and then you went and made the worst possible one."

"A political marriage. I did it to protect you." He sounds so dejected.

"You fed yourself to the wolves!"

"She's angry Bram cast her aside for you. She only wants to get him back. She took the changeling proposal off the table immediately. She's convinced three lords to stay here instead of going with Bram to England to torture humans. Already I'm getting more respect at court. I didn't know what else to do!"

"Anything but this!" Lydia shouts. "You deserve real love, Emmett."

"Ivy's gone." Emmett's voice goes quiet and his eyes well with tears. "Ivy's gone and she's not coming back, so let me do this. Let me help you."

More. Please. Even in my own head, my voice is nothing more than a broken whisper.

The scene lurches and I'm back in Lady Thalia's room. It's unbearable, but I have to know more.

Emmett is asleep in bed next to her and rolls over, exposing the long column of his throat. There, fresh and red, is the bruise I left when I bit him at the revel.

This memory is recent, I realize. It happened the night we

were both dosed with love potion. There's his long hair, his single earring, his familiar doublet discarded on the floor.

It's like my heart has been replaced with a hot coal and it's burning everything around it, ruining it until it crumbles to ash.

It would be one thing if Emmett had taken other lovers while I was gone and he believed me to be dead, but to be in another woman's bed just days ago is devastating in a way I didn't anticipate. For the first time, I hope that maybe I am dead. That way I won't have to go back and face him.

My heart isn't broken seeing a version of Emmett who doesn't love me back, it's that it no longer matters if he loves me. That's beside the point. He's gone from me, and I have to watch it all play out, vivid and gruesome in its detail.

I can take no more.

As quickly as I fell into the memories, I am spat back out.

I come to, shaking, sobbing on the hard dirt ground.

Blinding white light clears from my vision and I blink against the sun.

Bald tree branches sway gently above me, stark against the bright blue sky.

I'm outside the cave, I realize.

I gasp for breath, my stomach aching as if the wind has been knocked from me, but the movement only causes me to cough and the coughing causes me to vomit.

Someone pulls my hair off my neck. Their fist is cool where it rests against the base of my skull. "There, there, get it out.

You're all right. You're safe," says a soft voice.

I look up through watery eyes to find Lydia. She, too, is pale and shaky, but she's on her feet, which means she is faring far better than me.

"I'm alive?" I rasp.

Lydia's pale face consumes my field of vision as she stands over me, examining for any signs of harm.

"What did you see?" she whispers.

I push the visions of Emmett down; I don't want to remember. "You first," I answer grimly. She doesn't reply.

Lydia pulls me to my feet and wraps me in a tight hug. "You were in there for nearly an hour."

"And you?"

"They tell me I was gone only twenty minutes before I wound up here."

My empty stomach drops. "So, I won?"

Lydia nods gravely.

That's the thing about sisters; you can't hide anything from them. She knows I didn't want this. "You won."

CHAPTER TWENTY-ONE

Bram and his courtiers gather around me moments later. Emmett stands near the back of the crowd, his face grim with worry.

Rhion extends a hand to steady me, but I refuse it and stumble, my legs as shaky as a newborn fawn's.

"It's done," I whisper in his ear, and he gives me a single nod.

I pat the interior pocket of my cloak and find the comforting weight of Ferrinus there. Despite it all, we achieved what we set out to do today. It should feel like victory, but I am hollow.

"How'd it go?" Bram asks cheerfully, his tone eagerly intent.

Back in Bath, while the others delighted in torturing humans at the revel, it seemed that Bram was mostly above it. I see now that he enjoys the carnage just as much as the rest of them; his tastes just lean more personal. What good is pain when it's inflicted on a stranger? Up close, when it's me or Lydia or Emmett or his mother, it must be so much sweeter for him.

Perhaps that's why he let his court run so wild back home in England. My distress wasn't an unfortunate aftereffect, it was the point entirely.

I do my best not to recoil from him as my eyes meet his. There is glee glinting in his silver irises.

"It was horrible," I answer honestly. The sour taste of vomit lingers in the back of my mouth.

Bram slings a heavy arm around my shoulder and grins down at me. There's that single dimple, the one that used to make my heart stutter in my chest. "Good."

Unlike the last trial, I do not retreat into the carriages. I cross to the circle of silk settees around the roaring bonfire and I have a drink. I paste a smile on my face and do my best to look gracious at all the congratulations flung my way.

I can't bear to look at Emmett.

I feel the weight of his eyes on me across the roaring fire, but every time I glance back, I see him saying *I do*.

He's been married this whole time. The betrayal stings like a slap across the face, but deep down, I just feel so stupid for thinking I knew him better than this.

You really think my love is that fickle?

No matter the reasons he had for marrying her, he should have told me.

And Lydia kept his secrets for him, which is another blow.

The sun sinks low in the sky, casting the cliffside party in long shadows.

Without the sun, the breeze coming in from the roiling sea is properly bitter, and I am shivering despite my heavy cloak.

"Let's take this back to the castle!" Bram announces, and everyone shouts in agreement.

Emmett brushes by me on our way to the carriages. "Are you all right?" he asks under his breath.

I push past him without answering. I don't know what to say.

The hours-long ride back to the castle is a new kind of torture. I tremble with cold as the images of Emmett come back to me in a torrent.

Married.

Emmett is married.

He's been some other girl's husband this whole time.

I jump out of my carriage before it has come to a full stop and don't stop moving until I'm back up in my room, alone, with the thick curtains drawn.

I pull Ferrinus from my cloak and examine it in the light. It's nearly identical to the drawing we looked at in Lydia's room. A rough piece of metal, closer to a rock than a blade, has been sharpened to a crude point and bound to a golden hilt. From end to end it's smaller than my forearm.

I weigh it in my palm, finding comfort in it and praying I don't have to use it. Then I shove it under my mattress. I'll give it to Lydia later, per our agreement, but I don't have the strength to face her right now.

I pull the velvet cord to ring the bell and Eloree appears.

With gentle hands she plaits my hair into a long braid that falls down the center of my back and helps me into a silky nightdress.

"Eloree?" I ask when she's nearly out the door.

She pauses. "Yes, ma'am?"

"Where are Lady Thalia's quarters?"

Her brows furrow. "Why would you want to go there? She's so . . ." She struggles to find the words.

"Horrible?" I offer.

"Cruel," Eloree answers.

I know, I don't say aloud.

"Please, where does she live?"

Eloree sighs. "Her quarters are with the rest of the lords, in the east wing of the castle, past the central courtyard."

"Thank you."

She nods and closes the door behind her.

I sink down into my bed alone. Every time I shut my eyes, I see Emmett against the wall, Emmett in bed, Emmett vowing to love someone else.

After what feels like ages, I can bear it no longer and push myself up out of bed.

I crack open my door and find the hallway still and empty, though the revel below buzzes through the walls and up the stairs.

I knock on the door at the end of the hall first, but know I will find it empty. I understand now why there was no bed. He never slept there.

I pass throngs of partygoers on my way to the east wing. Tonight, they're dressed in shades of gold. Somewhere within the throne room, I have no doubt Bram is in costume as Midas.

A few try to press cups or sweets into my hand as I pass, but

I push through them and out into the cold air of the courtyard.

It's damp tonight. Not quite raining, but misting like the sky can't make up its mind. It clings to my skin and hair, so by the time I enter the foyer of the east wing, I'm shivering.

There's a servant girl tending to the entryway fire and I ask her the way to Lady Thalia's rooms.

"Second floor, last door on the left," she instructs.

The door is unlocked, which surprises me, but maybe after hundreds of years of living together, the faeries in Bram's court don't bother with locks.

The room is draped in greens so dark they're almost black. In the middle of the space looms the massive canopy bed from the visions in the cave. The sight of it makes my eyes water. I didn't doubt what the cave showed me, but here is further confirmation that it was real.

I take a seat in the hard wooden desk chair and wait.

It doesn't take long before the door creaks open, Emmett's tall form silhouetted in the entrance. I was ready to confront Lady Thalia, but I'm glad it's him.

He jumps as he sees me. "Ivy?"

"Tell me the truth." I'm desperate for my voice to sound cold instead of brokenhearted.

"What are you doing here?" he asks urgently. "You shouldn't be here."

"Tell me, Emmett. Is it true?"

"Is what true?"

"You know what!" My voice breaks. "You've been married

all this time and you never thought to tell me. *Married*, Emmett!"

His face crumples. "Ivy, please. I never meant for you to find out."

"That's worse!" I shout. "You do see how that's worse, don't you?" I turn, ready to leave. All I needed was confirmation.

"Ivy, wait," he calls.

This emotion, this need to *run* when things get hard, is so familiar it startles me. I have a vision of myself this spring, running to Queen Mor and asking her to make me forget Emmett. I felt just like this then, a trapped animal, and in making that bargain, I hurt Emmett more than I ever could have anticipated.

I don't want to be the kind of person who runs. I want to stand and face things.

I take a steadying breath and face him.

His face is so beautiful, it's heartbreaking. He's looking at me, wide open and full of grief.

"Can we just talk, please?" His voice is barely a whisper. "I didn't want to hurt you."

"You haven't just hurt me, you've made me a fool."

"How did you find out?" His voice is barely a whisper.

"The caves. It was emotional pain, as it turns out." I blink and there it is again: Emmett in that candlelit chapel, vowing his life to someone who isn't me.

He lets out a long breath. "Then you know I only did it because I was trying to protect Lydia and because I believed you to be dead. You have to believe me. I *never* would have done this if I thought you were still alive. I would have clung to the hope of you until my dying breath."

I throw up my hands, feeling half-crazed. "That's not fair. You were always going to move on, and you should have, that's your right."

"That's not true," Emmett says.

"I'm not upset about the marriage—" I pause. "Well, I am, of course I am, but I don't have a leg to stand on there. I'm heartbroken that you've been lying to me. You let me look foolish in front of everyone, in front of Lydia," I argue.

He presses the heels of his hands into his eye sockets and lets out a breath. "I never meant to hurt you."

"I want to believe that," I reply. "But does it matter what we feel? It's happened. It's done." There's a swooping sensation in my stomach like I'm falling from a great height. It's like the illusion from the bridge spirit, when I saw Emmett as an old man. The future I imagined for us in tatters.

Emmett pulls away from me, the air between us suddenly as cold as ice.

"I understand," he says flatly, his gaze pinned somewhere above my head.

"It's just—" I struggle to find the words. "You're *married*. I don't see how we overcome that."

"So are you." He looks at me, bewildered.

"But I never lied to you about it! Every moment I've been in the Otherworld, you've been lying to me."

"To protect you!"

"Or because I'm as disposable to you as the rest of them?" It's my worst fear, finally voiced aloud: that I am simply one in a long line of Emmett De Vere's girls. Another naive debutante who fell under his spell and let him make me believe I was special.

The words strike him. His voice is a whisper now, anger evident in every word. "Accuse me of anything you wish—you're right, I've ruined everything—but don't accuse me of indifference."

It physically hurts to look at his face. I can't stand another rejection. I'm simply not strong enough.

"She doesn't even care about me." Emmett's voice is louder now. "She was one of Bram's lovers before he married you and Lydia and she's jealous and petty and out for revenge. She married me to hurt him."

"I saw you with her, in *that* bed!" I point to where it looms in the middle of the dark room. "Why were you with her after I arrived here? I can understand when you thought I was dead, but I was alive. I'd *just* kissed you."

Emmett wrings his hands. "We shared a bed. I did not touch her, I swear it. I couldn't. It's you I want. Only you."

"I don't know what to do." My confession is thick with tears. "What if what we had back in England wasn't meant to last? It all happened so quickly." I don't mean it.

"Do you want me to let you walk away?" he asks softly.

"Yes," I lie.

The muscle in Emmett's jaw flexes as he clenches his teeth together.

He says nothing as I walk out the door, but I hear a crash come from his room just seconds after it shuts behind me.

It's nearly dawn when my door swings open. I jump in fright but immediately relax when I see it's just Lydia.

"How was the revel?" I ask.

She perches on the edge of my bed, her brown eyes lined with gold the same shade as her gown.

She sighs as she sees my swollen face. "I'd ask which one of them left you in this state, but I already know it was Emmett. He's just been to see me."

"How is he?" I can't help asking.

"Awful," Lydia answers. "And I'm sick of it. Sick of you both."

"Sick of it? You're the one who's been lying to me all this time. You and Emmett played me for a fool."

Her mouth is a grim line, but her eyes are soft. "I shouldn't have kept his secrets for him. I was trying to protect you both. I love the two of you so much, it causes me pain to see you hurting. I hate that I've contributed to that hurt. I want nothing more than to see you happy."

"We—" I start to argue, to tell her all the ways we're doomed, but she interrupts me by pulling a box from behind her back.

She sets it down next to me, and I peer inside to see rows of neatly folded paper.

Lydia rises and throws my curtains open, flooding the room with enough pale dawn light to read by.

"What am I supposed to do?" I ask.

Lydia pauses in the doorway. "Just read them. The rest is up to you . . . to you both."

She closes the door behind her. I reach out and open the top letter.

It's dated August 28, 1848.

> *Ivy,*
>
> *I wished to write you sooner, but I've been in prison and my broken hand has only just now healed enough to hold a quill. But you've never left my mind, all this time.*
>
> *If I were braver or crueler I never would have let you walk down that aisle and marry him. I'll carry that regret with me for the rest of my life. Could I have saved you?*
>
> *I find comfort in knowing you're somewhere better, that nothing can hurt you, that you're beyond Bram's grasp, but if there's anything left of you in this world, please haunt me.*
>
> *Yours,*
> *Emmett*

With shaking hands, I unfold the next letter.

October 1848

Ivy,

I dreamed of you last night. Was that you visiting me? We were back in Kensington Palace and you were kissing me like I was someone worthy of you.

Love,
Emmett

Winter 1848

Ivy,

Time has gotten so hazy. I don't know when it is, only that I feel your absence in every second.

Come back to me,
Emmett

Winter, still 1848

Ivy,

It's so cold and all I do is miss you.

Spring 1849, I think

The Others don't celebrate the New Year, but I believe a year has passed because it is warm again and it was warm when I lost you.

I'm trying so hard to take care of Lydia. It's almost like I'm taking care of you, but I think she's as sad as I am. We're a sorry pair and some part of me is glad you're not here to see it.

Summer,

Ivy, Ivy, Ivy, Ivy,

I may have said my vows to her but it was you who was on my mind. My very soul was rebelling against itself as I stood before her and promised to be hers because I've only ever been yours. I'll only ever be yours. Wherever you are, I hope you're waiting for me. I'm still doing my best to be someone worthy of you, but I fear I'm getting further from it. I didn't mean what I said to her, my love. The only person I've ever wanted to make a vow to was you. I picture our wedding all the time. I would have cried as you walked down the aisle. I would have made Pig bear the rings. You would have been so, so beautiful.

I'm sorry.
Emmett

Autumn Equinox

Sweetheart,

Do you remember the first night we met in the carriage? Did you know that I fell for you, right then and there? You probably did. You were always so much smarter than me.

Cold, again

Come back to me
Come back to me
Come back to me
I'll be better this time. I swear it.

There are dozens more, but I'm crying too hard to continue reading, so I pull the most recent one off the stack.

High summer

Know that you live inside my every heartbeat. You'd say that line was corny if you were here.
But you're not.
You're not.
That's the problem, isn't it?

Are you haunting me yet? Send me a sign.

I love you. You're the only person I've ever loved. Ever will love.

I should end this letter with goodbye but I am still not strong enough.

Emmett

I wipe my swollen eyes and know immediately what I must do.

With the letters clutched against my heart, I run down the corridor to Emmett's room and pound on the door. It's just like the first night I was here.

"Emmett De Vere, let me in this instant!" I command. I'm not even sure he's in there, but if he doesn't come to the door soon, I'll try Lady Thalia's rooms and then Lydia's. I will not rest until I have found him.

But he doesn't make me wait long.

The door cracks open, revealing Emmett's devastated face, his eyes rimmed with red.

I push past him and dump the letters on his desk. "I wrote to you too. All those months you were gone, I was writing you letters."

He looks to the mess of papers and then back to me. "I want to fight for you. Will you let me fight for you?" he asks.

"Yes." My skin buzzes; my heartbeat thunders in my ears.

"I am, and have only ever been, yours. I would have done anything to protect you."

I tip my forehead against his and we breathe raggedly, but in unison.

"I'm sorry," I say softly.

Emmett lowers himself to the floor until he's kneeling in front of me. "I have loved you and I have grieved you and now I am on my knees for you," he says. "Ivy Benton, if you believe only one thing let it be this: I am yours, down to my bones."

I brush my fingers under his chin and he rises. "Then can we both agree that we're stronger together than we are apart?" I ask.

He nods like he might start to cry again, his hazel eyes all glossy.

"I love you, Emmett De Vere."

He rises from the floor and leans in. "I lost you once. I'm not going to be stupid enough to lose you again."

It's like this that Emmett and I have always made the most sense: alone, in a dark room.

He wraps his arms around the small of my waist and tugs my body flush against his, then crushes his lips to mine, and I'm lost.

His mouth moves down my neck, to the sensitive hollow of my throat, and then back up. We both stand and he tips me against the back wall until I can feel every aching plane of his body.

"Wait—" I gasp against his mouth.

He lets out a sharp breath I'm not sure is a laugh or half a sob.

"What comes next? Your wife—"

Emmett groans. "Don't say that word. I'll get it annulled, I'll get a divorce— I'm not sure how the faeries handle it, but I'll do anything."

I sigh against his mouth. "And then you'll join me in my exile?"

He smiles back. "If you'll have me."

"All right, then. One more trial to lose. Two faerie divorces, and then forever?"

"Forever," he agrees, and kisses me hard. "I'll never deserve you," he mutters, his mouth moving against mine.

I pull back and shake my head. "If we play this whole *who is deserving of who* game, we'll forever be unhappy."

"Because I'll never deserve you?"

"Because love doesn't care if you're deserving or not. It just *is*."

He turns to face me and captures my face in his hands. They're large enough that they reach from my jaw to nearly the crown of my head.

"Let me love you, just as you are," I breathe. "You told me your love isn't fickle. Well, neither is mine."

Emmett lowers his mouth to mine, and there are no flames or sparks or comets shooting across a distant sky. His lips yield against mine, and the kiss is soft and slow.

It feels like coming home.

CHAPTER TWENTY-TWO

Rhion pulls me aside at a garden party two days later. Marion, Faith, and Emmett are already waiting. "Have I come last in a game of Sardines?" I ask.

But none of them crack a smile. "Oh no, this meeting seems grave."

"Now that we have the knife, we must act." Rhion is all business. I knew the peace I found with Emmett was as fragile and fleeting as ice on a pond, but it's still disappointing to see it shattered.

We're in the corner of a greenhouse containing thousands of blooming flowers, but through the glass, I see Lydia across the lawn. She's got white feathers in her hair and a crystal teacup in her hand. She's surrounded by courtiers, including Lady Thalia, who I've made a point of avoiding.

"Should we get Lydia?" I ask.

The rest of them share an uncomfortable glance and I can read the subtext in it.

"You think she loves him too much?" I ask.

Rhion sinks his teeth into his bottom lip. "I think she loves him, full stop. It complicates things."

"What will we do?" Marion asks.

"Bram is in England for the next day or two. When he comes back, we'll confront him. I'll call him for a meeting in my private quarters and we will threaten him with the knife and a choice. It is my hope he will choose to abdicate."

"And if he doesn't?"

Rhion presses his fingers into his temples and exhales. "I'm hopeful we can force him behind bars, just like his mother."

"And if we can't?" Emmett asks.

Rhion's bright blue eyes are grave. "I will do what needs to be done."

Across the gardens, Lydia smiles and laughs at something.

"Fine," I say, even as my stomach rolls.

Emmett nods slowly. Lydia may love Bram, but Emmett does too, and the pain he's feeling is evident. "We'll do what needs to be done."

Thock, thock, thock.

I'm unsurprised by the knock at my door, later that night. For the past two nights, Emmett has snuck away to see me while everyone else is reveling. We hold each other like shipwrecked sailors lost at sea, and when the morning comes, he leaves my room with a simple *I love you*, and I hold his hand until the last possible second as he walks out the door.

I tighten the tie of my cream silk dressing gown and bound

from my bed to answer.

Standing at my threshold isn't Emmett but Bram. I should have known: it wasn't the right knock.

I jump in shock, and he looks at me through the mop of his light brown hair, his mouth arched in a teasing half smile that reveals his dimple.

I do my best to arrange my face into a surprised grin, but Bram's expression flickers like he caught a glimpse of my dread.

"Hello, wife."

"Second wife," I correct him.

"Details, details." He arches a brow and leans against the doorframe. "Are you going to let me in?"

I pull the door open wider. "Of course, it's your castle."

"You're not happy to see me?"

"Just surprised." I keep my voice steady. "I thought you'd be in England until at least tomorrow."

He shakes his head. "No, my errands took less than an hour. I was merely collecting a few more members of my court who wished to return home to see the final spectacle."

He brushes by me, close enough that his intricately beaded doublet snags on the soft fabric of my dressing gown.

He shrugs off his doublet and hangs it on the fireplace fender, then turns to me.

"I've missed you," he says. "I feel like I haven't seen you in ages."

"It must be quite diverting, being the king of two kingdoms,"

I reply, trying to keep my tone light.

He pushes up the sleeves of his white undershirt. "Still, I miss your company."

Bram toes off his shoes and pulls off his socks, then his brown leather breeches, leaving him in nothing but his underclothes.

At that exact moment, Emmett knocks at the door. It's always the same—three sharp raps, a pause, and then another. Panic courses through my veins. The last time Bram caught Emmett and me together, it earned Emmett two months in a faerie prison.

Bram looks toward the door.

"Not tonight, Eloree!" I shout. "I'm quite all right on my own. My husband is here, bring a tray for two in the morning!"

I try to keep my breathing steady. I can picture Emmett so clearly outside the door, his face falling. I pray he doesn't feel betrayed, that he understands I have no other choice.

For a moment there is silence, and then the sound of heavy feet walking down the hall.

Bram slides into my bed and pats the space next to him. The mattress is much too thick to feel the knife I've shoved under it, but I'm terrified that Bram might be able to sense its magic somehow.

Lydia asked about it today, after the garden party, and I lied and told her I'd deliver it to her tomorrow morning. There's a pit in my gut every time I think about it.

"I'm tired," Bram says.

"Me too." My voice is too tense. I need to calm down or he's going to realize something is wrong.

I wasn't exactly warm to him back in England, but I did a better job of pretending than this.

I shrug off my dressing gown, leaving me in nothing but my nightdress, and slide into bed beside him.

Bram turns off the flickering bedside lantern with a snap of his fingers and blue darkness pours over the room.

I'm terrified he's going to touch me.

I don't know why Bram hasn't pushed the physical aspect of our relationship since our wedding, but I am grateful for it.

Perhaps somewhere, deep down, he retains some level of honor. Maybe he can tell I don't desire him in that way.

Or maybe he's getting his physical needs met elsewhere.

He lays a cool hand on the side of my face and my stomach drops.

"You're special, Ivy. You've always been special," he says softly.

"Did you ever love me?" I ask. Here in the dark, I can't help myself. "Or was I always a means to an end?"

He's quiet as he ponders my question.

"I don't understand what humans mean when you say the word *love*. To put someone above yourself seems very impractical. Why do you do that?"

"Because it isn't a choice," I answer. Emmett's face flashes through my head.

"Isn't everything?" Bram asks, his voice genuinely curious.

"Is that how it is for you? You choose your emotions? What you feel for other people?"

He sighs and rolls over, removing his hand from my face.

"I don't think I've felt anything in a very long time."

His answer chills me to my core. "But you sound so sad."

"Is that what this hollow sensation is?" he asks. "It's quite unpleasant. I keep trying to fill it with wine and laughter and bread, but nothing sates it."

"Maybe," I answer honestly.

"What does it feel like?" he asks after a moment.

"What does what feel like?"

An autumn breeze ruffles the trees outside my window. A log in the fireplace pops.

"Love," Bram says.

"You know that feeling, when you come home after a cold winter's day. When you're cold down to your bones, and your teeth are chattering and your shoes are wet, but you walk in, and there's a fire roaring. The heat begins to seep into your fingers, and right before they're truly warm again, there's that tingling sensation?"

He hums in understanding. "Love is the tingle?"

I sigh, frustrated by the lack of words I have in my brain to make him understand. Lydia would know how; she's always been the artist of the two of us.

"Love is the knowing, no matter how hard everything else is, you've got a soft, warm place to land."

"Then why don't you fall in love with your landlords?"

Bram asks.

I sputter. "Not a literal soft place to land. An emotional one." I bite my lip. "Let me try once more. You've said how fleeting human lives are. Well, we feel that, too. We know that our time is limited. When you love someone, you choose to be with them, witness them, even though you know your time together is finite. One person will always be left behind. But you do it anyway, despite the pain you know is coming. By loving, we offer ourselves up to the pain willingly."

Faeries must feel some version of the same thing we do—joy, love, pain, heartbreak, anger, longing. The feelings are universal except maybe loss. I don't think Bram knows what it is to lose something. I pity him for it. Can you truly feel something without knowing you'll one day mourn its loss?

"A sacrifice," Bram says.

"Yes." I close my eyes and picture Emmett. We're in the garden and the sun is shining in golden rays from behind him, illuminating his broad shoulders and all the planes of his face. His eyes soften when they look at me, and when he reaches out to touch my waist, it's as if my whole body sighs against him.

"Love sometimes feels like a frenzy, like you'll die if you don't get to touch them or be with them soon, but with the right person, I think it's different. It's so simple you can't imagine doing anything else."

The mattress groans as Bram turns on his side to face me. The shadows of tree branches dance over his face in the moonlight.

His eyes narrow in accusation. "And you feel that way about me?"

Love is nice, but your hate tastes so much better.

He must know I don't, which means this is a test that I'm failing. Alarm bells ring in my head. *He shouldn't be here. Why is he here?*

My throat tightens.

"May I ask you something?" If my clock has run out, there's one question that has gnawed at me since the caves. I need to ask it now, before I no longer have the chance.

"You don't need to ask permission. I am not a scolding tutor."

We're lying on top of the quilt, nearly nose to nose, but not touching. I take the opportunity to stare into the depths of his gray eyes, looking for *something*—but find nothing there. No depth, no emotion. It's like looking at the surface of a frozen pond.

"Why did you have my baby necklace? The one with the pearl *I*?"

He doesn't look surprised, but he presses his lips together like he doesn't quite know how to answer. It gives me a sick thrill of satisfaction to have thrown Bram off his guard.

"Did Lydia tell you?" he asks.

"Does it matter?"

He sucks in a breath through his nose. "No, I suppose it doesn't. But it is a rather long story, so I suppose you ought to settle in."

Bram's voice goes a shade softer, and for the first time since we were married, he sounds like the boy he pretended to be back at Kensington Palace, the one who walked me into a sunlit stable and spoke of magic.

"My mother left the door between our worlds open for the royal family when she fled this place and became queen of England, you know about that."

"I do," I answer quietly.

"Yes, well, I went back and forth rather frequently, in secret, before I puzzled out the marriage element of her original bargain and permanently joined her court. I'd visit England the way lords check on a seldom-used country home. It satisfied some sort of nostalgia, and I wanted to see how things were getting on without me. I always planned on taking the reins from my mother one day, and a good king keeps tabs on things."

"I understand."

"But it was lonely, you see. I was stuck wandering the woods like some sort of vagrant, or observing the palace through the bars of the gates like nothing better than a commoner."

"That sounds difficult." *Placate. Always placate with Bram.*

"Thank you. It was agonizing."

"I assume it was on one of these visits you found the necklace?"

He cocks his head slightly. "Always so impatient, Lady Ivy."

I'm not Lady Ivy anymore, but I don't correct him.

"Visiting England grew tiresome as time went on. Humans

used to have a respect for my kind. We were near gods. They'd flock to us, begging for bargains and boons and favors. They delighted in our music, our revels. My mother severed that connection and as generations passed, she also removed all evidence of us from libraries and historical records. People forgot. I was once regarded with awe and reverence, but eventually, no one even lifted their gaze when I walked into a tavern."

He takes a deep breath, lost in memory. "My mother's latest husband's family had a country estate not far from Oakham. I liked the feeling of the woods. The trees were nearly as old as I was, and the birdsong quieted as I strolled among them. It was there that I first found the offering on the edge of the forest. It had been so long since someone had left a gift for me, it felt like being doused with a bucket of cold water."

"Unpleasant?"

"No," he corrects me gently. "It made me feel *alive*—and what a feeling it was after being numb for so long. Time isn't always a gift, you must understand. After a while, it becomes a curse."

I can picture those woods that he describes so clearly. Our superstitious old cook refused to go in them at all.

"I was desperate to see who made the offering. I watched all day from the tree line. It was twilight when I first saw you. You came bounding out of the kitchen, just a child, near feral in your white dress and tangled hair. I knew the necklaces were your idea by the way you ran across the damp lawn to check on them before being sent to bed by your governess. Lydia appeared moments after you did, but she came through the kitchen door reluctantly and followed you like a beleaguered nursemaid. *Ivy*, she called after you. And once I knew your name, I took your necklace."

I can scarcely breathe, horror dawning on me that he's been watching me for so long. I thought I collided with Bram by accident—destructive, but decidedly a matter of bad luck. To know that by offering my necklace, I called him to me is too much to bear. I invited the monster into my life, held the door wide open and beckoned him in. Lydia didn't want to leave our necklaces on those tree roots. In chasing a childhood fantasy, I unwittingly doomed us both.

"I thought perhaps you saw me through the trees," Bram continues. "You paused and scanned the woods. I prayed you'd see me. But I didn't dare reach out. You were only a child, and I didn't wish to scare you. I watched your family for the rest of the day. You wailed as your mother ordered your cook to burn your book of faeries, and I resolved to track down another copy for you."

Faeries of the British Isles. I thought it was so romantic when he gifted it to me during our courtship, but now the thought is stomach-turning.

"I knew it wasn't yet time for me to make my reappearance at court, but I resolved to find you once I did."

"Why?" I ask, scarcely above a whisper. "It was only a necklace. A child's folly."

"No." Bram shakes his head where it rests against the pillow. "It was more than that. You were the first human in centuries to make me an offering. You *respected me*. You knew I was special."

"I was playing in the garden with my sister."

"It was more than that. You know it was," he snaps. His voice is heated. *Placate. I need to placate him.*

"Of course it was, darling," I soothe. I don't ask him to continue, but after a moment, he does anyway.

"I kept tabs on you through your upbringing. I'd check in every few years, peer through a window or from across a garden to make sure you were doing well. When I finally conceived of the plan to unseat my mother, I timed my arrival at court to coincide with your coming-of-age. I engineered it so that the season I would announce my intentions to find a wife would be the same year you turned eighteen. I was delighted when Lydia first arrived at the castle here, you know. From across the room, I thought she was *you*. You always did look so alike. Imagine my disappointment when I realized I'd have to make do with the other sister. But Lydia is special, too, in her own way, and in time I grew fond of her. I figured I could marry her here and not have to deal with all the tedious business of a royal wedding back in England. I was disappointed when my marriage to her didn't break my mother's bargains and end her rule, but some part of me was relieved, too. It was always meant to be you, Ivy. I've known it from the first moment I saw you."

I'm in shock, thinking of me and Emmett last spring, all our careful planning. We were so foolish. "So, I never needed to beg you to run away with me?"

He lets out a sharp laugh. "I thought I was going to have to beg you."

He reaches down and trails his fingertip over the gold-and-pearl ring I wear on my pointer finger. He once wore it on his pinkie, before gifting it to me during my season. At first, I treasured it as evidence of his affection, but in the months since, I haven't dared to take it off for fear of angering him. I wear it on the same hand as my rose-cut engagement ring and gold wedding band.

The seed pearl set in the middle of the gold glows softly in the moonlight.

My stomach drops. It's all I can do to stay here, still and listening, when I want to run from the room and vomit my guts up.

"You're saying this is—" I can't complete the sentence.

Bram nods, as reverent as I've ever seen him. "It's the pearl from your necklace. We've been connected this whole time."

Bram doesn't wait for me to say anything further. His eyes drop closed and he leans in to kiss me. His cool hand rests on the soft side of my neck.

Unable to take it, I spring from the bed.

"Why now?" I ask him.

"Because you are mine," he answers simply.

"I—" I scramble for an excuse. "I have a headache. Another night, please."

Bram rises smoothly from my bed and dresses swiftly and in silence.

He walks to my door, his face unreadable, then plants a dry kiss on my cheek.

He takes a step back and looks at me, his eyes narrowed. "Of course. Sleep well."

He shuts the door behind him, and I stand there, frozen, my pulse racing like a jackrabbit's.

I want to call for a bath or new sheets, but that wouldn't be very practical, so I grab an ice-blue quilt from the window seat and lie down on top of my covers.

Everything, even my own skin, feels contaminated by him.

Minutes go by, but sleep does not come.

Then there's a knock on my door, so soft I think I might have imagined it. But then it comes a second time.

I fear it's Bram again. Will he believe I'm asleep if I just ignore it?

"Psst, it's me, Emmett."

I wrap the quilt around my shoulders and rise from bed.

He's standing at my threshold, not in his nightclothes, like he usually is, but in a plain white shirt and dark breeches.

He looks worried. "Are you all right? I heard what you said when I knocked earlier."

I wave him quickly into my room. The relief I feel at his presence rushes through me.

"Bram came for a visit," I explain.

Emmett's brows knit together. "What did he want?"

"He asked me to explain what love was to him like he was some sort of child and then he tried to kiss me."

A look of alarm comes over his face.

"Don't worry, I shooed him off."

Emmett's shoulders drop in relief and he sits down on the edge of my bed.

"I was concerned. I had to make sure you were all right."

I step closer to him, and he winds his arms around my waist and pulls me down on top of him.

"You seem all right," he mutters into my ear, sending a shower of sparks down my spine.

"I'm all right now," I whisper.

His hands grow needier, more insistent as they grip at my thighs and pull my nightdress up around my waist.

He rolls us so he's spooning me from behind and lavishes kisses in a trail up my neck, then in the tender spot behind my ear.

I arch against him. "I'm tired of your teasing," I sigh, my body aching for more, always more with Emmett.

"Oh, Ivy. It seems only fair."

The voice makes me pause. Even the air in my lungs goes still with dread.

I know that voice.

And it's not Emmett it belongs to.

I don't want to look behind me, because I know the monster

I will see there.

I gather all my bravery and turn.

Bram is in bed behind me, his hair rumpled, his shirt hanging off his tanned shoulders, his face absolutely enraged.

He sucks on his lower lip as he regards me.

I spring from bed and do nothing but stare at him, my breathing ragged.

"So, you'll whore yourself out for my brother but not for your husband?" he asks, his voice icy with rage.

Hot tears spring to my eyes, but I won't give him the satisfaction of crying in front of him. He might not understand love, but he is well acquainted with pain, and he gets so much satisfaction from mine.

"I—" I scramble for an explanation, for anything that will protect Emmett. I don't care much what happens to me anymore, but I need him to be safe.

"I thought I was dreaming. You caught me half asleep."

He tuts his tongue at me like a nursemaid. "You'll have to do better than that. You've been in the Otherworld long enough that I thought you'd recognize a simple glamour."

"It's the truth. What do you know of human sleep?" The lie is thin and he sees right through it.

He laughs, and it's like the rumble of a storm cloud on the horizon, dark and awful. "More than you, apparently."

He rises from the bed and puts himself to rights.

As he smooths his hair, he walks toward the door. "We're going to have such fun at the next trial."

"Divorce me," I beg. "Let me go home. Punish me in any way you see fit, but leave my sister and Emmett out of this."

If I thought it would make a difference, I would drop to my knees in front of him and beg.

He doesn't break stride. "What fun would that be?" he says, and slams the door behind him.

CHAPTER TWENTY-THREE

I wait only thirty seconds, long enough for Bram to leave this floor, before I burst out of my door and race down the stairs, across the frozen courtyard, and up the stairs of the east wing.

I don't bother knocking, and the ornately carved door isn't locked.

The room is dark, and in the middle of the bed, Emmett's sleeping form is tucked under a pile of blankets. I am flooded with relief that there isn't someone next to him. I don't know what I would have done if I'd found Thalia here.

I shove his shoulder. "Emmett, please, wake up."

He startles awake. "Ivy?" His voice is gravelly with sleep and he rubs at his eyes.

"We have to go." I throw the blankets off of him, then snatch the jacket hanging on the back of his desk chair and toss it at him. "Get up, now."

I'm reminded of a night just like this, months ago. I burst into Emmett's room right after Queen Mor told me I'd lost the competition for Bram's hand. I was panicked then, too. If only I'd known.

"What's happening?" Emmett says groggily. His long hair hangs over his face. He makes an attempt to brush it away, but it flops right back.

"Bram knows." I pull shoes from the wardrobe and throw them to the edge of his bed. "He knows about us."

"How?" Emmett is moving, but too slow for my taste.

"He came to my room glamoured as you. I think he suspected it was you who was knocking earlier, so he left and came back." I swallow the sob crawling up my throat. "I thought he was you."

At this, Emmett springs from the bed and races over to me.

He captures my face in his hands and tips it from left to right, looking for any signs of harm. "Are you all right? Did he—"

"I'm fine. He didn't get far."

Emmett sighs in wordless relief, then slips on his breeches, his jacket, and laces up his boots.

He rises and grabs both my hands in his. We're both shaking a little, but neither of us acknowledges it.

"Are you ready?" he asks. His eyes are so soft, and in them I see how deeply he wants to protect me, how it kills him that he can't.

"It's time. It has to be now."

"Marion and Faith? Rhion? Your sister?" he asks, and a stab of pain bolts through me.

"We don't have time. Did you send Nan the letter?"

Emmett nods, his eyes swimming with grief.

"Then let's go," I say.

We race across the castle to my room, which feels tainted and wrong now. The bed is rumpled, the carpet corner askew from where I ran out the door. Mercifully, Ferrinus is right where I left it, tucked safely between the bedframe and the mattress.

I'm grateful Emmett and I had the foresight to create a backup plan last night, but I never dreamed we'd have to put it into action so soon.

He helps me out of my nightclothes and into a simple black dress, and I toss my blue cloak over it. I hide the knife in the interior pocket, its weight a steady comfort.

We take the back service staircase down into the dungeons, hoping to avoid Bram or his guards.

The first guard we encounter stands at the entrance to the dungeons; when he sees Emmett and me, he waves us by lazily.

I feign tripping over the hem of my dress and fling myself onto the ground at the guard's feet.

As he bends to help me up, Emmett uses his height to reach over his head and swipe the set of keys that hangs on the pegboard above the guard's chair.

The dungeons smell of rot and damp earth. Emmett is so tall, he must duck as we navigate the dark, narrow passages.

His breathing is ragged, his hands balled into tight fists

at his sides. I run a finger over his white knuckles and realize he probably hasn't been down here since he himself was a prisoner.

"Are you all right?" I ask him. "I can do this on my own if you need me to."

He grits his teeth and shakes his head. "I'll be fine." Then he glances back to the sliver of light behind us, marking the entrance. "Did you know they threw me down those stairs?" he asks softly.

"I'll kill them all for you," I whisper, surprised to find I mean it. Bram coming to my room in a glamour, touching me like his right to my body was inherent, has filled me with an inferno's worth of rage. My anger is no longer some simmering thing I can live with.

Emmett shakes his head. "No. You don't need to kill them all, you only need to deal with the one."

Our footsteps squelch through the damp earth until we finally reach the last cell. In the deepest, darkest bowels of the prison, she is illuminated by only a single, dim faerielight.

"Ivy Benton." Her voice is croaky with disuse. She looks to my left and laughs. "And Emmett De Vere. My, you two are predictable."

I have no time for small talk or her tricks. "This ends tonight. You need to take us back to England."

"That sounds rather difficult given my current predicament." She arches a perfect brow and waves her thin hand toward the bars of her cell. Without the trappings of her court gowns or bejeweled tiaras, she looks even younger than usual. Her flawless skin is wan and her dark hair hangs limp around her shoulders. Her doe eyes might read as childlike if not for the fathomless darkness within them.

"No more talking in circles," I declare. "We don't have the time."

I pull Ferrinus from my cloak and hold it up to the dim faerielight. She squints her eyes and then goes still. "Where did you get that?" she asks, a quiver in her voice betraying a crack in her armor.

"I will use it to kill you if you don't take me and Emmett back to England this very moment and lock the door behind you. You locked it four hundred years ago. I know you know how."

"Those are my options?" she asks, her voice steady. "Take you and the boy home or die?"

"And lock the door. But yes."

She sizes me up with her fathomless, dark eyes. "What about your sister? Your friends? Weren't you all thick as thieves?"

I place my hands on my hips and swallow the rising nausea. "You know nothing of love, so I won't waste time speaking of it to you."

Mor tilts her face, like a bird of prey examining a mouse. "Is that what you think? You know, you never asked me why I sent Lydia here the first time. I kept waiting for you to question me, but perhaps you're less clever than I'd hoped."

I can't help myself; I take her bait. "Why, then? If you're so eager to tell me."

"I may have shut the door between our worlds, but I never lost sight of who I was, or where I truly belonged. I might have found the mass torture of humans distasteful during my reign, but I understood that it served an important function in keeping the court sated. Do you think Lydia is the only misguided youth I sent to the Otherworld? There were hundreds just like her, begging for escape, and to some of them, I granted it. Every few years, I would pass a human through the door as a show of goodwill to the fae court. I believed my former husband was still ruling and I thought it a gesture of diplomacy. I didn't realize Bram had killed him long ago."

"Why are you telling me this?"

Queen Mor takes a sharp breath. "So that you understand where my loyalties will always lie."

I'm counting on that.

"Only Lydia wasn't supposed to come back to England. You Benton sisters ruined everything."

"Shouldn't you have known then that something was wrong?"

"I thought my ex-husband had sent her home. He did that from time to time, back when he was still living. As always, my love for my son blinded me to his true nature," she says.

At the thought of Lydia, a stab of pain shoots through my

chest. We've failed each other in so many ways, but I have to believe I'm doing right by her now.

"Bram has gone mad, or maybe he was mad to begin with. But he's found out about Emmet and I and he's going to kill at least one of us. We need to go, quickly, before we are discovered."

Queen Mor pushes herself up off the ground. In her dirty white chemise, threadbare blanket over her shoulders, she looks like a phantom.

Her black eyes rake over Emmett. "I always told you your soft heart was going to be the death of you, Emmett De Vere. You're so like your father."

"I wouldn't know." He growls. "I never got the chance to know him before you killed him."

"Oh, that." She sighs like she's sad about Edgar's death. "I figured one of two things was true; either that he'd helped Bram with his coup—I knew he'd been leaving you little hidden messages for years—or he hadn't, and Bram was going to torture him worse than I ever would have. It was a punishment or a mercy depending on how you look at it."

Emmett's face crumples. "It was murder."

"That doesn't mean I didn't care for him. I regret what I had to do to poor Edgar. He was one of my favorite husbands."

This is already going on too long; we can't let her goad us like this. I know her well enough by now to know there is a good chance she is biding her time, waiting for Bram to find us down here, to prove her loyalty to him.

I flash the knife. "The time for discussion is over. What will it be?"

She rolls her eyes. "I've always been rather invested in my own self-preservation. Open the cell."

Emmett produces the heavy brass key ring he swiped from its hook by the door.

The lock slides open and Queen Mor steps out of her cell with all the grace of a queen parading in front of her people.

She holds her hands out to us.

"Are you ready?" she asks.

We nod and take one hand in each. Like her son, her skin is the same cool temperature of the air. It's like holding hands with a dead body.

The air goes still, and it's as if I can faintly hear another far-off lock click open, and then the door materializes in front of us.

It first appears as a rectangle of light, appearing at eye height, about the size of a painting. Slowly, it expands until it's large enough for a human to step through.

It's daytime in England and the sudden change of light burns my eyes. Queen Mor tugs our hands, and without any fanfare, the three of us walk through together. In half a heartbeat we travel from the dungeons of the Otherworld into the grand foyer of Kensington Palace.

It's just as I remember it. The leaves on the tree that grows up through the staircase have turned from green to brilliant orange. They flutter gently through beams of golden sunlight, from the eaves to the black-and-white checkered floors. The front doors to the gravel drive are wide open, letting in the cool autumn breeze.

It smells just how I remember it, too, a mix of damp earth and floor polish.

There is no sense of relief, though. This is not meant to be a happy homecoming.

Emmett takes one step into the foyer, and I make no attempt to follow him before I am wrenched backward. Our eyes meet, and the space between us is charged with all the time we wanted but will not get.

Queen Mor grips my hand tighter and yanks me off of my feet.

I don't even have the time to gasp before I go tumbling back through the open door to the Otherworld.

"I'm sorry!" I scream. If he can't forgive me, I hope he at least understands, in time.

I hear one last thing: Emmett screaming my name.

Mor and I land with a thud in the great hall of the castle. The sky is dark and a revel is in full swing around us.

The band whines to a halt and the crowd gasps as they see Mor and me, fighting like alley cats in the middle of the ballroom.

I land a blow to her stomach and she jerks me back by my hair hard enough that her hand comes away with a fistful of it.

She holds me down, but I buck my hips and roll, briefly escaping, before she scrambles to her feet and brings her foot down on my hand, hard, shattering the delicate bones and pinning me to the floor. My scream echoes off the rafters.

Maybe it's her immortal strength, but it isn't much of a fight after that. For all my kicking and punching and biting, she hauls me to my feet, pins my hands behind my back, and pushes me toward the dais at the end of the room. I never stood a chance against her. I knew that.

Sitting in twin thrones are Bram and my sister.

My sister's face is parchment white, her hands gripping the arms of her seat, but Bram looks on with curious amusement.

Mor kicks the back of my legs, sending me to my knees. I try not to grimace as bone strikes marble floor.

I test the joints of my hand, but they scream in pain, completely useless. I say a small prayer of gratitude that it was the nondominant one she shattered.

"My, what exciting party crashers," Bram declares.

"If you ever wanted proof of my loyalty to you, here it is," Mor snarls, standing above me. "Your insolent wife came to me, begging me to help her and Emmett De Vere escape. She threatened to kill me if I didn't once again lock the door between our worlds."

Someone in the crowd boos and there's another smattering of nervous laughter.

But my eyes are trained on my sister. I mouth, *I'm sorry.*

Tears well in her eyes.

I love you.

She shakes her head and mouths *Why?* in return.

I'm not sure what she means. Why did I leave her? Or why didn't I tell her what I plan to do?

I suppose the answer to both questions is the same: I was trying to protect her.

"Kill your wife and be done with it," Mor declares.

Do it, I'm tempted to urge, but for this plan to work, I must be patient.

Bram glances from me to Lydia and then back to me.

Queen Mor leans over to one of the banquet tables. From between the half-melting chocolate cakes, waxy grapes, and picked-over chicken carcasses, she grabs a paring knife.

It's a delicate little thing, shiny enough to glint in the faerielight of the ballroom, sharp enough to slide right between my ribs.

"Please, no." Lydia's voice shakes as she swallows down tears. "I'll do anything, Bram. Just exile her, I beg of you."

I press my lips together and shake my head, just enough for her to see.

Please, I want to tell her. *Let me do this.*

"Send her away," I say to Bram. "Go ahead and kill me, but as one final kindness, do not make my sister watch." He remains expressionless.

"Ivy, no. Ivy, please." Once upon a time, all I wanted was for my sister to fight for me, for any evidence that she loved me just as completely and wretchedly as I loved her.

But I do not want her to fight here. Showing any level of loyalty to me will only put her at risk. She needs to be somewhere far from this castle.

Rhion stands on the edge of the dais, his face a cool mask. This wasn't his plan. It wasn't even Emmett's plan. It was the one I formulated in secret and prayed I'd never have to use.

I turn my gaze toward him and hope he can read the silent plea in my eyes. *Take her out of here.*

Rhion nods once and his deep voice fills the room. "I'll take the queen, Your Majesty." Before Bram has a chance to say no, Rhion has already scooped Lydia into his arms.

She flails her legs and arms, screaming, "Ivy, Ivy, Ivy!" I've never heard a noise like this come out of her. Not even in the darkest days right after her disappearance did she cry this hard, scream her voice hoarse like this.

I thought seeing visions of Emmett in the cave was the worst emotional pain I'd ever feel, but it's nothing compared to this.

I want to shut my eyes and cover my ears.

I want to disappear.

I want to be anyone but me.

But I have a job to do.

The door slams behind Lydia and Rhion, though her sobs echo distantly down the hall.

Slowly, Bram rises from his throne and descends the steps of the dais to his mother and me.

Mor tries to pass the knife to him, but he waves it away.

"Bram?" I whisper. I look into his storm-cloud-gray eyes one last time.

I take a step closer to him and extend my hands toward his face, like I'm going in for one last kiss. His eyes soften.

Then I pull Ferrinus from where it's hidden in the inner pocket of my cloak, and drive it directly into his heart.

CHAPTER TWENTY-FOUR

At first, I think my ears are ringing, but as the panicked roaring in my head clears, I realize it's Queen Mor, screaming behind me.

The heavy knife falls from my hand and slides across the polished marble floors, leaving a trail of dark blood in its wake.

When Emmett and I first conceived of this plan, I promised him I'd run after I stabbed Bram. That I'd find some way back to him in England.

I lied. I never had any intention of leaving this room alive.

Behind me is a crowd of courtiers so thick I have no chance of making it through them, and stationed at all the exits are royal guards in blue-and-gold livery, armed to the teeth.

And in front of me—

In front of me, Bram's crumpled body begins to stir.

I lunge for the knife, ready to strike another blow if I need to, but it doesn't make any sense—I struck true. I felt the sickening snap of his breastbone and the squelch as the knife drove its way into his heart.

Lady Thalia appears at the edge of the crowd and snatches the knife from the floor with a revolting grin.

I lunge, ready to throw my entire body weight at her, but a guard appears behind me and pins my arms behind my back.

I shut my eyes tight, ready for him to slit my throat, or let Queen Mor snuff me out like tallow candle, but nothing comes.

Then I hear laughing.

Bram pushes himself up off the floor and smooths his doublet.

It's got a sizable gash down the center from where the knife struck, large enough to see his bare chest beneath.

The skin there is the pale pink of recent healing. The blood splattered on his white undershirt is the only evidence there was ever a wound. His body is unmarked, whole and completely fine.

It doesn't make sense. This was my one chance.

Bram runs his tongue over his full bottom lip as he regards me, squirming in the guard's grip.

"Take her to the dungeons!" he commands. "I'll deal with her later."

Another guard glances to Queen Mor. "And her?"

Bram chews on the inside of his cheek, then gestures to the throne beside him. "She can stay. The party was awfully dull before you showed up."

An iridescent petal floats down from the eaves and lands

on top of Mor's dark hair. She smirks victoriously.

I don't bother struggling as the guards drag me down into the darkest depths of the castle. All the fight has leached out of my body the same way the unicorn's silver blood ran out of its neck and into the dirt.

I'm hollow, a husk of who I once was.

The guards toss me like a bag of rubbish into the last cell; the one that, until this afternoon, belonged to Queen Mor.

I slump against the dirt and examine my crushed hand.

It's bright red, the skin pulsing and hot. The pain is so intense, it radiates up my arm and into my shoulder, like a physical rope of aching fire.

I'm almost grateful for it; the agony gives me something to focus on that isn't the emotional pain of my failure.

The dungeons are a pit of darkness, with only the shadowy glow of the distant faerielight by the guard's station to see by.

I don't know how long I sit in that cell, slipping in and out of consciousness.

It must be at least a full day by the way my stomach starts gnawing at itself. My broken hand throbs with a burning pain so intense, sometimes it's hard to breathe.

I'm drifting somewhere in the hazy space between sleep and wake when I hear a soft ringing sound and look up to see Eloree knocking at my bars.

Her large eyes are frightened, but her voice is steady. "They won't let your sister visit, ma'am, but she did convince His Majesty to let me bring you some of your things."

In her arms she holds a blanket stuffed with objects.

Gently, she unfurls it and passes them to me one by one. A leather-bound journal, an inkwell and fountain pen, a glass carafe of water, and a pillow small enough to slip under the bars.

The last object, she handles with great care. It's glowing a dim blue, small enough to fit within the palm of her hand.

It passes under the bars with only a hair's breadth to spare.

I gasp softy, and the glow turns to a warmer shade of blue, the color of the sky on a crisp fall day.

It's the lux flower Emmett gave me, that afternoon he took me to the waterfall and told me this place could be beautiful. I ruined it by goading him into a petty argument, just like I ruin everything else.

I clutch the flower to my chest and find it slightly warm. It's the first comfort I've had, in this hole at the center of the earth. No, *not the earth*, I remind myself. England will be forever out of reach to me.

It's funny that the thought of rainy afternoons, a warm cup of tea, the Thames winding through the center of the city, is what finally makes me cry.

I'll never again see the Covent Garden arcade, or the trees of Hyde Park. I'll never walk through Belgrave Square with a parasol over my shoulder, or bound up the steps of my family home.

I'll never see my mother and father again.

I'll never see Emmett again.

I cling to the hope that Lydia is smart enough to keep her mouth shut about me, to send me down the river and protect herself and our parents. I am all right with dying if it means she gets to keep on living.

I made that decision days ago, when I first conceived of this plan, though I hoped it wouldn't go quite like this.

I feared if things went south and we didn't get the opportunity to implement Rhion's plan of threatening Bram with the knife and asking him to abdicate or face prison, we'd need a second option.

Emmett knew I planned to threaten Mor into opening the door, but he didn't know about the second part of my plan. I can't bring myself to regret it, not even now.

For all the time Emmett spent living under the same roof as Mor, I fear he doesn't understand her as well as I do.

Above all things, Mor loves her son. Even threatened with death, I knew she would not betray him.

Emmett believed we were going to return to London, all of us, and let Mor spend a few weeks ruling as she used to. We would then use our allies throughout the country to bind her in iron chains once more and have her cede power.

But she'd never do that, not if it meant leaving Bram behind forever.

When Bram caught me with Emmett, I knew he'd never let me close enough to kill him again. I had permanently severed what little trust he had left in me.

But I also knew Mor would betray me to him, giving me

the perfect opportunity to get within striking distance with Ferrinus in my hand. I believed it was only through her that I'd ever get close to Bram again.

Only I didn't expect that the knife would fail. I got it all correct except for that one crucial detail. I still don't understand why.

My certainty that I would be betrayed by Mor and need to kill Bram by my own hand is why I was fine leaving Lydia and the other girls behind. The less they were tied to me, the better. They needed deniability to protect them.

I wrote a letter to Nan and Fennick just yesterday begging them to shelter my sister and friends until Rhion could figure out a way to return them safely to England.

Eloree looks at me, startled, through the bars of my cell. She twists up the blanket until it, too, is small enough to pass through and I take it from her gratefully.

"Why are you crying, ma'am? I tried to bring you your dresses, but it was forbidden."

I choke out a watery laugh. "That was very kind of you, Eloree. You are welcome to take the dresses for yourself. I have the feeling I will not have use for them again."

Concern flickers over her face, but she curtsies and turns to leave.

"Wait—"

She turns back, face expectant.

"I need food," I say. "They haven't been feeding me."

She sucks on her bottom lip. "I'm sorry. I tried, really I did.

They told me it was forbidden."

"Who did?"

"The King's Guard."

Even crawling the few feet across the cell to retrieve the objects Eloree passed me has left me dizzy.

"Then tell His Majesty I request an audience."

She looks to the ground sheepishly. "Prisoners aren't allowed to make requests."

"I'm the queen of England. Tell him I demand an audience." I try my best, but my voice is too weak with hunger to carry any real sense of authority.

Her mouth wobbles with pity. I don't even have the strength to keep myself upright, so all I see is her mud-slicked slippers disappearing down the hall.

It's as if the darkness in the dungeon is a physical beast, swallowing me whole. Every moment I spend here I disappear a little more.

I don't know how many days I've spent in the dungeons before I notice the scratches on the far corner of the cell.

They're near the bottom where the stone wall meets the dirt floor. It's as if they've been carved with a sewing pin; it clearly took whoever wrote them multiple strokes to make each letter visible.

My vision is blurry, but the message is unmistakable:

Ivy Benton, 1830–1848
There was no one braver or more brilliant.

> *She was too good for this world and she was too good for me. But that didn't stop me from loving her. I loved her. I loved her. I love her.*

I reach out with my good hand and brush my fingertips over the cool stone.

This must have been Emmett's cell, I realize. He sat in this awful place and mourned me.

I'm surprised I still have enough moisture in my body to cry, but hot tears run down my cheeks and into the neckline of my filthy dress.

In the middle of the cell, the lux flower glows a deep, melancholy blue.

That day by the waterfall comes back to me. Emmett looked so beautiful with his face tilted toward the sun, the spray of fresh water making his hair even wavier than usual.

There was so much happiness in his voice as he told me he was good at being a regent. It was to him that I first admitted out loud that I was proud of my work as queen.

And I don't believe anyone deserves to rule a country, not in the way Queen Mor did, with a grip so tight it choked the life out of its people. But if Emmett and I had had more time, perhaps we could have created an England that was built for more than just the aristocracy. Where girls could aspire to more than just marriage and your family name didn't determine your fate. Perhaps if I'd had the chance, I could have been the kind of ruler who didn't speak the loudest, but amplified the voices of those who matter most, society's most vulnerable members.

It was easier when I didn't let myself want anything.

Once I started, I wanted everything too much.

Will Bram give me a funeral after I starve to death? I wonder. If so, what will my tombstone read? Ivy, queen of England? Or Ivy Benton, the most gullible girl in the world?

The lux flower shifts toward periwinkle.

I was queen. I laugh audibly at the thought, it's so ridiculous.

Whatever else happens, he can't take that away from me. I may have only ever been a means to an end, to him. But I was still queen.

Will he allow England to mourn me? Will he tell my parents? Will he open the door so that I can be buried there?

Rhion's words come back to me. *Bram is the door.*

I've long wondered how Lydia returned to London from the Otherworld if Bram didn't open the door for her. Vaguely, I figured Queen Mor must have been the one to let her return, as part of their bargain, but it doesn't make sense with what Lydia has since told me about her escape or what Mor said about assuming it was her ex-husband who sent her back.

But what if no one opened the door for Lydia? What if she opened it herself? After all, she was Bram's wife. She was queen of the Otherworld.

And Bram would have underestimated her.

What if in her panicked escape, she accessed the magic that was her right by way of marriage?

And if she escaped, maybe I could too.

I close my eyes and search through the deepest, darkest parts of me.

I picture Kensington Palace, with its checkered floors and grand staircase. I imagine my old attic room back at Caledonia Cottage with its narrow bed and window that looked out onto the green of Kensington Park.

I reach for it, my hand outstretched. I open my eyes and find—nothing. Nothing but the darkness of the cell and that flickering lux flower.

I take a steadying breath and attempt it once more. This time I focus not on what home looks like but how I felt there. My chest grows warm as I think of Emmett teaching me to waltz in front of a roaring fire, of Olive baking bread in the kitchen of the cottage, of Lydia helping me into my dress on my wedding day.

I've already lived the best days of my life, and I didn't even know it.

Agony pierces me. I can't help myself as I let out a wail of despair.

Something deep within me shifts. My hands tingle, even the ruined one. My head feels lighter than it has in days.

Perhaps it's death.

My eyes are so heavy that opening them seems like a herculean feat. It would be so easy to slip into the darkness, to let myself be carried away by the tide of it.

I could find Ethel and Greer and Emmett's father and the

girl in the deer mask and tell them how sorry I am.

It would be the easiest thing in the world. I know that with a certainty that reaches to my soul. I would be welcomed and made whole in death.

But what a waste it would be to give in to something because it is easy, when I've come this far.

The smell of damp earth and floor polish hits my nose.

With every last amount of strength I have, I pry open my eyes.

In front of me is a perfect rectangle of light, the grand foyer of Kensington Palace visible within it.

Emmett turns and gasps.

CHAPTER TWENTY-FIVE

Emmett hurls himself through the door the minute he glimpses me. There's no hesitation in his actions. One moment he's standing in Kensington Palace, and the next he's on top of me.

My broken hand screams with pain as I attempt to push myself upright. I look up through tangled hair. My dress is so thoroughly covered in mud, it sticks to my body like a second skin. "You landed on me," I rasp.

Emmett pulls himself off of me, then captures my face in his hands. "You're alive?" he asks with wonder.

"Barely," I joke.

"How?" He looks around the dungeon.

"The royal family is the door. I thought it just meant Bram and Mor, but I realized it meant me, too."

"Darling, sweetheart, brave girl," Emmett whispers as he presses a kiss to my filthy head. "Why did you do that? Why did you let her pull you away from me?"

"I knew she'd double-cross me. I believed it was my only

chance to get close enough to kill him."

"If I weren't so relieved to see you, I'd be very upset with you for that plan."

"Be upset with me later," I say.

"And did you kill him?" Emmett voice goes quiet. I can't tell if he hopes I did or not.

I shake my head. "The knife didn't work, I don't know why."

In my distraction, the door to England has winked shut, leaving Emmett and me trapped in the dungeons.

"I need to concentrate. I'll open the door to England again and get us both out of here." I close my eyes and reach for that strange feeling, but nothing comes. I'm too distracted at having Emmett here. Relief and terror course through me.

Focus, Ivy.

My stomach growls.

Emmett reaches into the pocket of his coat and pulls out a scone wrapped in a cloth napkin. "Olive and Ben baked them this morning."

I take a bite and resist the urge to groan as butter hits my tongue. It's the best thing I've ever tasted.

It's finished in just two bites. Emmett watches as I chew and swallow.

"How are they?" I ask.

"Right as rain. Olive has been stress-baking and Eduart wouldn't stop complaining about the number of cakes filling the house, and they miss you, of course. We were all so worried."

"I'm sorry. Can I say I'm sorry again?" I ask, and Emmett answers me with a quick kiss.

My focus is broken by the sound of footsteps crashing down the corridor.

Emmett can't be here; if we're caught—

I squeeze my eyes shut and reach for that place inside me, but the door won't come.

I curse under my breath.

A dark figure comes into view.

"Rhion?" I say as he presses his face against the bars.

"I'm sorry—" he pants, then stops at the sight of Emmett. "How'd you get down here?"

"Ivy," Emmett answers.

"Never mind," Rhion says. "Explain later, I've come to rescue you."

"How gallant," Emmett says.

I shoot him a glare and look back to Rhion. "How are Faith, Marion, and Lydia?"

Rhion gives me an uneasy smile. "Alive, but locked in their rooms. Bram has been in a rage, and I fear Mor is only encouraging him. We need to get you all out."

"I opened the door once, I can do it again," I say, and Rhion's eyes widen. "I just need the time to focus."

Rhion sorts through a ring of keys until he finds the right one and sticks it in the lock. "Then let's get you somewhere safe."

The cell door opens with a creak and Emmett helps me to my feet.

Rhion looks anxiously over his shoulder. "I knocked the guard out, but he won't stay asleep much longer."

Emmett's body is tense as we creep through the damp corridors of the dungeon, but he carries on without faltering.

We're to the stairs when Rhion pauses. "Wait—" He stops, his eyes wide, but we're too late.

The guard is awake, and he's sounded the alarm.

Dozens of guards stampede down the narrow staircase, blocking our only means of escape.

"Ivy!" Emmett screams. He lunges toward me, but the guards reach me first. My head snaps back as I fight, but they've pulled my hands behind my back and my broken hand makes it agony to pull away. They pull chains from their belts and bind my wrists while I wail in pain.

"Don't touch her!" Emmett yells. It takes four guards to restrain him, and six for Rhion.

For a beat they just hold us there, with our limbs pinned.

And then a silhouette appears at the top of the stairs.

Bram walks down slowly, relishing our fear and the power he has over us.

He comes directly to me and bends so his gray eyes are level with mine. "You wanted me dead?" he asks. His mouth is turned down, his voice thick with pain.

"You're going to kill us, what does it matter what I want?" I snap.

He leans in even closer, until our noses nearly brush, and I know he's savoring the hate coming off me in waves.

Over his shoulder, Emmett struggles in vain against his chains, and I hate myself for failing him.

With deep hopelessness, I reach once more for the door, and then I find it. That *click*.

A small square of light appears in front of me, between Bram and Emmett. Bram's back is to it, so he doesn't see, but Emmett's eyes go wide.

I nod, just barely. *Go*, I will him. *Save yourself.*

"Don't look at him, look at me," Bram barks, and my eyes snap back to his. My hold on the door is tenuous. I won't be able to keep it open much longer.

"Go!" I yell.

Bram's head whips around. Fury contorts his features as he sees the door.

He pushes my body up against the wall. "How are you doing that?" he demands.

"You gave me this power," I mock. "I should thank you."

The door is narrowing by the second. Emmett and Rhion need to go. "Now! Please!" I yell over Bram's shoulder at them.

Emmett uses his shoulder to knock a guard off his feet, then kicks his legs out from under him.

With all the strength he has, he lunges at Bram. "Do not touch her."

Guards have us both pinned to the ground in seconds. The door shrinks to nothing but a sliver of light and then winks out of existence entirely.

"No!" I shout through tears. "You fool, you idiot. You

should have saved yourself."

One guard shoves Emmett's face into the dirt and digs his knee in between Emmett's shoulder blades as he wrenches his hands behind his back.

Emmett licks blood from his split lip and gives me a grin. "Save myself? That's not what we do."

PRINCE EMMETT DE VERE

I'm locked in my office for two days before the summons from Bram appears.

It comes, as they always do, as a note slipped under my door.

Fencing, noon, this one reads, in handwriting that isn't even Bram's. He's dictated it to a servant like I'm not even worth getting ink on his hands.

On the rare occasion that Bram was in the Otherworld, we often met for various sports. We spent our time playing tennis, or horseback riding, or hitting croquet balls in the garden. There was one summer Bram magicked the wickets to run away, which was particularly annoying, but these were the times it was easiest to imagine the boys we once were in London.

I didn't expect to ever receive a summons like this from him again.

For the last two days, I've been out of my mind with worry for Ivy. I've torn apart my office, searching every book for anything that could help me save her, but I've come up empty. Every day, trays of food arrive, and in that regard, it's been unlike my previous stay in the dungeons, but I've never felt more like a caged animal.

My breakfast arrives with a set of fencing whites. I dress and sit on the edge of my bed, my brain wearing out the same thought over and over—*How do I save her? How do I save her?* There aren't any clocks in the Otherworld, so I don't know how long I wait until my door unlocks and swings itself open magically.

Two guards flank me on either side, so I'm unable to run to Ivy's room or the dungeons, but there's an air of inevitability about this meeting. I'm looking forward to facing Bram, all veneer stripped away, and, for once in our lives, being honest with each other.

Bram is waiting for me in the gymnasium, tugging on his white gloves, his nose tipped up in the air arrogantly.

"Just tell me if she's alive." My voice is little more than a snarl. It's taking every inch of self-control I have not to launch myself at him and pummel my fists into his face.

Bram gestures to the bench where my gloves and saber lie. "We can talk while we spar."

Seeing no other choice, I pull on my mesh mask and join him on the mat.

Bram lunges at me, but I parry, blocking him. "This is beneath you, Emmett," he drawls slowly, like this is just some brotherly spat we'll be over before dinner.

"Is she alive?" My tone is desperate, and I don't care. Let him know how desperate I am. He sidesteps my thrust, then parries back lazily, as if we are boys again and none of this matters.

"Yes, she's alive. Why do you care?" he snaps. "She's intolerable, and unfaithful, and you lower yourself by loving her. Do you not want to rule as my regent? You'd give all this up for *her*?"

"Yes." It comes out as nearly a shout. "I'd do anything for her, do you not see that?" It's foolish, perhaps, to admit, but he must know by now, and I see no sense in hiding it. If Bram is going to kill me, then I want to die with the truth on my lips. "It was always about her, everything I've done."

"No, you love *me*." Bram lunges again, something newly ferocious in his movements, and this time his saber strikes my torso with force enough to sting, even through my jacket. "We were brothers, weren't we? That's what you needed when I first met you. You were so small and weak, barely more than a child, and all you wanted was a family. *I* gave that to you. *I* became what you needed. In exchange, you were supposed to be loyal to me."

"I would have been." I feel equal parts rage and heartbreak at Bram confirming that our brotherhood was never anything more than another manipulation tactic. The worst part is, he's not wrong. I *do* love him, but I hate him more.

I lunge again, my slash crisp and precise as my old training returns to me. Bram and I had the same fencing master, once upon a time. "Are you going to kill her?" I ask.

Bram's maneuvers are sloppy, disdain and arrogance in every swipe of his saber. "She's going to die at some point. Your lifespans are so short, what does it matter if it's now or later?"

He waves his hand and knocks my mask off my face with magic. I block, but he flicks his saber up and slices a cut down my cheekbone. "You're all so fragile."

"You're pathetic." I throw my saber to the ground and lunge at him with my full body weight. My fist screams in pain as I land a blow to his sternum, but I draw my arm back and hit him again. "You have two wives and neither one wants you."

He rips off his own mask and hurls himself forward, forcing me backward onto the mat.

Bram lands one good punch across my face, but he's a poor student—and I've been the better fighter since I caught up to him in height, years ago.

I use my legs to hook his ankles, throwing him off-balance, then drive my entire body weight upward to get him off me. I have him pinned in seconds, his wrists under my knees.

"Do you understand what this kingdom has turned into while you were off in England, treating everything like a toy you can break? Lydia and I have held the Otherworld together with our bare hands and you don't even care."

Bram's eyes flash and in an instant, I'm tossed back against the mat. My lungs ache as the air is knocked out of them and I struggle to catch my breath. A few ribs are probably cracked, but I don't care.

Bram stands above me, grinning, and I recognize this look on his face. It's the same one he had that day when I was fourteen and he fought my bullies for me. I realize now, it's the violence he loves.

"You used magic, that's not fair," I groan. "Fight me like a man."

Bram kicks me with the toe of his boot. "Maybe I should force you to your knees, make you beg."

Of my own free will, I rise to my knees and tilt my throbbing face up toward him. "I will do anything for her. Let them both go and I'll stay here as your regent, forever. I'll let you beat me to a bloody pulp every day. Would that make you feel big?"

Bram curls his lip in disgust as he looks down at me. "You're not fun to play with anymore."

He waves his hands at the guards flanking the doors and they step toward me. "I'm finished," Bram snarls as he walks away. With his back toward me, he snaps his fingers, and I am knocked unconscious.

CHAPTER TWENTY-SIX

Iron bars have been bolted in front of the pale purple door to my room. They're rough-hewn and ugly, particularly monstrous against the feminine backdrop of my chambers. The wall has cracked in the places they were attached, like it was all done hastily, but they're solid, and I suppose that's what counts.

I hurl my body against the door a few times in an attempt to dislodge them, but they stay as immovable as granite, leaving me with nothing but bruised confidence and an equally bruised shoulder.

The diamond-paned window won't break, no matter how many objects I smash against it. Eventually, I'm not even throwing them as a means of escape, but because I can't quiet this raging storm inside of me and it feels better to scream my voice hoarse and destroy these beautiful objects than to lie down in bed and wait for my own death.

My floral teapot shatters against the window. I use every bit of my strength on my tiaras, which ricochet and leave dislodged gems scattered across the carpet like raindrops. I break the glass shelves they once laid upon with a single mighty swing of a rack from my wardrobe, wielded like a sword.

I look down at my broken left hand, disgusted at the sight of my wedding rings. My fingers are bruised and swollen, but I pull and pull, ignoring the screaming pain until they're finally off. In one fluid motion, I toss them into the fire.

I stare at the pearl ring on my index finger a beat longer, breathing heavily. How strange it is to look back at my six-year-old self with so much ire. How could someone so small have wrought this much horror? How could I have steered my entire life on a collision course with disaster and not even known it?

A shower of sparks goes up as I toss it into the fire as well, but it doesn't make me feel any better.

I rage until I'm damp with sweat and my voice is entirely gone, and then I lie amid the broken glass and stare up at the ceiling so long I start to see fuzzy shapes in the darkness.

The guards knocked me unconscious before they locked me in here, so I do not know what has happened to Emmett, my sister, or any of the others.

I have to grapple with the possibility that they are all dead. Well, except for Lydia. Bram will not have us deny him his final show.

For two days, I live in the wreckage I have made. I'm forced to wear shoes at all times because of the broken glass on the carpet.

I try to reach within me, to find that magical latch that unlocks the door back to England, but I can't do it. It's like it's been scooped out of me.

I wonder if Bram has some magic preventing me from reaching it, or if I'm just a failure.

I have the sad realization that if I was able to open the door from the dungeons, Mor could have as well. The bars were merely for show. She chose to stay in that dungeon for her son.

On the third day, Eloree arrives as the first pale pink of dawn peeks over the distant hills. Behind her are two other lady's maids, who carry a large leather trunk between them.

A guard pulls out a key, but before he unlocks the bars, he looks at me and says, "If you try to run, we'll kill her." And gestures to Eloree.

"I won't run." My voice is a mere whisper, still ruined from all my screaming.

He unlocks the door and the three maids shuffle in silently.

The trunk crunches on the scattered glass as they set it on the floor, but their faces remain stony. It's only Eloree who looks around the room, shock evident in her overlarge eyes.

"How is Lydia?" I rasp.

Eloree presses her pale lips together. "Worried about you," she answers.

But she is alive.

"And the others?" I ask.

Eloree runs a comb through my tangled hair, her eyes flitting down to the floor, then back to mine in the mercury glass mirror. "I do not know."

For silent hours, Eloree and her assistants work on me. There's much to do.

Eloree combs out each strand of my hair until my wild curls are a ball of frizz. Then she rubs a lotion that smells of herbs onto her hands and distributes it through my scalp and down the strands with gentle pressure. She uses a curling tong until each of my natural, wild curls has been re-formed into a perfect, cascading ringlet.

Her two assistants kneel at my feet, each one taking a hand. They scrub the dungeon dirt from under my nails, then cut and file until they resemble ten perfectly shiny crescent moons. I resist the urge to wiggle my fingers, which feel bare without my rings.

I am nothing better than a paper doll, blank and compliant as Eloree and the others slip my dressing gown off my shoulders, exposing my bare torso.

They rub oils that smell of honeycomb and violets into the skin of my arms and neck and collarbone. They do my legs next until every inch of me is glowing.

Eloree unscrews a pot of something white and cold and dabs it on the dark circles under my eyes. "Close," she says gently, then applies the rest to my swollen eyelids. She smears a pink salve on my lips and cheeks, bringing their sallow color back to life.

The tips of her fingers are cool and gentle against my angry skin, and it hits me that she will likely be the last person to ever touch me with kindness.

My stomach twists as I try my best not to think of the others. Eloree is being so gentle with me, and it would be rude to cry off all her hard work. I won't have my final actions be those of disrespect.

I'm numb as they guide me gently by my elbows to stand, and then methodically lace and button me into a gown.

It isn't until they're done that I glance in the mirror and realize what I'm wearing. It's constructed of layers and layers of whisper-thin, white, Swiss-dot tulle. Wide off-the-shoulder sleeves connect into a gentle V at the center of my chest. The waist is nipped in and tied with a grosgrain ribbon and the full skirts are embellished with intricate embroidery of wildflowers, white thread on white fabric.

"His Majesty selected it himself," Eloree explains gently.

But I already knew that, just by looking at it.

It's not the exact same, but it's the closest copy Bram could make in the Otherworld of my Pact Parade gown. I look almost exactly as I did the day we met. Well, I suppose it was the day *I* met *him*. He'd known me for long before that.

The only difference is my long, unbound hair and the golden tiara Eloree places atop it.

I look like a princess from a storybook.

And I am equally doomed.

I press my lips together and try to blink away the stinging feeling in my eyes. "Thank you, Eloree," I say. "You did beautiful work."

I look to the others, half cowering behind her. "I didn't even ask your names," I say with regret.

"Enid and Aspen, ma'am," the taller one answers meekly.

"Thank you, Enid and Aspen." I nod in their direction. "I apologize for my rudeness. You didn't catch me on my best day."

Eloree's green eyes well with tears, and she turns from me quickly, so I don't see them spill. "It's been an honor, ma'am," she says, then hurries out the door.

I'm afraid waiting will be its own form of torture, but the moment Eloree leaves, two large guards step into the room. One holds a delicate glass vial containing a few drops of silvery liquid. "We'll force you if you don't take it willingly," the guard says in a tired sort of way that implies he'd really rather not.

I keep my face blank as I extend my hand. He drops the vial into my palm. I'm surprised to find it's ice cold.

I don't hesitate as I uncork the vial and pour it right down my aching throat. I'm unconscious before I hit the floor.

LYDIA BENTON

My feet are buried in damp sand. Each pull of the tide toward the shore covers them further, and soon I've been sucked in so deep, I am completely unable to move.

Upon the horizon, a wave grows and grows until it crests so high, it blocks out the blazing sun, turning the daylight off like snuffing a lantern and casting the beach in eerie, sudden shadows.

"Help!" I call, but I turn my head and find that no one is there to save me. The dark sand stretches for miles in either direction, and I am completely alone.

"Help!" I call again. The wave is barreling toward me, picking up speed with every moment, now a solid, terrifying wall of water.

I pull and pull but my feet stay glued to the earth.

The rush of the ocean is deafening, dizzying.

I look down, and find myself, once more, in the body of my childhood. My white play dress is dirty with sand, and the pink ribbon around my waist is limp and ruined.

I raise my chubby hands to cover my ears, anything to stop the painful roar, but before I do, I hear something to my left.

"Lydia?" The voice is barely a squeak. I turn to see Ivy beside me, no older than six. Her golden curls whip around her face, picked up by the sea breeze. She's dressed identical to me, as we often were as children. Her round cheeks are pink from the force of the wind and her brown eyes are huge and terrified.

I'm moved by a bone-deep need to protect her, but my feet will not budge. I cannot move. I can't do anything but stand there as the wave barrels toward us.

"Don't look, Ivy!" I shout. "Look at me."

"Lydia?" she whines, her voice sharp with fear.

"Ivy!"

The wave crashes into us, pitching our bodies into its icy depths. I search for Ivy's hand in the dark waters, but my fingers slip through the surf and come away empty.

Reality arrives in splinters, but that incessant roaring noise doesn't stop. It's as if it's coming from within my own head. The volume causes such intense pressure, I feel like my skull might burst.

My vision is bloodred, the inside of my eyelids illuminated by blindingly bright light.

My hand lands on a plane of sharp gravel that bites into the flesh of my palm, and in my other hand, I hold a cool, smooth object.

I push myself fully upright, and force my eyes open,

ignoring the stinging sun.

For a second, I think I must be in another dream. My brain can't seem to make sense of where I am.

I've been dumped at the bottom of a bowl.

Well—not a bowl, I suppose. I search for the right word. I'm sure my father must have said it once during all our family dinners discussing history and archaeology.

A *coliseum*. The word comes to me with stomach-churning clarity.

Above me, circular stands carved from snow-white marble are filled with thousands of faeries. Our kingdom isn't particularly large; nearly everyone must be here—and they are the source of the roaring.

The nearest stand is probably ten feet above me; close enough to see the faces of the faeries who leer down at us.

They're open-mouthed and shouting, screaming with equal parts glee and terror. *"Get her!"* some yell, or *"Run, Queen Lydia, run!"*

I look down at my hand, the one not holding me up in the dirt, and find I'm clutching the horn of the unicorn I stabbed. It shimmers an iridescent blue in the beating sunlight. The wider end is ugly and jagged from where I tore it from the poor beast's body, and the other is a deadly sharp point.

Whatever sleeping draught they made me take to transport me here has left me feeling groggy and nauseous. The crowd goes absolutely wild as I finally stand.

I rotate in a slow circle until I find what I'm looking for

and—yes. There he is.

Bram lounges on a throne at the other end of the arena, the golden crown on his head glinting in the light.

Beside him sits Emmett, his white shirt dirty and torn, his hands and legs in iron chains, a gag tied around his mouth. From what I can see of his eyes from behind strands of his limp hair, he's fighting tears as he struggles against his restraints. Next to him is Rhion, also gagged and beaten black and blue. His bruised eyes bore into mine, that piercing blue visible even from here. I'm surprised by how much it hurts me to see him in pain.

On the other side of Bram is his mother on a brilliant golden throne, and beside her are Faith and Marion. They're not chained or bruised, but by the grim looks on their faces, I have no doubt they've been threatened with it.

And directly below Bram, her unconscious form slumped in the dirt, is my sister.

I take off for her at a full sprint, pushing my weak legs to their absolute limit.

I skid onto my knees as I approach her, absolutely shredding them, but I don't care. The pain is nothing compared to the panic. Is it possible Bram dumped me in here with my sister's corpse to torture me further?

"Ivy?" I shake her lifeless shoulders. "Ivy, please, please."

She awakens with a rattling gasp and I let out a sob of relief.

I pull her into a tight hug. "What's happening?" she

mutters groggily into my shoulder. We're dressed identically, like we're little girls again. Both of us in perfect replicas of my Pact Parade gown, golden tiaras on our heads.

Ivy is made up just like I am, with painted lips and rosy cheeks, so I know the lady's maids must have paid her a predawn visit as well.

The only difference is Ivy's left hand, the one Queen Mor broke the day Ivy attempted to kill Bram. It's wrapped in thick gauze, immobilizing it.

Her right hand, like mine, contains a weapon. Bram loves a joke, and this one is particularly cruel—he's armed Ivy with the crude knife she used in her ill-fated assassination attempt.

A boom echoes out through the arena, and I pull Ivy to her feet, careful not to jostle her broken hand, and sling an arm around her waist to keep her standing upright.

I hate the way fear ignites in her dark eyes as she takes in our surroundings.

Bram is standing now, and I realize the booming sound was the hilt of his sword striking the marble railing of his observation box.

"Dear guests!" He must have magically enhanced his voice to carry across the arena because an immediate hush takes over, causing my ears to ring in the absence of the crowd's roar. I force myself to focus on Bram's words over the buzz.

"I welcome you here to enjoy the finale of three trials to find my wife."

I'm already your wife, I want to hiss, but Bram is a coward and cowards will always bend the truth until it fits the narrative they want to believe about themselves.

"I was married both here and in England to free us from my mother's tyranny, but it left me in a rather interesting predicament," he explains. A smattering of laughter ripples through the crowd. I bet he loves it.

"A man cannot have two wives, and a land cannot have two queens. Both Benton sisters have fought bravely, but I am still unconvinced either possesses the devotion to put me, and our two great lands, above all else. Thus, our final trial is simple. To prove her loyalty to me, the last living sister will be declared the winner."

The last living sister? It takes me a moment to even glean his meaning, but Ivy puts it together faster than I do.

"You want us to kill each other?" Ivy shouts up at him with disgust. If she thought she could bridge the distance, she'd probably spit on him, too.

"Yes." Bram sinks down onto his throne. The jet-black beads of his ornately embroidered doublet jingle like soft bells.

Emmett struggles against his binds, but Bram doesn't so much as spare him a glance.

Oh, Emmett. My heart breaks for him, my faithful friend. He's only ever been guilty of having a heart that longed for love so desperately it left him, and everyone in his wake, bruised. I wish I'd gotten to see a world in which he and Ivy got to be together, settled and happy. They deserved it, but I suppose life doesn't always deliver what we deserve.

I know immediately what I must do, and I know I cannot hesitate.

The unicorn horn is still clutched in my sweaty palm and I raise it above my head, briefly blocking out the sun.

In that single heartbeat, a memory comes back to me with crushing clarity, perhaps one final gift from the universe.

It's my very first memory, a little foggy and pink around the edges. My father leading me by the hand into my mother's bedchamber. She was propped up against the pillows, a little sweaty, but glowing with happiness. I'd never seen her hair down before; that's what I remember being shocked by. I didn't even notice the wriggling bundle in her arms until my father scooped me up and placed me next to her.

She tipped the white blanket toward me, and inside was a sleeping baby. The sister they'd been promising me for months.

"She's mine?" I asked. *Happy.* That's how I felt looking at that chubby little face. Possessive, too. None of the other girls at the park had their very own baby sister. Anne had a baby brother, but he was always snotty and crying. This baby wasn't crying. She was *perfect.*

"Meet Ivy, your baby sister," my mother said gently, smoothing the bow I had tied in my hair. It had gotten all rumpled while I was playing on the floor with the kitchen cat.

"Mine." I reached out for her tiny little hand and she gripped my finger in hers like she needed me. When I think now about the two years before she was born, it seems unfathomable that

I ever existed without her.

"It's your job to protect her," my father said, looking at the three of us. I didn't understand why he was crying.

"My baby sister," I whispered with awe. It was the first time I understood why people cried from happiness. I knew then, I'd do anything for her.

Even this.

I take one last breath, one last glance at Emmett and Ivy. Then, before I have the chance to lose my nerve, I drive the unicorn horn toward my heart.

CHAPTER TWENTY-SEVEN

I'm still so dazed from the sleeping draught, it takes my brain a moment to catch up to the scene in front of me.

Lydia and I have been dumped in the middle of a coliseum, something right out of one of our father's mealtime history lectures.

The noise of the roaring crowd is enough to make me dizzy, and the sun is so bright, my eyes still haven't adjusted.

I've been dropped like a cat drops a dead bird for its owner, directly at the base of Bram's throne.

His wretched announcement rattles around my skull, and I'm attempting to puzzle some way out of it when an object glinting in Lydia's hand catches my eye.

I turn, to find her with the unicorn horn raised aloft. Her eyes are closed and there's something about her that's so still, like she's already made peace with what's happening.

"Don't look, Ivy!" she screams, and in one rapid motion, she drives the horn toward her own heart.

I don't think, I just run, throwing my body weight into her

in a side tackle, sending us both splayed out on the gravel.

Lydia pushes herself up, sputtering, and crawls, on her hands and knees, searching for the horn, which went flying when she fell.

"Lydia, stop!" I scream. "Please!"

I wish I could open the door back to England again and free us both from this, but the bowl of the coliseum is lined with sheets of iron, dampening whatever small magic I have within me.

"Let me do this!" she groans, still sifting through the gravel, looking for the horn.

But Ferrinus, the weapon Bram placed in my hand, landed directly behind me when we fell.

If she's not going to give me time to think of a plan that saves us both, then my next action is clear. I once snuck out of a warm town house and took off into a cold London night to search for her. It was the riskiest thing I'd done in all eighteen years of my life.

When we were children, for the first five years of my life, Lydia was the only person I spoke to willingly. It would drive our parents and governess mad, the way I'd lean over to Lydia and mumble in whispers only she could understand.

Lydia was the first person I ever spoke to.

I am glad she will also be the last.

"I love you, Lydia. I'm sorry," I say as I pick up Ferrinus, the knife that failed me so terribly, and hope it lands true. I strike before the fear of pain sets in.

The knife connects with my jugular vein, but just before it opens skin, something tears it from my wrist and knocks me back.

Lydia is on top of me, clawing like a feral animal. She drives her elbow into the wrapped palm of my broken hand, causing me to lurch in pain and drop the knife.

She picks it up herself, and I kick her wrist hard enough to hear it pop.

I can't even look at Emmett for fear I'll lose my nerve and not be able to do what I need to do.

A sharp pain rips through my head and I taste metal in the back of my throat, the eerie heat of magic suddenly crawling up my fingertips, through my shoulders, my collarbones, and up into my brain.

You hate her, a voice that sounds eerily like my own whispers. *You hate her. She abandoned you, she shut you out, she left your family's fate on your shoulders, then resented you for your power and fame. You were the one who dreamed of magic, but she stole your dream and became queen of the Otherworld. Emmett loves her. Maybe he's in love with her. While she's living, you'll always wonder if he wants her more. But you could kill her, kill her and be done with it. You'd be queen of England and of the Otherworld, just as you always imagined as a child. It was your dream. Not hers. Kill her, kill her, kill her.*

I claw at my hair and throw the tiara on the ground, desperate to get the awful words out of my head.

Kill her. She's jealous of you.

Kill her. She's never loved you as much as you love her. In fact, she doesn't love you at all.

"No!" I scream, just to drown out the voice. "It's not true!" I know it's not, because loving Lydia is an inexorable part of who I am, just as vital as my blood or bones.

It hurts to love a sister, but the only thing I've ever hated about her is the way she reflects the parts of me I can't stand, my living mirror. I hate that I can't lie to her, that I dread letting her down, that she's always been more honest than me. But I don't hate her. I couldn't.

I know what my sister is made of because I am made of exactly the same thing.

I turn to see Lydia in an identical battle, curled up in the fetal position, thrashing in the dirt, with her hands clamped over her ears.

LYDIA BENTON

The voice that is both me and not me slithers through my mind like a venomous snake, whispering the worst thoughts I've ever had like they're irrefutable facts.

Emmett and Bram chose her, but they should have chosen you instead. She never appreciated all you did for her. She's selfish. An attention seeker. Deliberately childish. She was cold to you when you came home from the Otherworld the first time and needed her comfort. She'll only ever resent you.

Kill her.

It'll be so easy.

Kill her.

This will all be yours. They'll both be yours.

I press my hands over my ears and scream as loud as I can to drown out the awful words.

I love Ivy, I remind myself. It's the foundation upon which everything else rests. *I love my sister.*

I love her so completely, it's not something Bram could ever corrupt, not with all the magic in the world.

The memories I saw in the Isern Caves come flooding back to me. Ivy might have seen Emmett, but I saw *her*. She was wrapped in her black cloak and Papa's scarf, lost, in the dark streets of London. In one shaking hand, she held my pearl baby necklace, the twin to the one she left at the base of the tree for the creature we now know was Bram.

She was looking for me, I realized with horrifying clarity. It was a memory from last winter when I was first in the Otherworld. I'd abandoned my sister, leaving her lost and alone. She was putting her very life at risk to search for me, all because of a selfish bargain I made on a whim. Ivy had never been outside alone before, but she was brave for me, because she believed I needed her.

I've always needed her. I wish I could tell her that now. I never should have left her. I should have let her in when I came home. I spent so many nights turning the lock of the door of my bedroom and then pretending to be asleep when I heard her knocking. I shut her out because she was the only person who truly saw me and I didn't want her to witness my shame. There's so much I have to apologize for.

As quickly as the voice in my head came, it dissipates like mist clearing a harbor. The crowd has gone silent as well, watching Ivy and me in stunned horror.

The faeries have a thirst for blood and chaos, but this seems to have surpassed even their taste for horror. There are many good souls among them; it is a shame that Bram's cadre so often drowns them out.

Rhion struggles against his shackles so desperately his wrists are dripping blood. There's a dirty rag around his mouth, but his eyes say everything.

Bram stands from his throne and stomps his foot. "You're not any fun!" he screams, the edge of his voice sharp, like a toddler screaming for a toy. "This isn't any fun! This was supposed to be fun!"

Ivy pushes herself off the ground and looks to where both the horn and the knife lie in the dirt, directly between us.

My eyes meet hers and I shake my head slightly. *Not yet.*

As I lift my gaze to Bram, it's hard to believe that just hours ago he was asleep next to me in my bed, breathing softly.

But as I see Bram now, his face contorted with rage, I realize I've been indulging in a fantasy. Bram might still be living, but that boy is long dead. He likely died centuries before I was ever born, and there is no amount of love I can pour into Bram that will bring him back to life.

"You've ruined everything!" Bram is red in the face, his hands balled into fists at his sides.

Ivy and I just stare at him. Maybe if we let him burn out his temper tantrum, we can all go home. But I know it's a foolish thought. It won't be that easy with Bram.

We've committed the most unforgivable sin; we've humiliated him by refusing to play his game.

"You want to be clever about it? Fine. No more games! Will that make you happy?"

He extends his ring-clad finger and points to Ivy, then me,

then back to Ivy, then me, where it comes to rest. I look up at this boy who I loved, who I *love*. Fury blazes in his eyes and before I have the chance to gasp or beg, or even cry out in surprise, he levitates Ferrinus and sends it flying across the arena, directly into my heart.

My breastbone cracks, and then I feel nothing at all.

CHAPTER TWENTY-EIGHT

I scream as Lydia's body hits the ground.

My legs move before I'm fully conscious of what I'm doing. I race for my sister and pull her into my lap. "Lydia, please, *Lydia*," I sob, but her body is nothing but a limp husk. She's not there anymore.

There is no death rattle, no fluttering eyelids, no last words on her lips.

Blood blooms around her like a great crimson flower.

Lydia was gone before she hit the ground.

My vision goes dark. The screams that pour from me are so animalistic, I'm not even certain it's me making the noise.

The crowd is deadly silent, the only sound is my wailing, and the crunching of Bram's boots in the gravel.

He's risen from his throne and hopped over the railing of his observation box into the arena.

His head blocks out the sun and he tuts with pity.

He nudges Lydia's limp foot with the toe of his boot. "What a mess you've made of things, Ivy. Look at what you've done."

My pain is so much worse than a broken hand: it's everywhere, all-consuming. I'm burning and breaking and numb all at once.

I tense, ready to spring up at him and claw his eyes out. I don't even care if it won't kill him; I need to see him bleed, make him pay.

My good hand is clenched, and I'm about to throw myself at him when the ground begins to shake, pitching me backward. Bram stumbles but remains on his feet.

Over his shoulder, still bound, in the stands, Rhion has spit out his gag and is screaming, but the noise is swallowed by a mighty groan as the land shudders from deep within its core, like it's a living thing. Then comes the soft sound of small rocks falling, skittering over the smooth marble, and the stands begin to crumble. The crowd shrieks as they run, frantically searching for safety and solid ground. Rhion covers Marion and Faith with his own body.

I can't see Bram.

The gravel of the arena shakes too, and then a crack rings out and the ground splits right down the middle.

Water pours in from either end, until it creates a roaring stream that bisects the coliseum. The ground ripples once more, and trees shoot from the ground up into the sky with another deafening crack. Vines snake around their growing roots, covering the gravel with tangled foliage.

Lightning pierces the sky as dark clouds roll in, dimming the daylight in a matter of seconds. They open up and sheets of torrential rain begin to fall, pooling on the ground and soaking me to the bone.

All around are the screams of people fleeing, but I'm barely paying attention. It crosses my mind that perhaps I'm dead too. A part of me wishes I was. I would trade my life for Lydia's without a thought.

I can't see anyone through the wall of dense green leaves. So I hold my sister, knowing these will be the last moments we have together, and pull her to my heaving chest while I sob. My tears run down my neck until they become indistinguishable with the rivulets of rain streaming over my skin.

A small gasp pierces through my trance and I look down, surprised to find Duddon. They're dressed just as they were the last time I saw them, in their silver fish scales, and their tiny face is lined with concern.

They suck a finger into their mouth and remove it with a *pop*. "More tears, my lady?" Their voice is wobbly with sadness and they approach me with trepidation and then run a tiny, sharp hand, heartbreaking in its gentleness, over Lydia's soaked hair.

"The land is crying, too," they say quietly.

"The land?" I ask, confused.

"She is our queen, she is connected to this place, to its people," Duddon explains slowly, like I'm a lost child.

I'm reminded of the memory I saw of Lydia and Emmett in the Isern Caves. Lydia was looking around the wilting castle gardens. *I think the land is sad when he's not here* was what she said about Bram and his frequent absences. Is there a chance she knew because she was connected to it, too?

Did Bram think so little of Lydia it never occurred to him to consider her the true queen of the Otherworld? Did it never cross his mind she might possess her own kind of magic?

"My heart hurts." Duddon clutches their chest. "The land cries out for her. It's mourning. All of the folk who are connected feel it too."

A shout of agony pierces through the driving rain, and my head snaps up. That was Bram's voice, I know it was, and this isn't over yet.

With as much tenderness as I can muster with only one working hand, I leave Lydia on a bed of vines that are bursting into brilliant pink flowers, and push myself to stand.

"Wait!" comes Duddon's tiny voice behind me.

I turn to see them crouched over the spring, pulling something heavy from out of its depths. Their body slumps and strains as they struggle to lift whatever it is, and then they turn, their face in a triumphant grin, their eyes still watery.

"A gift, in exchange for the tears."

They pull the object through the writhing vines and drop it at my feet.

I gasp as I finally see what it is. The blade is soaked, but still sharp. I bend, and grasp the hilt of the sword Bram gave me during the first trial to kill the unicorn—the sword I threw into Duddon's spring in a failed attempt to save the creature.

"Go. Be clever," Duddon instructs.

I pick up the sword, and on heavy feet, my shoes soaked through, take off in the direction of Bram's audible struggling.

I slash through the ever-growing forest that has sprung up in the middle of the coliseum. But it doesn't take long; Bram is only a few paces away.

"Ivy." His voice is agonized as I cut through the clearing and see him fully.

He's pinned to a massive tree, his back flush against the trunk, his arms and legs held in place by thick branches that have wound around him like claws.

He struggles against them, his wrists already visibly raw with effort, but they do not budge.

His eyes flash to the sword in my hand. "Cut me free, Ivy. Now."

But I do not obey. I stand there, looking at him in icy silence, the rain pouring down my face and arms, until it drips off the tip of my sword.

In his face, I search for the boy who kissed me in the garden at a ball, who made me feel so special and cared for at a time in my life when I felt nothing but small and lost and afraid.

Is Bram as good as you say?

It was one of the first questions I ever asked Emmett, when we were scheming to put him on the throne. I know the answer now. Bram's life has gone on too long, and whatever goodness that might have once existed within him has withered and atrophied and died, leaving nothing but a desperate creature who feeds on power and control like a predator.

Another branch sprouts from the tree and winds itself around Bram's neck, pulling tighter and tighter until he's sputtering. "Please," he rasps.

I march toward him, dragging my sword at my side, until we are nearly nose to nose, close enough to kiss.

In his gray eyes, I search for any flicker of regret.

"Why did you do it?" I ask him, my voice cracking around the question. "Why pit us against each other like this?"

Bram's eyes drop closed, his lips growing pale. "I only wanted you to fight for me. Why didn't you fight for me, Ivy?"

"What about Lydia?" My question comes out in a sob.

Bram doesn't answer and the tree branches keep squeezing tighter, digging into the tender flesh of his throat.

"Is this what pain is?" His voice is barely a whisper now. "No wonder you go to such lengths to avoid it. This is awful."

I look up at the top of the tree. Its branches are swaying in the driving storm. It's a solid, sturdy thing, and if I hadn't just seen it grow myself, I would have assumed it was hundreds of years old.

The realization strikes me that this is the land's revenge upon Bram for killing their beloved queen. It's never going to let him go.

I could leave him here, stuck and suffering for the rest of his eternal life, or I could put an end to this.

I look down at the silver blade of my sword, at the raindrops running down its sharp edge.

Cold iron.

We thought that meant unforged, but maybe we were wrong.

This sword has never had a drop of blood spilled upon it.

Bram's eyes are fully closed now. His chest rises and falls with great effort as water runs down the delicate beading of his doublet. "I only wanted you to love me. Didn't you love me, Ivy?"

I lean forward and press one final kiss to his cheek. "I hope this is a mercy," I say, and then drive the sword into his chest. I don't stop until the blade hits the solid trunk of the tree behind him and Bram goes limp.

CHAPTER TWENTY-NINE

As quickly as it began, the rain ceases and the clouds part, revealing calm, sunny skies. It's as if the air around us lets out a sigh of relief, leaving nothing but the green smell of fresh trees and a gentle breeze off the sea.

The vines stop moving, the trees go still, the brook slows from a roar to a gentle babble.

I slide my sword out of Bram's body and fall to my knees, sobbing.

He picked the wrong girl to kill. If it had been me, nothing would have happened. The land wouldn't have cared and he and Lydia could have both gone on living, but instead, they've left me here, alone, to deal with it all myself.

The bloodstained sword slips from my limp hand and falls to the ground with a clatter. I give one final look to the tree, where Bram is slumped. His eyes are closed, and his face is peaceful enough that he could be sleeping, if not for the tree branches holding his hands aloft, pinned above his head.

I don't regret what I have done but I know I will also mourn

Bram, the person I believed him to be and the person he could have been, for the rest of my days. I will also mourn the girl I was before our paths collided. He killed the version of Ivy who believed in magic and goodness just as surely as I killed him.

I then turn and trudge through the vines back to Lydia's body and sink to my knees.

Duddon is there, standing guard, stroking her damp curls, and I hold her, not knowing what else to do.

Eventually I will have to rise and face the consequences of my actions, but then Lydia will have to be buried and that will really mean she's gone and I can't bear it yet. So, I steal these final moments with my sister.

Heavy footsteps crunch through the vines toward us. I look up, prepared to see Queen Mor in a rage, ready to kill me for what I did to her son, but instead I see Emmett, free of his binds, pushing through the dense greenery alongside Faith and Marion.

Emmett's face crumples in relief upon seeing me, but when his eyes land on Lydia's body he releases a bloodcurdling howl of pain and falls to his knees beside me.

I feel so stupid for all the time I spent being jealous of the relationship he had with Lydia; now, I'm just grateful to hold her with someone who loved her, too.

"Oh, Lydia," he weeps. "Lydia, no."

Rhion follows closely behind him, and collapses, weeping into her hair. "I'm sorry," he cries in a voice that's just for my sister. "I failed you."

His bloodshot eyes meet mine. "I never even told her that I loved her."

"She knew."

Faith and Marion make their way through the crowd soon after and silently sink to the ground next to me, laying their hands on my shoulders. Tears stream down both of their faces.

"Emmett?" a voice calls, but Emmett can't manage to answer. Seconds later, Nan bursts through the trees, Fennick at her heels.

Eloree appears next, tears in her eyes. Then others I recognize vaguely from the castle, staff and courtiers.

One by one, they fall to their knees, until the entire arena is filled with faeries and other small folk like Duddon. Even the Redcaps are there, on their knees, mourning for their queen.

Bram may never have respected Lydia's authority as queen, but it doesn't matter—the residents of the Otherworld did.

The ground shakes once more, like it's weeping alongside us.

The vines upon which Lydia lies ripple and writhe like green serpents. I shout in surprise, but Duddon stills my hand. "Just watch," they instruct in their tiny voice, and I force myself to do just that. If Lydia is connected to the Otherworld in this way, then it seems only right I let it take her, no matter how it pains me to see her go.

The thick green vines snake over her feet, her legs, wrapping around her hands and arms until they reach her torso and cover her bloodstained dress and the place where the killing blow landed. The vines then wind up her neck, her face, her hair, until every inch of her is covered.

I turn away. I don't want to look as she's pulled under the dirt, but Duddon places their slimy hand on mine again. "Watch."

Someone in the crowd cries out, "Long live Queen Lydia," and it echoes from all around. *"Long live Queen Lydia!"*

It's then that the vines begin to glow. First, a dull, sunset pink, then vibrant orange, then sunny yellow, until Lydia's body is covered in white light so blinding I have to squint to keep looking at her.

The earth shudders again, a mighty quake that causes the leaves around us to shake and the crowd to cry out in surprise.

Then it stops, as if exhaling in relief, and the vines around Lydia's body retreat.

They ripple back, a perfect reverse of the way they moved before, until they reveal my sister, looking perfect and whole once more. Her curls fall around her like a golden halo, dotted with small white blooms, and her skin is flawless and glowing. She's even got a dusting of rosebud pink along her lips and the tops of her cheekbones.

I brush my hand against the cool skin of her forehead.

Her eyes snap open and she gasps awake.

CHAPTER THIRTY

"Lydia!" I shriek, and pull her into a tight hug.

She coughs sharply, like she's just been saved from drowning, then takes a heaving breath.

"Ivy?" She blinks against the light.

"You're alive." I weep into her shoulder and grip her tight.

She looks down at her bloodstained gown and clutches at the place in her chest where the knife landed. "I died." She says the words softly, marveling at them. "I was dead."

"What happened?" Emmett asks gently.

Lydia blinks as if the memory is already slipping from her. "I saw Bram. I walked past him on a road lined with flowers, and then I was back here. Something—" She pauses and searches for the words. "Something gave me the choice, to go or stay, and then a tether of golden light pulled me back into my body."

"The land, Your Majesty," Duddon pipes up from behind Lydia's head. "It didn't like that you were gone. It brought you back."

There's so much about this place that I'll never understand, but with my sister here beside me, miraculously whole and beautiful and perfect, all I can feel is gratitude.

"Long live Queen Lydia!" Duddon's tiny voice shouts again, and the chant catches like wildfire until the whole arena is chanting for her.

Rhion offers his hand, but Lydia pushes herself gingerly to her knees, then her feet, and raises her hand to wave at the crowd. They all drop to their knees before her, even me and Emmett. A mighty wind blows in off the sea, sending the tender green leaves from the trees raining over Lydia, and I might not be connected to the Otherworld in the same way Lydia is, but it's obvious, even to me—it's happy.

The cheering continues, but I turn to Emmett with a sick turning in my stomach. "Mor?" I ask. I'm expecting her to barrel into the crowd at any moment to finish what her son started.

Emmett pulls me to my feet. "Come with me," he says gravely. "I'll show you."

We push through the crowd until we reach the edge of the arena.

Bram's marble observation box has cracked down the middle, and is half hanging off the stands, dangling into the coliseum.

Inside the box is Bram's tipped-over throne, the remnants of Emmett's shackles, and something else I can't quite see.

I hike up my skirts, kick off my sodden shoes, and begin

to climb. It's not far, only as high as a few rungs of a ladder, but I feel the heat of Emmett's hand hovering behind me protectively.

I hoist myself up and Emmett follows. It's immediately clear what he was referring to.

On the floor of the observation box is a tangle of bloodred lux flowers. They've grown in a near perfect circle, about three feet wide, exactly where Queen Mor was sitting next to her son.

"What is this?" I turn to Emmett.

"I'm not sure. In the chaos, none of us saw. When Bram—" Emmett can't choke out the words *killed Lydia*. "The trees started growing, everything happened so fast. Faith snatched one of the guard's swords and demanded he undo my chains or be run through. Once I was free, I began looking for Mor, terrified that she'd be looking for you, but all we found was this." He gestures again to those strange flowers, swaying gently in the breeze.

From our higher vantage point, I can look out past the coliseum. We're on a flat plain between the edge of the forest and the sea, near enough to the Isern Caves that I can see their silhouette in the misty distance. "She could have bolted," I say.

Emmett shrugs. "She could have, but would she have not stayed to defend Bram?"

It's true, but maybe she saw the writing on the wall. *I've always been rather invested in my own self-preservation* may have been the truest thing she ever told me.

I stand on my tiptoes and strain to look over the edge of the coliseum. The fall would kill a human, but what do I know of immortals? But I make the decision in that moment not to let it consume me. I prod at the tangle of flowers with my toe. "Good riddance," I say. If it is her, I hope she's found the only peace she ever really wanted—a place where she can be with Bram.

Emmett helps me down from the ruins of the stands and we make our way across the arena to Lydia.

She's standing now, supported by Rhion.

Her skin is so luminous it's as if it's emitting light, but her face is still a bit queasy.

"Mor?" she asks.

"Gone," I answer without elaborating.

Lydia steps from the shadow of the trees into the light and her skin glimmers slightly. She clutches the place in her chest where the knife drove through and winces. "I don't feel like myself," she says.

"Shh," I soothe her. Rhion and Emmett exchange a tense glance over Lydia's head. "You've been through so much, you only need to rest."

There are carriages waiting outside the gates of the crumbling coliseum, and the remaining King's Guard drop to their knees the moment Lydia steps out into the clearing.

"Long live Queen Lydia!" they shout, then pull out their swords and lay them at her feet, her slippers still damp with her own blood. "We pledge our swords to you, Your Majesty."

Lydia dips her chin regally and they part for her like the tides.

In the jostle of the crowd, we end up in separate carriages on our way back to the castle, so I have no way of speaking to her.

Emmett peers at me, worried, as the carriage starts to move. Across the bench, Faith and Marion look equally concerned.

It's only once I'm alone with them that I allow myself to shatter.

CHAPTER THIRTY-ONE

Upon returning to the castle, Lydia retires to bed without speaking to a single one of us. That night, no revels rage in the castle, but from down in the valley below, flickering torches light a celebration among the faeries who live outside of court.

It's past midnight and Emmett is sleeping soundly beside me, but I can't settle. Every time I close my eyes I see Lydia falling to the ground, the knife stuck in the center of her chest, blood blooming around it.

On quiet feet, I pad out of bed and down the staircase to her room.

I knock softly and wait.

The door creaks open a minute later, revealing Lydia, in her robe with her hands covered in paint, a streak of white along her cheekbone.

"Can't sleep either?" she asks, and opens the door wider.

I plop down on the edge of her bed and she returns to her painting in the corner, a field of flowers so dense, it's nearly abstract in all its colors.

"Have you come to ask me if heaven is real? Rhion beat you to it."

"I didn't think faeries believed in heaven." The whole immortality thing makes the entire concept baffling to them.

Lydia adds a streak of orange across the sky of her painting. "They don't, but Rhion heard all about it from humans and finds it a fascinating concept."

"What did you tell him?"

She shrugs. "The truth, I suppose—that I'm still not sure."

"Did Rhion tell you anything else?" I prod.

Lydia turns to face me, her brows knitted together in confusion. "Like what?"

I sigh against her pillows. "Come on, you can't really be that dense."

Lydia flicks her paintbrush at me. "Don't do that. I hate talking around things. If you have something to say, just say it."

"Did he also tell you that he's hopelessly in love with you?" I say only somewhat sarcastically. It's glaringly obviously by now.

Lydia's cheeks go pink and she glances at the floor. "I don't have time to think about those things. Not yet, at least."

"I don't think he has any problem with waiting for you."

I watch her paint for a few minutes, then break the comfortable silence. "I'm sorry about Bram."

Her back is to me, but she goes still and her shoulders fall. "Don't be. He brought it upon himself." He did, but it doesn't lessen the rope of guilt, pulling like a noose around my heart.

"I'm still sorry. I know you loved him."

She's quiet for a moment as she paints a patch of pink flowers with the tip of her brush. "I loved who I believed him to be, but I don't think that's the same thing. What about you?"

I sigh. "It was only ever Emmett for me, that was part of the problem."

After another long beat, I continue. "I have something else to tell you."

She nods, her back to me. "Anything." There are no more secrets between us now, there can't be.

In the dark of her room, I confess what Bram said to me. "He saw me first on the edge of the woods. I was six and you were eight," I begin.

Lydia listens carefully as she paints clouds over her canvas. Her back is to me, but her breath hitches like she might be holding back tears.

"He timed his arrival at court to my coming-out in society. He spent a decade watching me, planning this." I'm crying too, but I don't stop to wipe the tears until my story is done.

When I'm finished talking, I feel as if I've been wrung out. "I'm so sorry. I brought this upon us. It's all my fault."

Lydia turns to me, her eyes puffy with tears. "If I told you to forgive yourself, would it make a difference?"

I let out a sad laugh. I'm so sick of crying. "Probably not," I confess.

Lydia turns back to her painting. "I'll say it anyway. It

wasn't your fault. I do not blame you. If it wasn't us, it would have been some other poor pair of girls and—" She swallows hard. "I'm glad it was us, Ivy. I've grown to love this place. It's given me a purpose."

It's plain to see. She's got a glow about her, like she's more at home here than she ever was in London. I might have been the one who longed for magic, but it's come to Lydia like it was always meant to be hers.

"You will come home, though, won't you?" I ask the question a shade quieter, suddenly terrified of her answer. I've never considered a life in which we might be apart.

Lydia sets down her brush and turns to me. Her jaw is clenched, her brows furrowed.

"I don't think so." She presses her lips together until they go white. "That is, I mean, I don't think I'm able to."

"I don't know what you mean," I respond, but the panic from earlier returns, crawling up my throat.

"I think something . . . changed in me," Lydia says.

My first instinct is to comfort her. "You—" It takes everything in me to say "*died*" without sobbing again. "I think anyone would be changed by that."

"No," Lydia whispers. "I think I came back different. Not wrong—" She searches for the words. "But not . . . what I once was."

My blood turns to ice. I force myself to look at Lydia more closely than I have been. Her back has been to me for most of our conversation, but now I truly see her.

Her skin glows so dimly, it would be easy to convince myself I was imagining it, and in her eyes, there's a spark of light, as if from the Otherworld's double moons.

She is still my sister, but I can also sense that she's more than that somehow.

"What do you mean?" I ask in a whisper.

"This place brought me back to life. I can feel its magic flow through me now, like blood in my veins. We're tied together."

"No, *you and I* are tied together." My voice breaks.

Lydia's face crumples. "Not like this."

The joy at seeing my sister alive is swallowed by a wave of sadness.

"You don't know that," I argue, my voice sharp. "Don't make assumptions with no evidence. Go on, open the door. Just try."

Lydia sighs like she's placating me and waves her hand in an arc.

A portal to Kensington Park opens in the middle of the room, showcasing a great oak tree, ablaze with orange leaves that flutter to the ground. The gentle breeze floats into Lydia's room and scatters the stack of sketches on her desk.

I stand and thrust one foot through the door to England, so I'm straddling our two worlds. I offer Lydia my outstretched hand and she sighs, but takes it obligingly.

Cool autumn air envelops me as I step through completely, but the pressure of Lydia's hand in mine disappears, floating away in a wisp of white smoke. When I turn back, she's staring at me sadly through the portal, feet firmly in her room in the Otherworld.

"No," I rasp.

Lydia offers me a sad smile. "You can always come visit me."

"But Mama and Papa—" I hiccup as a cry I can't stop escapes my lips. We'll never again drink tea in our family's drawing room together, or snicker behind our fans at a bad pantomime, or walk through Belgrave Square arm in arm.

It feels as if I've lost her twice in one day.

Lydia's eyes shine with tears. "Mama and Papa can come visit, as can you, any time you wish. In fact, I insist upon it."

I step back through, into the warmth of her room, and seal the door behind me. "But I'm going to miss you so much."

Lydia wraps me in a tight hug. "It was always going to be this way, whether I married Percival Chapwick or became queen. Life was always going to force us away from each other. But it'll be better this way, won't it? Knowing that I'm exactly where I'm meant to be."

I sleep next to Lydia that night, but by the time I'm awoken at dawn, the space next to me is cold.

Eloree nudges me gently awake and dresses me in one of Lydia's gowns, something pale pink and gauzy. "Is everything all right?" I ask blearily.

Eloree nods. "Your sister requests an audience."

In the great hall, I join a crowd of equally exhausted-looking courtiers, in various states of dress.

Emmett finds me quickly and pulls me into a crushing embrace, then plants a kiss on top of my head. "I missed you. Do you know what this is about?"

"I thought you might," I reply, and he shakes his head.

"Oh, there you two are!" Rhion's voice pierces the crowd. Emmett and I walk over to him and are joined by Marion and Faith in quick succession.

"Any idea why we've been dragged from our beds?" Faith asks.

The double doors to the throne room swing open.

Lydia sits on her throne, a candy-pink sky behind her as the sun rises in the Otherworld, on the first day without Bram and Mor.

She looks settled, so herself, that the sight of her nearly brings me to tears. She's wearing a simple gown of pale purple with a golden circlet laid on her head. She needs no other jewels to communicate that she is queen; the look in her eye is enough.

The throne room is soon filled with most of court, including the staff.

"Thank you for joining me." Lydia's voice rings out true and clear. "I apologize for the early wake-up call, but there was no time to waste."

The crowd settles into a reverent hush.

"I wanted to make my intentions clear as quickly as possible, and so I saw no reason to delay. The cruelty of Bram's reign is over. The use of humans for sport is now forbidden. The door to England will remain locked, save for a few carefully selected ambassadors. The small folk are to be treated with the same respect as any citizen. Any grievances will be dealt with directly by me."

As if to echo her statement, a mighty gust of wind shakes the castle walls. The first light of the day beams through the stained glass window high above Lydia's throne, casting her in a halo.

"If you have any objection to these new rules, you are welcome to leave my court. In fact, I insist upon it."

There's a scoff of indignation from the back of the throne room, but Lydia's steely face does not waver.

"Those who have been participants or complicit in the torture of humans will have letters delivered to you today, outlining your upcoming trial dates."

"You can't do this!" Lady Thalia shouts. Two guards flank her and direct her toward the door. "Emmett!" she yells.

Emmett doesn't even turn around. I reach across the space between us and squeeze his hand. There are some wounds that you feel for a lifetime, and I'm sure Emmett and I will forever bear the scars of our disastrous first marriages, but what a relief it is to be rid of them.

Lydia sinks back onto her throne and folds her hands neatly in her lap. "Any questions?"

The crowd bursts out into riotous applause. Someone magicks flower petals to fall in a shower from the ceiling.

Rhion is the first to sink to his knees to bow to her, followed quickly by Emmett, and then everyone else, until all of the court of the Otherworld is kneeling at Lydia's feet.

I look up at my sister, both our eyes glimmering with tears, and I have never loved her more.

CHAPTER THIRTY-TWO

Only slightly the worse for wear from Lydia's coronation revel, Emmett and I meet Marion and Faith the next morning in the great hall. Emmett carries a trunk of remnants from his life here in the Otherworld, mostly books, clothes, and a few earrings (I insisted upon it), but the rest of us are traveling light.

Rhion and Lydia wait for us at the base of the staircase, standing on the polished marble floor bathed in a streak of sunlight beaming in from the high windows.

Rhion wears a guard's uniform, a sword hanging at his side, and Lydia looks something like an angel next to him, in her white gown and gold diadem. Her blond curls hang loose around her shoulders, made even more beautiful by the faint otherworldly glow she has about her now.

"Great party, Lyd," Emmett says, and she laughs.

"There's only one way to win over this court."

Rhion shakes his head. "Nonsense. They were already in love with you."

I raise my brows and shoot him a knowing look. His eyes flit to the floor as he ignores me conspicuously.

"Ready?" I ask the gathered group.

Rhion places his hand on the hilt of his sword. "Ready."

Marion looks around the great hall, smiling sweetly. "I don't know. I think I might miss it."

"Which part?" Faith asks. "Us being tortured or watching Ivy be tortured?"

"The food." Marion rolls her eyes.

Lydia lays a hand on her arm. "You're welcome anytime."

Lydia then looks to Emmett.

"I'm going to miss you, Lyd," Emmett says, a shade quieter.

She opens her arms, and they embrace. "You'll visit so often, there won't be time for all that," Lydia replies briskly, but her voice is thick with tears.

They pull apart, and then she turns to me. "And you."

I wave my hand dismissively. I've never been good at goodbyes, not when they hurt this much. "No more tears, I can't take it."

"See you soon, then, yes?" and I reach for that space inside of me I still don't quite understand, where the door resides, just to make sure it's still there. I brush over it mentally, and it gives me comfort.

I nod, my eyes stinging. It feels so unnatural to leave her behind, even if it is what she wants, even if no other future is possible for us.

"I'll see you soon." It's a promise.

I open the door and the rest of them follow me like good little soldiers. Lydia waits until the very last moment it closes, waving the whole time, silent tears sliding down her cheeks and a smile on her face.

Rhion is back in England as her official emissary to track down the members of Bram's court who remained here. We're lucky that most of them returned to witness the spectacle of the trials, and Lydia will handle them back in the Otherworld, but Rhion is here to deal with any stragglers who remain.

London is still and sleepy after the sparkling chaos of the Otherworld, but when Emmett and I slide into bed that night with Pig nestled between our legs under the covers, there is no doubt that I am home.

It's at breakfast the next morning that we're startled by a pounding on the door. A footman opens it to reveal a palace guard in full regalia, clutching a scroll in his hand. I set down my toast and look at him with raised brows.

"It's for you, ma'am." I unfurl it as Emmett looks on silently.

"So?" he asks after a sip of tea.

I sigh. I knew this was coming but I'd hoped we'd have more than a few meager hours back home before it did. "We've been summoned to Parliament," I say glumly.

Emmett sighs and rolls his head back. "Then we'd better get dressed."

Lottie is still in Bath, so I have a skittish housemaid help me into the most regal gown I can find in my old wardrobe, something made of cream silk with a square neckline dotted with pearls. On my head, she places a tiara fashioned of diamonds in the shape of ivy leaves I received as a wedding present from some lord or another.

Emmett is waiting for me in the foyer, looking unfairly handsome in his black frock coat, his dark hair tucked behind his ears. He's kept his earring in. His hands are clasped behind his back and he turns as I descend the great staircase.

"You look perfect," he says, and kisses me.

I push him off with a playful shrug. "And you look distracting. How am I supposed to do any political dealmaking with you in the room?"

We walk out into an uncommonly sunny October day. Emmett laughs and helps me into the awaiting carriage.

It's a little dizzying to see London unchanged when I feel so different. What has been weeks for us in the Otherworld has only been three days here.

Our carriage slows in front of the Palace of Westminster and we can hear the roar of voices inside from the road.

"Surely that's not all for us?" I ask, nervous energy suddenly coursing through me.

Emmett pulls the folded-up summons from his breast pocket and reads it once more. "We're in the right place, it says the Painted Chamber."

Hand in hand, Emmett and I enter the ancient palace on the banks of the Thames.

There's a section of roof caved in from where a faerie's firework show got out of hand a few months ago. I remember asking Bram to fix it and he said he'd get around to it eventually, but never did.

But most of the hallways are still intact and Emmett and I walk in silence until we reach the main chamber.

I brace myself, then press the doors open, and at least one hundred eyes snap to me in unison. They take a collective breath upon seeing Emmett and me. Lord Langley stands in the middle, in front of the central desk, paperwork fanned out in front of him. The rest of the lords are on either side of the room, sitting on risers.

"Good!" he barks as Emmett and I enter. "Let us begin."

Emmett and I are waved to two chairs next to where Lord Langley stands. We sink down into them, passing a tense glance between us. It's as if we're on trial.

Like the palace, Parliament, too, bears the scars of Bram's brief rule. Every face in the crowd looks drawn and sallow. I can name at least three different lords in my direct eyeline who lost property or business to bad bargains with Bram's fae court. Lord Dudley even lost his wife, who ran off with one of them.

"Now that the children are here, we can commence with the day's agenda," Lord Langley says.

"Which is?" Emmett asks.

Lord Langley looks down his nose at us. "Determining the future of England."

A cry goes up from the crowd, one hundred voices shouting in a collective roar.

Lord Langley bangs his walking stick on the floor

three times, sending a boom echoing throughout the long, rectangular meeting space. "Silence!"

A hush falls and Lord Langley continues. "We have never been in a more precarious position as a country. Queen Mor may have had her flaws—"

Another cry of dissent goes through the crowd.

"—but she also kept this country stable and at peace for four centuries. As we look toward the future, we desperately need a monarch who can guide this ship with a steady, capable hand."

Again, Emmett and I share a charged glance.

Lord Langley shuffles through the paperwork on his desk. "Through the line of Edward the Fourth of York, son of our last human king, the crown should pass to Wendell, the tenth Duke of York."

In the crowd, the duke, a balding, owlish man, blinks a few times in surprise. "Oh—" he sputters, and stands from a riser on the right side of the room. "Oh, well, I suppose . . ." he bumbles.

Emmett springs from his chair. "This is ridiculous!" he shouts.

Lord Langley turns to him, his brows upturned. "Do you have something to say about these proceedings, Mr. De Vere? You've been conspicuously absent these many months we have suffered." From somewhere in the crowd someone snickers and mutters something about the prince desperately needing a haircut.

"Of course I have something to say," Emmett roars. "You already have a queen!"

He gestures to me. I straighten my back, unsure of how I want this to go. I have a strong sense of duty and a vision for justice and a better world, but I am so very tired, and perhaps it would be nice to leave someone much older than me in charge of fixing Bram's great big mess.

"Ivy is not a queen, she is a queen regent." Lord Langley adjusts his spectacles.

"Bullshit!" Emmett yells.

"Decorum, Mr. De Vere," Lord Langley snaps. "I won't be disrespected by an irresponsible drunkard who is barely more than a boy."

Emmett's face is deadly serious as he stares down Lord Langley. "Is that where you think I was? You believed Bram's gossip that I'd slunk off to drink myself to death in a country estate?" His voice is venomous and low, barely more than a whisper. "I was in the Otherworld, which means I know exactly what true power is, and you may sit here and attempt to insult us, but Ivy has it."

Emmett turns around and glances back at me, aching love evident in his face. "It is *Queen* Ivy who killed Bram, freeing us from his tyranny. We owe her a debt of national gratitude."

A chorus of gasps echoes through the room.

"He won't return?" Lord Langley asks.

I shake my head as guilt crawls up my throat. "He won't return."

"She alone was brave enough to face him and powerful enough to defeat him," Emmett says.

"That is not evidence she should be queen," Lord Langley retorts.

"Not on its own, it's not." Emmett walks to the front of the room, sidestepping in front of Langley and his papers.

"But Ivy is more than just brave. She is kind and just and steady. She held this country together while Bram attempted to turn it to ashes. You all bore witness, so do not deny it. Her first thought is always of others, and she turns those thoughts into actions. England needs a ruler who is not only powerful, but just and *kind*. No one in this room fits that description other than her."

I blink back a tear threatening to escape. My first instinct is to respond with humility and shyness to Emmett's impassioned speech. I've been raised and trained all my life to be sweet and agreeable. But why would I want to be sweet? The only thing being sweet has ever done for me is make me easier to consume.

I take a steadying breath and rise. "Lord Langley, who looked over your railway proposals? Lord Bexham, who arranged for more wheat for your tenant farmers? When Bram's actions threatened to plunge this country into darkness, it was I who stood with you all. I continued to respect this institution enough to meet with you all, to help where I could, even as chaos reigned." I pause and look up and down the risers, meeting as many of their eyes as I can manage. "I don't believe that any one person has inherent right to rule over another, but if you insist that this country have a figurehead, let it be me. Together, we'll build something for the people, a government that serves us all."

About half of the room starts clapping, but Lord Langley silences them swiftly with a strike of his walking stick against the floor.

"Are we really going to hand our country over to an eighteen-year-old *girl*?"

"Queen Mor was a woman, and she ruled for centuries," I point out.

"Yes, but she always had a regent."

"She'll have a regent." Emmett's proclamation cuts through the room like a blade, leaving silence in its wake.

He turns to me, blinking and stunned. "I planned to have a ring when this happened. I commissioned one first thing this morning."

"Is this a proposal?" I whisper in shock.

"I meant for it to be more romantic than this."

I beam back up at him. "It's all right. I've always been the practical sort."

I turn back to the room. "Well, there you have it. You know who I am, and I see no use in a drawn-out debate. Let's put it to a vote and be done with it."

Lord Langley sighs heavily. "All in favor of letting Ivy continue ruling as queen?"

Overwhelmingly, the council cries out. Their voices echo

through the Painted Chamber and pierce me right down to my bones.

"All opposed?"

A few scattered "nays" sound out around the room, but the verdict is clear.

Lord Langley pounds his walking stick against the floor one last time. "God save the queen!"

"God save the queen!"

Emmett looks at me, his eyes shining.

"Don't you dare say it, too." I laugh and wipe the tears from my eyes.

It's raining on the day of our coronation. Heavy gray clouds hang over the city like an embrace and raindrops fall gently down the windows of our carriage.

Emmett and I insisted on taking the same one, despite Lord Langley's protests. My fiancé sits across from me now, every inch the prince. He adjusts the diamond star pin on his royal-blue sash and glances up at me.

"Like what you see?" He smiles.

"I'm sad you cut your hair." I pout.

Emmett runs a hand across his head. "I'll grow it back out for you."

"This is hardly the time to be flirting with me, Emmett De Vere. We're on our way to the most important moment of our lives."

His gaze flits down to the engagement ring I wear on my

left hand. "What about the wedding?" I sigh against the plush seats of the carriage. From outside the window, thousands of people have gathered to shout well wishes as we pass. The snow-white horses that pull us are adorned with golden saddles and white feather plumes on top of their heads.

I understand the purpose of all the pomp and circumstance, but that doesn't mean I enjoy it.

"Can't we just elope?" I groan. "I can't imagine doing all of this again next month."

Emmett reaches across the gap between us and places a reassuring hand on my knee. "You can convince me to do anything. But you'd break poor Rhion's heart. He's assigned himself as my best man."

"Seems prudent for diplomatic purposes."

Emmett pulls a face. "I don't think it's that. He read about human wedding ceremonies in a book and desperately wants to take me on a stag night and give a speech."

One of the things I love most about Emmett is that he always makes me laugh, even at the tensest of moments.

The carriage slows as we reach Westminster and the doors swing open, revealing a plush, crimson carpet leading into the abbey.

"Brace yourself," Emmett says, and leans forward to give me a quick kiss the moment before the doors swing open.

He hops out first and extends a hand to help me down.

"We met in a carriage," he says under his breath. "You looked just as beautiful then."

My feet hit the ground and I gaze up at him, amazed that I ever got this lucky. There is so much work left to do, but I take comfort in knowing he will be by my side through all of it.

The orchestra swells. Hand in hand, we step through the door.

I have his heart and he has mine. There has never been a fairer bargain.

EPILOGUE
London, 1868

The oil in the lantern is burning dangerously low, and I pray it will last the length of this letter. It's the final correspondence I need to complete before retiring to bed, but if the prime minister doesn't have it by morning, it'll be my staff that has to deal with his ire, and I'd really rather avoid a confrontation.

"You're making the rest of us look bad." I look up to find Emmett leaning against the doorjamb, wearing a loose white shirt, his formal coat discarded hours ago.

The lantern burns out with a snick, leaving the fireplace on the far side of my study the only source of light. Emmett laughs gently and pulls an extra well of oil from the cabinet by the door, crossing the room to my desk.

"One of us has to work around here." I nudge his elbow as he pours in the fresh oil and reignites the lantern.

He leans down and places an affectionate kiss on my head. "I'll have you know I spent all morning in the mews examining the new carriages for Lydia's first trooping of the guard."

"You *love* the horses—and then you spent the rest of the day chasing the children around the garden. I could see you from here!" I bite back the smile pulling at my lips. After nearly twenty years of marriage, Emmett still manages to surprise me every day, but I was never surprised at the doting father he became. Each and every one of our children has him completely wrapped around their fingers.

"Not true," he retorts. "Lydia's much too tall for me to chase now."

"That trait came from your side of the family."

Lydia, our oldest, turns eighteen next week, and will begin her official duties as a working royal. She won't come out in society as a debutante like I did. I ended that practice the first year of my reign.

Like every girl her age, she has the opportunity to determine her own future. We gave her the choice to become a dancer or a poet or a banker, or even to permanently join her aunt and namesake at court in the Otherworld, where she has enjoyed many happy holidays, but she insisted she wanted to go into the family business. It didn't particularly surprise me or Emmett, as Lydia has always been the most responsible of our children. Her sixteen-year-old sister, Elizabeth, is her opposite. She told us last week she intended on becoming a pirate or a dressmaker, or a dressmaker with her own ship, like some kind of floating modiste. She spends much too much time with her aunties Marion and Faith, who encourage her, but Emmett's no better. He's already enrolled her in sailing lessons.

I finish the last sentence of my letter and sign it with a flourish while Emmett perches on the edge of my desk, watching patiently.

When I am finished, he arches a brow, and after all these years, it still gives me butterflies. He looks just the same as the day we met, with the addition of a few smile lines around his hazel eyes and a dusting of gray at his temples.

"I never get sick of looking at you," he says.

"You're a shameless old flirt, Emmett De Vere."

He bends down and kisses me, too long and too passionately for a room with an open door where any one of our multitude of children could walk in.

He pulls back, his eyes shining. "Just one of the many things you love about me, Ivy De Vere."

I rise from my desk, smiling. "I know, I know. Did you interrupt my work just to seduce me?"

Emmett holds the door open for me and I step through past him. "Seducing comes later. The children want you to say good night. Pippa has demands."

"She always does."

"She takes after you in that way."

Emmett and I walk hand in hand, down the long, carpeted hall of Kensington Palace, into our private family apartments.

"When do Greer and Joseph arrive from Scotland?" Emmett asks. My childhood best friend, Greer, was presumed dead after Queen Mor staged a suicide during the competition for Bram's hand. But Greer and her stable boy Joseph were successful in fleeing over the border to Scotland. She came back to visit England two years into my reign as queen, a wiggling baby in her arms and her doting husband by her side. The day she arrived in my throne room remains one of the happiest of my life.

"Tuesday morning, they'll be staying with us for a week."

Emmett shakes his head. "I don't like the way their second son looks at Elizabeth," he says in a mock whisper.

I roll my eyes at him. "You should be more worried about the poor lovesick boy. She'll eat him alive."

We reach the drawing room, aglow with firelight and filled with the laughter of our two middle boys, who are sprawled out on the carpet playing with Emmett's childhood toy soldiers. Our children might be being raised under the same roof as my husband once was, but their childhoods bear no resemblance to the iciness of his own.

"Mama, Edmund is using magic!" Henry shouts as I walk into the room.

I look to see Edmund laughing uproariously, a little toy soldier beside him marching across the carpet. Fennick gifted it to him on a recent trip to the Otherworld, and I find it a little creepy, but Edmund adores it.

"Stop complaining and use it back, then." I scoop up a clever little butterfly toy from the mantel and pass it down to him. It was also a gift from Fennick, who has absolutely no respect for the peace of my household.

Henry tosses it at his brother, and it takes off flying,

sending them both squealing and running in a full circle around the drawing room.

"And you say I rile them up." Emmett sinks back onto the sofa and smiles over at the boys.

"Don't bump me! I'm reading!" our second-youngest, Amelia, cries from the window seat, where she sits most evenings, with a blanket on her lap and a book in her hand.

"Fifteen minutes, then bed!" I call in her direction.

"Let me finish this chapter!" she retorts without looking up.

I sigh fondly and plant a kiss on top of her head. I'd better get Pippa down before I attempt to wrangle the rest of them.

"Good luck in there!" Emmett calls as I walk down the dark corridor to the children's rooms.

"Don't let the rest of them push you around while I'm gone."

Henry jumps onto his father's lap and Emmett lets out a good-natured cry of pain. "It's impossible. We're so outnumbered."

Pippa, our youngest, is only six—but the fiercest of all our brood. She's sitting bolt upright in bed as I enter her room, with her favorite doll clutched to her chest.

"You made me wait." She's got Emmett's dark hair and my wild curls, but her bright eyes are all Lydia. Sometimes it feels like I'm looking at my sister in miniature. I wouldn't be surprised if Pippa one day chose to leave England for the Otherworld and find some land in need of a queen, just like her aunt.

We've made no secret of our personal past or our nation's history to our children. It would be impossible not to, what with the frequent holidays to the Otherworld and the history dripping from the walls of Kensington Palace. Emmett and I made a conscious decision not to scrub the evidence of Mor and Bram from our home. Their portraits still hang in the great hall, and the throne room is still painted with frescoes of the Otherworld. We kept the statues in the garden, and though most of the money has my face on it now, there are still a few bills and coins circulating that portray Mor instead.

No matter how badly things ended, Bram was once Emmett's brother, and it was important to him that our children knew Bram was loved. On nights that are particularly cold and stormy, Emmett will gather our children around the fire and tell them stories of the time Bram taught him to play billiards or the fight they once got into on my behalf at a gambling club. That one is a particular favorite of the boys.

"I'm sorry, darling." Pippa's soft mattress sinks as I sit down next to her. I pat the space next to me and call, "Come here, Piglet," until the scraggly little dog bounds from where she was lying by the window and leaps up into bed next to us.

Pippa climbs onto my lap and cups my face in her tiny hands. "Mama, I missed you all day."

I press a kiss into her soft cheek. "We had lunch together, silly, and tea after that."

She frowns, her brows crinkling over those warm brown eyes. I brush a tangled curl out of her face and begin a loose braid down her back.

"I know," she sighs. "But I want you with me all the time."

"I want that, too, sweetheart."

She reaches up and touches where I'm plaiting her hair. "Papa does a better job than you," she says. "Yours always fall out."

I laugh. "You have a very talented papa."

Once her hair is finished, she climbs off of me and settles back into her pillows.

I look toward the teetering stack of books by her bedside. "What story tonight, my love? Only one, and then it's lights-out."

She nibbles at her bottom lip with her baby teeth and I already know what she's going to say. It's been the same for months now.

I pull the book with the worn green cover from where it sits at the top of the stack. *"Faeries of the British Isles, again?"* I ask incredulously.

I thumb through the pages, their illustrations now long faded with time. "Which chapter would you like?"

She burrows into my shoulder and presses her lips to my ear, her sweet voice asking what it does nearly every night. "Tell me again, the story of the faerie king."

ACKNOWLEDGMENTS

First, thank you to the readers for following both me and Ivy into the unknown. Writing a sequel is honestly a little terrifying, but your kindness about *The Rose Bargain* carried me through many long nights. Every day, I get to live my dream because of you, and I'll never stop feeling grateful for it.

Thank you to my incomparable agent, Hillary Jacobson, who has been by my side through every step of my career (and honestly, most of my adult life). Thank you for your unwavering support, your faith in me, and for being the fastest reader I know.

Thank you to my editor, Erica Sussman, for captaining the *Rose Bargain* ship. I'm endlessly grateful for your incisive notes, your steady hand, and for never letting me lose track of the heart of this story.

Thank you to Clare Vaughn, who works tirelessly for her authors.

Shepherding a book into the world is no small task. Thank you to everyone at HarperCollins, particularly Sean

P. Cavanagh, Nicole Moulaison, Audrey Diestelkamp, Molly Fehr, Joel Tippie, Erika West, Mary Magrisso, and Anna Ravenelle.

The entire Electric Monkey team in the UK is an absolute joy to work with. Thank you to my editor, Sarah Levison, for all your guidance. Getting lunch with you is one of my favorite things in the world.

Thank you to Hannah Penny and Lila Nicholson for joining me on a mad dash tour around the UK and for all the M&S train sandwiches. Thank you also to Aleena Hasan, Lindsey Heaven, Lucy Courtenay, Olivia Adams, Emily Sommerfeld, Sophie Porteous, Ingrid Gilmore, Josephine Knipmeijer, Dan Downham, Francesca Lucci, and Leah Woods. Please know my mom and I frequently talk about how much we love you all.

Thank you to the team at CAA: Sarah Mitchell, Filipa Vaz, Josie Freedman, Berni Vann, and Gaby Sheiner.

To my colleagues, whom I respect and adore: Stephanie Garber, Rachel Griffin, Adalyn Grace, Ayana Gray, Isabel Ibañez, Allison Saft, Kerri Maniscalco, Shelby Mahurin, Ava Reid, and Chole Gong, thank you for saying such kind things about *The Rose Bargain*. Thank you also to Rebecca Ross, Hannah Whitten, Andy Darcy Theo, Kika Hatzopoulou, Zeena Gosrani, the London Girls Book Club, Joel Rochester, and Katherine Webber for joining me on the *Rose Bargain* tour.

Thank you to the booksellers, librarians, influencers, and bloggers for getting *The Rose Bargain* into the hands of readers and for all you do for the bookish community. I was a deeply nerdy kid who found refuge in the shelves of bookshops and libraries. To know that my books now exist on those same shelves will always fill me with awe.

Thank you to Celine and Anna. I know we were just on Zoom, but it felt as if you were quite literally holding my hand as I wrote every word. You took time away from your babies to sit with me well into the middle of the night, and cheered me on hard enough to believe I could write this book. Your friendship is a gift.

Thank you to Susan, Jenna, Serena, Emma, Hannah, Mary, and Emily. I'm starting to run out of ways to tell you how much I love you and how grateful I am for your presence in my life.

To Emilie, always. I'd be lost without you.

To my family, I'm so lucky that you're always the ones cheering me on the loudest.

To Casey, who sat with me on the floor of a lime-green room in Bath, England, and asked all the right "what if" questions. This job (and this life) wouldn't be nearly as fun if I didn't get to do it with you.

To my husband, Charles, who shows me what abiding, true love looks like every day of my life.

And finally, thank you to my dog, Billie—you actively hindered the writing of this book, but I love you anyway.

SASHA PEYTON SMITH

is the *New York Times* best-selling author of fantasy novels for young adults including *The Witch Haven* and *The Rose Bargain*. Her work has been translated into more than a dozen languages world-wide. She lives in a 100-year-old house in the mountains of Utah, with her husband and (allegedly) two ghosts, though she has yet to see them.